THE COMPLAINTS DEPARTMENT

THE COMPLAINTS DEPARTMENT

A NORTHERN NOVEL

Susan Haley

GASPEREAU PRESS
PRINTERS & PUBLISHERS
2005

ALSO BY SUSAN HALEY

Getting Married in Buffalo Jump
A Nest of Singing Birds
How to Start a Charter Airline
Blame it on the Spruce Budworm
Maggie's Family
The Murder of Medicine Bear

◂ 1. COMPLAINTS ▸

Robert Woodcutter, aged forty, and Haga, a down-and-out of fifty or more, without, as far as anybody could remember, another name, were standing outside the band hall in the night-long summer dusk, chanting dolefully to the drum music as they warmed themselves beside the fire. The drumming and the stamping of feet suddenly came to an end in a chorus of cheers, handclapping and hoots.

"Well—may the best man win, that's what I always say," remarked Robert.

Haga was too weird a person to qualify as Robert's friend—or anybody else's—but he was one of the ten people who had voted for him in the chief election.

Robert's younger brother, Danny, had recently returned to Prohibition Creek after working in Yellowknife a few years. Since most of the Band belonged to the Woodcutter family, his election was pretty much assured. Not even Robert's mother would have voted for Robert.

Danny came down the steps of the band hall to stand beside them.

"No hard feelings," he said.

"Nope." But Robert merely looked at Danny's partly outstretched hand. He was not going to shake hands with his brother.

"Now that I'm the new chief I'm going to make some changes in this place. I'm really going to do something."

Robert didn't like to hear this.

"We're going to get rid of the apathy around here," said Danny. "Throw out the booze."

"Yeah!"

"Okay!" There was some handclapping from the people standing around. To Robert it was like a Protestant prayer meeting.

"I'm going to make everyone work together: the nurse, the police, the social worker, the hamlet office – all the departments together on a big committee."

Danny had a degree in business administration from a university in Saskatchewan. This, plus his years working in the territorial government in Yellowknife, made him talk like a whiteman who had lived in the North for three months, from Robert's point of view. Robert had quit school in grade ten, but he read things. He was the only person in town who had a subscription to *Time* magazine.

"Once we get everybody cooperating we'll be able to get some things done."

Robert thought cooperation was not the right word. Collaboration was more like it. Letting the whiteman run the town.

"Don't you think there's something you're forgetting?" said Robert. "I guess every organization needs one. Didn't you get some kind of a university degree in this?"

"What is it you're trying to tell me, Robert?" Danny expected people to agree with him immediately because he knew he was right.

"I mean you need a Complaints Department, that's all."

"A what?" Danny was taken aback.

The dance suddenly became much louder, as someone took to the dance floor inside and the drummers stood up. All at once they were both shouting over the drums.

"A Complaints Department!"

"What for?"

"Complaints!"

As suddenly as it had begun the music ceased, and they were standing there, looking at one another foolishly.

"Look, I've got to go in there now," said Danny. "Maybe you'd better come down to the band office tomorrow. We can talk about your department then."

He walked quickly across the grassy lawn and up the steps onto the porch, disappearing inside the building. Robert was now feeling very foolish.

A Complaints Department. What had he meant by that anyway?

Inside the hall Danny was making a speech in their language. They couldn't hear it out by the fire, but his voice made it sound convincing enough. Robert was quite surprised to hear him speak the language so well after all those years away.

They had both had the same traditional upbringing, living in Prohibition Creek as children in the fifties and sixties when people still went out on the land. Now, in the nineties, the skidoo had replaced the dog team, the bottom had fallen out of the fur market and that life was disappearing. People lived in town, unemployed and watching TV, and even the language was getting lost.

"He sounds like a preacher," said Robert moodily. "Not a chief."

"So what can you do about it? Can't do nothing," Haga remarked.

That was what people in Prohibition Creek said about residential schools, fur prices, the game laws, government red tape, the Housing Corporation, bears in town, TV interference, loose dogs, no cigarettes in the store, bushmen, UFO sightings, the oil companies, unemployment and, for that matter, employment.

"You've got to do something sometimes," said Robert irritably. "There must be some kind of a thing you can do. Start a Complaints Department."

"Well, Danny doesn't want one, that's for sure."

Danny's speech inside came to an end and there was another session of revival-meeting clapping and chanting before they all came out.

Robert's mother, Rachel Woodcutter, was standing right beside him all of a sudden.

"Ama," said Robert.

"What are you doing outside in the darkness? You should be celebrating because your brother has won the election."

"I'm just standing here with Haga." Robert was trying not to sound defensive.

"It's okay, Ama," said Danny. He had been discussing what to do about Robert off and on all week with his mother. "Robert is going to help me out," he continued. "He's already got some ideas."

Rachel was looking from one of her sons to the other. She well understood the bad will that was between them. It had been there ever since Danny was five, and old enough to notice what a troublemaker Robert was, and since Robert was fifteen, old enough to be a serious troublemaker.

"I am going to sing now," she said suddenly.

Rachel had gone to the convent school in Fort Resolution after being orphaned as a baby. She had loved it, even though other people, with their own more or less terrible memories of residential school, could hardly believe that was possible. She had been a petted favourite of the nuns, and with her beautiful voice she had seemed made for a life in the Church. But when she was twenty, she suddenly came home to Prohibition Creek and married Robert's father, to the shock and sorrow of the sisters who had brought her up.

She was now singing a hymn in French with great simplicity, her voice soaring, and in spite of himself, in spite of Danny and the election, Robert felt a shiver of pleasure run up his back.

◂ ◂ ◂

Robert followed the chief election up by going on a six-week hard-drinking spree that consumed the rest of the summer. He financed it largely by collecting on poker debts, although he ended up doing a lot of fruitless bumming in the last week or so.

Throughout the whole experience he had babbled continuously of the Complaints Department, with Haga at his side as witness and assistant, until people even began taking the name to denote an entity; and now in this more or less forlorn stage of the binge, small children mocked him with the name, calling it after him on the road through town.

Robert was not an alcoholic; he had been saved that fate by the game of poker, to which his father had introduced him at the innocent age of six. Gambling had ruined his life in quite a different way from drink. So it horrified him now, in the semi-consciousness of his present state, how many weeks he had spent with the bottle. In addition to that, his wife was furious with him for coming or not coming home drunk day after day, and his eighteen-year-old son had vowed to kill him.

Meanwhile Danny, having applied for and received a grant for a drug and alcohol prevention program in the name of the Prohibition Creek Band, had started holding AA meetings and organized a drop-in centre for teenagers in the basement of the Pentecostal church. The government then sent in a social worker at his request to help out with AA and set up a counselling program. She was a young woman named Rebecca McCrae, fresh out of training at Thebacha College in Fort Smith. She was also Danny's second cousin on his mother's side.

The police truck stopped on the road. Dave, the cop, got out and opened the back door.

"Robert. Hop in," he said.

"What for?"

"Something. You look pretty rough, Robert."

Robert was looking very rough, and this was not only because he had been up all the previous night, but also because he had drunk something that Haga gave him in the morning that had turned out not to be liquor, or even homebrew, but some type of medicine. He was now hoping that it had just been cough syrup, not liniment.

"Where are we going?" Robert knew the police could not arrest a person for having a hangover or being nauseated, but he was still on the defensive.

"Just down to the detachment." Dave was whistling. "By the way Robert, I heard about your idea for a Complaints Department."

"Oh yeah?" Robert was in the back seat of the crew cab, trying to relax. He didn't like the fact that there were no handles on the doors back here.

"Yeah. I just thought it was a pretty good idea. Hey, this is Rebecca McCrae. Did you meet Robert yet, Rebecca? She's the new social worker. I've just been giving her the tour of downtown Prohibition Creek."

Robert had not had time to see the face of the woman in the front seat. But he had already been wondering, in some part of his mind, whether she was pretty.

The truck pulled up outside the detachment. Dave got out and opened the door first for Rebecca. He pretended to forget Robert trapped without any door handles, then went back for him with a grin.

"Come on in, Robert."

"Like I said, what for?"

"Like I said, you'll see."

They went into the detachment and Dave immediately disappeared in the direction of the cells. Rebecca and Robert were left standing in the outer office.

She was pretty.

"You must be some kind of cousin of mine," remarked Robert. "What's your Dad's name?"

"Elijah McCrae."

Elijah McCrae was a well-known Protestant lay preacher, a fundamentalist. Robert had met him one time years before when he was hanging around with his father in Yellowknife, playing poker every night with the Chinese.

"I probably saw you one time," said Robert. "In Yellowknife about twenty years ago. You were a baby."

"I'm twenty-eight," said Rebecca. "That baby must have been my brother. I was eight if it was twenty years ago," she added.

A cell door slammed. Then there was a scuffing sound down the hall and Dave reappeared, propelling Bobby, Robert's teenaged son, in front of him.

"Well, look who's here," he said to Bobby on Robert's behalf.

Robert didn't like the way the policeman was holding Bobby's arm. He said nothing. Neither did Bobby.

"Now he's going to sit down here and behave himself like a good boy. Right, Bobby?"

Dave gave Bobby a little jerk and he sat down suddenly in an office chair.

Bobby had been on probation since the early summer because of a fight he had got into when he was drinking with some of his friends. Robert was rather afraid of him these days. From being a silent child, always sticking around with his mother, he had turned, almost overnight, it seemed, into a moody, violent young man with a drinking problem.

"Were you drinking again?" Robert asked.

"Sure was," said Dave. "Tell him what else, Bobby. Or has the cat got your tongue there?"

Bobby didn't answer. He was looking at the floor. Unexpectedly, he made a little noise like a sob.

"Well, I'll tell your dad, then. It was break and enter, first of all. Him and a bunch of punks broke into old Arthur's trailer. Stole the booze and beat up the old man. Then he got into a fight with one of those pals of his—using a couple of two-by-fours. That was later on, down by the lake. Which makes two counts of assault. He's going to jail just as soon as we can get him on a plane."

This didn't seem fair to Robert. He thought there had to be a trial before they could ship people off to jail like that.

"Isn't someone innocent until proven guilty, according to those laws of yours?" he asked.

"He broke his probation." It was Rebecca who spoke.

Robert had forgotten she was even there. But he realized, now, that she knew all about this. Like the nurse, like the teachers, like the priest, the social worker was one of those agencies or departments Danny wanted to have cooperating.

"Who's she?" said Bobby.

"She's the new social worker," said Dave.

"Why'd you bring my dad here?"

"He's got to know, that's why."

"He doesn't care anyway," Bobby said. "He doesn't care about anything I do."

It was true that Robert had been staying away from Bobby more and more lately because of the violent things he said he was going to do—he was going to beat people up, he was going to kill them. Even when he was drunk himself, Robert was cautious enough to stay away from people who talked like that all the time.

"I got nothing to say to him and he's got nothing to say to me," said Bobby abruptly.

Robert looked at the floor. All around him was office: grey metal filing cabinets, metal desks and chairs, typewriters, thick stacks of the pink, white and blue pastel forms used by the police.

"Hey, Bobby, maybe you should just give him a chance to talk," said Dave.

"That's all he ever does. Talk." Bobby's voice began to rise. "He doesn't care about me. He never cared about me. And I hate him, see? So get me out of here."

Bobby had started panting again. Now he made the noise that was like a sob.

"Well, you heard him, anyway, Robert," said Dave. "There was a complaint for you."

He nodded his head abruptly at Bobby who got up out of the chair and preceded him out of the main office, his face averted from Robert. The cop did not have to touch him. He was going back to his cell voluntarily.

Robert looked after his son, walking away from him, and a mental image of Bobby as a small child came into his mind suddenly. He was holding Robert's hand as they walked uptown to the store when Herod McCrae's red truck passed by. "Truck!" he exclaimed, pointing excitedly. It was his first word. There had only been a few trucks in town back then.

Robert became aware of Rebecca standing beside him. She just stood there, hesitant, embarrassed, perhaps even sympathetic.

Dave came back. He sat down at his desk and switched on the radio.

"Sorry about that, Robert." He was also a little embarrassed now. "Why don't you talk to the social worker here," he said after a moment. "The Complaints Department isn't going to help you, is it?"

After this, Robert went home and told his wife, Mary Ann, about what had become of Bobby, who was their only child. He was expecting her to have a strong reaction, but not quite the reaction she did have. After uttering a long list of recriminations she had apparently been harbouring for years, she packed him a kit bag full of his old *Time* magazines, a change of socks and his winter jacket, and told him he had to go live somewhere else.

◂ ◂ ◂

Robert was sitting on a log in the woods with no home at all for the first time in his life.

He was still arguing with his wife in his mind. She had no right to throw him out. They were both Catholic, and had been married in a Catholic church. Of course he knew that divorce was legal in Canada, but the Church wouldn't recognize it, certainly not when there was a child.

He realized that all this was beside the point but he had this kind of legalistic mind; Robert could not help arguing.

She would stay on in the house, as it was Bobby's home; she had pointed this out quite forcibly. Their financial affairs were quite separate, as Robert made only enough from card playing to keep on playing cards, while she eked out a living for Bobby and herself with sewing, janitorial work, working at the store during inventory, and taking her cut of the communal meat supply. Really, they had had almost no contact in recent years at all, since he was usually out all night and only came home to sleep in the morning.

It surprised him how articulate Mary Ann could be when she put her mind to it. Robert was wishing he had thought of some good replies to what she had said. Of course, he realized even as he thought of them that it would have made absolutely no difference. He would still have been here, sitting on this log in the bush.

His chief emotion was bewilderment. Robert had read in *Time* magazine of the mid-life crisis, but it seemed something that would happen to fat, middle-aged whitemen in cities in the south, not to forty-year-old Robert Woodcutter, a Dene man living in Prohibition Creek, N.W.T.

Separated from his wife.

With a son who hated him.

When Robert was growing up they had been told they had to respect the elders, and that didn't just mean being polite. People were expected to do what they were told; they were scared not to. Robert had rebelled against this when he was a teenager. He had had a wild time in his twenties. But he had never gone to jail. He had ended up getting married as the Church and his parents had commanded. And now he had a son of his own to whom commands of that sort were meaningless. Of whom he himself was even afraid.

It had not really struck him so forcibly before that the order had changed, changed utterly, and with his generation. It came to him with a kind of grim humour that when he was growing up the elders were the boss and now that he was grown up the kids were the boss. He had got stuck in the middle somehow.

Someone was coming, not taking any care about keeping quiet, plunging through the bushes. Robert sat still on his log. Presently Haga emerged onto the path beside which Robert was sitting. He stopped abruptly when he spotted Robert. Then he jumped back with a look of terror.

Robert laughed. He guessed that Haga thought he was a bushman.

Haga seemed to be in the hallucinatory phase of whatever it was he had started out drinking that morning. He began to run away, crashing into the undergrowth.

"Wait!" shouted Robert. "It's just me. Robert."

Haga paused dubiously.

"You kind of sound like Robert," he said.

Robert grinned.

"Well, if I was a bushman pretending to be me I guess I'd try to sound like me, wouldn't I?"

Oddly enough, this seemed to make Haga think, even more, that he was talking to Robert.

"What are you doing out here in the bush?" Robert asked him.

"Going to my house."

It was news to Robert that Haga had any kind of a home of his own. He thought Haga lived with his married older sister, at least in the sense that he went to her house to sleep sometimes.

"She threw me out," said Haga. "Told me I snore too loud." They started walking along together, going down the old road to the fish plant.

Robert said: "Well, Mary Ann threw me out too."

"I heard Bobby went to jail," said Haga.

Everyone, of course, would have heard.

"Did you ever go to jail?" asked Robert.

"Nope," said Haga. He would have been terrified to go to jail because of the whitemen there. Whitemen were almost as bad as bushmen to Haga.

"Well, I never did either."

"Do you snore?" asked Haga suddenly.

"Yes," said Robert. Mary Ann had put that in her list of grievances.

"Well, heck, you can move in with me then."

They had come into the clearing where the abandoned fish plant stood. Most of the building was derelict, but there was an outbuilding, a sort of shanty by one wall, that had been used as a storehouse for surplus unprocessed fish. Haga opened the door with a flourish.

Robert preceded him inside and looked around while Haga stood by in proud and expectant silence.

It was a mess. The floor was covered with glass, broken linoleum floor tiles, some garbage indicating that it had been in use by adolescents for sex and smoking. The furnishings were a wood stove made out of a gas can, and an overturned pair of bunk beds.

"Boy, what a junk hole," said Robert.

"What do you want?" demanded Haga. "The Yellowknife Inn? It's got walls."

But Robert saw that it wasn't bad in a number of other respects. It was completely surrounded by firewood—on the trees, but nevertheless, there for the taking. And its distance from town was another good thing about it. A life of freedom, self-reliance, independence. It was not just that this was appealing; it was the only option.

Robert began looking around for a good place to stow his *Time* magazines. The braces in the studding of the uninsulated walls provided plenty of shelf space.

"Gee, a bookcase," said Haga.

With a good deal of effort they succeeded in setting up the bunk beds. One bedspring was gone, but there was a piece of plywood that fit. Haga was trying to heave his ragged bedroll up onto the top bunk.

Robert had a vision of Haga falling out of bed when he was drunk. He could hardly get up there even now.

"I guess I'd better take the top," he suggested.

"Why?"

"You drink too much," said Robert bluntly.

"Hey, you're getting kind of personal there, aren't you?" Haga turned around, his arms full of ancient, smelly sleeping bag. "You aren't so much better than I am."

"No, I guess I'm not," said Robert, surprised.

"You snore too," continued Haga. "Wife threw you out. Got beat in the chief election by your little brother."

Robert just stood there, taking it.

He wouldn't have been so humble only a few hours before.

"Well, okay, that's settled," said Haga. "So you can take the top bunk."

After they had got their bedding arranged, the place began to take on a more home-like appearance.

Robert found the stump of an old broom and began sweeping up the floor.

Haga hunkered down with his back against one wall. He took a letter out of his pocket and withdrew it from the envelope.

"Look what I got here," he said. "A letter."

Haga couldn't read. He might have travelled with the letter for several days before finding someone to read it to him.

Robert had spotted something that could be turned into a table again. It had obviously been a table at one time before. He began pulling it out in front of the bunks.

Haga sat down on the bottom bunk and put his elbows on the table.

Robert had seen a bucket in a corner. He turned it over and sat down opposite Haga. It was only a little low. He looked around with considerable satisfaction. The place was not clean but it was a lot neater.

"Okay," he said. "Now what about that letter?"

> Dear Sir,
> According to Bylaw NO. 245-07 of this Hamlet, called the Dog Bylaw, no dog shall be permitted to range freely by its owner. The fine for a first offence against this bylaw shall be $20.00.

> Your dog, a black, white and brown mongrel with four eyes, has been spotted on three different occasions at the dump: Monday, July 21, Tuesday, July 22 and Wednesday, July 23.
>
> You are therefore asked to appear before the Justice of the Peace on Friday, September 1 at 2:00 p.m.
>
> > Yours very sincerely,
> > James McCrae
> > Town Bylaw Office

September 1 was tomorrow. It seemed like short notice for Haga to come up with twenty dollars.

• 2. TEACH ME HOW TO CRY •

Once a month Herod McCrae presided over JP court in the school gymnasium.

As well as justice of the peace, Herod was also the mayor of Prohibition Creek, and had been so since the place became large enough to have a mayor. He was a relative of Robert's through his mother. Most of the Metis in town were McCraes; the treaty Indians were Woodcutters. The difference was not reflected in closeness of family ties, for there was considerable intermarriage, but it was deeply felt all the same. The Metis families believed that the way they ate and drank and worked and spoke and made love was superior; and the treaty Indians felt a similar, or even—if that were possible—deeper scorn for the Metis ways.

All the cases the court was taking up today—and in fact this was usually its whole function—were under Bylaw NO. 245-07, the Dog Bylaw. It might be said that the town government of Prohibition Creek existed more out of the need to institute rules about the restraint of dogs than for any other reason.

The arrival of the skidoo in Northern Canada had brought with it a technological change that could be compared to the invention of the automobile for the rest of North America. Just as the automobile had rendered the horse obsolete, so had the skidoo dealt the dog a mortal blow—which unfortunately had not in fact been mortal, for the dogs lived on. Unlike horses, dogs could not be butchered for food, they did not become status symbols or expensive pets, and the unobtainability of veterinarians made it impossible to prevent them from reproducing. In a Northern town after sunset the sound of the dogs howling, so mournful and romantic and full of Jack London to a stranger, is but a reminder to the outnumbered human inhabitants of the multitude of dogs that must be shot—or else somehow fed and kept in chains—each year.

Robert was sitting beside Haga in the middle of the chilly, echoing school gymnasium. There were about ten chairs of a common metal and plywood variety in a slightly jumbled array situated along the centre line of the basketball court. In front of them, Herod McCrae sat behind a table of the same sort, with the dog officer at his right hand.

"Haga. I guess you're up next."

"I'm acting for the accused, Your Honour." Robert stood up.

There was a small, pleased stir in the audience behind Robert as everyone realized this was going to be worth watching.

"I call James McCrae, dog officer for this settlement, as my first witness."

James stood up. "I don't see how I'm going to be a witness for Haga," he said.

"That's none of your business, James," said Robert. "Just as long as you answer some questions. Now, this is the most important question in the whole case," he continued. "James McCrae, have you got a dog that could be described as a black, white and brown mongrel with four eyes?"

"Well—yeah." James nodded, taken aback.

Robert was suddenly moving in for the kill. "Now was this dog of yours seen at the dump on these dates: July 21, July 22, July 23?"

James was apparently dumbfounded by this line of attack. He stared at Robert in silence.

"Was that your dog?"

"Hey, of course not!" James had found his voice again. "That was Haga's dog."

"Well, all you tell us in this letter—" Robert opened up the letter and studied it with a frown, "is that a black, white and brown mongrel with four eyes was seen at the dump."

"What are you getting at, Robert?" Herod was impatient.

Robert grinned at the JP. "I'd say the dog officer here has got a motive to accuse Haga, when it was really his dog all the time. Wasn't it, James?"

"Objection!" shouted the dog officer furiously.

Herod leaned forward over the table and gazed at Robert above his half glasses. He was a man of about sixty, ponderously fat, a dignified and slow talker, who commanded considerable respect in the community. He scrutinized Robert for a short while.

"You say he's got a dog like that?"

"So does he. You heard him." Robert was unperturbed. He was enjoying himself. Of this type of tricky argument, he was a master, even if it was something no one in the community appreciated.

Herod turned to the dog officer, who was his nephew. "Was it your dog, Jimmy?" he demanded.

"No! He's trying to pin it on me to get Haga off."

"Well, I'd say it was you trying to pin it on him, not the other way. When you accuse someone in a court of law you're supposed to prove what you say," Robert said.

There was a long pause. The large hand of the institutional clock high up on the wall made a startling advance of several minutes with an echoing click. Herod was staring at Robert again.

"Okay." He brought down his gavel. "You get off this time, Haga. But keep your dog tied up, okay?"

"Okay. Sure," said Haga, overjoyed.

Herod looked at the grinning faces in the little audience out in front of him. Then he brought his gavel down again. "That's all for today. The court is dismissed."

"Gee, thanks, pal," said Haga. "I sure didn't have the money for that fine."

Robert was feeling very pleased with himself as he went out the door of the gym.

It was a very nice day—crisp, early September weather. The schoolyard was ringed with yellow poplars and birches, the burnt orange of the larches bright against the deep greens and reds of the muskeg and the bush beyond. It was duck-hunting weather. It reminded Robert of the pleasure of fall camps from his childhood: taking out boats on the lake in the sunshine, eating the split, drying fish anytime you felt like it all day, good duck soup, rich with grease, in the tent at night; and the sunsets, magnificent and sad, like funeral orations on the death of summer.

There was a little crowd leaving the school, participants in the court proceedings and a few spectators. Suddenly Danny and the new social worker caught up with Robert and began walking alongside. Robert was still feeling pleased with himself, but Danny started right in.

"You know what really annoys me about you, Robert? It's the way you're wasting your time. You're a smart guy, know that? You're a guy who could be really useful to me now that I'm chief. But you spend your time hanging around with half-crazed alcoholics like this. Going to court to get his dog off, for God's sake. This place can go to hell as far as you care."

"Half-crazed alcoholics like this?" repeated Haga.

"I've been wanting to talk to you, Robert. Everyone knows you're going through a lot of trouble. Now you're living out in the woods like a bushman with this deadbeat here—"

"I'm sure not a bushman," Haga said.

"This trouble I'm in that everybody knows about, Danny," Robert said angrily. "You know, the way we were brought up, someone was in trouble, you knew about it, sure, but you didn't go up and tell him in front of a hundred other people."

It was an unspoken rule, or one that did not usually have to be spoken.

"That's the attitude I'm trying to change," said Danny. "If you're in trouble, it's not just your business, it's the business of the whole community. Everyone's going to pitch in and help."

"Well, if I want everyone's help I'll ask everyone myself."

"You were talking about the way we were brought up. Well, that was then, and look at what's happening now. Drinking and dope and substance abuse. Everyone up all night playing cards. No one looking after their kids."

There was a lot of truth in what he was saying. Robert knew that. But what was Danny going to do about it, after all? Bring in a lot of social workers and drop-in centres and extra police, and start people snooping into one another's affairs at AA meetings and prayer camps? Danny was Dene; he ought to know better. He wanted to solve the problems of this town by turning people into whitemen.

"No one's bringing anyone up any longer. And your own boy, Robert, your own boy too," Danny said.

His own boy. Robert was suddenly very agitated. It was a blow beneath the belt: Danny's speech had actually taken his breath away. This was his brother, after all, and he was going too far.

Haga now took Robert's part.

"Boy, people sure have been calling names this afternoon. And that's not the way I was brought up. I may be a half-crazed alcoholic deadbeat bushman, but the way I was brought up—" He was looking tactfully away.

Robert was still struggling to regain control over himself, remembering that scene in the police detachment, his own son saying those terrible, final things in front of the cop and this woman here. He had been hating himself ever since.

As a matter of fact, a change had already taken place of which he was not yet aware. Since he had moved in with Haga he had not been to town to play poker, and it was now close to three days since he had had a drink.

However, Robert did not know that he was in any position of moral strength to argue. He just wanted to get back at Danny.

The first thing would be to do something about this woman with him. Danny had brought her in here; she was obviously his property.

"What the heck are you doing here, anyway?" he said to her. "See, the chief here thinks that because you have a diploma and an office you're qualified to tell people what to do. But I wonder if you actually know what you're getting into."

"If we can all work together—" Danny began.

"What I mean is," Robert interrupted him, "people are going to tell you all kinds of stuff that maybe you can't handle. Maybe you think turning this place around is going to be simple. But it isn't simple."

Rebecca was listening to him quite seriously, and Robert suddenly felt like trying to convince her of something and not just trying to get at Danny.

"Sometimes people have got a problem," he went on. "But then sometimes you think they've got a problem, but actually it's everyone else. Maybe it's even you."

She had been looking at the ground, but she raised her head sharply.

"Just look at Haga here. I guess you think he's a hopeless case."

Haga gave Robert a look of outrage and surprise.

"Well, it might surprise you, but according to Haga here, you guys are the ones that are all messed up." Robert was grinning. He had come up with a very good example.

"You think he's a bum," he said. "But really—he's an individualist."

Haga grinned as well. Rebecca began to smile.

Danny was opening his mouth to speak when Haga said suddenly, "Hey, Robert, it's Lassie! That's my dog over there!"

He pointed toward the school garbage cans, a couple of rusty forty-five-gallon oil drums perched crazily on the roadside, tilting into the ditch. A black, white and brown mongrel was poking among them, probably looking for candy papers. The dog came around the side of a can and Robert saw that it had four eyes.

He began running toward it, Haga on his heels.

The dog spotted Haga and turned to make a dash for freedom. Robert attempted a football tackle on its hindquarters and the tilting cans fell in on him as he flew past them, horizontal in the air.

"You okay, pal?" Haga pulled a couple of cans off Robert and he got to his feet, knee-deep in ditch water. The dog had already emerged with a yelp from the scene of collision and was now some distance off down the street.

"Why didn't you tie her up, you jerk?"

"I didn't even see him till now."

Robert decided to try calling the dog, who was still within earshot, although disappearing rapidly.

"Lassie! Lassie, come here!" he called. It made him feel silly. Probably calling the dog Lassie was Haga's idea of a joke.

"He won't come if you call him that."

Haga began to run after the dog again, and the animal, with a glance over its shoulder, disappeared into an opening between two houses and was gone.

Robert was beginning to get the idea. It was not a joke at all. Only Haga would think a black, white and brown male mongrel with four eyes looked like a female collie on TV.

He climbed out of the ditch and followed Haga into the driveway. There was now no sign of the dog at all. Robert remembered that there were some garbage cans on the other side of one of the houses. The dog would probably stop there for a pee and a sniff and they could get him if they adopted a pincers strategy.

"He's got his own name—in dog language," Haga was explaining.

Without having to discuss it—after all, Haga was supposed to be a moose hunter too—Robert began to implement his tactic, going back around the house, and leaving Haga to scare the dog toward him.

As he had expected, the dog came pounding toward him as soon as it noticed Haga approaching from behind. Robert pounced on it, the wings of his jacket spread wide. He was afraid that Lassie might bite him this time, so he held the dog down firmly with his whole body, his knees straddling its back. His shoes were full of water and the wet knees of his jeans ground the dust of the road into mud.

The dog yelped and began licking his ear.

Haga came up, panting.

"Gee, that was good thinking, Robert," he said.

"Where's your rope?" demanded Robert. He was now merely holding the dog by the collar, trying to hold it at arm's length, in fact. It was a very affectionate dog.

"The only thing I've got is my belt. And that's holding up my pants," Haga said.

Robert studied him for awhile. Haga had a cigarette butt he must have found when they were both scrabbling in the school garbage. He lit up, his face serene, unclouded by thought.

"So am I going to have to take off my belt?"

"Okay. Sure," said Haga. "Hey, thanks a lot, Robert."

"Haga, I don't know what to call you, but you sure are some kind of a—!"

"Well, what you said back there to them was that I was an individualist," said Haga. "So I guess that's what I am. Some kind of an individualist, Robert."

The two individualists led the dog out of town to their home in the old fish store on the end of Robert's belt and tied him up outside to a tree. Then while Haga went to attend to a snare line which kept him well supplied with rabbits at this time of year, Robert made a fire in the stove and fell to some serious housekeeping, using a mop and pail borrowed from his mother.

It still did not occur to him that he had not had a drink for three days.

◂ ◂ ◂

At the end of the week Robert went to a meeting in the band hall. It was billed as an AA meeting, but he went not so as to confirm his own sobriety, of which he was still hardly even conscious, but because he had heard that the self-styled Alcohol and Drug Abuse Committee were intending to make an intervention.

Intervention was a technique used in community encounter sessions of this type, where someone's family and friends were invited to hold him up to public opprobrium in front of a committee composed of the officials of the town, most of them white: the nurse, the priest, the police, the social worker, the mayor and the chief.

Robert had already heard all about how this worked from his drinking and poker-playing buddies, who had been joking about it—and dreading, at the same time, that it might ever be applied to their case—in the weeks after Danny's election.

Robert would never have gone to one of these sessions merely out of curiosity, for this idea was absolute anathema to him. It violated all the understood rules of his culture: not to interfere, to mind your own business—the part of their upbringing he had been trying to remind Danny of during their conversation in the schoolyard.

However, the meeting was being held over his younger brother, Michael.

Michael was twelve years younger than Robert, the last child of their parents before his father had left home. He was a poker player like Robert, and a drinker. However, unlike Robert, and even their father, who had also been a gambler and a drinker, Michael beat his wife, Sarah. They had two children at this time and she was pregnant with a third.

After Sarah, Robert's mother got up to speak. She explained how she had tried to bring up her children to be good people; but then she broke down and wept, covering her face with her hands.

The old women in the hall, most of whom had remained stoical throughout Sarah's incoherent presentation, now broke down as well and cried with Rachel.

Danny would have spoken then, and Robert saw that he had tears on his face too, but Michael got up, crying, and hugged his wife. He hugged his mother. Danny hugged him. Michael apologized to them all.

His wife appealed to the policeman present—not Dave, but the one who was billed as the mean one—and charges were informally dropped against Michael. Then Danny spoke, followed by the priest, who said a prayer.

The meeting was over, its mission accomplished, and there was a joyous note in the air. Michael went out of the hall hand in hand with Sarah. Rachel was talking and laughing with some of her friends. The white officials were making arrangements to see each other home; they would probably all talk about the meeting together later at one of their houses.

Robert got up from his place by the door feeling like an outsider in his own community. It was a sour feeling: he knew that what had been accomplished tonight was good, but his heart was sore with embarrassment for his younger brother and his mother.

"Hey, wait a minute, Robert." It was Danny; he had followed him out the door.

"What do you want?" Robert was gruff.

"Nothing. I was surprised to see you here, that's all."

"I just wanted to know what you were going to do to Michael."

"Well, it was nothing bad. You saw him. He said he was sorry."

Robert was still trying to get away; he preceded Danny down over the dark lawn of the hall. Then he stopped under the street light. The nights were dark again and they stood there in the pool of light under the power pole.

"Do you really think it's going to change everything, Danny? Hauling a guy up in front of a bunch of people and making him cry and say he's sorry?"

"You've got to start somewhere, Robert," said Danny. "The first thing is to make the guy see he's done something wrong. A lot of them don't even know that."

He was right, but the way they did it reminded Robert of something he had read in *Time* magazine about China. If there was a person in the village people didn't like, they hauled him up and threw rocks at him till he crawled out in front and apologized. Then if they still didn't like him they killed him and ate him right there.

"It made me feel pretty lousy, that's all," he said.

"Look, our brother Michael beats up on his wife. He's got a disease called alcoholism. He doesn't even know he's sick. Or he didn't know it yesterday." For Danny the revival meeting was still going on.

"Maybe Sarah should just throw him out." Robert knew he shouldn't have said that, because Danny pounced on it instantly.

"The way Mary Ann threw you out?"

Robert had never beaten his wife. He had merely neglected her for twenty years, losing interest in her from the day of their marriage; she had already been pregnant with Bobby at that point. But Mary Ann was a very tough person and she had responded in kind, ignoring Robert, calling upon him for nothing, not even financial support. Robert was insulted by Danny's comparison of this—a kind of silent, but nonetheless dignified warfare—to Michael's treatment of Sarah.

"Maybe she's going to want you back sometime."

"How do you know what she's going to want?" Robert demanded angrily.

"I've been counselling her," Danny replied.

Did everyone have to know everything about everyone else? Were they going to try to get him in there and make him cry too?

They were, and Robert saw that it was happening right now. He and Danny had been alone, but they were joined all at once under the street light by the social worker who was leading, almost pushing, Robert saw, his ex-wife. This had been planned.

Robert and Mary Ann looked at one another.

"Hello," he said.

There was a silence and Robert felt with a certain hopefulness that Mary Ann had as little stomach for this kind of thing as he did.

"Talk to him," Danny prompted.

"My boy is in jail." Mary Ann spoke abruptly. "It's your fault."

"My God, Mary Ann, how can you say that?" said Robert.

"You never talk to him."

"I do. He won't listen." He had even been afraid to talk to Bobby lately, however. He was bigger than Robert, irrational and mean.

Mary Ann spoke out of the certainty of her upbringing: "You're the father. If you talk, he's got to listen."

"No he doesn't. It isn't like that anymore, Mary Ann." But to Mary Ann, he knew, the wisdom of the elders was an eternal verity. She couldn't credit, any more than his mother could, that all that had passed away in the span of a generation.

"You don't care about my son," said Mary Ann. "You're the father and you don't care at all."

It might have seemed to her that this was true—Robert could see how she must think it—but it was not true.

"For God's sake, Mary Ann—" By now Robert had forgotten the other people present. He had begun to cry, partly because of the way she had called Bobby "my son"—no longer his, or even theirs.

"It's all your fault."

"Okay, it's all my fault. But I do care about him," he managed to say.

Robert had covered his face with his hands. He cried helplessly for a minute or so. Mary Ann continued to stand in silence a few paces in front of him, not weeping, her hands hanging loosely at her sides.

"Mary Ann—" Danny said. He was trying to prompt her again. He wanted her to make up with Robert now, to hug and kiss, like Sarah with Michael.

"I'm going home," she said flatly.

Embarrassed now, Danny was offering to walk Mary Ann home.

"I've got to get home myself. The kids like it when I'm around to put them to bed," he told her.

From a dark place inside his head Robert heard them go crunching off. He stayed there in that place for a little while, recovering himself, or trying to.

It was a clear night of the new moon. The aurora began to appear and the coloured shafts and columns shifted across the glittering background of the starlight.

Robert began to feel a dawning embarrassment. He remembered how he had cried—just like Michael. He turned and walked, almost without consciousness anymore, toward the fish-plant store while the mysterious lights of the high North cracked above his head.

◂ ◂ ◂

It was duck-hunting season and Robert's whole extended family would soon go to their camp at Joker Lake for several weeks for what was by all odds the best season of the year: the fall time. They would dry fish, shoot a moose if they could get one, pick cranberries and eat gallons of delicious, thick, rich duck soup. It was a time for taking boats out on the lake, for lazing around in the last of the sunshine before winter brought the dark; a time of gourmet eating. This was the cream of life for hunting and gathering people.

Robert was going to go hunting with his family this year; he usually did not go hunting because of the demands of his poker-playing schedule. But as he was no longer playing cards he had a lot of time on his hands and was restless for some kind of activity. He was intending to go out with his mother, since he had gambled away his own boat and motor some years before. They usually went to the camp by boat through a complex of lake and river systems travelled winter and summer by their ancestors for thousands of years.

But in the three days before he departed he wanted to fix up his home for the coming winter, the old fish store. It needed an outhouse.

He had spent all of one day and part of the next scrounging

materials and tools: lumber, plywood, a door of some kind, a hammer, a saw.

Another big job was to get Haga involved in the project. He would be needed to help with the digging, but Robert was too wise to mention this. Instead he had entrusted Haga with five dollars to purchase some nails at the store the previous day.

It was now early afternoon and Robert had come home with the picks and shovels he had managed to borrow. He made a fire in the stove and boiled the billy for tea. Then he munched on a piece of bannock, looking at Haga, who was still asleep, lying on his back and snoring without inhibition.

"We've got an outhouse to build," he said.

Haga snored a little louder.

"C'mon, let's get going."

Haga sighed and rolled over to face the wall.

"Get up," commanded Robert. He took hold of the foot end of Haga's sleeping bag and hauled the whole thing down onto the floor, Haga inside coming with it. Haga hit the floor with a good-sized thump, then sat up indignantly.

A moment later he got out of the bag and bundled it up on his bunk. He was fully dressed since he usually wore everything except his boots to bed.

"Well, now you're up," said Robert.

Haga went to get himself a cup of tea in dignified silence. He added sugar, sipped experimentally, then added more sugar.

"Look, winter is coming. You're going to like having that outhouse just as much as me."

Haga had begun his usual early morning throat-clearing routine; it was his only ritual of personal hygiene, for he never shaved, washed, changed his clothes, or as far as Robert could tell, even took them off. Sometimes, irregularly, he combed his hair, using Robert's comb.

Throat clearing for Haga started with a prolonged snuffle, during which he seemed to draw his vocal chords up behind his tonsils, an expression of pained surprise appearing on his face. Then he let go in a full-throated hawk, which was designed to propel the accumulated ball of phlegm up onto the back of his tongue. He would savour this for a moment or two, rolling his eyes, as he checked it for size and viscosity. After that he went to the door, hawked lingeringly once more, and spat the giant blob in a satisfactory and aesthetically pleasing arc onto the moss.

For a moment he lounged in the doorway, cleansed and ready to start a new day. Then he sighed, yawned, belched slightly and said to Robert:

"All right, let's see what you got."

Much relieved at being forgiven so quickly, Robert followed him outside into the clearing. It was a wide opening in the bush, now slowly filling in with willow and poplar, but with a good prospect of the lake. A ruined teepee stood in the graceful frame created by beach, lake and bush.

The fish-store shack was really a sort of lean-to attached to a much larger structure, the packing plant. About fifteen years before, the packing plant had been rendered obsolete with the arrival of more modern means of transportation bringing food from the south, and the marketing boards, which set prices too low for export. The building had been allowed to fall into decay: little boys broke the windows with stones, teenagers used it as a place of assignation, then it was robbed for lumber by home builders such as Robert. There was not much left, except the bare structure with the lean-to hanging off its back.

Robert had scavenged most of his lumber here. Then he had unofficially borrowed some large scraps of plywood from a Housing Corporation construction site and found half a roll of tar paper at the dump.

Haga inspected the accumulated trove of materials.

"Got tools too?"

"Borrowed them from Herod." In addition to his positions as Mayor and Justice of the Peace, Herod McCrae ran the Department of Public Works depot, which meant that he drove the grader and operated the only mechanical workshop in town.

Haga had moved on to inspect Robert's best find: the door. He had come across it on the beach, where it must have fallen down the bank off somebody's junkpile. In a town as off the beaten track as

Prohibition Creek, people were in the habit of collecting all manner of odds and ends and keeping them for a rainy day. It was a full-sized wooden interior door in good repair, and it had two perfectly straight hinges, with screws still in them.

Haga was looking at the shovels, the pick and the crowbar, his hands in his pockets.

"I gave you five dollars yesterday, remember? To get nails at the co-op."

"Oh yeah."

"You got them, right?"

"The store was closed."

"Closed?" Robert exclaimed. "On Friday afternoon?"

"Well, I was busy. You can't expect me to do everything." Haga was uneasy. He turned away from Robert.

"So what did you do with the money?" Robert confronted him, and Haga turned away again. "I guess you spent it."

"I gave it to a person in need."

"A needy person with a brew pot," said Robert in disgust.

He stared at Haga's back and kicked the pile of digging tools. After a moment, he put his own hands in his pockets and turning away too, began to whistle. There was no point getting upset about things like this. He could go into town for a game anytime and win the money for a bag of nails.

He was not going to do that, but just because he didn't want to bother.

A truck came jolting toward them in low gear along the rough track through the undergrowth. It was a red one—Herod's Ford. He pulled up and jumped out, puffing. Herod was a very fat man who never walked anywhere; he needed his truck to get around, keeping his finger on the pulse of Prohibition Creek.

"Hello, Robert. Haga." He nodded at Haga, who was staring in surprise.

"I heard down at Housing that you boys were going to build yourselves an outhouse," he continued. "So being that I'm the mayor, I thought I'd bring you the paperwork."

"Paperwork?" said Robert, startled. Herod was handing him an application form.

"Yeah, we've got a zoning bylaw now. Means that you've got to apply. Now this is a commercial use here, since it's the old fish store, but I figure the Council would let an outhouse application through. After all, the employees would have to have some place to go."

"The employees?" said Haga.

"That's us, I guess," Robert told him.

It was a three-page form, calling for "an architect's drawing, including floor plans, of the proposed structure."

"She's only an outhouse," remarked Herod. "I guess they'd let you off that. Just write down how many holes she's going to have."

Robert took the pen Herod offered him and sat down on a fallen log to read the rest of the form.

"Describe relationship to any nearby buildings indicating position of water, sewage and electrical lines," he read. He looked around at the clearing, full of the golden leaves of autumn, at the hulk of the old fish plant, at the little lean-to clinging to it crazily, the stovepipe coming out of the roof. There was probably an old electrical line somewhere, and perhaps there had once been tanks for water and sewage—no one knew where they were any longer, though.

"All bathroom and kitchen facilities must conform to minimum standards set by CMHC," Robert read.

Whether the Canadian Mortgage and Housing Corporation would regard an outhouse as a bathroom was debatable. Robert paused, his thoughts whirling. If they did think it was a bathroom, then by their regulations it probably couldn't be an outhouse. But if it was not a bathroom, what was it then?

Haga was displaying the tools to Herod. Herod was looking gratified; they had all come from him in the first place.

Robert read, "Outbuildings must preserve a forty-foot fire separation from existing stuctures." Forty feet was a long way to go in the winter.

"I was just wondering if you'd happen to have any nails," Haga was saying.

"Well, sure. I guess I can spare a few nails."

They got up on the back of the truck and began to rummage for the nails. Surprised and impressed that Haga was taking some initiative, Robert went back to his reading.

"Specify type of heating and indicate position of chimneys, exhaust systems or provision for venting of fumes."

It was the first question he had been able to answer. He wrote in "The Great Outdoors" on the top line of the space.

Herod had found a whole box of nails in the tool chest on the back of his truck.

"Gee, thanks," Haga was telling him.

Robert gave back the application form and the pen. "I did my best with this, Herod. There were a lot of spaces I had to leave blank." Aside from his name at the top of the front page, the form was almost entirely blank.

"I guess they're used to that in Yellowknife," said Herod.

"What's Yellowknife got to do with it?"

"You don't know? The Department of Local Government made up a town plan for us last year. Now everything's got to be approved by headquarters."

"Why the heck did you let them do that?" said Robert in disgust.

Herod sighed and sat down beside him on the log.

"To tell you the truth, I don't know the answer to that one myself," he said. "Seems as though we're always doing something that ain't in the town plan nowadays."

"It's the same old story," said Robert. " Look at this—whiteman even wants to tell me where I can shit next winter."

"Well, the Council here isn't going to turn you down, Robert, that's for sure."

"Yeah, but what about Yellowknife? The Department of Local Government sure won't think much of the way I filled in that form."

"Local Government's supposed to come in and have a big meeting at the end of the month. I don't guess they'll look at the paperwork till then."

"This outhouse has got to be finished before that. I was thinking of going to Joker Lake at the end of the week."

"Well, you could just come to that meeting."

"Yeah, I think I will. I might have a complaint about this," said Robert.

"I guess I might have one too," said Herod with a sigh. "Anyway, you explain your application to them."

"So they can go ahead and make us install running water and electric lights?"

"I'd kind of like you to come to that meeting anyway, Robert. We're going to talk about the airport too."

The Prohibition Creek airport had been a running sore for years in discussions between the local councils and the government. A dirt strip situated in a firebreak, it was a mudhole in spring and summer, and full of snow all winter, and was notorious among the local airlines for its accident potential.

"Sometimes I get mad at meetings like that," Robert remarked.

"Well, maybe that's why I want you to come."

Robert was surprised to hear this. He liked Herod and he knew that Herod liked him, but in terms of local respectability they were almost at opposite poles, especially after what had happened recently.

"I always like it when you begin talking in that highfalutin way of yours," Herod explained.

Someone else was using the Complaints Department for its proper purpose.

Herod got up off the log and lumbered to his truck.

"You boys all set up to go now?"

"Sure. Thanks."

"Yeah. Gee, Herod, thanks a lot."

The red truck rattled and bumped its way over the rough wood road out of the clearing.

Haga had picked up a shovel and was attacking the ground right where he was standing.

"I guess it's time to get started on this thing," he said.

Robert stared at him in astonishment, putting his hands on his hips. Haga paused to grin at him sheepishly, then fell to again.

"Got some nails, did you?" Robert began to swing the pick.

"Yep."

"Well, that was good."

The work in the hole was too hard for them to go on talking. After about an hour, going at it steadily, and dislodging several boulders from the layers of frost, they had a hole wide and deep enough for their purposes.

Robert was cleaning the earth off the tools. Haga belched, spat, squinted at the sky, then started to go into the shack.

"Hey, where are you going?"

"Time for lunch," said Haga. He came out again a moment later, grinning, with a bannock in his hand, and sat down on the rotten board that constituted their doorstep.

"Oh. Okay." Robert sat down beside him. "I was just worried that by the time you finished lunch it'd be suppertime, that's all."

Haga continued to sit for a while after he finished eating. Robert got up and wandered restlessly around. As usual, Haga was operating on a timetable of his own.

"C'mon, Haga, I just want to get this done before the snow comes, okay?" he said at last.

"Okay," said Haga. He stood up. "But just remember, without me, this whole thing would have been a disaster," he continued.

"What do you mean by that?" demanded Robert.

"I got the nails," said Haga "You can't put up an outhouse without nails, Robert."

• 3. CINDERELLA •

Things in Prohibition Creek were on the up and up. Danny and Rebecca had got the Alcoholics Anonymous meetings started and many people were attending. The story of Michael's conversion to sobriety and how it had been achieved had caused quite a stir. People were generally in favour of what Danny was doing. The fact that he had begun his work with his own family gave rise to approving comment as well; it was a reform that was taking place from inside the community for a change.

Rebecca had her work cut out for her. There was all the usual paperwork connected with welfare, but on top of that she had a full slate of counselling sessions every day, and AA meetings at night. She was living in the old Department of Public Works trailer on the edge of town, and she had spent a lot of time trying to get it fixed up so that she could live in it; small apartment on one side, office on the other.

On Sunday morning she was in her office, trying to get the files in order. There really weren't any files. The last full-time social worker to stay in Prohibition Creek had left in an alcoholic haze, and whatever paperwork there was now Rebecca had brought in with her, or was currently constructing through her counselling.

There was a knock at the door, which immediately flew open revealing a good-looking young whiteman of about twenty-three, in hip waders. It was Don, the pilot employee of the infamous Red Baron who operated an airline at the Forks. Don had brought Rebecca into Prohibition Creek in the Red Baron's Beaver and she had seen him not quite by accident several times since; he liked her, she knew.

As with many young pilots, the North was part of Don's apprenticeship. The terms of his employment were that he did hard work for low pay seven days a week and had a wild time with the local girls whenever and wherever he could.

Rebecca knew this about him as well.

"Hey, Rebecca, I got a day off," he said. "And the Red Baron let me borrow that broke-down piece of crap he calls an airplane."

This was not just one of the coincidental chats they had been having over the past few weeks, she decided. She was looking up into his face and she liked his brown eyes, his short brown hair, his good teeth. He looked to her like a person who didn't have many problems.

"So what I came all the way over here from the Forks to ask you was: want to go somewhere in the sky?" It was an invitation for a date.

"Where?" Rebecca asked carefully. She couldn't go to a bar with this whiteman.

"Well, it'll have to be some lake, lady," he said.

She recalled that the Beaver was on floats. It was not a conventional proposition, although she knew there was a proposition in it somewhere down the line.

Suddenly she was filled with the desire to get out of her office. The pilot saw from her expression that she was going to say yes.

"Okay!" he said. "Close that drawer, braid up your hair and put on those big rubber boots. We're going to go flying."

It was a wonderful day for flying, a blue day. Under the pontoons of the plane, the colours of the bush unfolded like an Oriental carpet: the red of muskeg, the gold of the poplars and the dense green of the swamp spruce.

Prohibition Creek was a boondocks town, not on the Arctic coast nor in the valley of the Big River, but way out in the middle of nowhere. White government officials wished it didn't exist at all, and had been trying to move it for years, but the location had a rationale. It had been a meeting place of the wandering bands for several thousand years. Through the sinuous waterways that wound and opened out into shallow lakes, the fish ran backwards and forwards in their ancient spawning patterns. The ducks came to feed, minks and otters played on the mud banks, beavers built dams and brought the muskrat, moose stood hock deep in the weedy backwaters. Rebecca was peering down at this panorama as it opened out beneath them.

"Having a good time?" Don asked her in dumb show. The engine noise was loud and he was wearing earphones.

A moment later the plane went into a nose-dive. Rebecca clung to her seat and the doorframe beside her, pleasurably terrified.

Don pulled up a few feet off a lake and they went skimming across the surface, then rose over a couple of boats. Rebecca saw the horrified expressions on the faces of the people in them as the plane rose up just in time. Then Don pulled the plane way up, skimming the tree tops, and around, slipping sideways to finally come down on the water, speeding scornfully past the boats in the other direction with a shower of spray.

"You were trying to scare me!"

"Sure makes you look pretty." He made a grab for her, but she dodged.

He settled back in his seat with a good-natured chuckle.

"Are we going to stop here?" They were taxiing into the mouth of the river.

"I think those people are hunting duck," he said. "I love hunting duck. Maybe I can borrow a boat here for, say, all afternoon."

He nosed the plane up into a mud bank and Rebecca saw that there was an encampment in the grassy clearing above: some log cabins and a teepee. An old woman stood staring at them with a basin in her hands, her arms covered in blood to the elbow.

"They must have got a moose. I'm going to get my gun out of the back," Don said. He jumped out on the floats and held the door for Rebecca.

Rebecca realized that the old woman was Rachel Woodcutter, Danny's mother. Robert now stood up in one of the boats moored beside them on the riverbank, a look of surprise on his face as he noticed Rebecca teetering behind the pilot on the pontoon of the plane.

"You'd speak English, I guess," said Don to Robert. "I'd like to borrow your boat, my friend. I've got an appointment with some ducks."

"Sure," Robert replied. "If you don't mind paddling, my friend. The kicker's on the fritz."

"On second thoughts, I think I'll walk." Don was getting out his gun. "We'll just leave the plane here for a while, if you don't mind."

Rebecca jumped off the front end of the float and scrambled up the bank. "Hi, Rachel," she said.

Rachel looked blankly at the pilot, then at Rebecca. "Hello," she said.

"C'mon, c'mon. Let's go blast some of those flying rabbits." Don was trying to take her arm to hurry her along.

The camp was on a pretty grassy field above the mouth of the river within a few hundred yards of the lake. Rebecca was looking at it in curiosity. So this was Joker Lake, the ancestral camp of the Woodcutter family. She had heard about it from Danny; she had also heard about it from some of her McCrae relatives, who had fished and hunted close by here for a hundred years or more, and married into the Woodcutter clan. Her father had virtually grown up here, although he never came here now, and her mother, who was from Yellowknife, knew nothing of the bush.

"Stay and have tea with Ama, Rebecca." Robert was watching the pilot's efforts to hurry her along with disapproval. He jumped up on the bank and stood beside her, folding his arms.

"Come into the teepee, Rebecca," said Rachel, leading the way.

"Oh, okay," Don called after Rebecca. "We'll do something romantic later."

Inside the tent Rachel sat down on her heels and after hanging a hide from a hook on one of the poles, began slowly scraping it into the basin of water with an enormous curved knife.

A fire made of punk smouldered under the fish hanging to dry above their heads. A billy was perched on the edge of the grate.

"Is this tea?" Rebecca was investigating. She found some cups and a bag of sugar, an open tin of evaporated milk, all neatly arranged on a scrap of plywood. She poured out two cups of tea, and politely put milk and sugar in for Rachel before passing her one of them.

"Masi," said Rachel.

"Masi," Rebecca said in return. She did not really like tea, but drinking it was an important part of good manners with Prohibition Creek people.

Rachel was saying nothing. Neither she nor Robert had liked to see Rebecca with the pilot. He had a certain reputation. However, it was not her affair.

There was the sound of a revving boat motor outside. A moment later Robert ducked his head and came into the teepee.

"I lent him the spare kicker," he said to his mother. "I guess that guy wouldn't bother to pick up any of those ducks he shot if he was walking."

"More ducks," said Rachel in a dry voice. There was a large pile of ducks, still unplucked, beside her on the floor.

"Yeah," agreed Robert. "It isn't as though we didn't have enough already."

He was putting tea in a cup for himself and there was a little silence, the only sound the lapping of the water and the fast receding roar of the boat.

"Who shot the moose?" asked Rebecca.

"Me," said Robert. "That was yesterday. The rest of the family's out on the lake today but I stayed here to fix that boat motor," he went on.

Rachel continued scraping, taking her time. Warm fall sunshine came in the triangular door of the teepee. Rebecca sipped her lukewarm tea. There was a distant shot, then another.

"It's nice here," said Rebecca. "I've never been out in the bush."

"But you're Dene." Robert was shocked.

"We used to go for picnics in our boat. But we didn't have a camp like this."

"Well, this is our place. I was born here," Robert told her.

He was sitting on his heel with one knee up, and now he rested his teacup on the knee, smiling at her.

"It must have been kind of scary. To have a baby without a doctor," Rebecca turned to Rachel.

"The first one is the hardest," she replied. "My mother was dead but I had my sister Mary."

"Yeah, and Aunt Mary didn't know what to do at all," said Robert. "She was just running around in circles."

"How do you know? You weren't there yet," Rachel said to him.

They all laughed.

"At least I was with my family," Rachel said to Rebecca. "Nowadays they go to the hospital in Yellowknife. They leave their other babies to be cared for by strangers."

"But it's safer, isn't it?"

"Ama doesn't think they do anything better nowadays."

"They don't," said Rachel, and they all laughed again.

Rebecca was thinking that Robert was nice.

She looked at him with attention for the first time. He was about ten years older than herself, old enough to have been born in the bush, not a hospital. And he was quite good-looking; she had not noticed that before: bright eyes, longish black hair, a broken nose slightly marring, but also drawing attention to his handsome face.

"Back then we had our own ways," said Robert. "The old women knew more than those hospitals. We had our own medicine."

Rebecca was amazed. For her the system of taboos and shamanism that had prevailed among the Dene before Christianity was wrong. She had never heard anyone speak of it favourably before.

"What do you know about that—about the medicine men?" she asked.

"Well, for one thing they're all gone," said Robert. "Maybe that's our problem."

"But do you really think it would be better if we still had them? What about the taboos?"

She knew that the taboos had dominated all of life: how you could hunt, live, eat, even whom you could speak to. This had always been described to her as a system of utmost falsehood, a kind of devil worship.

"I don't know about that," said Robert. "But when you're out in the bush—or when you look up into the sky—there's more to this than just our puny little ideas about who we are."

"So you think the medicine men knew—they understood everything?" The conversation touched on something deeply alarming and also deeply fascinating to Rebecca.

"The medicine men were like scientists. They were trying to understand."

They were both unconscious now of the soft scraping of the knife, the puff of smoke from the punky little fire, the soft, flickering light that entered the teepee through its canvas sides.

"I always thought they were preachers," she said.

"Maybe they were both," said Robert.

They stared at one another, surprised. Neither of them was used to a conversation of this type, following where the truth led them. Robert was used to arguing. He always argued to win, and so did Rebecca, who usually lost and then resented it forever.

"It's a funny thing though," he said after a moment. "We had nothing back then and we were completely happy. They say no one was even sick before the whiteman came."

"In the old days people had respect." Rachel spoke suddenly.

"Self-respect," said Rebecca.

"No." Robert had no use for this vocabulary: self-respect, role model, initiative, work ethic—these were all terms that the whiteman used to beat up on native culture, in his view. "What Ama means is that they did what they were told. Because of medicine, and then later, because they were afraid of hell."

"At least people took care of their families back then," said Rachel. "That is the most important thing. To take care of your family, Robert."

She spoke pointedly. Robert looked at the ground and for a moment there was only the distant sound of the boat motor, getting louder.

"My grandson is in jail. And your wife won't let you live in your own house. That is why she is not here with us now. You are staying in a dirty shack with that Haga. It will burn down sometime because he smokes in bed."

Robert still had nothing to say. Rachel continued her slow scraping.

"Old people like me, no one listens to us. And to us, so much that is happening has no meaning. All there is now is this modern life that we don't understand. Jail and divorce, and people going to AA."

"Well, at least you don't like that either, Ama."

"Be quiet. My son, the chief, has started this AA. He and this woman here are trying to do good for us. Your father must be proud of you, my girl," she said to Rebecca.

Rebecca was embarrassed. The conversation they had been having had deeply interested her; she had forgotten all about Robert's disgrace.

The boat was roaring outside on the river; then the sound was suddenly cut off. A moment later Don came into the teepee and threw down an armload of ducks beside the pile that was already there.

"Boy, that was good," he exclaimed. "See how many I got? Pretty good shot, eh? All in half an hour or so. These are for you, granny."

"Too many ducks," muttered Rachel.

"You like duck soup, Rebecca?" asked Robert.

"I've never had it."

"Well, like I say, you can keep 'em," said Don. "I never eat stuff like that. I just like to shoot 'em." He reached down to help Rebecca to her feet. "All set to go, sweetheart? We've got a table for two reserved on the next lake."

"Don't go," Robert said to Rebecca. He stood up too. "You could stay here and have soup with us. I make a pretty good soup. We could take you home by boat tomorrow."

"Are you kidding? She's got a heavy date with me."

"I have to go to work tomorrow morning," Rebecca said to Robert.

"Yeah, and we got a few other things to do before that," said Don.

She went out of the teepee and down the bank to the plane, where it was tied up beside the boats. Don helped her onto the float and then opened the door. She turned around to wave to Robert who stood on the bank above; his arms were folded again. Don pushed off without help, then jumped up into the cockpit. A moment later the engine roared to life and they were off, leaving Robert behind, still standing there on the riverbank with a frown on his face.

As for Rebecca, she knew quite well what the pilot was hoping to get out of their plane ride together. On the next lake they went fishing for a while from the floats of the airplane, until she announced that she had to go home. But after he walked her to her trailer, she permitted him only a brief kiss on the lips, and when he showed a disposition to demand more, she told him not to be a bad boy and went inside, locking the door.

She knew from Rachel's blank face, from Robert's folded arms, from what Danny would say, but even more from the voice of experience, that she should not get sexually entangled with this young man. It would spell disaster for her job, for what she was trying to do in Prohibition Creek. It might also spell disaster for her life if she got involved in his wild ways, if she started to drink again.

But Rebecca also liked flirting with disaster.

◂ ◂ ◂

The boat entered the river mouth and they slowed down as they passed between the mud banks; then the willows ended on the right and they were at the boat landing, nosing in where the floats of the plane had lodged and left their marks the previous weekend.

Rebecca was going to Joker Lake again, this time by boat, with Danny. It was several weeks into their counselling program and he was alert to the possibility that she might burn out. What they were doing was draining them emotionally; it was hard to find the time or mental space to have any kind of a personal life. But their counselling program was so successful that they both thought they were beginning to turn the town around.

A small crowd appeared at the top of the bank and a little girl began to scream delightedly, "Daddy! Daddy!" This was Jamaica, Danny's four-year-old daughter.

Danny hugged his wife, Roseanne, then the rest of his kids, two little boys of six and eight.

"Have something to eat," said Roseanne. "We just finished. Robert made duck soup again."

There was an open fire burning in a trench in the middle of the campsite, and they walked toward this. Rachel was ladling soup out of a cauldron on the grille. Rebecca took her bowl and sat down with it on a chrome kitchen chair that was perched beside the logs around the fire.

Danny was still excited to see his children. "How are my kids? How's my little girl?"

Jamaica squealed with delight as he tossed her up in the air.

"All right. I'm going to eat," he said at last. "Then it'll be family time. After that, bedtime."

Danny was always organized about time.

"This soup is good," he remarked.

"That's what we all used to think." Roseanne spoke rather dryly. She was a pretty, intelligent woman of about Rebecca's age, who had been a daycare organizer in Yellowknife until Danny had moved the family to Prohibition Creek in the spring of that year.

"Come on, Roseanne. Us Dene can't have too much duck soup."

Both Danny and Robert regarded duck soup as a kind of passport to the Dene Nation.

Rebecca was still finishing her first bowlful. It was good, hot and rich, with a tangy, gamey taste. There was nothing in it but duck meat; no vegetables, no seasonings but salt.

"Did Robert shoot a moose? Or was that you, Michael?" Danny gestured toward the hide, now fully scraped and drying over a pole.

"It was Robert," Rebecca said.

"How did you know that?" Danny asked in surprise.

"Oh! I was out here last Sunday." She had to tell him now and get it over with. "With that pilot. Don is his name."

"With the Red Baron's pilot?" Danny spoke slowly and she felt his surprise and disapproval.

There was a short silence. The two of them had really just been talking to each other, but everyone was clustering around Danny, listening to whatever he said.

It was beginning to get dark earlier in the evening. The visible flames flickered in the firepit and long shadows fell from the spruce trees. There was a sunset over the lake that was like blood streaking the sky.

He finished his second bowl of soup. "Okay. Family time," he said. "Let's go in our tent."

"Wait, Daddy," cried Jamaica. "Robert's going to tell us a story now. He always does."

Robert had just been putting wood on the fire. He went back to the woodpile for more.

Jamaica made him tell a story every night.

Danny was again somewhat taken aback. "Oh," he said. "Well, go ahead, Robert. Then we'll go in the tent for family time."

The whole clan was kneeling or sitting there on the logs beside the fire, looking at Robert expectantly. It was not just Jamaica who wanted a story.

Robert paused a moment, looking at them all.

"There were two brothers," he began. This was the beginning of many stories.

"They were you and Daddy, weren't they, Robert?" Jamaica guessed.

"They were out looking for duck down. As far as they knew, it was just something that hung on the branches of trees or lay on the ground."

"Didn't they know it came from ducks?" the little girl demanded.

"Just wait," said Robert. "I'm coming to that. They went a long way from home. The older brother lost the younger brother. He was looking for him when he walked right off the edge of the earth."

"Luckily he grabbed a tree root. Then the younger one showed up and pulled him back. But boy, that younger brother was unreliable. He got lost again. And this time, he got into trouble himself. He got stuck under water in a fish net. Some otters came along and gnawed him out. So that was lucky for him."

"This story is weird, isn't it, Mummy?" Jamaica said.

"By this time the brothers had gotten pretty old. They came to a tent, and there sat a beautiful young woman beside a campfire. She said she was their grandmother."

"Didn't you tell us she was a young woman?" interrupted Danny.

"Just listen to it, okay?"

Danny was silent. In this area, Robert was the older brother even if he didn't live up to his other responsibilities.

"Actually she was the Day Sun—that means the winter sun. She told them to wait for her husband, the Night Sun."

"Did he come?" asked Jamaica.

"Of course he did," Robert replied. "He just had to wait for the summer. Then he flew the two brothers back to their own country. And he gave them some feathers to wear. The way the story ends is, since that time little ducks have always come down from the moon."

Robert sat down and there was a pause. The story was over.

Rachel said, "That was a good story."

"It was weird. Wasn't it, Mummy?" said Jamaica.

"Where did you get that story, Robert?" Danny asked. "I don't think I ever heard it."

"I read it somewhere," said Robert.

"Read it somewhere? There aren't any books about us Dene. Where did you read it?"

It had been in a book with a green cover, a thin little book that was arranged with chapter and verse almost like the Bible. It was in the school library and nobody else ever bothered to look at it because it was small and strange. Robert had found it one day years before. It was true that there was nothing else about the Dene in the library; they were not even mentioned in the encyclopaedia.

"As far as I know, most of the books in the school library are in Inuktitut," Danny remarked. "Anyway, that was a pretty good story."

He looked around at the smiling faces in the firelight, then glanced at his watch.

"Okay, now it's family time. Let's go," he said.

His wife and children got up obediently.

"Goodnight, Robert!" cried Jamaica, being borne off on Danny's shoulders. "Goodnight, Rebecca!"

Rachel went into the teepee. Michael's wife and kids went off to their own tent. Michael lit a lantern and went down to his boat.

The campfire was crackling. Robert put on another piece of wood and poked it with his foot. Then he sat down on his heels across from Rebecca, one knee up.

The moon was still low in the sky and there was a luminous green glow over the dark treetops, the remnants of the sunset.

"Hi," said Robert finally.

"Hi yourself, Robert," she said. "You're a good storyteller."

"Yeah, maybe I am. But my dad's a great storyteller," he said.

Rebecca had already been wondering about Robert and Danny's father, who he was. Rachel lived alone in Prohibition Creek, and Danny never spoke of his father.

"He lives in Yellowknife." She hadn't asked, but Robert was answering anyway. "Probably Danny didn't tell you about him. They don't get along too well. My dad's kind of a crazy guy."

"Oh," said Rebecca.

"I know what you're thinking." Robert was defensive. "Sure, he drinks and parties all the time; he never gave a damn for my mother. I hated him once for all that. But, it's a funny thing, we kind of get along now."

"It's hard to hate your father." She spoke reflectively.

Robert was looking at her with attention but she said nothing more.

"You know what I think is funny about my parents?" he said after a moment. "They were kind of like my children when I was growing up. I felt like the whole thing depended on me. When I began to act up—Poof!—it fell apart, just like that."

"My parents aren't like that at all," said Rebecca.

"I guess not. Your dad's a preacher."

"Yes." But Rebecca couldn't talk about it, even though she felt he would be sympathetic. The struggle she was having with her father was still going on. There was no way that she could summarize it as—Poof!

"The thing is both of them are elders now," Robert continued. "The last time I saw my dad, he was talking just like Ama does, about religion and everything. You know," he went on, "I don't think I'm ever going to be an elder. I think no one will even know what that is by the time I'm old."

He shrugged and then grinned.

"But the way you tell stories—" she said. "I've never heard anyone but an elder do that."

"Yeah. But they don't get them out of books."

Rebecca said hesitantly, "Don't you think Bobby will see you that way sometime?"

"You mean, the Bobby who's in jail?" asked Robert in irony.

"Yes, I mean him," she said. "Maybe he'll be sitting beside a campfire some night and he'll say: my dad's a great storyteller."

Robert shrugged again. "Yeah. Maybe," he said.

But he was sad.

The little boy who had been the perfect audience for stories, the way Jamaica was now, had disappeared into the youth, his eyes dull with boredom and inattention when he sat around the house, who was capable of beating up an old man for drink—or maybe just for the hell of it; whom Robert couldn't connect with at all. He didn't even seem to like girls. Not the way Robert had liked them when he was a young man. Of course girls were very different now too; they hustled in bars, they drank as much as men. When Robert was young, girls had been more mysterious; they withheld sex and that could drive a man crazy.

He looked across the fire at Rebecca, who had resumed thinking about her own troubles, and her pure features, her downcast eyes, the oval of her face, reminded him of the strange woman in his story, the Day Sun. She might have looked a little like Rebecca.

"Why was she old, that girl who was the Day Sun?" he asked aloud.

Rebecca looked up.

Danny suddenly reappeared in the circle of firelight. He stared at them for a moment, surprised to see them talking together. He had actually come back because he felt that he had been neglecting Rebecca, leaving her out of the family circle.

"I didn't understand that part either," he commented, sitting down on a log.

Robert was rather annoyed to see him.

"But do you have to understand a story?" asked Rebecca. "Isn't it just like—something that happens?"

"No. It's more like a parable," Danny said. "Like the stories Jesus tells in the Bible."

A curiously stubborn expression had crossed Rebecca's face and Robert looked at her attentively. He had already divined that her father's religion was a problem for her.

Elijah McCrae had turned renegade on his Catholic family and become a Protestant lay minister. He conducted prayer meetings at which people spoke in tongues or lay on the ground and howled, according to what Robert had heard. He was still a scandal to older people like Robert's mother.

"A parable is a story with a moral," Danny went on. "It's supposed to tell you something."

"Yeah," agreed Robert. "Maybe that younger brother could use a few hints."

Danny laughed good-naturedly. Then he said to Rebecca, "You were out here on Sunday with the Red Baron's pilot?"

Rebecca raised her chin. "He wanted to go duck hunting. I stayed in the teepee with Rachel."

"Yeah, she was talking to Ama," said Robert.

He was assuming that Rebecca had slept with the pilot and he didn't like it much—a Dene girl going with that crazy whiteman. But he wanted to cover for her somehow. He felt it was none of Danny's business.

Rebecca laughed suddenly. She understood perfectly what was on both their minds.

"We went fishing. Then he took me home," she said. "And right after that he went back to the Forks."

"Well, that was fast," remarked Robert, relieved.

Rebecca smiled. "I used to be married to a whiteman. Maybe I could tell you about that some time," she said. "After I think of how to make it into a story—a story with a moral."

Rachel had suddenly appeared in the circle of firelight.

"Rebecca, you are going to sleep in my cabin."

Rebecca nodded obediently.

"Danny, Roseanne says Jamaica has an earache," she continued.

"Oh no." Danny got to his feet. "Have we got any Aspirin out here?"

"Where am I supposed to sleep, Ama?" Robert spoke plaintively. He had been sharing his mother's little log shack with her.

Danny turned around. "On the ground, Robert," he suggested. "That wouldn't be anything new, would it?"

Robert got his bedroll out of the cabin and lay down beside the fire to sleep. Rachel and Rebecca had taken the lantern into the house with them; after a while they turned it out, and all was quiet except for the slight crackling of the low fire and the muted sounds of distress from Danny's tent.

◂ ◂ ◂

At midnight, Roseanne and Danny were out by the campfire with Jamaica. She was crying continuously now, no longer merely whimpering. Her parents were having an argument.

Rachel emerged from her cabin and entered the circle of firelight. She was wearing a flannelette nightgown, her hair in a skinny grey braid. Roseanne appealed to her:

"I want to take Jamaica into Prohibition Creek. She has an earache."

"We're not going to town," Danny contradicted her.

"I've been out here for two weeks straight, Danny. That's enough for me," said Roseanne.

"Look, we can't go now. It's still dark." Danny was trying to be patient.

Roseanne hugged the grizzling child on her lap and attacked him. "You've been in town all this time. We were out here with your mother and your weird brother."

No one had been paying any attention to Robert, rolled up in his sleeping bag on the other side of the log. Now he unrolled himself from his blanket.

"Which weird brother?" he asked. "Michael or me?"

"Oh!" Roseanne jumped and turned around, dumping Jamaica off her lap. "See what I mean?" she said to Danny.

"I was just sleeping here," said Robert.

"You don't think this guy is weird, Danny?" cried Roseanne. "I don't want to stay out here with these people. I want to go back to Yellowknife."

"Hey, wait a minute. We went through all that."

"I had a job in Yellowknife. Now you expect me to live in this boring little settlement and go into the bush with your horrible family."

Jamaica had stopped crying. She was standing between them, looking from one to the other, clutching a ragged baby blanket.

"You know I think I can really do something important here." Danny was still trying to be reasonable.

"You can do something important, but what about me?"

Roseanne got up and ran for the tent, weeping. Jamaica stood beside the fire, looking after her, crying again and pressing her blanket against her hurting ear.

Rachel went into the teepee with the lantern. She came back with a bottle of Aspirin.

"Jamaica, take this pill," she said.

Jamaica backed away.

"Take the Aspirin like Ama says, Jamaica." Danny tried to pick her up, but the little girl pushed him away.

Rebecca came out of Rachel's hut. She was also wearing a winter nightgown, her hair loose on her shoulders. She sat down on the kitchen chair and began to coax the little girl.

"Come here, Jamaica," she said. "Come and sit on my lap."

Jamaica looked at Rebecca and then back at Danny. "No!"

"Here is water." Rachel approached with an enamel cup. "Now take the pill."

Jamaica was trying to escape, pushing away Rebecca's arms. Danny grabbed her before she got away completely.

"All right, I'm holding her," he said. "Now take the Aspirin, Jamaica."

The little girl was fighting him, kicking, trying to bite his wrist, crying wildly.

"I hate you, Daddy! Stop!"

Danny held her head while Rachel forced the pill between her lips.

"This will help you get it down," said Rebecca, offering the cup of water.

Jamaica drank some of the water, and gagged. The pill had gone down, however. After a moment Danny let go of her and she sprang away from him panting and sobbing.

"Now come with me, Jamaica. I'm going to go in the tent with Mummy," Danny said.

He turned his back on the fire and walked toward his tent, but Jamaica didn't follow.

"Sit on Granny's lap," suggested Rachel. She patted her lap.

Jamaica had not forgiven anybody. "I'm going to sit with Robert," she said, after a moment.

"All right, sit with Robert," said Rachel. She went back into the teepee with the pill bottle.

Jamaica went over and stood in front of Robert, waiting for him to sit down on the log so she could climb up on his knees.

Danny and Roseanne were continuing their argument in the tent. The people left by the fire could hear her voice raised in tearful accusation, his voice, low and patient, replying.

Jamaica nestled on Robert's lap, pressing her ear against his chest, and he hugged the little girl gently. She had taken refuge with the Complaints Department.

"I hate medicine," Jamaica said into his shirt front.

"Me too," he agreed.

"Why did they make me take it?"

"I don't know. It made me want to throw up, just watching."

Robert had not witnessed a medicine-taking like that since he was young enough to be the victim of it. If Mary Ann had ever forced Bobby to take a pill, she had known better than to enlist Robert for assistance.

The child tipped back her head to look at him. Her eyes were tearless, her face bland and calm. The Aspirin was already beginning to work. "Tell me a story," she demanded.

Robert was still feeling queasy. "Maybe someone else will," he said.

"No one else tells weird stories like you do," she said.

Rebecca was still beside the fire, sitting quietly on the kitchen chair, her eyes downcast. She was feeling bad about the pill, and also about the argument between Danny and Roseanne.

"Rebecca could probably tell you a story," Robert suggested.

She looked up in alarm. "The only story I know is Cinderella."

"I already know that one," said Jamaica.

"Maybe she can tell you a different version," said Robert.

Jamaica was curled up in Robert's arms and they were both looking at Rebecca very seriously, expecting her to tell some kind of a story.

Rebecca laughed suddenly. She had thought of something. "Okay," she said. "I guess I could tell you a different version. For a start, Cinderella in my story was Dene."

"Get to the part where she meets the prince," said Jamaica.

"The prince was a white guy. He liked to party, and he had one of those big Elan skidoos. So they got married."

"Is that the end of the story?" asked Jamaica, disappointed.

"No. After they got married, Cinderella went right on dancing and partying. The prince began to get mad at her for staying up all night and having fun. He didn't like the way she danced with other boys too."

"Yeah," said Robert dryly.

"Besides, that fun stuff Cinderella was doing was making her get kind of ugly. She was tired all the time, and she drank a lot. Sometimes she couldn't remember what happened the night before. She was spending all the prince's money, and he was mean to her about that."

She had stopped talking and was looking into the fire. There was a silence.

"Hey, this is supposed to have a happy ending," said Robert.

"It does. Cinderella went to the detox centre."

"That's a happy ending?"

"Jamaica's asleep anyway."

They sat opposite one another, not talking. Robert bent his head down over the head of the little girl. He was wishing that story of hers had turned out a little better.

"Rebecca's a good name," he said. "Do you know the story about Rebecca in the Bible?"

"I don't know much about the Bible."

"You must have heard of Abraham?" Robert asked, slightly scandalized.

She nodded.

"So I guess you've heard of Isaac too. Well, Abraham wanted to get a good wife for Isaac, his son." Robert was in his element once again. "He sent an old servant with some of his camels to go find the right woman. It was kind of a dry country, I guess. The servant was old, like I said, and pretty soon he stopped to rest. As he was sitting there he prayed to God that a girl would come and give him a cup of water. That way he would know she was the right one."

"What happened?"

"Well, a girl came with a cup and offered him a drink of water, and she gave the camels water to drink too. So he knew she was the right one."

"But how did that prove it?" asked Rebecca.

"Don't you see? It came true. It was like a dream. Like the dreams of those old medicine men of ours."

Danny came back from the tent.

"All right," he said, sighing as he sat down. "We're going into town as soon as it gets light. Rebecca, I'm sorry about this. It's not much of a day off."

"That's all right, Danny."

He stood up again. "Give me Jamaica, Robert," he said.

"But she's asleep. She's okay on my lap," protested Robert.

He liked the feel of the sleeping child, warm and heavy in his arms. It reminded him of Bobby, and also of other times, when as a child he had held his younger brothers and sisters, even Danny sometimes.

"She'll be better off in bed. For what remains of the night." Danny scooped her up.

"You know, I sometimes wonder whether you're a real Dene, Danny," said Robert, instantly contentious. "All this bedtime stuff. Dene don't have bedtime."

Rachel had appeared again, looking little and old in her nightgown, but also curiously commanding.

"We have had enough arguing already tonight," she announced.

She followed Danny and Jamaica toward the tent, carrying Jamaica's blanket.

◂ ◂ ◂

Danny took Rebecca and his wife and children into town the next morning where Jamaica saw the nurse. Then, for a while, there was tranquility in their family, for Danny was a home-loving man and a good father, and Roseanne truly appreciated those qualities in him; even though she found his mother and his brothers backward and strange to the point of being frightening, and even though she rebelled against her humdrum life in Prohibition Creek.

Robert stayed in the family camp at Joker Lake for several more weeks, and throughout this lazy, contented time of harvest, he did not dream about poker, or wish for his town persona, his crazy stay-up-all-night life of the last few years. But he had to go back into town for the meeting at the end of October. He had not forgotten that Herod had called upon the Complaints Department.

Accordingly, one afternoon he borrowed his mother's boat, the motor of which he had in the meantime repaired, and took it down the Kalonde River to John the Baptist Lake and then to Prohibition Creek, arriving at the beginning of a snowstorm, the first snow of the winter.

• 4. HAGA'S DREAM •

There was never a good time for a meeting in Prohibition Creek. In the summer people were too busy fixing things that should have been fixed all winter and trying to make a little money in seasonal employment; fall was, of course, time for hunting; trapping took place in the winter; spring was fish runs and duck hunting. But the Department of Local Government, operating on its own insane nine-to-five, five-days-per-week-except-Christmas-and-national-holidays schedule, was always surprised when nobody showed up to meetings.

The Hamlet Council was sitting around a large, new oak table. Spectators and government officials were expected to sit on the overstuffed furniture, a sofa and chairs packed closely together around the walls of the room. The room had once been a classroom and some of its furishings were still in evidence, including a picture of the Queen and a blackboard.

Although it was only a town of 250 people, Prohibition Creek had, in effect, two separate governments, the Dene Band Council, funded by the federal government, and the Hamlet Council, largely a function of the McCrae family, and funded by the territorial government. The settlement had become a hamlet recently; the Department of Local Government had decided to make all the settlements hamlets, at some considerable expense, and without regard to any absurdity in the notion "becoming a hamlet."

The Band and the Hamlet Council made sporadic attempts to govern the community together despite the haze of bureaucracy that separated them. This was in fact a combined meeting; almost the whole Band Council was present and about half the Hamlet Council.

Robert was the only spectator. There were also two officials from Local Government present, a skinny little whitewoman named Shelagh, who usually handled their affairs, and a fat whiteman named Mike, who had been sent in tonight to troubleshoot.

Herod cleared his throat. "I guess I'll call this meeting to order, being that I'm the mayor. That all right with you, Danny?"

"Go ahead, Herod. It means I can talk."

Herod was making the people around the table introduce themselves to the white officials.

The Band began: "Danny Woodcutter," "Arthur Woodcutter," "Fred Woodcutter," "George Woodcutter," "Elvis Woodcutter."

The last name provoked laughter, even though it was an old joke to those at the table. His real name was William Woodcutter, but he had been known as Elvis since the mid-fifties. He was also Robert's uncle, the surviving half-brother of his father.

The Hamlet Council, similarly, was almost entirely made up of members of the McCrae family.

"The big item on the agenda is this deal about the airport," said Herod. "Maybe you can come up here and talk about that, Shelagh."

There was a pause while the two officials held whispered consultation.

"Couldn't you tell them, Shelagh? You're the one they're used to."

"Are you kidding? I wanted you to break the news."

"Okay, Mike," said Herod. "Let her roll."

"I guess you all know about this airport. We've spent the whole year doing feasibility studies and site planning. But we struck a little snag."

"A little snag, eh?" Herod looked anxious. Danny sat up straighter. They really needed a new airport and they had been on the list for a long time.

"The site that we've been working on turns out to be federal land."

"So what's the problem?" said Herod.

Mike looked harassed. It was always very hard to explain these things. There weren't any legal minds out here in the middle of nowhere. "It's the type of federal land involved," he said. "A Department of Indian Affairs reserve."

"Pardon me," interrupted Herod, "but did you say reserve? An Indian reserve?"

Mike nodded slowly.

"There aren't any reserves in Prohibition Creek—not that I'm aware of." Herod spoke intemperately. He had known who held what land in this place for nearly sixty years; and in any case, as a Metis he was very much against the whole concept of reserves.

"Wait a second," said Danny. "Are you telling us that the airport land actually belongs to the Band?"

"Are you the chief?" Mike asked.

He eyed Danny, who eyed him right back. Danny was wearing a crisply-pressed blue and white striped shirt and a clean navy blue windcheater. In front of him was a clipboard and pad of lined paper. The pencil in his fingers was long and freshly sharpened.

By contrast, Mike was wearing a hooded sweatshirt with a kangaroo pocket pulled down over his paunch, and grey track pants.

Robert had been sitting on the edge of the large armchair by the door, getting mad, as he had predicted. He was suddenly surprised to find he was glad Danny was the chief. His brother looked good; he looked like a person who could handle this whiteman.

"Maybe I can explain this to you," Mike was saying dubiously. "The land doesn't belong to the Band. It's federal land held in reserve for the Band."

"Let me get this straight." Danny was being definite. "You're saying that the new airport is on a piece of land the federal government is keeping away from us?"

"Okay. You can put it like that." Mike had no brief to defend the Feds at this meeting. "The point is, though, that we're going to lose our mandate to go ahead with this if we can't complete the studies. We can't do studies on federal land."

"Well, this is the first I ever heard about Indian reserves in Prohibition Creek," Herod burst out.

"I think this is the first time the Band ever heard about that too," said Danny.

"Well, I don't belong to the Band and I've sure got a problem with the idea of Indian land."

"You could belong to the Band, Herod. You know about the new rules in the Indian Act."

Herod said now, "Yeah, I know about the new rules. But I'm never going to belong to the Band."

He spoke with finality. He did not regard himself as an Indian and he would never become one.

"When did the Feds start holding this land for us?" Danny asked.

"In 1918." Mike cleared his throat.

"You mean they didn't get around to telling us about that in seventy-five years?"

Herod broke into this, "Look, I'm getting to be an old man and I don't claim to be a deep thinker," he said. "What you're telling us is that we can't get the new airport?"

"Unless the Band will make a resolution to release the land."

There was a long pause.

"That's it?" Danny spoke disbelievingly. "We'd have to give back the land?"

"Yes."

There was another pause. Herod's face was purple with suppressed rage.

"Okay, Herod, I guess the Band will have to have a separate meeting about this." Danny was staring intently at the tip of his writing pencil.

Shelagh said, "Wait a minute. There's a land-use application too." Mike had been just about to sit down.

They began going through one of the briefcases they had brought and there was the dry sound of rustling papers.

To Robert, used to birdsong, fresh air and water noises, everything about the room was somehow dry: there were the desiccated little sounds of throats clearing, chairs scraping, a dry scent of cigarette smoke in the air.

"I've got it right here. Application to erect an outhouse by the fish store shack," she went on.

"Okay, this thing is pretty simple, isn't it? Just an outhouse," said Herod.

"The problem here is that the application is for land you've set aside for commercial use in your zoning bylaw," Mike explained.

Herod sighed.

"Robert, you'd better come up here now. It's your outhouse."

Robert stood up in the narrow space between his armchair and the table.

"Well, maybe you didn't read your zoning bylaw too closely—" Mike began, addressing Robert directly.

"I never read it at all," said Robert.

"It clearly specifies that a bathroom on commercial premises has to be heated and have a flush toilet." Mike had turned to Herod. "And there have to be two of them."

"Two of them?"

"Yes. For the male and female employees."

"Hey, wait a second," protested Robert. "That fish plant hasn't been operating for fifteen years."

Mike shrugged. "It says in your zoning bylaw—" he repeated.

"Maybe we could fix this right here," said Herod in exasperation. "We could just vote on it, and let Robert have an outhouse."

"Amend your bylaw, you mean?" Mike asked alertly. Ever since the zoning bylaws had come in, the hamlet councils had been trying to escape their consequences. No one in these little places understood how laws were supposed to work, thought Mike.

"Nope, I just mean let him have an outhouse," said Herod, speaking to Mike's thought.

"You'd have to amend your bylaw." And there was no way they were going to let people build outhouses on commercial premises. Yellowknife would see to that.

"Look," said Robert, speaking directly to Mike, "I needed to build an outhouse. Just like we need to have an airport."

Mike decided to start again at the beginning: "It really isn't that simple," he explained. "You see, Prohibition Creek passed a zoning bylaw this year—"

Robert gave up suddenly.

"I think it's time to move the whole town, Herod. Just get her out of here."

He had lost his temper and begun to speak in that highfalutin way of his.

"Where are we going to move to, Robert?" Herod was delighted. "There's a lot of bad countries out there."

"You're right," said Robert. "Let's take her to the moon."

Mike, who had been taking him seriously for a short while, suddenly sat down. The Department of Local Government had been trying to move Prohibition Creek out of the swampy lowland where it was situated for years. But they couldn't afford to send it to the moon. Yellowknife would never stand for that.

"Good idea," commented Herod.

"Except probably they have some set of rules that wouldn't let us get her on a spacecraft."

"C'mon," someone suggested. "Let's just move her across the lake."

"That'd be all right if we didn't tell the government where we were going."

"We wouldn't have an airport."

"And that'd be good. Then no one from Local Government could come in here and bother us," said Robert.

"You see? Solves the whole problem," he added a moment later.

No one laughed. There was a moment of rather heavy silence.

"This meeting is adjourned," announced Herod. He stood up ponderously, slapping the table.

◀ ◀ ◀

It was a wild night. The wind skirled around the corners of the small wooden building; it was pitch dark except in the pools of light under the street lamps where the driving flakes of snow reflected back a million sharp points of light. Robert pulled his jacket up over his head like a hood and started to walk through town to the wood road that led to the fish plant. He could have gone to his mother's house to stay the night, but he was worried about Haga, who had not been home when he had arrived earlier that evening.

It was the kind of storm, unexpected and the first of the season, when people like Haga, who tended to sleep in ditches or on the beach, wherever they were felled by whatever they had been drinking, froze to death or died of exposure.

Robert went from one house to the next on his way through town, looking for Haga. He might have taken refuge anywhere tonight. It was a big storm.

He opened the door on a poker game and walked in. The voices greeted him joyously.

"Hey, Robert, want to play?"

"Nope."

This wasn't true. He felt an instant surge of desire to sit right down and play through the night. It was lucky he was worried enough to be looking for Haga.

"Anybody here seen Haga?" he demanded, gruff, fighting with that poker monkey.

"Haven't seen him tonight."

They weren't too interested in Haga, or him either, if he wasn't going to play. A dozen men sat in a large circle on the bare floor, the chairs and other few sticks of furniture the room contained pushed back against the walls with the spectators, mostly the women and children who lived there, perched upon them. The room was well-lit, a warm room, almost too warm, and full of loud rock music.

"C'mon, Robert, play a couple hands."

Robert backed out the door, after a lingering glance at the disposition of the hands he could see. But he had to find Haga.

He was out in the wind again, fighting it.

No lights in the next house. It was Michael's house and he was at Joker Lake.

Haga didn't seem to be anywhere in town. But he could be out at the shack. The meeting had taken a long time. Robert hadn't been there since before dark.

He had been walking backward to keep warm. Now he turned around into the wind. A tall, thickly-clad man—looking almost shaggy, the way his woollen clothes blew in the driving snow—was coming toward him, the last street light behind him.

"Hey, pal have you seen Haga tonight?"

The huge figure—whoever it was—didn't bother to answer. It swerved past him on the run, apparently being blown down the road.

Robert turned around in surprise to look after it, but it had gone. He stood stock still for a moment, the little hairs on the back of his neck standing up, straining his eyes to see. But there was nothing in the street anymore, just his eyes blurring in the slantwise gust of the wind.

A bushman had gone past him on the road.

No, it couldn't have been a bushman, Robert reasoned with himself. What would a bushman be doing out on a night like this? They were smart the way animals were smart, and stayed in their dens when it was storming like this.

He began to slog onward, feeling his way with his feet as he left the street for the path through the bush. He had gone hunting in the bush as a young man. It was not true that there was nothing to be afraid of; that was a lie people used to soothe children. There was a great deal to be afraid of, and the thing was to make fear work for you. It kept you alert, ready for anything. Learning how to use fear was what made you into a man.

▴ ▴ ▴

Robert was not wrong in his surmise that the storm had overtaken Haga when he was least prepared for it.

Since Robert had left him to go with his family to Joker Lake, Haga's life had been rather lonely. He and Robert had a little housekeeping routine that Haga had even begun to enjoy. He wasn't taking much pleasure in his old life of mooching around, and there was nothing at all to drink.

He had finally, that very afternoon, secured from his sister in a tour de force of lying half a bottle of painkiller (the kind—it was his favourite—with the picture of the doctor on the label, marked FOR EXTERNAL USE ONLY), and he had not gotten far out of town before he had gulped it down.

After that—just as Robert feared he might have done—he had sat down with his back against a log and gone to sleep.

The freezing sweep of snow on the wind finally began to wake him up.

"What am I doing here?" he muttered, struggling with the vapours of painkiller in his brain.

It seemed to him at first as though the wind had music on it, a wild Dene drum dance chant. But this ceased and changed and it was TV music that he heard, the prelude to the program called *Star Trek*, which had many followers in Prohibition Creek.

"What's going on? Where am I?" cried Haga, struggling against the painkiller.

There were electronic noises on the wind, as well as the scary music and then bright lights were shining in his eyes. The whole path was lit up suddenly, as though with automobile headlights, except that the quality of the light was white, not yellow, of an unearthly, ghastly whiteness.

A pack of men in masks rushed out at him from every direction and he had time to see that they were dressed conventionally as spacemen, except for their feet, which were the feet of dogs, the high furry heel descending to a paw, no boots. They leapt on him, scratching and clawing him, tearing his clothes.

The electronic music continued. Haga was struggling but the dogs carried him inexorably down the path through the bush to a huge spacecraft parked at the opening of the fish plant clearing.

Haga had given up trying to fight them and had his eyes shut. All he could hear was the scratchy sound of the dogs' claws on the smooth floor of the corridor through which they were dragging him.

They threw him down all at once, and Haga opened his eyes in pain and fear. He was in a great round room, illuminated with that same unearthly glare. Before him stood a giant woman, totally naked except for her long thick black hair which hung down her back to well below her hips. In one hand she carried a long, highly decorated dog whip like one which had once belonged to Haga's father, before he lost it at a stick-gambling session on New Year's Day in 1947.

He was inside a flying saucer with this woman and these dog men.

"Have you brought me more to eat, my sons?" The woman addressed his captors, who stood around Haga, panting like dogs.

"Who—who are you?" Haga cowered on the smooth floor in front of her.

"I am the Woman Who Married the Dog. My sons have brought you here for me—to devour you!"

Her horrible peals of laughter rebounded in a limitless echo from the walls of the room.

Haga was already crying. Now he heard himself screaming for mercy.

"Be still, food!" snapped the giantess.

The dogs around her feet began to yap and then to howl.

"No, please! Please don't! Please don't eat me!"

"Sons, get your father," ordered the woman.

The dogs ran with clicking claws to do as she told them. They returned with an enormous dog, who paused when he spotted Haga and howled horribly.

The huge woman had retreated to a throne high up on the wall of the room and sat down. The Dog King bounded toward her and leapt upon her chest, between her wide-spread knees. He began licking her mouth and then suckling at her thick black nipples. It was a hideously erotic sight to poor Haga, who suddenly conceived an idea of how all these dog men around him had come into existence. He began to vomit.

The woman suddenly threw the giant dog off her, standing up and kicking it with her enormous bare feet. It cowered in front of her, growling, as she kicked it a few more times, until at last it lay down and let her place her foot upon its back.

She clapped her hands:

"Bring me the food now, slaves."

The little men in masks ran to pick Haga up under the arms. They began to drag him toward the giantess, and the Dog King opened his huge black-lipped mouth to drool and slaver at the sight of him, his long red tongue lolling out.

"No! No! Please!" Haga was begging and praying as he was dragged forward. The Dog King, his neck ruff erect, was rising to his feet.

"Haga! Haga! Wake up!" Robert had found Haga lying across the path and was trying to shake him awake.

"This is a miserable underfed little Dene you have brought me, dogs," shouted the giantess, shaking her fist.

Haga had roused himself sufficiently to struggle. He was aware that he had somehow escaped being torn apart by the Dog King, but he was still trying to fight Robert off him.

"Hey, look pal, I know you don't want me to leave you out here to freeze." Robert was relieved to find that Haga could still move by himself.

"His skin is blue but we shall soon see if his blood is red," shouted the woman. But her horrible laughter faded away on the wind.

Haga found himself lying on the ground, only half dressed. His jacket was gone, his shirt half off, and he was wet all down the front where he had vomited on himself. Robert was holding him in a gingerly embrace.

"Robert! Is that you? How did you get me out of there?"

"What are you talking about, Haga? I nearly fell over you on the path. Where's your jacket? And you haven't even got your slippers on."

Grunting, Robert heaved Haga onto his feet. They began to stagger toward the shack, Robert still supporting him.

It was hard going against the wind. Haga's feet were too numb to stand on properly and Robert had to drag him the last fifty feet or so to the doorstep. He dropped him to open the door and then turned around to lug him inside.

Haga lay collapsed in a heap on the floor as Robert shut the door again. They were in total darkness while Robert felt his way to the stove and lit a match. A moment later he had a small fire going. Then he found the lamp, turned up the wick, and lit it. The room sprang into existence around them, cave-like and secure against the storm, but reassuringly square, wooden—not a *Star Trek* interior.

"Let's see what's wrong with you, pal." Robert was now busy heaving Haga up on the bed. He was surprised at how easily he was able to move him around. Haga looked bigger than he was, since he wore many layers of clothes to meet the exigencies of a rough life.

Both Robert and Haga had the big-chested, broad-shouldered

physical profile of the mountain Dene, although Robert, who was younger and had been better nourished in childhood, was the taller and much the stronger of the two.

Haga groaned. Robert was peeling off his ragged socks to inspect his feet.

"Where's your shoes, for God's sake?"

"Maybe those dogs took them," said Haga.

His feet were blue and it looked to Robert as though he might have a couple of frozen toes. However, his toes were like moose antlers, so dirty and covered with callouses that it was hard to tell. Robert covered them up in disgust, then pulled Haga's sleeping bag over him.

"There, you ought to get warm pretty fast now."

He went to adjust the draft on the stove.

"Am I here?" asked Haga pathetically, looking at Robert's back.

"Yeah, you're there."

Robert dipped water out of the butt into the billy, then set the billy on the stove and adjusted the draft again.

He felt good about being here too. It was his place, in a way that the house he had rented for the last eighteen years from the Northwest Territories Housing Corporation was not. Even though it lacked lights, oil heating, plumbing, refrigeration and had only the most rudimentary furnishings, he was king of the castle in this place.

Since everything was all pretty much the way he had left it when he went to Joker Lake, he guessed that Haga hadn't spent much time here while he was away. It was just good luck that Robert had come back tonight in time to find him.

"I was on a spaceship." Haga spoke weakly from his bed.

Robert was interested. He took a seat on the side of Haga's bunk. "I've always wanted to see one of those things," he remarked.

"I got dragged in there by men in masks who had legs like dogs."

"No kidding?"

Robert thought that Haga must have been having quite some dream on whatever it was he had drunk: painkiller, mouthwash—he wouldn't have put it beyond Haga to drink shoe polish.

"They dragged me down a tunnel and threw me on the floor in a big room in front of a giant woman. She had long hair that hung down to her ass and she was holding a dog whip in her hand."

"Was she Dene?" Robert asked. The story was beginning to remind him of something.

"I dunno. She said she was the Woman Who Married the Dog."

There was a story about her in the little green book in the library. A cannibal woman who lived inside a mountain—Haga must have got that spaceship idea from somewhere else—with her husband who was a dog. Maybe Haga had heard that story from one of the old people at a camp in the mountains when he was a little boy.

"Then—but this was the worst part, Robert." Haga's voice dropped to a hoarse whisper, and Robert's skin crawled and he felt his gorge rise too as Haga told him the worst part.

"It made me throw up," Haga concluded.

He still stank of vomit. Disgusted, Robert got up to make the tea.

"Boy, that was awful," said Haga. "I thought I was a goner that time."

"If I hadn't come along just then you might have been a goner."

"Gee, thanks, Robert." Haga was unusually humble.

"You must have gone to sleep there on your way home."

Robert took a couple of tea bags out of the box and dropped them in the billy. Then he pushed the tea off the stove to steep.

Haga lay looking up at the underside of the bunk above, a sense of relief gradually dawning.

"You figure that was all just a dream I had?"

"Yeah."

"Never went on that spaceship?"

"Nope."

Robert poured tea out of the billy into their cups. There was sugar, even a can of cream. He handed Haga the hot sweet milky brew.

"Masi."

Haga lay in silence, sipping occasionally and still looking up at the underside of the bunk above. It hadn't happened, he was thinking; none of it had happened, not even that really bad part. Dogs didn't marry women; they wouldn't want to. It stood to reason that dogs would only want to marry other dogs. So the dog men whom she called her sons couldn't have been real either. It was all just something the painkiller had thought up for him.

"You still look pretty rough," Robert remarked. He took Haga's empty cup. "Just go to sleep now."

Haga had closed his eyes experimentally, but there were no dog men in there. He dozed off, and soon his snores were competing with the loud gusts of the wind.

Robert sat by the stove, having another cup of tea. He had a feeling of security. The roof had not come off yet, and so the chances were good that it wasn't going to come off.

They got this kind of storm at least once or twice in the autumn. For him it would have made no difference in recent years; he would have been in a circle of poker players inside some warm, loud house. But it was a night when women waited up anxiously for the menfolk to come home. Mary Ann would have been waiting for Bobby on a night like this, worrying, wondering whether he was lying out somewhere like Haga.

Robert felt a sense of repentance for this. He had never spared a moment's thought on anybody's whereabouts but his own, not for years. It seemed as though he had not even been alive in the past few years; he wondered how long he had been dead. It had been since Bobby was old enough to hate him.

Haga snored, a long, racking indrawn nasal rattle, followed by a trumpeting expulsion, like the roar of a charging elephant. He was in the habit of snoring this way, off and on, sometimes for hours at a time. Robert went to the bed and shook him by the shoulder, whereupon he gave a curiously child-like sigh and rolled over.

Robert began thinking about Haga's dream again. It was certainly like something out of an old story. But the old stories were supposed to have been about things that had happened. What was the difference between a dream and a vision? The medicine men, after all, had seen things like this and worse, and no one thought they were lying when they said so.

Robert remembered suddenly that he himself had seen a bushman that very night. The hair on the back of his neck prickled at the recollection.

Then he laughed. It was a good thing he hadn't told Haga about that. Haga would still have been awake; he would probably have been awake for the rest of his life if Robert told him he had seen a bushman.

• 5 • MARRIAGE IS FOREVER •

Robert went back to Joker Lake briefly to collect part of the meat from the moose and caribou he had shot, and to pick up some ducks. Then he had formulated the plan of going hunting in the mountains with some of the other men of the community, taking Haga with him.

When he returned in his mother's boat he took the meat straight to his wife, not having given it much thought beforehand. Robert was Dene, and the idea of not sharing food, through any degree of estrangement, would not really have occurred to him. Besides, Mary Ann had a large freezer.

Robert put his head in the kitchen door. Mary Ann sat at the kitchen table, her glasses on, sewing beads. "Oh. It's you." She spoke flatly.

"I brought you some meat."

He flung the leg he was carrying on his back down on the table, and went outside for more. When he came back in, Mary Ann was putting the whole thing in a black plastic garbage bag. She had some more of these laid out on the floor. They filled the freezer up together until it would hold no more.

"You must have had a good hunting trip with your family," she said.

"Yeah. I got a moose, a couple of caribou. Here, want these ducks?"

There wasn't any more room in the freezer.

"They're all plucked and everything," said Robert, holding them out by the feet.

"Give them to your girlfriend," she suggested.

"I haven't got a girlfriend," Robert said, startled.

He knew that there had been a time when Mary Ann was very jealous of him; and she had had just cause to be so. After they got married, Robert had fallen out of love with her once and for all, because he felt, quite unfairly, that she had trapped him. He went through a phase where he slept with every pretty girl he could find. It had actually been one of the most successful periods in his life. He had discovered that he could be attractive to women; he was, in fact, devastatingly attractive. Only poker could have lured him away from all that—and it had lured him away from it entirely in the end.

He had not had anything to do with other women for several years—in fact it had been Mary Ann herself with whom he had last had relations, more than ten months ago, on New Year's Eve—and she ought to remember that, if he did; he had been slightly drunk at the time. It was before he went out to play cards.

Robert stood looking at her now, nonplussed, and Mary Ann, sitting again by the table, returned his look with hostility.

"Could I sit down?" he said. It seemed as though they ought to be able to get this straight, after all these years, and now that they were no longer living together.

"Maybe I could have some of your tea."

She looked at the kettle on the stove, but Robert was already going over to help himself.

"Masi," he said, sitting down with the cup.

It was not a very cozy kitchen; a small old-style electric stove and refrigerator were the only furnishings beside the table at which they were sitting. There were no decorations of any kind except for the crucifix over the door leading into the other room. The cupboards were equally barren, and there was nothing in the refrigerator aside from the open can of cream to which Robert had helped himself with his tea.

This was the way Robert had lived with Mary Ann, and in fact it was probably what they had most in common—a lack of interest in wealth and possessions. Everything in the house that reflected Western material culture—the stereo, the TV, the picture of Jesus at the Last Supper over the back of the sofa in the other room—either belonged to Bobby, or had been purchased by him. In Mary Ann's case, religion superseded everything else in her life; she was like Robert's mother in this way. As for Robert, gambling deprived him of the wherewithal to acquire anything, or to keep it, once acquired.

But their lack of materialism had even deeper roots than this: they were both Dene. The bags of meat they had been stuffing in the freezer represented virtue to both of them, and the only kind of wealth worth having.

"Have you come back now?" Mary Ann put the question to him baldly.

"No," said Robert. "You threw me out, didn't you?"

"This is your house."

It was not, in fact, his house. It was a government house, and since both Mary Ann and he had next to no income, the rent was nominal. Like many other people in town, Robert did not see this as a good cheap living arrangement, but as a thing that had been forced down his throat by the whiteman, like the school, the store, the church. He had hated the house since they moved in, almost eighteen years before, and this was reflected, to some extent, in its state of repair.

"The doorknob has been broken since January," said Mary Ann.

This was not intended as a reproach for Robert's lack of handiness around the house, however. Robert had broken the doorknob last New Year's Eve. Coming home drunk, he found that Mary Ann had locked up and gone to bed. After he had rattled and banged for some time, and it was clear that she would not get up to let him in, he had kicked it in. Since then, whenever they attempted to talk to one another about anything, the doorknob came up.

The jamb had since been patched with a board by Bobby, or Mary Ann herself, and she had also gone to the Housing office and gotten a new lock, but no one had installed it. And as it had become clear to Robert that everyone regarded this as his penance, it had become equally clear, in the grinding reality of household probabilities, that he was never going to do anything about it.

"Get me the screwdriver," he said now.

Mary Ann rose and found the screwdriver in a drawer. It had the wrong type of head but it was the only one they had. Kneeling grimly in front of the open kitchen door, Robert began to work the lock and knob into position.

"If I go to Housing and say: fix the door, they ask me: where's your husband?" remarked Mary Ann.

"It's always that way with Housing," agreed Robert, struggling to make everything fit.

"I'm not a widow. Housing will say, 'You got a husband. Get him to fix your door.'"

"Yeah," said Robert.

"Then I'll say: but my husband, he broke the door."

"Okay, okay. I'm fixing it now. See that?"

He had, somewhat to his own surprise, managed to do quite a good job of fixing it. What was needed really, as they both knew, was a new door, a new jamb, a whole new frame—an uninsulated hollow wooden door with ancient weatherstripping did not do much to keep out the cold. These houses had been quickly and cheaply built out of poor quality materials, and they had to withstand rather hard usage because of the contempt of their tenants.

Robert stood back and looked at the finished job with pride. He had been doing a lot of things like this out at the shack lately: weatherstripping the door, cleaning the stovepipe, putting plastic over the outhouse window—getting ready for winter.

"There's your door," he said, giving Mary Ann the screwdriver.

It seemed like a good end to their interview. She put the screwdriver away. Robert pulled on his jacket. But she detained him.

"You're going to go on living out there with Haga?" she said.

"Yeah," said Robert.

"This place been my home for eighteen years. It's Bobby's home too."

"Well, okay." He didn't really see what she was getting at.

"Bobby's in jail now," she continued. "He doesn't even know you're not living here anymore."

"I guess not."

"Maybe that's going to hurt him too. But I guess you don't care."

"For God's sake, Mary Ann—!" Robert pulled himself together. "Look, you told me that before. I said I was sorry. I even had to say it in front of a whole bunch of people."

"Think that's going to help him where he is now?"

"No. But Mary Ann, you can't blame me for everything that went wrong with him. It's—I don't know—this place—the way things are—"

"You never take him hunting. Never tell him anything—not till it's too late. Play cards all night and come home drunk. Break down the door. That's what he sees."

He was astounded by her articulation.

"You say you're sorry—that's just talk. For me it's too late for talk," she said.

"Well, what do you want, then? What do you expect me to do?"

"I just want to stay here, in this house," she replied. "Until he comes home. This is his place, see? As long as I'm alive, he's still got a home here."

"Well, sure," said Robert. "I'm not going to take it away from you."

He was looking at her in surprise. She had thrown him out, but the idea of any kind of revenge, or even further action, had not crossed his mind. She could stay in the house, go on getting mail addressed to Mrs. Robert Woodcutter; he had never thought of anything different than that.

"Marriage is forever," he remarked. "That's what they say."

"Eighteen years—that's been like forever to me," Mary Ann replied.

She watched him zip up his jacket.

"Well, okay. So long then."

Mary Ann said suddenly, furiously, "Take these ducks to your girlfriend." She had snatched them up off the table and held them out to him at arm's length.

In a moment she would drop them, and Robert had a superstitious feeling about meat on the linoleum floor. There was an old taboo against throwing meat around like that. He took them from her to prevent it, even though she was intending their return as an insult.

"Hey, I don't have a girlfriend. Who do you think—!"

He had been backing out the door as he spoke, with Mary Ann advancing upon him. Now he was outside on the porch with the ducks, and the door slammed in his face. A moment later he heard her locking it.

"Mary Ann, I don't have a girlfriend! For God's sake—!" Robert realized that the only people he was telling this to were the neighbours.

▲ ▲ ▲

Robert began to walk disconsolately along through the snow, carrying his ducks, going nowhere in particular.

Mary Ann had got the things she wanted. She was going to stay in the house, even though he was the one who was renting it. And apparently she had wanted to be able to lock him out; that was the first thing she had done, at least.

He knew that he hadn't been much of a husband. But it came to him with pleasure that he had taken her almost all of the meat he had brought back from Joker Lake. It was like heaping coals of fire on her head. She would have to add that into the calculation when she decided how bad a man he was.

He had not been hunting at all in recent years. She would have to see that now he was doing something different, something good.

Robert walked on, thinking hard.

Suddenly he walked right into Rebecca, coming out of the post office, colliding with her quite violently.

"Sorry!"

"You okay?" He began looking to see whether he had hurt her, holding onto her arm.

"I was thinking about something," she said. "I didn't see you."

Since he was looking into her face, Robert couldn't help noticing that she had been crying. There were tears in her eyes, and it was not from the pain of their collision, for they were also red, as though she had been crying for a little while.

"What's the matter?" he asked. "Something bothering you, Rebecca?"

"No. It's just—" She made a gesture to indicate the futility of further explanation "—my job. Sometimes it gets to be too much."

"I guess it's getting you down. It would get anybody down."

What he said was quite true, although it was not, in fact, what had been bothering her.

"People telling you a lot of stuff," he went on. "Things you don't want to hear. No one wants to hear that garbage. All you can do is sit there and listen, right?"

"I'm kind of tired, that's all," she said. "I'm okay." She put the letter from the Justice Department in the pocket of her parka.

She didn't look okay to him at all. He turned around and began to walk beside her toward her trailer.

Rebecca was still close to tears. She tried to start a conversation about something else.

"What are you doing here, Robert? I thought you'd still be out at Joker Lake."

Robert explained how he had come in for the meeting. And about how he had found Haga out in the storm.

"He hasn't changed his ways," he remarked.

"No. Nobody has," said Rebecca. "Maybe nobody can."

"What do you mean by that?" Robert was moved to argue, as usual. "I hear half the town is going to AA. Look at Michael. He's doing good."

She wasn't going to last long if she was already breaking up like this, he thought.

He was worried about her. Robert liked things to stay the same, however they were at any given time. Rebecca being the social worker in Prohibition Creek had become part of the landscape as far as he was concerned. He didn't want her to go away.

"You're not drinking and partying these days, are you, Robert?" she said.

"No."

"Do you miss it?"

He didn't really miss any of that. What he missed was gambling—poker, in particular: the trickery, the calculation, the cunning required to play a game like that really well.

"Do you miss it?" he asked, thinking of the story she had told at Joker Lake.

"No. But it seems as though there's no one I can really talk to these days."

"At least I've got Haga." He laughed.

"You must be the only person in the world who likes Haga." Rebecca laughed too.

"I didn't really tell you what happened to him. He went on a spaceship."

"What do you mean?" Rebecca tilted her head to look up at him, the fine snow brushing her face.

"He was lying out there in the bush without a jacket—he didn't even have slippers on—and some dog men came and picked him up."

"Dog men?" said Rebecca. She was just like his niece, Jamaica, Robert noticed, the way she listened to a story.

"They dragged him on board the spaceship. A giant woman called the Woman Who Married the Dog was on there and she wanted to eat him."

"How horrible!"

"Well, she was horrible. She's in our old stories. Her man was called No Fire. And there was this other guy, White Horizon, who was always trying to rape her. But she got away from both of them. She ate people, really had a taste for it. Finally, a giant dog took her for his wife. And Haga saw him doing—you know, doing things to her," Robert concluded.

"Dog men—I don't even believe that! Haga just dreamed it." Rebecca was revolted.

They had reached Rebecca's trailer. They stopped and stood facing one another in the lightly falling snow.

"Maybe he did. But there's a lot of truth in those stories," said Robert. "You just think about what it was like back then. They had to live out there on the sides of those mountains. The place wasn't a national park. They had to steal women just to keep themselves going. They didn't really eat each other for fun. The stories help you make sense of all that."

"I suppose so." Rebecca had lost interest suddenly. The letter in her pocket was foremost in her mind now that she was home. "Goodbye, Robert," she said.

Robert saw that something was bothering her again. Obviously she couldn't tell him what it was; he didn't even want to know, if it was connected with her job. But he was moved to help her somehow.

There was something in his hand. He remembered he was still holding the ducks.

"Here. Would you like these ducks?" He extended them to her, holding them by the feet. "I shot them and I couldn't give them to—well I couldn't give 'em away."

"How do you cook them?" Rebecca asked dubiously.

"They're all plucked. All you have to do is boil them."

Would she be able to do it? He eyed her clean parka, her high leather boots. He himself was in the same pair of greasy coveralls he had worn into town from the bush.

"Masi, Robert." Rebecca spoke formally, taking the ducks. Robert sometimes seemed like an elder to her. He went hunting, he told old stories, he had a strange friend like Haga.

But Robert was still struck by her clothes. She was dressed like a whitewoman, she even looked like one when she had her hair done up in back like that. She did not seem like the same Rebecca he had been talking to a moment ago. He was embarrassed to think what he had been saying.

"Well—goodbye," he said abruptly, turning away from her in the snow, which was still falling and falling.

Rebecca entered the part of her trailer that was her house and taking the letter from the Justice Department out of her pocket, spread it on the table beside her dirty plate from breakfast.

It did not mince words. The court continued to uphold the injunction against her children visiting until "she had been working steadily for six months and provided testimonials of continuous sobriety during that time from police, teachers, justices of the peace, and community leaders."

◂ ◂ ◂

There was a Band meeting the next day in Danny's office at the band hall. It was late in the afternoon and they had a fire out in the stove in the big room, the hall, since it was cold; it was still snowing.

Michael was humming the tune of a hymn, his feet up on Danny's desk.

"Can't you hum something a man would sing instead of this religious stuff?" Robert said, irritably. He was in a bad mood.

"What kind of songs would a man sing, Robert?" asked Danny. "I guess you mean songs about drinking and truck driving and cheating on your wife."

"I mean Dene songs," Robert said shortly.

Michael now began to sing "Michael Row the Boat Ashore."

"Oh, for God's sake!" exclaimed Robert. "You sound like a Protestant."

"So what?" said Danny.

"How were you brought up anyway, Danny? I hear you're getting everybody all mixed up with this AA of yours. The priest from the Forks, and an RC nun, and then that medicine woman you invited— I heard about her. And you've got the Pentecostals in there too."

"It's the same God," said Danny.

"No, it isn't."

"Yes, it is."

"No, it isn't." Robert was aware that this was childish, but he couldn't stop himself.

"I want to start this meeting," Danny said.

"Look, they don't think it's the same. That's why they're different," said Robert.

"Could we get started?" Danny was exasperated.

The atmosphere of this meeting was more informal and relaxed than the hamlet meeting.

"Okay" said Danny, pulling his chair up tightly into the kneehole of his desk. "The only reason we're here is to talk about this airport land deal."

Michael removed his feet from Danny's desk. "Well, we need an airport. The Red Baron won't use the old strip. Which means the only plane we can get is the Beaver on floats. Flown by that cowboy, Don."

"I don't want to give up the land," said Danny. He looked around and there was a murmur of assent from the older people sitting on the sofa, and on the straight chairs around the wall.

Danny's office was well-furnished: a large desk, many filing cabinets, a Xerox machine, a fax, a computer with a printer on his desk. Danny looked like a new-style Indian in his clean, freshly pressed shirt and his clean moosehide jacket with the fringes and beadwork. He wasn't like the old-time chiefs with their snuff-stained teeth and their broken English; he could actually use all the equipment in his office. And this was, in fact, true of nobody else in the room, including his two brothers.

"Why can't we just sell 'em the land?" asked Michael.

"I asked about that when I was talking to Ottawa on the phone. It seems they're keeping this land for us, but we can't have it. We'll only actually own it after the land claim comes through."

"If the land claim comes through, you mean," Michael corrected.

"You know, I've been wondering about that," said Robert crossly. "Right now we have to talk to the territorial government and the Feds. When we get the land claim, does that mean we're going to have to talk to a third government on top of those two?"

"What third government do you mean?" asked Michael.

"Us."

"Well, at least we'll know who we're talking to," said Danny

"Guys like you, you mean, Danny," said Robert.

There was a hostile pause.

"Anyone else want to say something?" Even though there was a quorum of Council members present, only Danny and his brothers had been doing any of the talking. Danny's eyes swept over the jacketed figures sitting around the walls. A blank look crossed his face as he carefully avoided meeting the eyes of his father's half-brother, the one they called Elvis.

No one said anything.

Michael said, "Well, we've got to do something about that airport. Sarah's pregnant. This'll be the second time she has to go out of here and come back with a kid on that Beaver."

It came to Robert suddenly in a blinding flash, a brilliant idea that solved everybody's problems at once.

"That piece with the fish plant on it," he said. The co-op had only been leasing the land for the fish plant. It was still Crown land; it wouldn't have been taken over by the territorial government because of the wrecked building on it. "Maybe we could trade the airport land for that."

"But why would we want it?" Danny was looking puzzled. "No one lives out there except—Oh yeah, you."

"Me and Haga," agreed Robert. "That would make two Dene living on the Indian reserve here."

"Get serious," said Danny.

But Robert was entirely serious. If his outhouse was on an Indian reserve he wouldn't have to go to any more meetings about it. The point of having reserves was so that people could live on them the way they wanted, after all.

He shrugged his shoulders. "Somebody want to second the motion?"

"You're making that into a motion?" Danny was frowning.

"Sure," said Robert.

"Well, I'll second it. I think Robert has a pretty good idea there, Danny," said Michael. "At least we might get an airport out of the deal."

"Okay," said Robert quickly. "Any further discussion? Question! All in favour? The motion is carried. There, your meeting's over, Danny."

Danny was looking like a thundercloud.

Robert was very pleased with himself, no longer irritable and unhappy, the way he had been feeling earlier.

The other people at the meeting were getting up to leave. Danny remained seated, the look of annoyance fading from his face. Robert began putting his jacket on to go too. His uncle Elvis was standing by unobtrusively, waiting for him to get ready.

"Well, okay, maybe it wasn't such a bad idea after all," said Danny.

"Thanks," said Robert.

Danny had not spoken with sarcasm and Robert was surprised.

"I'm pretty tired," Danny remarked. "I already had a couple of meetings before this today."

"That's the kind of stuff that goes with the job, I guess," said Robert lightly. "Me, I'm going hunting in the mountains with Haga—and with old Elvis here."

"You're taking Haga hunting?" said Danny. But this was not really what was on his mind. Once again his eyes swept past Elvis.

"Sure," said Robert. "Only Haga froze a couple of toes Monday night, so we had to wait around till the nurse said he was okay."

"Isn't he kind of—accident-prone?" said Danny.

"I know what you mean," Robert said. He laughed. "It's been snowing all week, perfect weather, and we couldn't get going because of him and his toes. But once we get out there it'll be all right." There was no brew pot, no galaxy of household fluids out in the mountains.

"I'll get my skidoo now," said Elvis, quietly.

Robert nodded, and the old man went out. Danny continued to sit where he was, allowing his shoulders to slump; he was exhausted.

"Want us to drop you off home, Danny?" said Robert. "When Elvis comes back he'll probably bring the toboggan."

"I've got to stay here and do a couple more hours work."

Looking at Danny's office, the changes he had made since he moved in, Robert couldn't help being impressed. Danny was showing he could handle the job of chief; and the arrogance he frequently expressed was, after all, Robert's own arrogance.

They had not been close as children. They were nearly ten years apart in age, and Robert had been fonder of his two younger sisters than either of the other boys. The way they didn't connect had something to do with their parents' relationship too. From the time Danny had been a toddler, his mother and father were fighting openly, and Danny had loved only his mother. Robert was a teenager, and seeing himself as the centre of his parents' disagreements, he became increasingly hard to handle.

"Why are you going hunting with Elvis?" asked Danny.

He put his hands up to his eyes and smoothed his eyebrows, a gesture of detachment, of boredom.

Robert was not deceived.

"For one thing he's an old-timer. He knows a lot. Why?"

"You know why." Now Danny yawned.

Danny hated Elvis because he was having an affair with Rachel, his mother. He had just become aware of this since he had moved back to Prohibition Creek this year, although the affair was of many years' standing. It was a clandestine affair, but like most clandestine affairs, everyone in town but the whites knew all about it.

What Danny didn't like about it, what filled him with jealousy and an intolerable fury, was that Elvis was their father's stepbrother, and he had been a member of their family circle for years, off and on since Robert was a little boy, before Danny could remember. It was impossible not to speculate that this affair had started long ago, before their father had left home.

Although he was pretending to be casual, Robert knew exactly how Danny felt, since he had had some of the same emotions some years ago himself, when he first became aware that Elvis was sneaking into Rachel's house every night. It had seemed indecent—these two old people having a sexually passionate affair like that. And he too had wondered how long it had been going on.

"Well, I guess I know what you're getting at. But what's the matter with it, Danny?" he said. "So what?—after all these years."

"Don't you think it's wrong? They're old, for God's sake. And Ama's still married to—to Dad."

"Well, what the heck. Our dad's been gone for years. He's never going to come back. It's not as though he didn't have a few girlfriends himself in the meantime. They didn't break up on account of Elvis, that's for sure."

Danny was looking at Robert with attention. This was the first time they had ever talked about their parents; it was really the first time they had ever had an intimate conversation. Just as Robert sometimes couldn't help being impressed by Danny, Danny now felt a kind of respect for his older brother.

"How do you know?"

"I thought about it," said Robert. "And I was there, remember?"

he went on. "You were only eight years old back then. I was nearly eighteen."

"So why did they break up?" asked Danny.

"It was me," he said. "The way I was acting."

"Why do you think that?"

"She just couldn't stand it. That I was turning out the way I was. She blamed the way I was acting on him."

"Well, maybe she had something to blame him for," said Danny.

"Yeah. Sure." Robert spoke dryly. Danny sounded like Mary Ann.

But Danny surprised him.

"The point is, however you were acting, and even if that did make them break up, it wasn't your fault, Robert. You were only a kid."

He had been a kid, and Robert remembered just how wild he had been. But it was true, he had not intended, he had not anticipated in any way, that his father would just get up one day and leave them all forever. That had been a time of emotional chaos for Robert; it had taken him a decade to recover from it, and by that time he was married and acting roughly the same way his father had acted all his life.

But he had recovered; at least, in a way. He now perceived that Danny had not.

"I kind of like Elvis, that's all," said Robert.

"Well, I don't," Danny replied.

"She's never going to marry him, Danny. Isn't she being punished enough?—She's like you. She thinks adultery is a sin."

"I don't know whether I think it's a sin," said Danny.

"They're not bothering anybody."

"Well, it bothers me. She knows that."

The outer door opened quietly. Elvis was standing in the big assembly room out beyond the office.

"Did you bring the sled, Elvis?" called Robert.

Elvis gave an affirmative grunt.

Robert glanced at Danny, but he had suddenly swivelled his chair around and opened a filing drawer. It was true that he had a lot of work to do, even though he was already very tired; he didn't have time for this problem as well. If Robert was going to go hunting with Elvis, so be it. He would not be eating the meat.

In fact, he was not really on speaking terms with his mother at the moment, having discovered her together with Elvis in her house one night lately, after she had come in from Joker Lake. Danny had not merely been taken aback and embarrassed at finding them like that, he had been deeply, seriously wounded, jealous, and very angry.

He pretended to be too busy to notice Robert taking his leave. There was no reason why he should respect Robert's opinion of Elvis, since he did not respect Robert.

• 6. DANNY AND REBECCA •

"Boy, that was a long day," said Danny.

Rebecca pushed in her desk drawers. She was tired too, but working together with Danny made her feel energized. He was so enthusiastic—when she was with him it seemed as if they were getting somewhere. The mass of information they had together here was awesome; but even more, they could see that they were making progress from the attendance at AA meetings, from the number of people who had given up drinking, the number of people who took counselling and the teenagers who came to the drop-in centre every day.

"I had a meeting with Indian Affairs in the morning over this stupid airport land deal," said Danny with a sigh. This matter was a sinkhole, in his opinion; he already had a folder full of email on the subject.

"Then at lunchtime I took Jamaica to the nursing station for her needle," he continued. "After that I had a meeting all afternoon with the nurse. She's got a problem with what she can tell the police, for God's sake. She can tell them this, she can't tell them that."

"You must be pretty tired, Danny." Rebecca was sympathetic.

He put his booted feet up on the other side of her desk and crossed them, then smiled at her impishly, and removed them again.

"Do you know what I've got?" said Rebecca. "I've got duck soup. And it tastes really good."

She had made it just the way Robert did, using all the ducks he gave her. Just meat, not even an onion; all the flavour came from the rich oily taste of the duck meat.

"Well, I want that." Smiling, Danny waved his hand in a 'get it for me, slave' gesture.

"You could come in. I cleaned up my place." Rebecca hesitated in the doorway to her living quarters. No one had ever visited her there. She seemed to live only through her job.

Danny was already following her through the door.

"You've really fixed this up, Rebecca." He was looking around appreciatively.

She *had* really fixed it up. It had been a mess when she moved in: a bedspring and a disgusting, stained mattress, a disconnected gas cookstove, a honey bucket, the sink and shower not hooked up to the pump, the floor of the one main room knee-deep in trash. In the first week after she moved in, Rebecca had got the appliances connected and working, washed the walls and the floor, bought a new mattress and covered it as a daybed, laid down some cozy rugs, and a clean oilcloth for the table, and set up her CD player and her TV conveniently.

Presently it was in apple-pie order. After she had got that letter about her kids from the Justice Department, she had done a ferocious day of cleaning.

"What do you think of my picture?"

Rebecca was putting two bowls of soup in the microwave. She came over to look at the picture with Danny. It was a strange picture, very abstract, and she wanted to hear what he would say about it. But he had already turned away. He sat down on her bed, bounced a few times, and they both laughed.

She brought him the soup, and he continued to sit on the bed to eat it. Rebecca sat down in the only chair beside the table in the little kitchen area.

"I bought that picture in the West Edmonton Mall," she remarked. "I think I like it because it isn't about anything."

Danny looked at it again and shrugged. He returned to the soup, eating with pleasure.

A little disappointed, Rebecca got up to put on a CD, which she had also bought at the West Edmonton Mall.

"I like your place. It's so relaxing."

"It is now—after I cleaned it up," said Rebecca, laughing. "It was a mess last week. I just didn't have time."

"I know. I know how hard you've been working, Rebecca."

"It's—sometimes it's pretty tough to listen to—to all this stuff." He would know this too, since he was also doing some counselling. He was not really supposed to, since he didn't have the training, but nobody was going to tell the chief what to do with his own people. Rebecca needed all the help she could get. "And then what can you do?" she continued. "It's like putting on a bandage."

"You have the power of love," said Danny. "The power of love can change everything."

"Do you really think so?" She knew he had his own theories, which were not the theories she had been taught at Thebacha.

"Sure," he said. "It's all anybody needs. What you get from your parents, your friends, your wife. That's the only thing that counts."

Rebecca began to think about Roseanne, Danny's wife. She had heard them quarrelling out at Joker Lake, and from what she could tell, Roseanne was still not happy here. She was not very friendly to Rebecca either.

"What are you thinking?" he asked. Rebecca had rested her cheek on one elbow, a wistful expression on her face, and he was gazing at her with an appreciative smile. It was a pleasure to work with someone who was as pretty as Rebecca.

"Nothing," she said now, sitting up straight and smiling.

She had not been unconscious of Danny's eyes on her. He was attractive to her too: tall and handsome, and somehow sure about everything. That was a quality she deeply appreciated about him—when she was with Danny she felt that she too was sure.

"I was thinking about Roseanne," she corrected herself. "Don't you think she wants a job?"

"She wants a job," agreed Danny. "But who's going to look after our kids if she gets a job? There isn't any daycare."

"That's true." Rebecca had been formulating a project to get a daycare going somehow. And she knew that Roseanne had been a daycare worker in Yellowknife.

"There's nothing more important than your family," Danny said. "Your wife, your kids—especially your kids—they're your whole life."

Danny didn't know Rebecca's history, because she had never told him. She had been intending to: in fact she had been thinking of doing it right now. He was the only person here in whom she could confide, and he was in a position to help her. But when she heard him say this, her blood ran cold. He would not understand, he could never understand a woman who had deserted her own kids.

"Do you think some people are really bad?" she asked abruptly.

"You ought to know better than that," he replied. "But people sometimes do things they can never make up for."

Rebecca felt that everything had gone well for Danny, all his life. He had never partied wildly every night, or drunk so much that he couldn't remember, or slept with people he didn't care about, sometimes just because they would give him a drink. Rebecca realized that if she told him those things about herself he would be repelled and disgusted.

Danny wondered what was causing her to look so distraught all of a sudden. She fiddled with her hair when something was on her mind, and it was coming down in tendrils around her face. He was thinking that she was even prettier like that, with her hair in a mess.

As a matter of fact he had something on his mind as well. There was no one he could confide in better than Rebecca at the moment.

"Robert has gone hunting with Elvis," he said. "He doesn't care. It doesn't bother him about that old man and my mother."

"Rachel? And Elvis?" Rebecca was surprised. She had, of course, heard the rumour, but she had thought it must be untrue. Rachel was very devout, and both of them were old people—very old, from Rebecca's perspective.

"I don't know when it started," he said. "Maybe it began a long time ago. When I was still at home."

Rebecca was still surprised, but she wasn't shocked.

"But why is that so wrong?" she asked.

"She shouldn't do it. She's married."

"And marriage is forever?"

"Yes. It is. I believe in marriage," he said.

Danny was agitated; his voice was shaken by something like tears.

Rebecca was more taken by his tone of voice, by the fact that he was making a confidence, than by the content of what he had said. He loved, he cared, he too could be hurt, his voice told her, and she wanted badly to talk to somebody like that. She began again to tell him about herself.

"Danny? What if there was a woman—?"

Danny was smoothing his eyebrows, that gesture of his that imitated boredom. He was still trying to compose himself.

"She was like your mother. She couldn't live with her husband."

Danny was alert now. He knew she was talking about herself.

"Well, I can understand that," he said.

"She had two kids, a boy and a little girl."

Danny was staring at her. "Where are they?"

"They're with my husband. And he—the court won't let me take them, not even for a little while."

There was a long pause.

"Why not?" Danny asked.

"I'm not a bad woman. Don't think that!" Rebecca cried. "You said there weren't any bad people."

She was almost crying. It was too late now to try to tell him exactly what had happened to her as a young woman, her rebellion against her father, her foolish marriage, the way she had fallen deeper and deeper into a cycle of drunkenness and irresponsibility.

He just had to understand—the way he would have if she had been a woman he was counselling. She was floundering, trying to see what had happened, why it was that Danny couldn't accept what she was saying to him, why he was refusing to help her now.

She went over to the CD player and switched off the music.

"You think that woman should go back to her husband, don't you? But he wouldn't have her. And she doesn't want to."

Danny had got up and they stood opposite one another in the middle of the little room. Then Rebecca put her hands on his shoulders. He took her by the waist; it might have been to push her away, but there was an electrical charge in both of them that was excited by their closeness, by his touch, that went through them like a wild shock.

The kiss went on and on. They broke off for an instant, long enough for her to pull the clip out of her hair and let it fall down on her shoulders. Then they were clinging to one another again.

For Danny, discovering that Rebecca was a bad woman liberated him from the constraints he had been putting on himself for weeks, and he felt wildly that he was free to have her. As for Rebecca, it was the exercise of power that excited her; she had always used sex to get what she wanted, to anger her father and humiliate her husband.

Danny suddenly pushed her away, gasping. Rebecca stumbled backwards, nearly falling. Then he was standing by the door, his hand on the knob. His face was pale, and he was breathing heavily.

"This never happened," he directed. "We've got to forget this ever happened."

Rebecca began to cry.

"I'm going to walk out that door," he said. "And neither of us is going to remember it after that."

Still weeping, she nodded obediently. This Danny was the one she knew, the one she trusted, who took command and always knew what to do next. It would be all right again, if only they could both manage to do what he said.

He was gone. The door banged behind him.

Rebecca stood there for a moment, crying. Then she began to walk around in circles in the middle of her room, wringing her hands. She felt that she was like that horrible woman in Robert's story, who had done things that were so awful they put her outside the bounds of human compassion.

◂ ◂ ◂

On Sunday afternoon Rebecca went down to the town float dock. She had heard an airplane landing and taking off from there at regular intervals since that morning. As she had expected, Don was working there, in hip waders, unloading meat from his airplane.

"Hi," he said briefly, and went on working, ignoring her as she stood there.

It was a nice day, clear weather, good for flying. Last week's snow had almost gone from the ground. The birch and poplar trees across the lake were leafless, and stretched away toward the mountains, their grey and brown and blue diluting the definite blacks and reds of spruce and muskeg.

There was a hunt going on out there in the mountains, seventy or eighty miles away, but only half an hour by air.

"What are you doing here?" the pilot asked at last. He had made a neat conical pile of caribou hindquarters on the dock. There was no one there to pick it up yet; the trucks in town were busy making deliveries to the various recipients of the last load.

"I just came down to look at the lake," Rebecca said.

He studied her for a moment, but she continued to look innocently at the water, and after a moment he swung around to look at it too.

"Notice the ice all over?" he demanded.

Rebecca nodded.

"Well, the Red Baron likes it to be three inches thicker before he takes this junk heap off of its pontoons."

Rebecca laughed and Don grinned. He wasn't sure what she was doing here. She hadn't panned out the way he was expecting last time, and she was giving him conflicting signals again.

"I kind of had the impression you were through with aviation after our last date," he remarked.

"That was our first date," Rebecca corrected him.

"Our first date?" he said thoughtfully.

Rebecca tipped her head back to smile at him. He was male, he was handsome, he liked her; she felt she was willing to take a risk on him now.

Since the day Danny had visited her, she had been keeping her head down in work, fighting her anxiety. She was desperate for someone to talk to; Don would have to do.

The pilot was talking.

"—Thought I just wanted to get you in the sack," he was saying. "But come on, sweetheart. I think you're smart as well as beautiful."

In spite of what he said, she knew he had just wanted sex before. But even if that was what he wanted, she still might be able to talk to him.

"Are you going somewhere with the plane now?" she asked.

"Let's see," he replied. "First I fly half an hour in that direction. Then I pick up a load of dead animals and fly half an hour in this direction. Then I unload them here. Then I take off again and fly half an hour in that direction—Would you like to come for a little ride? For say, half an hour?"

He jumped down on the float and opened the door for her. Rebecca jumped down after him and clambered into the cockpit.

The plane reeked of fresh meat, a warm dense odour, not unpleasant to Rebecca. They were flying into the westering sun and it was hot in the cockpit. The swampy lowlands gave way to hills, and then, surprisingly soon, they were in mountainous country, not very high, but at these latitudes the treeline was only a few hundred feet up. The peaks rose jagged all around them in the brilliant colours of erosion: orange and rose, sienna and burnt umber.

There was no need for Don to use the radio; they were the only aircraft flying as low as this over the rough country. He took off his earphones. With one hand resting casually on the stick he turned around sideways to face Rebecca, close enough to kiss—which they did for a moment, lightly, their lips just touching. But neither of them said anything because of the loud throbbing of the engine; it was an invasive, harmful noise against which they would have had to shout.

Rebecca was thinking hard. He might have some problems himself; a girlfriend down south who wanted to marry him, an alcoholic parent. Surely they could talk about some of those things too, and then she could tell him about herself. She would like to break through the conventions by which they were bound—man and woman, whiteman and native woman—to try to understand and be understood.

Rebecca spoke at last, raising her eyes, and he glanced at her.

"Do you think a man and a woman can be friends?" she asked.

He smiled. "We'll just go down here first. Maybe I can answer your question then," he said.

She was sitting demurely, her knees close together, eyes lowered; she looked very pretty like that, fiddling with her hair, her face irradiated with the warm bright sunshine and he thought she was trying to tease him.

They had nearly reached their destination. Don swung around in his seat, preparing to take the plane lower into the valley they had been following. There was a deafening kind of silence as he reduced the power.

They were landing on a river in a deep, wide valley of the mountains. The plane was down in a strong current, its engine roaring to make headway. Finally Don brought it against the shoreline, crunching on the rocks. It was a forbidding place, the boulders along the shore, the valley cold and dark in the shadow of the surrounding peaks with the sun almost down, the wild rushing of the river loud in their ears.

Don jumped out of the cockpit with a rope, and went ashore to tie up to the willow bushes growing in the clay patches on the icy beach. He had brought the plane in behind a wide bend where the current swung out into midstream, but still the machine was dragged against its ropes by the water.

Now he waded out to the pontoon, up to his thighs in the rushing water.

"This is one heck of a wonderful spot to load up a bush plane. See all these rocks? Well, that's why they chose it, no doubt," he remarked.

He held out his arms and Rebecca saw that he was intending to carry her to shore. She looked toward the beach, where a high pile of meat lay waiting to be loaded. It was too far to jump, and the water was deep. There was no other way but to let him take her.

She put her arms around his neck, and he caught her up neatly under the knees. She was frightened by the depth and swiftness of the water, afraid he was going to drop her—and it would be cold; she could get carried away in the current. She might drown.

But he was sure-footed and for a moment, just before they mounted the beach, she was enjoying the thrill of it; taking a risk like this in the arms of a man who was almost a stranger.

Don set her down on the gravel beach and a moment later he was kissing her, a hard, sexually demanding kiss. He had felt the way she yielded to him when he was carrying her; the fact that she was resisting all of a sudden was just part of the cat-and-mouse game she had been playing with him from the start, as far as he was concerned.

"Come on, sweetheart. Don't I get some kind of reward?"

At this moment Rebecca caught sight of Haga, coming out of the thin bush above the beach and called to him.

He was panicked by the unexpected sight of Rebecca with the whiteman, who seemed to have been attacking her. Hesitating, he looked around for help.

"Haga!" she called. "Is this your camp?" and then, as Haga gave vent to a terrified yelp: "It's only me—Rebecca!"

He hesitated an instant longer, then ran off into the bush without replying.

"Friend of yours?" asked Don. He was moving in on her again.

"I know him," she said, backing away.

Her hair had fallen out of its clip, her cheeks were pink and she was breathing hard. She looked very desirable to the young man.

"That question you were asking me. You know—about whether a man and a woman—"

He had caught her in his arms and was coaxing her rather roughly to let him kiss her. But she was disgusted with him now; his lack of finesse, the way they had been struggling with each other when they scared off Haga. She saw how grossly he had interpreted her decision to go flying with him again. She had been wrong in thinking that she could make him care about who she was, and this frightened her. Perhaps there would never be anyone to whom she could talk.

"Come on, sweetheart. Just—one—little—kiss." Don was trying to make her raise her face up with one of his hands under her chin. As he loosened his embrace, she pushed against him and he stumbled backwards on some rocks.

Robert and Elvis now emerged from the bush. They saw Rebecca struggling against the whiteman. Apparently she punched him, for he fell down. Robert began to run toward them.

"Hey!" he shouted.

A moment later he was standing over Don, who had been getting up, but subsided gracefully on the beach when he saw Robert rushing down on him.

"It's okay, my friend. There's no harm done," said Don.

Robert continued to stand over him fiercely. Then he looked at Rebecca, who turned away, embarrassed.

Robert turned away as well, and the pilot got to his feet, ostentatiously dusting himself off.

Robert and Elvis, like Haga before them, had heard the plane and come down to the beach to help load it from the high pile of meat that lay waiting. They now formed a chain and began to work, passing the meat to Don in the water. No one had to speak; it was something they had been doing all afternoon, whenever the plane came in.

Rebecca wandered disconsolately up the beach.

She had wanted to open herself up to the young pilot; but it had been a mistake. She might even have let him go ahead and have her, simply out of despair, except that they had been interrupted. Now all her anxiety had returned. She had not succeeded in freeing herself, even for a short while.

Don came striding up the beach, the straps of his hip waders clacking and snapping as he walked.

"Let's go, Rebecca. I'm all finished here." He spoke coldly. He had been thinking too, as he worked.

She knew that he despised her now and she didn't want to go with him. She needed to be alone for a while.

"You have to come back in an hour, don't you?" she asked.

He nodded.

"Then I'll stay here," she said.

"Well, it's your decision, I guess," he replied. He waited an instant, then turned and went clicking off down the shingle to the plane. She sat with her head down. The door of the cockpit slammed, and the engine roared to life.

After the plane took off and rose away it was very quiet in the valley. Rebecca had found a boulder to sit on. She wrapped her arms around her legs and folded her jacket close about her; it was cold even though a little sunshine still found its way down the snow-covered slopes of the hills. Up here in the mountains it was deep winter already.

Feet crunched up the beach toward her. Rebecca raised her head. It was Robert. She had almost forgotten that he must be still there. She couldn't see Elvis, but then she spotted a curl of cigarette smoke coming up from behind a rock some distance away. He had taken refuge out of the wind to smoke.

"What are you doing here?" she asked.

"Loading meat." Robert was taciturn. He had seen what he had seen, after all, and he too had been thinking about it.

"Did you shoot all this?" The pile of meat on the beach still rose head high. It was caribou meat, woodland, not barrenland caribou; the larger animals.

"There's quite a few of us hunting out this way," he replied. It was their custom to bring the meat to a spot like this on the river and go in on the cost of the plane together.

"Where's your camp?" Rebecca was taking an interest in her surroundings again. It was a surprise to meet Robert here on this wild beach. He was looking rough and dirty; his parka was stained with blood and the juices of the meat he had been hefting. Underneath the dirt his face was tanned to a deep walnut shade of brown.

Robert was upset.

"Are you still screwing around with that pilot?" He spoke aggressively.

"I'm not screwing around with him," she replied. "I just wanted to go for a ride."

"I thought you knew something about whitemen. You told us you were married to one. So you should know—they never do things for people unless they get paid."

Robert was scolding her, but strangely enough, this made Rebecca feel better.

"I just needed to go somewhere for a change, that's all." This was at least partly true.

Robert was also feeling better now that he had said what was on his mind. He sat down on the rock beside her.

"Haga ran away when he saw me," she said. "Why did he do that?"

Robert laughed. "Probably he thought you were a ghost or something."

He could imagine the shock Haga had sustained, seeing Rebecca's ghost on the shore of Gravel River. It had been rather a shock to him too, coming out of the woods and finding her there fighting off that whiteman.

"Are you having a good hunt?" she was asking.

"Pretty good."

"I made soup with those ducks you gave me."

The conversation was very strange to him. For one thing it was in English, and he had been speaking his own language all week, with Haga and the other men. And out here no one had to talk much about anything; if they were hunting they knew what to do and they acted together. The work was hard and cold, and when they weren't working they were almost always eating or asleep.

Rebecca was not discomfited by his silence. She didn't have normal expectations of Robert anyway. It was for this reason that she decided to ask him the same question she had asked the pilot earlier.

"Robert—do you think a man and a woman can be friends?"

Robert was interested.

"You mean without one of them wanting to—?"

"Yes. I mean, just friends."

He pondered. "I don't know. Men and women are pretty different."

"But would that stop them from being friends?"

"If they could understand each other."

"Maybe it would be interesting," she said. "Trying to understand."

He nodded. "Yeah. I see what you mean. When you're married or something, the woman is kind of—well—almost your enemy."

Rebecca said, "If you like someone it doesn't matter if you're different."

"Yeah," agreed Robert. "I don't think any woman could be as different as Haga."

They both laughed.

In a way he had changed the subject, or at least he was trying to indicate that he didn't take this seriously. But she thought that he did take it seriously.

"I want to tell you something," she said suddenly, directly. She turned around to face him, the top of a boulder between them like a table. "I've got two kids. My son is eight. My little girl is five."

"Where are they?"

"They're with my husband. He has custody." Rebecca spoke baldly.

"But they're Dene kids," Robert protested.

"Part Dene. I was trying to get them this summer. To come up here with me. But he—he took out a restraining order. I can't have them." Rebecca was trying not to cry.

"You're the mother." Robert was scandalized. He felt the mother should have her children. A mother was a mother, in his view.

"They don't really even know me." Rebecca had covered her face; she spoke through her fingers.

"They're still your kids," he argued.

"That's not what he says."

"What does he say?"

"I neglected them. I deserted them. He says they don't have a mother."

"That's not true," said Robert. But he knew his words were hollow. Rebecca was sobbing now, her face in her hands, and Robert for a change, had nothing to say.

Rebecca was wiping her eyes with her fingers.

Robert was thinking about his father. While his mother had scolded him and talked to him and given him good examples to go by all his life, he recalled scarcely any of it; while he could remember every occasion on which his father had talked to him seriously or given him advice.

"Maybe someday, when they're older, your kids will come looking for you," he said. "They'll want to find out who you are."

"To find out who I am? Their mother?" Rebecca said bitterly.

"Like me with my dad. I hated him for a while after he left us. But later on I went looking for him."

"But isn't this one of those things you can never make up for?" she asked.

They could hear the drone of the plane returning.

"Don't you think I'm a bad person?" she asked.

Robert had never been asked to judge anyone before, although he had himself often been judged, and on these very terms. Once again, he had nothing to say.

The plane was landing. Elvis arose from behind his rock. Robert started down the beach as the pilot emerged from the cockpit. A moment later Don was up to his hips in the water, directing them as they pulled in the plane.

"Okay, let's load 'em up," he said, and the men formed a chain as before.

Rebecca drew her knees up under her chin, huddling in her parka. It was getting colder. The sun had gone down finally behind the canyon walls, and the bright sky overhead, streaked with orange and mauve and lemon, made the rock she was sitting on, the beach, the landing place, seem darker, colder and even more desolate.

These last two years, during which she had gone back to school, trying to determine the direction of her life, had not been easy ones. She already knew who she was, or she could never have done it. The next step was no different, then. She had to do what the court said—keep her job and not fall back into her old ways. She had to prove to them that she could do that. She was determined to get her children back, whatever that took.

Don came up the beach toward Rebecca. He had recovered his temper during the flight. Rebecca was a weird girl, but most of them were weird, in his view—they didn't know what they wanted from one moment to the next.

"You've got to come this time, sweetheart," he said good-humouredly. "Last trip."

She followed him in silence down to the landing place. There was a moment's hesitation as he turned around to face her. She put her arms out and he took her up to carry her through the water to the pontoon of the plane.

Then she turned around to look for one last time at the beach, so wild and lonely by the mountain river, where she had taken a new resolve. Her counsellors and teachers had told her that she would have to make decisions like this, some of them—like sobriety—on an almost daily basis. But this one was momentous, and it had been made here in this lonely place by the rushing mountain river.

Robert spoke to her quietly from the beach. "Remember what I said, Rebecca."

"What did you say?" He had not given her any advice.

"What I said about whitemen."

Rebecca looked at him in surprise.

"Don't pay him." Robert spoke even more quietly.

She burst out laughing, and the pilot, who was busy untying the ropes on the willows, turned around to look, startled.

"It's okay. I won't," she said to Robert.

• 7. WHITE FLOWER •

Elvis and Robert had made their camp not far away from the plane's landing place that night. It had already been almost night in the canyon when they had loaded it up for the last time. There was also the question of where Haga had gone.

He stumbled into the camp as soon as they had got the fire going, and it emerged that he had been hiding in the willows all afternoon.

After he finished supper Robert went hunting for driftwood down the beach. Haga was eating a piece of roasted meat and telling Elvis about his experience of the afternoon.

"She had long hair that fell down loose over her shoulders," he was saying.

"What was she wearing?" asked Elvis.

"I dunno." Haga thought for a moment. "Maybe she was naked," he said.

"Naked!"

Robert had been listening to them talk as he came back up the beach with an armload of wood. He came into the circle of light and dumped it down beside the fire.

"Did she say anything?" Elvis asked, poker-faced. It was impossible to tell what he was thinking from his expression, but Robert knew his uncle: he was playing Haga along.

"She called my name," said Haga.

Robert was still standing over them and his uncle looked up.

"Haga saw some kind of ghost on the beach today," Elvis informed him.

"Do you think it was the same one you saw that other time?" asked Robert, expressionless as well.

"Maybe that's how she knew your name," said Elvis. He had already been told about Haga's near-death experience with the dog men on the spaceship.

Haga reflected. "She wasn't ugly this time," he said.

"She didn't say what her own name was, by any chance?" asked Robert.

"I ran away too fast," Haga replied. "There was a strange man there too. He had a pale face and long yellow feet like a duck. He didn't look like a Dene."

Robert was thinking of a story he knew, another one out of that little green book. It might have happened right here on this part of the Gravel River.

"Maybe that guy was one of the Kollouches," he said.

Even old Elvis had never heard of the Kollouches. He looked inquiringly at Robert. Everyone—especially the old people—liked to hear Robert's stories.

"The Kollouches were a bunch of bad people who used to live out here and steal our women."

"There were a lot of men who stole women back then," agreed Elvis.

"One time there was a girl they stole named White Flower."

"Do you think she was the one I saw, Robert?" asked Haga, somewhat pathetically. He had lost the dramatic advantage, and he was sure that he was going to get scared when Robert told his story.

"Maybe," Robert shrugged. "White Flower had two husbands."

"Two husbands? How could that work?" Haga demanded.

"Well, it sure makes a lot more sense than a man trying to have two wives. When you think about it."

Haga thought about it. "Oh yeah," he said.

Elvis was nodding.

"The Kollouches cut off the heads of both her husbands. Then they gave her the heads to play with."

"Geez, Robert," whined Haga.

"One of the Kollouches became her new husband. She had to sleep with him, of course. But she wanted to get home. So one night she told him to lie on his back. Then she cut his throat."

"What about the other people in the tent? Didn't they hear it?" asked Elvis.

"They just heard a little noise from the knife sawing through his neck, but they thought it was the dogs outside gnawing on some fish."

Haga made a little whimpering noise in his throat.

"Okay," said Robert argumentatively. "But she was Dene. She didn't want to have to stay with the Kollouches."

There was black darkness all around them now; the moon had not yet risen above the steep sides of the valley, and they were alone with the wild, endless rushing of the river. In the little circle of light cast by the fire, Robert perceived that both his interlocutors were rivetted by the story.

"Anyway," he continued, "her mother-in-law yelled at her to go outside and chase the dogs off the fish. Instead she took a canoe and hid somewhere down the river behind some rocks."

"I think it must have been this river here, Haga. She was one of us, see?"

Haga whimpered again, more loudly.

"After the Kollouches found the guy with his throat cut, they got into their boats and paddled after her. But by that time a great white wolf had come along, and he carried White Flower up the river on his back. When she got home—I think that must have been Wrigley Lake, or somewhere like that—she recognized the place by the fishnets all over. But she'd been away a long time. So a little later, when her father came paddling past in his canoe, she wasn't sure it was him."

"Couldn't she say something to him?" asked Elvis.

"Maybe she'd forgotten how to talk our language. But the father kept hearing a little bird sing: White flower, tchi! White Flower, tchi! So he took some dry fish from his wife and put it out for the bird. White Flower ate the fish and then she lay down on the path singing, Tchi! Tchi! That way her dad knew who she was."

The other two were looking at the fire, comforting themselves with its brightness. Elvis carefully adjusted a small piece of wood on the embers. It flared up briefly.

"Go on, Robert," Elvis said.

"There was a whole bunch of men in that camp, and the father was afraid White Flower might get kidnapped again. So he kept her hidden till her baby was born."

"That baby must have been from the Kollouches, though," protested Haga.

"Well, it was a good-looking boy, anyway. Then her dad let the people in the camp know that White Flower was the mother. And all the men wanted her because of that baby. So her Dad got her a new husband."

"But that baby was from the Kollouches."

"Come on, Haga, you know we don't care about things like that," said Robert. "Dene people adopt babies even if they're whitemen."

"You figure these Kollouches were people, do you?"

"Well, if White Flower could have a good-looking baby with one of them, they must have been some kind of people."

There was a long silence. Then Elvis said, "Do you think Haga saw one of those Kollouches, Robert?" There was a trace of a smile on his small smooth old face.

"Nope." Robert laughed.

"Well, why'd you tell that story then?" Haga cried, indignant. "Geez, Robert, that story made my skin crawl. She was playing with their heads."

"Oh yeah, I forgot to tell you," said Robert. "She talked to the heads as if they were still alive, and then she dragged them around by the hair, and made them jump up off the ground."

"You're just making that up." Haga was galvanized.

"No, I'm not. She was pretending she'd gone nuts. She didn't want the Kollouches to kill her."

Elvis got up and put a whole armload of wood on the fire. There was a bright blaze and they were cheered by its warmth.

Robert yawned and began to unroll his sleeping bag.

"Well, just about time to turn in for the night, I guess."

Elvis began to set himself up for the night too. They were moving from impromptu camp to impromptu camp and they had no tent. If it snowed before dawn, they would simply get up and move on; but if there was a storm they would make themselves a lean-to or even a proper teepee. One of the advantages of travelling with Elvis was that he had the know-how for all this; back in the old days it had simply been his life with his family. Even though Robert had gone hunting in the mountains and to the camp at Joker Lake since he was a child he would never be as self-reliant in the bush as Elvis.

"How do you expect us to do any sleeping now, Robert?" Haga complained.

"This is the first time I ever heard you having trouble sleeping," said Robert.

"You didn't see one of those Kollouches, Haga." Elvis told him. "That story Robert told happened a long time ago."

Haga regarded him doubtfully.

"You just saw the pilot of that Beaver. He was wearing yellow hip waders."

"Oh yeah. I never told you what the Kollouches looked like," said Robert.

"Well, don't tell him, okay?" Elvis was already in his sleeping bag. "We'll be up all night. And we haven't got enough wood."

Robert took off his boots and his parka and got into his sleeping bag too.

"Who was that beautiful naked woman with the long hair?" asked Haga. He began slowly undoing his bedroll.

"That was Rebecca," said Robert. "And she wasn't naked," he added.

"Rebecca?" Haga shot Robert a suspicious glance. "That social worker?"

"Yeah. She hitched a ride out here with the Red Baron's plane."

Haga got into his sleeping bag without bothering to take off his parka or his boots.

The fire crackled brightly and by its light the wild rushing of the river was a less lonely sound.

"Sleep now," said Elvis.

Robert doubled his parka up under his head and snuggled down into his bag. They were camped on the beach, but Elvis had taken the trouble to make a spruce mat underneath, and Robert was comfortable and quite warm.

Haga began to snore, a horrible sawing noise.

Robert went right to sleep, by now quite used to this.

◂ ◂ ◂

After such days of travel and hard work they were in the habit of sleeping early and long; the time of daylight was short and they had to be well rested to maximize the hours they had for hunting. Usually Robert slept dreamlessly, or at least could not remember his dreams when he woke up.

But tonight he dreamed; and what he dreamed was that he was standing on the part of the beach where they had made the pile of caribou pieces, and he saw Rebecca. She came toward him, and even though she was wearing whitewomen's clothes and a store parka, with her hair down on her shoulders, she seemed like a Dene girl.

She spoke to him, as she usually spoke, with natural friendliness. "I made soup with those ducks you gave me."

But he was surprised; he couldn't understand how she had got out here in the mountains.

Then they were sitting side by side on the rock, and still speaking in that intimate but natural way, she asked, "Do you think that a man and a woman can be friends?"

He didn't answer; it seemed as though he couldn't answer her aloud, but he knew that he wanted to. What he wanted to say was that he was her friend even though he was a man.

"I have to tell you something, Robert." She spoke confidingly. "I've got two kids."

Again, he wanted to speak. He wanted to say that he would help her if only he could. He would use all the arguments he had to help her.

"But isn't this one of the things you can never make up for?" She had turned toward him pleadingly, and the smooth skin of her forehead was wrinkled up in distress. Then she was crying into her hands.

"There were a lot of things I did like that," he said.

"Do you think I'm a bad person?" Rebecca wept, and all he could see was her bent head and shoulders as she turned away.

"I know you're a good person," he said.

Robert was waking himself up with the sound of his own voice. He repeated firmly, "I know you're a good person," and opened his eyes in the firelight.

Haga also had woken up with a snort.

"Robert was talking in his sleep," said Elvis.

They were both sitting up. Robert sat up too, bewildered. That had happened, it had all really happened, hadn't it? he was thinking.

But then he remembered that it hadn't happened exactly that way. He hadn't said what he said in the dream. He had just sat beside her, uselessly, saying nothing.

"You were talking to someone," said Elvis. The other men were both looking at him strangely.

"Who was it?" Haga demanded. "Who were you talking to?"

Haga was still alarmed from being woken up so suddenly, and Robert saw he was all set to be frightened.

"Well, it was a beautiful woman," said Robert. "She was Dene and she had long hair that fell down loose over her shoulders."

For an instant Haga looked terrified, but then he perceived by Elvis's ironic silence, or perhaps by some minute twitch in Robert's expression, that somehow he was being had.

"Geez, Robert! Isn't that enough of that for one night?" he said in disgust. He lay down again.

Robert laughed. The funny thing was that it really had been about that woman. He lay down too, snuggling back into the warm depths of his bedroll.

It had been an interesting dream and his people had always assigned prophetic significance to dreaming. It was the first time he had ever had such an experience, so lifelike and intense—a dream that altered the future by changing the past.

◂ ◂ ◂

On Saturday of the following weekend Rebecca was at home, washing dishes. She was taking a whole day off and cleaning up her place.

Once again she had been working very hard all week. But things were going better. She was on an even keel again with Danny, after a little awkwardness in their first encounters, and it was he who had suggested she take the day off.

She was no longer having anxiety attacks, although she was sometimes depressed, and she attributed the fact that she was feeling better to her conversation with Robert, to that feeling she had had while they were talking that she could save herself, that she didn't have to be rescued.

It was a bright, sunny day. The cold weather of November had not yet really arrived and they were having a respite, a little Indian summer, as the residents of Prohibition Creek acknowledged to one another with irony.

There was a knock on the door. Rebecca looked out the window over the sink but Danny's wife Roseanne was already coming in through the door.

"Oh, it's you, Roseanne." Rebecca hesitated, conscious of a false note in her voice.

"I came to visit."

"I'll make tea." Smiling, Rebecca plugged in the kettle as Roseanne sat down beside the table.

"What's this?" Roseanne asked in surprise.

"Duck soup."

Rebecca had had it for breakfast, and there was the remains of a bowl of it still on the oilcloth.

"I made it a long time ago—last week." It was not so very long ago, Rebecca realized. "Robert gave me some ducks," she explained.

"Robert?" Roseanne raised her plucked eyebrows in surprise. She was a pretty woman of about Rebecca's age, slim, with an oval face.

Rebecca removed the bowl and spoon, and wiped the table with her dishrag. Then she poured boiling water into the teapot and set it on the table with the sugar bowl and an open can of cream.

"Danny's looking after the kids this morning. He said I should come over and see you."

"He did?" asked Rebecca carefully.

"He said you're lonely."

It was true that she was lonely, but Rebecca wondered if there was another motive in this besides kindness.

"He said I was getting burnt out. Staying home with the kids all the time. So that's why I should get together with you."

Rebecca relaxed all of a sudden.

"Danny is a good man, isn't he?" Rebecca said.

"Of course he is," replied Roseanne. "It's just too bad you had to hear us having a fight that time at Joker Lake," she added.

"Oh, I wasn't listening to that," replied Rebecca. "Besides, your little girl was sick. I guess that's the way people act sometimes when they're worried about—" she faltered suddenly.

"Their kids." Roseanne finished her sentence. "But you don't have any kids, do you?"

Rebecca was silent.

"Well, you're lucky," said Roseanne. "They tie you down. I just wish I had a job too."

Rebecca had been thinking about getting a nursery school going in Prohibition Creek ever since she had arrived. Danny didn't care for the plan, and neither of them had time for it, but she was aware that Roseanne had experience as a daycare worker. She had been intending to talk to her about this sometime.

But this was not the time, she realized. They were supposed to be having a day off, both of them together, arranged by Danny.

"I want to go see that medicine woman who's in town," Roseanne remarked. "But I'm scared to go by myself."

"She isn't very scary," said Rebecca. "I met her."

"I know," said Roseanne. "That's why Danny told me to go with you."

Rebecca was surprised and slightly amused to see how much Roseanne was under Danny's influence.

"Let's go see her then," she said.

She began finishing up the dishes, rinsing the dishpan, then the sink.

"Could we take Mary Ann with us?" asked Roseanne.

Rebecca nodded, looking at her interrogatively.

"You don't know her very well, do you?" said Roseanne. "She's Robert's wife. She used to be a friend of my Aunt Alice. Alice was telling me about her. Mary Ann was the bravest girl in the school residence."

Rebecca had disliked Mary Ann ever since the failure of the reconciliation she and Danny had tried to arrange between her and Robert. Mary Ann had struck her as cold and narrow, almost cruel, in her denunciation.

"She went hunting like a man. She wasn't even scared of mice. But now she never goes anywhere."

"Maybe she'd like to go with us," agreed Rebecca. She wanted to be fair.

As Rebecca finished up her chores, Roseanne watched her with a secret sense of—not malice exactly—but she too had negative feelings. She knew that there was something between her and Danny—she could feel them both compensating for it.

The two women put on their jackets and went out of the trailer. They walked into town, to the elderly subdivision in the town centre where Robert's house stood, chockablock with the other government houses of its age. Rebecca stood on the packed earth out in front, waiting, while Roseanne went up on the porch.

Roseanne didn't bother to knock on the door. She opened it and put her head into the kitchen. Mary Ann was sitting at the kitchen table, sewing beads, as usual.

"Come out with us, Mary Ann."

"Who have you got with you?" asked Mary Ann suspiciously.

"Just Rebecca," said Roseanne. "You know—the social worker. Everybody likes her. Even Robert likes her," she added, her eyes sparkling. "He gave her some ducks last week."

"Did he?" Mary Ann put down her sewing and stood up in agitation.

"We're going to see that medicine woman." Roseanne watched Mary Ann pull her jacket roughly down off the hook, then fumble with the zipper.

"Why do you want to go see some old woman like that?"

"They say she knows what's going to happen. I'm kind of scared of her."

"What are you scared of?" Mary Ann spoke loudly and boldly as they came down off the porch. "She's just some old woman."

The three women walked on together in silence, a somewhat hostile silence between Mary Ann and Rebecca, a delighted, wait-and-see silence on the part of Roseanne.

The medicine woman was living in a teepee behind the band hall and she was sitting cross-legged in front of the door in the sun when they came up. She was a fat, dirty old woman with untidy hair that straggled down to her shoulders. She was too eccentric and frightening to be invited to stay with anybody. In fact, her tenure in Prohibition Creek was almost over, because it was getting too cold for her to live in the teepee. Soon she would fly south, carrying with her the harvest of dried caribou meat and dry fish, beaded slippers and belts, rings, watches and money that she had reaped up north over the summer.

"We came to see you, eh ts'on," said Rebecca, feeling that she should manage the introductions.

The medicine woman grunted, looking them over from under the heavy lids of her eyes.

"This is Roseanne. She's Danny's wife. This is Mary Ann."

"Robert's wife," interjected Roseanne.

"Whose wife are you?" the medicine woman demanded of Rebecca, as she lumbered to her feet.

"She isn't married," Roseanne said.

The medicine woman stood aside from the entrance to the teepee, indicating that they should go in.

Mary Ann whispered to Roseanne, "This teepee is a mess."

It was very dirty inside: old bones lay around on the floor, as well as a mass of junk, refrigerator trays, and old furnace parts that had been thrown down there from time to time and that the old lady had not bothered to take out when she moved in. There was no proper spruce mat on the floor, just a piece of an old rug laid down on the dirt beside the fire ring where the old woman now took her place.

"What do you want to know?" she demanded.

Mary Ann was feeling indignant not only over the state the teepee was in, but also at the woman's rudeness. She had not offered them tea.

Rebecca had already determined that she was not going to ask any questions, especially in front of Mary Ann. In any case, there was only one thing she wanted to know, whether she would ever get her kids back. It was all she thought about now.

Roseanne laughed nervously. "I want to know how many kids I'm going to have, I guess."

"Four more," said the old woman promptly. "That'll make seven."

"Four more!" Roseanne gasped

"Who else wants to know something?" said the medicine woman.

"How did you know I already have three?" said Roseanne, but the woman ignored her, gazing at Mary Ann.

"Do you know things that already happened too?" Mary Ann asked, skeptical. "How old was I when my mother died?"

"You want to know about your son, Mary Ann."

Startled and confused, Mary Ann said nothing.

Besides the unpleasant smell of rotting meat in the teepee, the air was thick with smoke. The slow fire burning in the centre was made of punk; the smoke opening above was choked with bicycle tires thrown up over the poles by the bad boys of the community.

The woman watched Mary Ann lazily through the thick atmosphere.

"You want to know everything about him. Whether he is smoking that dope in jail, how soon he will get out, what girl he's going to marry, how old he'll be when he dies."

Mary Ann caught her breath: "How old will he be when he dies?"

"An old, old man," said the medicine woman. She picked up an old tobacco can off the hearth and spat into it.

The other two felt how the woman had caught even the skeptical Mary Ann off guard. All three of them sat there on their heels, somewhat dazed by the smoke and the dimness, waiting for the medicine woman to say something more.

"That's all," she said abruptly.

"Masi," said Mary Ann.

"Masi," Roseanne followed suit obediently.

But the medicine woman had turned to Rebecca. "Do you want to know something too?"

Rebecca, in her heart, wanted desperately to know something. But she couldn't ask, not in front of the others, especially after she had lied about it to Roseanne.

She swallowed and closed her eyes. When she opened them again it seemed as though the cold, smelly dimness in the teepee had given way to dense whirling smoke with the sound of drums beating in the distance, and then of nothing but darkness and the wind roaring across a wide space.

"Come on, ask her something, Rebecca," urged Roseanne, but Rebecca, her hands clenched, her eyes wide open now, said nothing.

"This is very strange. Where am I? Why can't I see anything?" Rebecca spoke to herself, in that place where she was, and the others didn't hear her.

The rushing noise of a mountain river now came into the mournful noises of the wind. She knew from the sounds that she was in the mountains again. But how had she got there?

She heard men talking now.

"I'm going to use that fancy telescopic sight on the 30-30," said Robert. "Bring the sled over here, Elvis."

"It's too far. Those caribou are way down in the valley." It was Haga.

Why could she only hear, not see them? Rebecca turned her head to one side and the men came into sight. She was seeing them with one eye, not stereoscopically, and her eye, she suddenly realized, was the eye of a deer, not a human being, which was why she had not registered vision before. She was a caribou doe.

"Well, what do we do now?" Robert was asking. "Go down there?"

"Let's make tea," Haga suggested. "Maybe something'll show up."

Rebecca saw that they were on a high ridge up ahead of her, looking down the other way. She herself, and two others—these were her fawns, she knew without looking—were frozen in place, having just spotted the hunters.

"Thanks for the wood," Robert said to Elvis, who was getting an armload from his toboggan. "Here, I'll put the billy on."

The fire began to crackle. The men were still turned the other way, looking down into the valley. It must be the small herd she grazed with that they were looking at and Rebecca wondered how she and her children had got so far from them. What were they doing here alone on this hillside?

"Up here all we'll see is stragglers anyway," remarked Haga.

"That's true. We'll have to go down, I guess. It's a long way, that's all."

Rebecca whispered to her little ones, "We can't move. They'll shoot us."

Haga whistled. "A long way down. Then a long way up again."

The little ones were curious. They were too young to know about hunters yet. They moved forward cautiously, watching the men.

Haga had turned around with the kettle. "Gee, Robert! There's a doe standing right behind you. Elvis, got your gun there?"

"That's a good-looking doe."

"Elvis!" cried Haga. "What're you doing with that gun? Stirring your tea?"

"She's running away now. Hey, she's got two little ones."

"All right, give me the gun," Haga yelled.

"Don't shoot her!" Robert was shouting. "She's got little ones, Haga."

There was a sound of gunshots behind, but Rebecca was away, pounding down the slope, her heart on fire with fear.

Then suddenly she was back in that dense darkness with only the mournful sounds of the wind and the rushing of the river. She had gotten away somehow. But what about her babies?

She emerged out of the swirling smoke into the dim, dense air of the teepee, and she was kneeling on the ground beside Roseanne, who said, "Come on, Rebecca. Aren't you going to ask her something?"

The old woman across the fire was regarding her with interest. She knew that something had happened to Rebecca, and perhaps she even had a good idea what it was. Things like this did happen quite frequently in her presence, and she was a shrewd judge both of character and of what might be on someone's mind.

"Ask her a question," urged Roseanne. "Why don't you ask her if you'll ever get married and have kids."

The medicine woman smiled, a crafty, pleased smile.

"I have answered your question," she said. "Haven't I?"

Her deep-set eyes met Rebecca's, and Rebecca stared at her, horrified. If that was the answer to her question, then what did it mean?

"No, you didn't!" said Roseanne. She was emboldened by the fact that she was about to give the old lady a gift in payment. But in her opinion, Rebecca had not got her money's worth.

"Tell her," said the woman to Rebecca, jerking her head at Roseanne.

"Did she answer, Rebecca? I didn't hear her say anything."

"Yes, she did."

"What did she say?"

"Oh, I don't know." Rebecca tore her eyes away from the ironic gaze of the medicine woman. "She said yes, I think. Let's go."

Roseanne took a can of chewing tobacco out of her shoulder bag and put it on the ground.

"This is for you, eh ts'on," she said, and the old woman answered, this time quite politely, "Masi."

They got up to go. Mary Ann whispered loudly to Roseanne as they went out the door, "That's a lot—for what she told us."

Rebecca was already outside, breathing the clean crisp air, trying to shake off the miasma of the teepee and clear her mind. She walked home unseeing, forgetful of the others. Mary Ann and Roseanne watched her go and then, shrugging at each other, went to have tea together in Mary Ann's kitchen.

Rebecca, meanwhile, lost in her own thoughts at home, was finding it strange that she could have understood the men talking while she had the vision and hearing of a caribou. She heard Haga struggling with Elvis to seize the gun, and then Robert shouting, "Don't shoot her! She's got little ones!"

It was so vivid; it seemed as though it must have happened.

◂ 8. REHABS ▸

Robert was driving the Housing Association's flat-deck truck through town. He was surprised to see Herod McCrae on the road, walking, and stopped to pick him up.

Herod never walked anywhere. He had always had a truck, ever since Robert was a small child and Herod a young man; before the skidoo had become universal, before ATVs, before anyone else had had one, Herod had been driving a pickup.

Robert leaned over to open the offside door and Herod climbed in, puffing.

"Thanks, Robert. I thought you were still out hunting with the boys."

Robert had come in from the mountains earlier than he intended and then he had taken a job with the local housing authority. The Northwest Territories Housing Corporation had lately allocated money for the repair and upgrading of houses of a certain vintage; to insulate their plywood walls and roofs, put in double windows, exchange their ancient oil furnaces for new ones, install plumbing to replace the tank and spigot system, and generally upgrade things to a standard that Prohibition Creek people customarily saw on their TVs.

"Taking a walk for your health or something, Herod?" Robert remarked.

"Nope. Some crazy dingbat stole my truck last night and drove it over the riverbank."

This was a typical description of crime in Prohibition Creek.

"Whoever it was didn't get a scratch on him," Herod continued. "Turned my truck into a little pile of sardine cans, but the guy himself didn't even get hurt. There wasn't any blood lying around when the cops found it."

The police would probably not be able to charge anyone, although it might become a matter of common local knowledge who did it. In this case, charging him would depend more or less upon whether the criminal himself remembered doing it.

"We've been doing pretty good in this place all fall. Just about everyone's on that temperance kick of your brother's. Nothing's going on. So why my truck, that's what I'm asking." Herod spoke in disgust.

"Where can I take you?" Robert asked.

Herod glanced at him, a worried frown suddenly appearing on his face. "I'm going over to evict your wife."

"Evict her?" Robert said in surprise.

"Housing asked me to handle it for them. Being that I'm the JP."

"Didn't she pay the rent or something?"

"Nope, it isn't that. She won't move out."

Robert didn't see why she had to move out.

"You're working for Housing, aren't you? So you ought to know," said Herod impatiently. "It's this rehab project."

Robert understood suddenly. Mary Ann would have to move out while they were fixing the house.

"Why do we always have to start building houses after there's snow on the ground?" he commented.

"It's Housing in Yellowknife," Herod replied. "Can't do nothing."

Robert drew up in his own dooryard.

"Here you are," he said. "Wait. I think I'll come with you."

After hardly a moment's thought Robert had arrived at the

conclusion that Mary Ann wasn't going to like being evicted. It was not his business, except that it was his house—and she was his wife.

"Sure. Good idea," said Herod. "Maybe you can talk to her better than anyone else."

"Are you kidding?"

They were standing on the packed earth, now lightly dusted with snow, in front of the high gravel pad upon which the house was perched. Mary Ann suddenly came out the door onto the porch and fired a shotgun into the air.

Panicked, Herod ran away several steps. Then, bravely, he turned around again.

"Stop it, Mary Ann!" shouted Robert.

"Is she going to point that thing at you?" At first Herod had feared it was himself; now he was convinced it was Robert.

"Come on, Mary Ann. You don't have to do that!" Robert was also alarmed but he knew he would already be dead if Mary Ann had been aiming the gun.

"I'm getting out of here!" yelled Herod, and Mary Ann fired a parting blast over his head as he turned and fled.

She lowered the gun and glared at Robert, her hair disarranged, panting slightly.

"Just put down the gun, okay?" Robert started up the porch steps slowly.

"You're working for Housing." Mary Ann was aggressive.

"Driving the truck," said Robert.

She retreated through the open door behind her into the kitchen and Robert followed.

"They made me move into this house eighteen years ago. They can't make me move out." She had begun to cry, and this was not typical of Mary Ann at all.

"Just put your gun down here on the table," he said.

"You remember," she went on. "I wanted to stay in that place of my parents. But they said, no, you can't. It's just a shack. Everybody's going to get sick with TB. Go into a new house. So I said yes."

Robert found himself looking at his wife of eighteen years as if she were a stranger. He had not considered her appearance for many years; it surprised him slightly that she even had an appearance. She showed no trace of the good looks she had once had: her eyes were swollen, her hair coming down out of the smooth braid she customarily kept wrapped around her head, and she was dressed like an old man, in ill-fitting work pants and a checked shirt.

And she was almost hysterical.

"Where's your tea?" he demanded, turning aside from this spectacle.

"I didn't want my son to get sick." Mary Ann was insistent.

"Okay, I'm going to make the tea," said Robert.

He went into the furnace room for water from the tank, carrying the kettle. When he came back, Mary Ann had put down the gun, but she was still standing in the middle of the floor.

"So now they come to me and say, you can't go on living in that house the way it is. It's just a shack."

"Well, it doesn't have running water or anything." Robert put the kettle on the stove and got out the teapot and a couple of cups.

"I never had running water. I'm not missing anything."

"Maybe they'll put in new windows too. And you've been complaining about that broken porch for years."

"They can fix the porch. I don't have to move out."

"Look, it's just for a little while. Then when you move back in it'll be a lot better. Warmer and everything." He had the feeling he was not getting anywhere. Mary Ann was incredibly stubborn.

"Where am I going to go?" she said.

"You could stay with somebody," Robert suggested.

"Maybe they'll move me back into a different house," she said.

It was true that they might do that. The house had three small bedrooms, and she was now single, with no visible dependents.

"My son has a bedroom," she said. "His things are all in his room. He wouldn't like me to move them."

"Is that it?" asked Robert.

"My son's going to come home. He's in jail. But at least he's still got a home."

"That's it, isn't it?" said Robert.

The kettle was boiling. He made the tea and poured Mary Ann a cup. He put in sugar and cream, then stirred it for her.

"Masi." She sat down at last.

They both drank reflectively. Robert and Mary Ann belonged to the last tea-drinking generation of the Dene. The younger people did not crave tea; if they wanted comfort they turned to chocolate bars or pop. To the elders, giving tea to someone was kindness itself.

"I went to see that medicine woman," she said.

Robert thought she was changing the subject, but he was interested.

"What happened?" he asked. "Did she tell you something?"

"I went with Roseanne," continued Mary Ann. "And that girl you gave the ducks to."

Robert didn't know what she was talking about for a moment. "Girl I gave the ducks to?" he repeated.

"Don't you remember your girlfriend's name?" said Mary Ann.

"For God's sake, Mary Ann," Robert was disgusted. "Rebecca isn't my girlfriend!"

Mary Ann spoke serenely, ignoring him. "The medicine woman said Bobby is going to live to be an old man."

Robert laughed. "What did you give her for telling you that?" he asked.

There was the sound of a truck stopping outside, but neither Robert nor Mary Ann was paying attention.

"Roseanne gave her a can of chewing tobacco."

"That was a lot," said Robert.

"I thought so too."

Someone outside was barking through a megaphone. Slowly it began to dawn on Robert that he and Mary Ann were the ones being barked at.

ALL RIGHT. WE'VE GOT THE PLACE COVERED.

"Oh, for God's sake!" he said.

COME OUT WITH YOUR HANDS UP.

"Come on, Mary Ann." He stood up. "Let's go out. Bring your teacup." They went out through the kitchen door.

It was the constable, Dave. He was standing beside the police truck, raising the megaphone, but he put it down when he caught sight of both of them.

"Where's the gun?"

"She was just shooting it in the air," said Robert.

"Domestic dispute, eh?" Dave came running up the porch steps.

"No," said Robert shortly.

Herod had been in the front seat of the police truck. He climbed out and came to stand at the foot of the steps, giving Robert a sheepish look.

The cop followed Mary Ann into the kitchen. Robert went back in too, and Herod came as far as the doorway.

"Look, all that happened was she fired the gun in the air," said Robert. "She wasn't pointing it at anyone. You know Mary Ann can handle a gun. Tell him, Herod." He turned to Herod. "I'd have buckshot in my back teeth if she'd been aiming at me."

"What's it all about then?" demanded the cop.

"Listen. Housing made her move into this house eighteen years ago because it was so much better. Now they're trying to make her move out because it's poorly insulated, got no running water, no double windows and the porch is broken. But in the meantime, she started liking the place, don't ask me why. Oh yeah, and for some reason she doesn't want to live outside till March, or whenever they finish the rehab project."

"I don't see any of that as the police's problem," Dave said.

"Herod, you know what I'm talking about." Robert again appealed to Herod. "You know what it is with the rental housing; it's the government making us give up our things."

"Okay, talking about it is one thing," said Herod. "But there's no cause to fire off a gun."

"That's Robert," Mary Ann spoke bitterly. "All he ever did was talk."

"Once you're living in a government house, you've got to do what they tell you."

"And he's still talking." She didn't understand that he was trying to get her off the hook.

"It makes you lose your pride, living in a government house."

"I never lost my pride," said Mary Ann, bridling.

The cop had withdrawn a pad of official forms from his jacket pocket. He now began writing busily.

"Okay. Firing off a firearm inside the hamlet boundary is an offence. We're going to give you a ticket for that, Mary Ann."

Soundlessly Robert made his lips into a Phew! He didn't agree with this ticket, but on the whole he was relieved. Left to handle her own defence, Mary Ann might have ended up in jail.

"Busy day, eh?" he remarked, watching the cop filling in every line of the form.

"You said it!" Dave looked up. He had a sense of humour. "First there was Herod's truck. Now this. But that's what we're here for. Detecting crime and capturing criminals."

He finished writing the ticket.

"There. That'll probably be a fifty-dollar fine, Mary Ann. So make your statement some other way next time."

"You mean she's got to pay a fifty-dollar fine for shooting her gun in the air?" Robert was indignant. As far as he was concerned what you did with your gun was your own business. If Mary Ann had been some crazy teenager who didn't know how to hunt it would have been different. But she was a grown woman, and it was the shotgun she had inherited from her dad. She had been handling guns since she was a little girl.

"You don't like that, tell it to the JP," replied Dave. He put the ticket down in front of Mary Ann on the table, and walked briskly to the door.

Robert swung around, still in the mood to argue. "The JP? But the JP is Herod here."

The cop went on out and Robert was left staring at Herod, who gave him a feeble half smile.

It was another court case, he realized, a case for the Complaints Department.

The next day Robert picked up his brother, Michael, as he was driving the Housing truck through town.

"Take you somewhere?"

But Michael was going nowhere in particular. "Where are you going, Robert?" he asked. "Maybe I'll go there too."

Robert said, "I got this job driving the flat-deck for Housing. So I'm taking stuff all around town."

"Hey, Robert, why are you doing that? You spent pretty nearly all fall in the bush. Aren't you going to take some time off and—you know."

Play poker—that was what he meant. Michael was only twenty-eight, the youngest of them all. In the opinion of Danny, his mother and their sisters, Robert and Michael were the most alike. They were the two who were screwed-up, the oldest and the youngest.

Michael liked to play poker almost as much as Robert. However, he was not nearly as good at it because he got drunk while he was playing, and he didn't concentrate enough when he was sober. He was still in a woman-chasing phase, even though he was married and had two kids.

"I heard that Mary Ann was shooting at you the other day," he remarked.

"Come on," said Robert. "She wasn't shooting at me. I'd be dead. You know how Mary Ann can handle a gun. She just fired in the air."

He began to explain what it had been about. Michael listened, nodding. Resentment against Housing was universal. "So the cops gave her a fifty-dollar fine under the bylaw, for shooting off a gun in town."

"Well, can't do nothing, I guess," said Michael.

"What do you mean, can't do nothing?" demanded Robert. "I could sure do something."

Accustomed to his brother's crazy ideas about things, Michael merely raised his eyebrows and looked out the window.

Robert had already had an argument about this with Mary Ann, which she had won by announcing that she was going to pay the ticket, whatever he tried to do in court.

But he couldn't help thinking about what he could do, and the thinking had grown into a full-fledged daydream. The scene, of course, took place in JP court in the school gym. In his mind he had added some TV music as part of the background, from a documentary program called *Family Court*.

He began running over this daydream once more; it was so good, he couldn't help it.

HEROD: *(Brings his gavel down)* All right we've got this case of Mary Ann firing a gun inside the hamlet boundary. It's a fifty-dollar fine for that.

ROBERT: *She's not going to pay.*

HEROD: *We didn't get to that part yet, Robert. Mary Ann, how do you plead?*

MARY ANN: *(Aggressively) I'm not pleading with anybody.*

HEROD: *I mean are you guilty or not guilty?*

ROBERT: *She pleads not guilty.*

HEROD: *How's she going to plead not guilty? She fired a shotgun off her front porch. I saw her.*

ROBERT: *Okay, call some witnesses to what happened.*

HEROD: *I just said what happened. I was there. You were there too.*

ROBERT: *You're the JP You can't be a witness in this case.*

HEROD: *(Sighs) All right, I'm calling Robert Woodcutter as a witness. Is he in the courtroom?*

ROBERT: *Yeah, I'm here, Herod. But I'm her husband. You can't make me testify against her.*

HEROD: *(Exasperated) Okay, we'll skip that part then. Mary Ann, I'm finding you guilty and the fine is fifty dollars. Wait a second, I'm going to read to you. (He puts on his glasses and clears his throat.) "Failure to pay a fine assessed by a Justice of the Peace under the bylaws of an incorporated municipality may result in prosecution by a higher court." That's from the Municipalities Act.*

ROBERT: *Wait a second.*

HEROD: *That's all there is to it.*

ROBERT: *No it isn't. You can't be the JP and the mayor, Herod.*

HEROD: *I've always been the JP and the mayor. You know that.*

ROBERT: *Listen to this: "No acting member of the judiciary may serve as councillor or mayor of an incorporated municipality."*

HEROD: *Where's it say that?*

ROBERT: *In the Municipalities Act. (Pause) I declare a mistrial.*

"So what can you do?" asked Michael idly. "You're not going to go to court over it?"

"Nope," said Robert. "Mary Ann won't go along with that. She's making a pair of slippers now so she can pay the fine."

Michael shrugged.

"She won't even let me talk about it," Robert continued. "It just makes her mad."

"Well, I guess I'll get out here," Michael said in a bored voice.

They were coming up on a house where there was always a card game going on, night and day.

"I thought you stopped living the life of a gambling man," said Robert, watching his brother watch that house.

"You used to like it yourself, remember? Want to come in for a while?"

Robert shook his head. He had finally given this some thought. Abandoning poker had at first been a kind of involuntary thing, in revulsion at himself, at his whole way of life. He had received a severe shock when Mary Ann threw him out, after Bobby went to jail. But it was no longer an involuntary thing. He wanted to play poker so badly sometimes that his hands would sweat and he would get headaches.

Robert knew that if he went into that house and sat down, even for one hand of whatever game they were playing, he would be hooked again. In no time flat he would be living the same wild life again. Poker tugged at him; he wanted the cunning, the trickery, the calculation of it, the emotional up and down, the visceral thrill of winning big.

He drew the truck to a stop. Michael opened the door and began to get out.

"Come on in. Just for a couple of hands. You don't have to play or anything."

Robert couldn't help noticing, now that he was looking directly at his brother, that he looked hungover.

"So you're Mr. Clean, eh?" Michael snarled. "Boy, Danny sure didn't like it when you went hunting with Elvis," he continued. "He won't even eat any of that meat."

"That's his problem," Robert replied.

But he thought he might as well tell Michael what he thought about this.

"If you want to learn how to hunt you've got to hang around with the old-timers," he said. "And if Elvis likes Ama, that's none of my business. I started going hunting with him a while ago. And now I'm going to go on going hunting with him."

Michael shrugged, getting out of the truck. He didn't care about this one way or another. Both his brothers were delivering sermons these days. He much preferred the old Robert, arrogant loudmouth that he had been.

◂ ◂ ◂

Robert pulled up in front of Mary Ann's house. He got out of the truck, slammed the door, and ran lightly up the porch steps.

Mary Ann was in the kitchen, the pieces of a pair of slippers traced out on a scrap of moosehide on the table in front of her. She looked up as he came in the door but said nothing. They were not in the habit of saying hello to one another.

"I had another idea last night."

A look of irritation crossed her face. She thought he was going to tell her about what he would say in court again. But Robert was related to Herod, and he didn't really want to hurt his feelings. In fact, he now had quite a different idea.

"This idea I had is great. I think it'll work," he continued.

Mary Ann went on bending over the cutting she was doing. She was looking better but Robert had again ceased to notice how she looked at all.

"My sister gave me this piece of moosehide," said Mary Ann. "I'm going to sell a pair of slippers to pay my fine."

"Well, good," he agreed. "But this idea I had is about something different."

She raised her shoulder at him in a gesture of indifference, taking the shears around a tricky curve.

"What you really want is to stop them from messing around in Bobby's room, right? Plus, you need a place to stay until next year, or whenever they finish fixing up the house."

"I'm not going anywhere." Mary Ann spoke flatly.

"Well, that's my idea," said Robert. "We could put up a tent in Bobby's bedroom."

"A tent is for outside," she said.

"See, you could put all Bobby's stuff in it. Just the way it is in his room." Robert had been expecting to have to persuade her. He had already guessed that she wouldn't take to it at once.

"His blanket, his volleyball, the rosary over the door—"

"But where am I going to stay?" she asked. She did seem to be getting the idea.

"Well, I was thinking you could stay in another tent out here in the kitchen," said Robert. "Then, after awhile, if that got in the way of the carpenters, you could move into Bobby's tent."

"Where would I sleep?"

"Come on. I don't think he'd mind if you used his bed for a little while."

Mary Ann was thinking it over slowly. There was no prejudice in her mind against tents as a form of shelter; she had lived in tents off and on all through her childhood. The chief consideration in her mind was whether Bobby would like her to do this.

"Of course you'd have to have water and heat," Robert was going on. "But you don't need much in a tent. Just a little stove. You could keep water in a fuel drum. Have them deliver it too. They could put the hose in through Bobby's window."

"People would think I was crazy." She was wondering whether Bobby would think she was crazy.

Robert shrugged. He cared even less now than he ever had about what other people thought.

"Where's your tea?" he asked.

Mary Ann had tea on the stove. She got it for him and poured out a cup for herself too.

"Masi."

This more usual way of doing things—her bringing the tea to him and not the other way around—gave them both the sense that the emergency of yesterday was over. She was going to do what he suggested.

"I borrowed a wall tent from the Band," said Robert. "Where's that little tent of Bobby's?"

"It's in his closet."

"You could put the big one up in the kitchen for a start."

"Which way?" she asked.

"I think you should put the front flap over here by the kitchen door."

"It would be facing the wrong way."

They hadn't been out in the bush together for some years and Robert had forgotten what a pain in the neck she could be.

"You've got to be able to get in and out somehow." He was trying to be patient.

"But it won't get any sun in the morning."

"Okay, okay." She was right about that. "Turn it around. You could come in by the living-room door."

They both sat contemplating the imaginary camp over their teacups.

Someone came up the steps. There was a moment's hesitation, then Herod opened the door.

"You here, Robert?" He stuck his head inside timidly.

"Yeah. I'm having some of Mary Ann's tea. Want some too?"

Mary Ann got up immediately and went to the teapot on the stove.

"Masi," said Herod.

He came in fully and after a momentary pause, during which he cast a glance of surprise over the domesticity of the scene, he sat down at the table.

"I heard you're up to some crazy scheme," he said to Robert. "So I walked over."

"Yeah. Mary Ann's going to camp here this winter," said Robert. "But—" he looked at Herod, a new thought forming, "—she's going to need a stove."

Herod nodded thoughtfully. He had been feeling terrible about the events of the previous day.

"Well, I've got a stove she could have," he said. "But I'm just wondering how to set up the stovepipe. Maybe you could put it out through the window."

"Which window?" Mary Ann pounced on this proposal in her usual contradictory spirit.

"I've got the tent," said Robert. "Let's bring it in. Then we can see how it's all going to fit."

He went outside and got the tent off the back of the flat-deck. It was a good-sized white wall tent the Band used sometimes during hunts. Robert had borrowed it from Danny that morning.

Herod helped him lay it out on the kitchen floor.

"There," said Herod, standing back. "I think this'd be the window for the stovepipe."

"The tent has to be the other way around," announced Mary Ann.

"How come? Then you'd have to come in through the living room."

Robert had already lost this argument.

"Forget it, Herod," he suggested. "We'll just turn it around, okay?"

They got it turned around, then all working together, began to set it up.

About half an hour later they finished up by putting the kitchen table inside. Mary Ann could still cook on the stove and use the cupboards and refrigerator if she went outside the tent. Later on, of course, these things would be removed, and she would have to rely on her wood stove for cooking as well as heat.

Herod sat down, puffing, on a kitchen chair. The interior of the tent was clean and white; it was quite airy in there.

"By the way," said Robert, addressing Herod in the spirit of irony: "Isn't this against some rule in your zoning bylaw?"

"I don't see any problem," Herod replied. "This is a residential use."

"I guess there's no problem till you have to put up an outhouse, is that it?"

"Oh yeah." Herod frowned. "You can probably use the neighbours', can't you, Mary Ann?"

"We better try out that stovepipe now," he said a moment later.

"Well then, I'll go get it. I've got Housing's truck," said Robert.

He hesitated. There was something he wanted to ask Mary Ann to do for him this afternoon. Now that there was a certain burden of obligation on her side he felt better about asking, although he still wasn't sure she was going to say yes.

"Hey, Mary Ann, would you do my laundry?"

She nodded blandly.

Robert was relieved. He wanted to have some clean clothes quite badly. He could have done laundry at his mother's house, but Robert had never washed his own clothes; he didn't know how to use a washing machine.

Herod was looking at them with attention. He had by now woken up to the fact that Robert was helping Mary Ann; they were even trying to get along. As a happily married man with many children and grandchildren to show for it, Herod thought it was high time these two resolved their differences—whatever they were; it was none of his business.

"Hey, are you two going to make it up?" he said.

"Make what up?" Robert was instantly defensive.

"Whatever it was you were fighting about." Herod shrugged.

"I wasn't fighting with anybody," said Robert. "And I'm sure not going to live in this tent here," he added, grinning.

"His girlfriend won't do his laundry," said Mary Ann.

Robert was so irritated by her saying this that he jumped up to leave right away.

"Mary Ann, for the last time, I don't have a girlfriend!"

"For the last time," Mary Ann repeated evenly, for the benefit of the astonished and embarrassed Herod, as Robert departed, slamming the door and leaping down the porch steps.

But he was going to get his dirty clothes.

◆ 9. THE TWO BROTHERS ◆

Robert came home from work that afternoon with a bag of clean clothes. He washed himself, using a kettle of warm water and a towel, and then trimmed his hair. Finally he shaved carefully, using a new razor he had purchased at the store.

They had just finished eating supper—boiled caribou meat—and Haga lounged on his bunk, picking his teeth.

"Are you going somewhere tonight?" Haga had been paying no attention at first, but now he was watching his friend curiously.

"I'm just going into town."

Haga continued to watch as Robert put on a clean shirt.

"Who washed your clothes?"

"Mary Ann."

Haga now got the idea that Robert was intending to exercise his conjugal rights.

"She still hates me as much as ever, though," Robert remarked.

Haga was relieved to hear it.

"Maybe I'll come with you then," he said.

Robert had been looking at himself in the tiny square of mirror glass they had stuck up on the wall. He was noticing that he could still look quite good if he took the trouble. He turned around quickly.

"No, don't."

"Sounds like a poker game." Haga yawned. It was odd that Robert was being so evasive about a poker game. Haga did not fully grasp in what relationship Robert found himself with poker, although he knew that he had not been playing cards lately.

"Nope."

"So where are you going then?" He was driven finally to ask outright.

"One thing about living out here with you, Haga," said Robert. "A man's got freedom. No one to nag him and ask him questions all the time."

Haga lay back down discontentedly.

"Want to hear something I heard?" he asked after a moment, watching Robert dip his comb in a glass of water.

"That's another thing: nobody tries to tell you any gossip," Robert added.

"So you don't want to hear, eh?"

Robert said nothing; he wasn't going to ask, that was for sure.

"I don't want to gossip about your family."

"What is it?" demanded Robert, turning away from the mirror again.

"Sure you want to know?" Haga asked, teasing him.

Robert came and stood over him. "All right. I want to know. Tell me."

"Michael fell off the wagon last week."

"I was wondering about that. How long it was going to take." Robert remembered his conversation with Michael the previous afternoon.

"There's another thing too."

"He's playing cards again, I guess," said Robert.

"No. This other thing is bad. They're saying he went on a joyride. In Herod's truck."

"In Herod's truck? But Herod's truck got all smashed up. Somebody drove it over the riverbank."

"Yeah. Your brother Michael."

Robert considered. It was a shock to hear that Michael had wrecked Herod's truck, and he felt bad about that. But his first obligation was to his brother, to see that he didn't get caught.

"Who told you?" he demanded

"A little bird that went Tchi! Tchi!" Haga replied.

Robert was alarmed. "You think a lot of people know about this?" he asked. That could still be okay—or not, depending upon who they were.

"A lot of bad people. Not a lot of good people," said Haga, answering his thought.

"Well, let's just keep it to ourselves then."

Haga nodded. "Us bad people, you mean."

"Yeah," agreed Robert. He laughed. "Us bad people."

◂ ◂ ◂

A short while later, Robert found himself standing in the snow outside Rebecca's trailer. Now that he was actually here he was feeling a lot less sure of himself. For one thing he was realizing that she might notice how he had cleaned himself up to visit her; she might think he was making a fool of himself. But he couldn't have paid her a visit in his dirty old clothes, the ones he had been hunting with; that would have showed a lack of respect both to the real Rebecca and to his dream about her.

It would have been easier if they had just met in the street.

On the other hand he wanted to talk to her about his dream. He really had to tell her about it. And he could not have done that on the street.

He knocked on her door.

Rebecca was inside in her spotless apartment, getting dressed up for a party. She was wearing big city evening clothes for a change: a tank top with spaghetti straps and sequins, palazzo pants. She had put up her hair in a French twist and was admiring herself in the bathroom mirror, feeling excited, and wondering whether it was foolish to like the way she looked.

"Coming," she called, hearing the knock.

She ran to the door and opened it.

For a moment Robert and Rebecca just stood there staring. They were each almost wondering who the other was. Robert was surprised and confused by Rebecca's clothes, her bare shoulders; she was even wearing makeup. And Rebecca truly didn't recognize Robert for a second. He could be, as he had seen for himself in the mirror, very good-looking when he chose.

Robert broke the silence rather awkwardly. "You're all dressed up."

"You're all dressed up yourself, Robert," she said.

"Are you going someplace? Maybe I'd better not come in." It had occurred to him that perhaps she had another male visitor.

"No! Come in." She stood aside, throwing the door wide open. "Please come in. I'd like you to."

"Oh well, okay then," he said.

But he was still uneasy. He entered and stood just inside the door.

Then he noticed the picture she had up on the wall. Obviously it was modern art; Robert couldn't help commenting.

"What kind of a crazy picture is that?"

Rebecca was delighted. "Oh, do you like it?" she said. "I really like it myself."

"It looks like sand," said Robert. He tilted his head. "Whichever way up, it still looks like sand. A picture of sand."

She laughed. "That must be what I like about it. It's so—sandy," she said.

They were still feeling extremely awkward with one another. Rebecca went to put on a CD. She thought that would make Robert feel more relaxed. She started to play the track she had played for Danny the previous week.

Instantly she felt that it was not the right piece of music for Robert at all. She quickly took it out, and put in something else but that was unsuitable too, and she stopped it on a slur.

"Please. Sit down. Let me get you some—pop or something."

She got a can of pop out of the refrigerator and pulled the tab for him, conscious all the time that he was watching her, and that this was a very unfamiliar Robert. He must have got dressed up to visit her and this meant he cared whether she found him attractive.

Somehow his clean clothes were putting a barrier between them that had not been there before. She wanted to be back on the same terms they had always been on.

"Robert, this isn't like you," she said. "You're not saying anything." She sat down on the sofa bed, then got up again quickly, realizing that he would probably not want to sit there beside her.

But if Robert's clean clothes were presenting a problem for Rebecca, this was nothing to the barrier her whole appearance presented to him. He found himself hating her beauty, wishing she didn't have it. He could hardly talk to her because of the way it distracted him; and she was dressed like a whitewoman.

"I wanted to tell you about something that happened when I was in the bush," he said. He looked away from her, standing there in front of what was obviously her bed.

"What was it?" Rebecca said quickly, thinking of her vision in the medicine woman's teepee.

"It's just that it's kind of hard to get into when you don't look like the same person. On the Gravel River you looked like a Dene girl, not a whitewoman."

"But I am a Dene girl, Robert," she said gravely. She sat down again on the bed, as he continued to regard her from beside the door.

"The way you were then—with your hair loose over your shoulders—I saw you again later that night."

Rebecca was still thinking of her own experience. "Was it a vision?" she asked.

"No. It was a dream, I think—Remember that talk we had?" he said.

"Yes. I remember." She remembered that it had helped her just to have that talk.

"We had it again. Only better."

"What do you mean, better?" she asked.

"Well, when you asked me if there were things a person could never make up for—I said there were a lot of things I did like that."

He was looking at her intently, afraid she might not understand now. He had to expose himself in order to tell her. But she did understand.

She nodded. "The dream made you honest."

"Then remember how you asked me if—"

"If you thought I was a bad person." She remembered this very well.

"What I said in the dream was, I know you're a good person."

There was no way to say this other than to say it, he realized. It was what he had come to tell her.

"I wanted to tell you ever since. I just didn't get a chance before this because—" He made a gesture with his hand and arm meaning that he had been working, that he had to live out in the shack with Haga, that he had not had any clean clothes up till now.

Rebecca really couldn't speak.

Robert saw that she would cry if he went on.

But that was all. He had told her everything.

He thought of something else he could say, knowing it would make her laugh.

"Oh yeah. Haga really did think you were a ghost that time."

Rebecca laughed.

"I helped him out a little," said Robert. They had got past the difficult part and suddenly he was feeling quite easy again with Rebecca.

Her eyes were bright and she was smiling at him as she listened.

"There's a story about a Dene girl who was kidnapped out there. He thought he'd seen her by the time I finished telling him about it."

"Were you trying to scare him, Robert?" She was only pretending to disapprove.

"Yeah, but it's okay," he said. "He likes to be scared."

They both laughed.

There was a knock at the door. Then it flew open and in came Danny, Roseanne, Jamaica and the two little boys. They wore party clothes too: Danny was in a light blue cashmere sweater, Roseanne and Jamaica were wearing dresses under their parkas.

"We came to pick you up, Rebecca," said Danny.

"We all came." Roseanne was breathless, her cheeks pink in the cold air. "Danny said we should all come."

"We've been cooking all day," said Danny. "Me, Roseanne—"

"All of us," said Roseanne.

Jamaica had noticed Robert beside the door.

"Daddy! Robert is here!"

"Oh." Danny swung around. "What are you doing here?" he demanded, surprised at first, then becoming jealous instantly when he saw Robert's clean white shirt, his well-combed hair.

"Look, Daddy! He's all dressed up to visit Rebecca."

"Yeah, he is." Danny spoke grimly.

"Robert can come with us too, can't he?" cried Jamaica.

Roseanne looked at Danny. Danny was almost glaring at Robert.

"What's this?" Robert was confused. Why were all these people here?

"It's a party," explained Rebecca. "Danny and Roseanne are having a Christmas party."

"Only we decided to have it three weeks early," said Roseanne. "Danny and Rebecca are going to Yellowknife next week for a workshop. And then we'll be too busy at Christmas to have a good family time."

"Robert can come too, can't he, Daddy?" Jamaica was tugging at Danny's hand.

Danny said to Robert, speaking rather dryly, "So you're back from the bush?"

"Yeah. For more than a week."

"What made you come in so early?" People usually came in just before Christmas.

"We had to come back because of Haga," said Robert. "That guy sure is accident-prone."

They were all listening to him, but Robert looked at Rebecca. He had been intending to tell her about this next anyway.

"We were up on a ridge above the Gravel River having tea when Haga saw a caribou. She was actually standing right behind me—only a couple of yards away. Haga grabbed Elvis's 30-30 and fired it off without stopping to get a good grip. The kickback just about dislocated his shoulder."

Rather to Robert's surprise, Rebecca had turned pale.

"Did he—did he kill anything?" She almost whispered the question.

"Nope. I was kind of glad too. It was a doe with two little ones." He couldn't quite understand why this was having such an effect on her. She looked as if she might begin to cry all over again.

"I don't like killing 'em when they've got calves," he said. "Some guys don't care. Haga just lost his head when he saw that doe standing there. She was only a couple of yards off."

Rebecca had caught her breath, but then she recovered herself completely. "I'm so glad he didn't shoot the little ones," she said.

"Let's go," said Danny impatiently.

"Well, I guess I won't hold you up any longer," said Robert.

"You're not holding us up," said Roseanne suddenly. She had been watching the way Robert looked only at Rebecca when he talked, the way Rebecca had responded to him as though they were alone in the room, and she had made a decision.

"Come with us," she said. "We all want you to come. Rebecca wants you to come too," she added slyly. "Don't you, Rebecca?"

◂ ◂ ◂

An hour later they were all sitting around on the floor in Danny and Roseanne's living room, where they had just finished eating a traditional Christmas dinner: turkey, dressing, mashed potatoes, cranberry sauce, olives, jellied salad, macaroni salad and pies, two of them, pumpkin and apple.

Danny lay down on his back, patting his stomach. "Boy, that was a good meal," he said.

"Who made the pies?" asked Rebecca.

"Danny. Pie-making is not my thing." Roseanne got to her feet and began carrying things into the kitchen. Rebecca got up to help her.

"Turkey and salad. Pie. That isn't real Dene food," remarked Robert.

Danny sat up. "Come on, Robert. We've been having turkey at feasts as long as I can remember."

"Yeah, but it's kind of like the way you take a piece of rhubarb to chew on in the springtime—to make your mouth taste something different. Dene food is meat, you know that."

"Well, I like meat myself." Danny was frowning.

"I hear you aren't eating any of that caribou Elvis and I came back with," said Robert.

"You gave it to Ama," said Danny shortly.

"It was to share. You know that."

"I'm not dependent on Ama for food."

"You're not dependent on Elvis, you mean."

"No, and not on you either." Danny was about to lose his temper.

Roseanne came back from the kitchen. "Let's talk about something else," she said.

"I want Robert to tell one of his weird stories," said Jamaica.

"Rebecca likes your stories too, don't you, Rebecca?" Roseanne said.

Robert looked at Rebecca and she nodded, sitting down on the floor again.

He paused for a moment, not only for dramatic effect, but because he was not quite sure what story he should tell.

"There were two brothers—" he began.

"They were you and Daddy, weren't they, Robert?" said Jamaica, interrupting.

Robert laughed. He had thought of a story to tell all of a sudden.

"These brothers were twins," he said. "And they were always

fighting with each other. They were even fighting inside the woman's belly—before they were born. What they were fighting over was who was going to be the older brother. When they came out, the first one was all covered with red fur, like an animal."

"Robert, that's horrible!" cried Roseanne.

"The second one came out holding onto the older one's heel. He was still trying to get ahead of the other one, and be older."

"Well, I'm the youngest," remarked Jamaica. "I don't like it much."

"Yeah, but I'm the oldest. That's no picnic either."

"Well, get on with it, anyway." Danny was impatient with this.

"The father loved the oldest one the best, in spite of the way he looked, with that fur all over him. He taught the older brother to hunt and when he got to be a pretty good hunter, the father didn't have to go out anymore."

"What about the younger brother. Didn't he teach him anything?" asked Danny, interested in spite of himself.

"No. The younger brother just hung around the camp with his mother." Robert looked at him blandly.

He knew he had picked a good story, seeing the expression on Danny's face.

"Well, one time there weren't many caribou in the country. The older brother had to go a long way looking for meat, and even then he didn't find any. When he came back from the trip he was just about starving."

"Maybe he wasn't such a great hunter after all."

"Maybe not," agreed Robert. "Anyway, he saw his brother with a bowl of soup. It was only made out of roots, because that was all they had. But the older brother was just about fainting from hunger, so he said to his brother, 'Can I have some of your soup?' And the brother said, 'Yes, if you'll let me be the older brother.' Well, the older brother was so sick and faint that he agreed, and that was a great mistake that he made."

"What does it mean?" demanded Jamaica. "How could he trade being older for the soup?"

Danny knew this story now. He said, "The older brother showed he didn't care about being the older son as much as he did for a bowl of soup."

"But he was starving," protested Jamaica. "That wasn't fair. I think it was a trick."

"Well, that was only the first trick the younger brother did," said Robert.

"Yes, that younger brother was a bad guy." Danny spoke with irony.

Robert grinned. "Well, maybe he wasn't so bad. His mother liked him."

"Okay, just get on with it." Danny lay down on his back again.

"Well, the father was getting old and sick, and he was already half blind. But he loved fresh meat, so one day he sent his older son out hunting, and he told him to make a stew with the meat he brought back. He just loved the way that son cooked a stew. And the father said that after he had eaten he would make a prophecy. He was a chief and the son of a chief himself, see, and he was going to pass his power to his son."

"What does that mean, pass his power?" asked Jamaica.

"It means his medicine power. This was a long time ago when the chiefs had that."

"But what is it, medicine power?"

"Hush, Jamaica, and listen to the story." Roseanne glanced at the rapt face of Rebecca.

"Well, the mother heard all that," continued Robert. "So she went and found some meat that was in the camp and made a stew with it, and she was a pretty good cook too. And then she dressed the younger son up in the skins that the older one usually wore at home, and she even tied the skins onto his hands and the back of his neck. Then she sent him to his father with the stew."

Jamaica guessed. "It was another trick?"

"It was another trick," agreed Robert. "Because the father was half blind, like I said. He was kind of surprised when he got the stew so soon. And the voice of the younger son wasn't quite right either. But when he felt his son's hand, which was all covered in fur, he said, 'Oh this is the hand of my older son.'"

"So then he made a prophecy and left him all his power," said Jamaica.

"That's right."

"And then when the older one came home—" Danny interrupted.

"I'll finish the story, Danny. When the older one came home and found out what had happened, all he could do was cry. Because there was nothing left for him. He'd be a hunter all his life and live on the ground and out in the rain. Oh yeah, and he might get the chance to help his brother out sometime when he was in trouble."

There was a short silence. Danny was lying on his back on the rug, one hand over his face. Robert's eyes rested on him for a moment.

"Go on," Danny said, still lying there. "That isn't the end, Robert."

"Okay," said Robert. "You're right, that isn't the end. The older brother got really mad and said he was going to kill the other one. A lot of stuff happened in here, because the younger brother was afraid and he ran away and lived in another country. They lived away from each other a long time. And the funny thing is, they both didn't do so badly, not even the older brother. The younger brother came off the best, of course. He had two wives and a lot of sons, and besides that he always had meat in camp and people wanted to stay with him."

"And he wrestled with God, don't forget," added Danny.

"Wrestled with God?" exclaimed Jamaica.

"Okay, but that's another story too. If you want to hear that—get him to tell it," Robert said to her. "Finally, after being away for years and years, the younger brother had a big argument with his wife's relatives," he went on. "They said he stole meat from them."

"Probably he did too, that tricky guy." Danny had begun to enjoy himself, in a strange way.

"Well, I think he did," said Robert. "But the thing was, he had to leave that country in a hurry, and he had nowhere else to go but home. But he was scared of his brother. So he sent him a lot of big presents, meat and that. He was trying to buy him off that way. And then he made everybody else walk on ahead of him and he came last. He said it was so his brother would see how well he had done and get all the presents first, but really—"

"He was afraid the older brother was going to kill him," interrupted Jamaica. "What happened, Robert? I want to know what happened." She tugged on his arm in her impatience.

Robert laughed.

"The older brother was so glad to see that man when he finally showed up that he ran toward him and he hugged him and kissed him in front of everybody."

Danny sat up, grinning at Robert.

"Well, that was what happened. Don't ask me why." Robert shrugged. Then he began to grin back.

Everybody else was laughing.

"Hey, doesn't anyone here recognize a story from the Bible?" demanded Danny. "What are you teaching the kids, Roseanne? What about you, Rebecca? Your father's a preacher."

"But wasn't it about the Dene?" Rebecca asked, bewildered.

"That was just the way he told it," Danny said.

"Robert tricked us," said Jamaica.

Danny was in a very good humour now.

"Yeah, and you should be in bed. I'm going to take you there one-two-three!" he said to Jamaica, catching her up suddenly.

Rebecca also began to get up, to help Roseanne carry out the last of the dishes. But Roseanne looked at her slyly and said, "Don't bother to help me, Rebecca. Why don't you stay here and talk to Robert?"

Danny had already gone off with Jamaica and the two little boys. Robert and Rebecca were left alone together again, as they had been before, on the margin of Danny's family.

"I didn't know that story." She smiled at him.

"It was the story of Jacob and Esau," said Robert. "They were the sons of Isaac and Rebecca. Remember, I told you about her?" He turned, sitting cross-legged, so that they were exactly facing each other across the sheet Roseanne had spread out on the floor as a tablecloth.

"Sometimes I feel I don't know anything about either side of me, the Dene or the whiteman," she said.

Robert nodded. "There's a lot of history there. On two sides like that."

But he was thinking about something else.

"You're going to Yellowknife?" he asked.

"Next week. I'm going to the same workshop as Danny," she said.

"So will you see—your kids?" he asked softly.

She nodded, and he saw a shy, eager expression cross her face.

Robert now realized that perhaps he was the only person she had told about her kids. She wanted to talk about it.

"Well, someday I'm going to tell them a story," he said.

"Do you think you'll ever get the chance?" asked Rebecca, with a more intense expression on her face, a yearning, hopeful look.

"Sure," he said. "Sometime you'll get them to come up here. Maybe next summer. They'll probably want to stay on with you too."

"Do you really think so?" It was all she had been thinking about for weeks, all she wanted to hear.

"Why not?" said Robert. "That whiteman can't keep them away from you forever. I already told you. They'll come looking for you in the end, whatever he does to stop them."

Rebecca was smiling at him, eyes bright.

"Robert, I never had a friend like you before."

She was lovely as she sat there, propped up on one arm, with her legs curled away under her, her eager pretty face turned up to Robert's. But he was no longer finding that her beauty got in the way at all.

"Well, I never had a friend like you either," he replied.

◆ 10. GOSSIP ◆

The following Monday morning Robert was fired from his job by the local Housing Association secretary because of the tents they had set up inside Mary Ann's house the previous Friday afternoon. There was now no way the housing authority could get her to move out for the rehab project, and the carpenters and plumbers and electricians were going to have to manoeuvre around those tents all winter.

He went to the co-op to visit the post office. His *Time* magazine had not come for three weeks now.

There was almost nothing to buy in the co-op these days because the Red Baron was conducting a feud with Prohibition Creek and the Northwest Territories government over the condition of the airstrip. He had been refusing to land his planes all summer on anything but water. Now that the lake was closed with ice, the Beaver couldn't come in there, and the Red Baron wouldn't send any of his other planes.

It was getting close to Christmas and everyone was complaining about this state of affairs.

There was still no mail, so he turned away from the wicket, and met up with his sister-in-law, Sarah, between the empty green-painted shelves of the store. She was quite pregnant; she would be going out right after Christmas to hospital, but that again depended upon the resumption of their air service.

"What are you doing here, Robert? Christmas shopping?"

Sarah spoke with irony. Everyone knew that Robert and Haga lived on rabbits in a dirty shack out in the woods.

She was a tall thin woman with no front teeth. She was slightly older than Michael, and they had got married in much the same way as Robert and Mary Ann, after they had a child together, and because the old people and the Church had finally forced them into it. Like many unhappy people, she enjoyed meddling in the lives of others.

Robert now felt almost as though Sarah had got him cornered there among the shelves. She was speaking in a low voice.

"You should move back in with Mary Ann, Robert."

"That's my business," replied Robert.

"You're married. You ought to stay with your wife."

"Who says?"

"Everyone's talking about it."

There was no way he could escape from this conversation without turning rudely on his heel and walking all the way back up the aisle to the post office wicket.

"Mary Ann isn't coming to AA anymore. I think the reason she quit is because of you and that social worker." Sarah had lowered her voice another notch.

"What do you mean by that?" Robert demanded.

"The way you and that social worker are carrying on," she replied.

"I'm not carrying on with anybody." Robert had never liked Sarah and he usually kept her at a distance. Since he couldn't help talking to her right now, he was getting angry. "Who said so?"

"Roseanne."

Robert suddenly saw how his behaviour was being studied and interpreted by these women—Mary Ann too. He started to walk away from it; he had no use for gossip at all, and he didn't care about anyone else's opinion. But then he bethought himself. Even if it meant nothing to him, this kind of thing could hurt Rebecca. He turned back.

Speaking in a normal voice—it seemed abnormally loud to both of them now—he said to Sarah, "I like Rebecca. I'm a friend of hers. So what?"

"You're a man. She's a woman," cried Sarah. "You can't just like each other."

Was that true? Was it so unusual?

He knew it was unusual and so did Rebecca. But not in the way this woman meant.

"Boy, what a world!" Robert said. "A man and a woman can't even like each other." He shrugged.

His brother Michael came around the corner.

"Hi, Michael," said Robert. "I was just talking to your wife here. But don't get worried. It isn't because I like her."

Sarah now began to question Michael about what he had done with some money that had been in her purse the previous day. Still feeling angry, Robert continued to stand there. He was not listening to this, but somehow he didn't know how to get away any longer.

"Well, I don't have it. See?" Michael was exhibiting his empty wallet.

"Where's that money then?" She didn't believe him. Robert didn't believe him either.

It reminded him of himself and Mary Ann, although Mary Ann had more dignity than Sarah; she would never have pursued the issue in public like this. But Mary Ann had sometimes given him money, and he had spent it, every cent of it, on gambling; and if she left something like a cheque lying around the house, well, he had spent that too.

Michael was denying, just as Robert had denied, that his gambling habit made him into a thief. "Well, I'm going home to look in the house. But if I don't find that money, Michael—!" Sarah turned away, almost in tears. She disappeared around the corner of the shelves and the door banged as she went out. Bernard McCrae, the co-op manager, came down the aisle from the post office. He was Herod's nephew, a rubicund man who was probably in line to become the mayor himself some day.

"Are we going to have Christmas, Bernard?" remarked Robert. He and Bernard were about the same age. They had been in school together at the Forks. However, Bernard had taken the trouble to finish; Robert had dropped out when he was eighteen.

"The trouble is, they can't get parts for the grader till the Red Baron gets in here with his plane," said Bernard.

"Plane can't come in till they grade the runway," said Michael.

It was a Catch-22. But no one felt particularly indignant; this kind of thing happened all the time. Bernard grinned. Michael shrugged.

"Well maybe that's good," Robert went on. "We could have a real Dene Christmas—without all that wrapping paper and stuff."

"Yeah. But what about the kids?" said Bernard.

"Heck, they'd be better off," said Robert. "Candy is no good for their teeth anyway. And those fancy toys like remote control cars or dolls that walk and crawl and say things out loud—all that stuff gets broken the day after anyway. Caribou meat instead of that turkey and jello—"

"It would put the store out of business," remarked Bernard.

"Just over Christmas. It'd be like the old days," said Robert.

"Yeah. We used to have a lot more fun in the old days. Remember the slide we had down there on the riverbank, Robert? Boy, that was fun."

"We never even had any sleds. Just boards and stuff we made for ourselves."

"Nobody goes sliding down there anymore," said Bernard. "Of course there was that guy that drove Herod's truck over the cliff. Maybe he thought it was a sled."

They all laughed.

"Herod sure misses his truck," Robert said. He looked curiously at Michael.

"Yeah, Herod's going to turn into a skinny little fellow with all the exercise he's getting," said Bernard.

"I wonder if that guy who did it feels bad. What do you think, Michael?" Robert asked.

"Oh, he was so drunked up he probably doesn't even remember he did it now," remarked Bernard. "He must have been pretty well out of it. Otherwise he'd never have walked away from that wreck."

"Probably that was it." Robert nodded. "Right, Michael?" he said.

"Yeah, he just crawled up the hill and into somebody's house," said Bernard. "Had a nice long nap and woke up feeling like, 'Where's my breakfast?'"

"Okay, but I think he knows who he is," said Robert. "Even if they don't catch him. I bet some other people know too. They always know, don't they, Michael?"

Robert didn't want to expose Michael, but it had annoyed him when he laughed. In fact everything about the way his brother was behaving annoyed Robert right now.

"Well, maybe they'll catch him at that," agreed Bernard. "Herod was telling me when he was in here this morning that that cop, Dave—You know that one?"

The other two nodded.

"Well, he's a real keen one," said Bernard. "He thought maybe they could find some fingerprints. So they took out the steering wheel and sent it to the forensics lab in Ottawa. If the guy has any kind of a police record—they'll get him."

Michael turned and walked away now, disappearing as suddenly as his wife had done. Bernard gave Robert a what's-got-him look, raising his eyebrows, and Robert shrugged. He turned to follow, catching up before Michael finished jumping down the porch stairs of the store.

"Hey, wait up, Michael! You're going home, right? Not to a poker game or anything?" said Robert.

"Look, I don't need you following me around too."

"It's just that I know something about you that you don't know I know."

Michael turned his head away. It was snowing again and they plunged through the thick falling flakes side by side, hands in their jacket pockets.

Michael still did not speak.

"You were the one that drove Herod's truck down the bank, weren't you?" Robert spoke bluntly.

"Who told you that?" Michael stopped and looked at him, nothing in his eyes.

"Haga."

"Oh him." Michael was dismissive. He paused. "They're not going to catch the guy who did it," he said.

"What about the fingerprints?"

"Maybe the guy was wearing gloves, Robert. It was a cold night."

"I wonder if the guy who did it remembers whether he was wearing gloves, Michael?"

"He's pretty sure he was." Michael was grinning.

"Am I supposed to be glad?" Robert stopped. They were standing facing one another in the middle of the road.

"You're my brother, aren't you?" said Michael.

Robert already fully understood the obligation this imposed. "But what about all the other guys who know?" he asked.

"What other guys? There's only you and me."

"And Haga," said Robert.

"Oh yeah. Haga."

"And the guy he heard it from."

"Okay, okay!" cried Michael. "But no one's going to tell."

"I hope not." But as a matter of fact Robert wasn't sure what he hoped. He was in a very strange position these days.

"Look," said Michael. "It isn't as though I meant to steal anything. His keys were in the lock."

"You remember that, do you?"

"Well, his keys must have been in the lock," responded Michael sheepishly.

"You're kind of old for a stunt like that, aren't you? Twenty-eight. Three kids."

"Are you going to preach to me like Danny?" demanded Michael.

Robert had not been intending to preach. He said, "You know what I was reading in *Time* magazine once? Some really smart guy like Einstein or Henry Ford said this: Intelligence isn't just something inside you. It's how you use information."

Michael wasn't in the mood for advice.

"Look, you can take your *Time* magazine and—!" he snarled. "Hey, I'm getting off here, Robert."

Michael turned away. After a moment he began to run back toward the house Robert had dropped him off at the other day. There was always a card game going on in that house.

Robert walked on, his head down, pondering grimly. The trouble with a town like Prohibition Creek was that sooner or later you couldn't prevent yourself from hearing things you didn't want to know. And this morning he had been forced to listen to a lot of garbage about himself too.

He had never even thought of carrying on with Rebecca. He was married, more than ten years older, and the way he was living now put an affair with a woman almost entirely out of the question. In Robert's opinion, the reason his sisters-in-law—and his wife—had dreamed all this up was as a kind of revenge against Rebecca for being young and pretty, and so much nicer than they were.

This was what he was thinking when suddenly Rebecca herself

overtook him on the road. She had been running after him, and she came to a halt abruptly beside him and began to slip. She almost fell over backwards, then grabbed his arm.

"Hey, don't fall down!"

Rebecca was laughing breathlessly. "I saw you when I was coming out of the drop-in centre. Didn't you hear me calling?"

She let go of his arm now, and they began to walk along, side by side. "You must have been thinking about something pretty hard, Robert."

"I get pretty fed up with living here sometimes," he remarked.

Rebecca looked at him inquiringly.

"I lost my job with Housing this morning. That secretary was even yelling at me," he said.

"Was that because of what you did for Mary Ann?" she asked.

"How do you know about that?" Robert was surprised.

"I heard. I hear everything sooner or later," she said.

He nodded. She did, of course. That aspect of her job repelled him.

"Why did you do it?" she asked.

"Mary Ann didn't want Bobby's things to get messed up." Robert spoke shortly.

"Bobby will be coming back for trial after Christmas," Rebecca said. "Did anyone tell you yet?"

This was another thing he didn't like about Rebecca's job. She was hand in glove with the cops.

"I was thinking of trying to get a job with Sasquatch Drilling after Christmas," said Robert.

"But you'll stay around to see Bobby, won't you?"

"Maybe he doesn't want to see me."

"You know that's not true."

"Well, it's just another thing to feel bad about," said Robert moodily.

There was a short silence between them. Rebecca felt sorry that she had trespassed on the subject of Bobby.

There was something she wanted to say; it was why she had run after him. She didn't know exactly how to start, but it had been on her mind for several days.

"Do you really believe in medicine power, Robert?" she asked.

He looked up. "Yeah. I guess so."

"Do you think it's around now? I mean, that medicine woman who was here this fall. Do you think she had power?"

"Well, it might still be around. I don't know about her, though," he replied.

"So you don't think—?" Rebecca had heard the note of skepticism in his voice.

"I don't know." Robert shrugged. Then he smiled. They had stopped walking along and she was gazing at him seriously, her face surrounded by a knit cap and yards of knitted muffler.

"I could make a prophecy about you," he said.

"What?" She was alarmed, clasping her gloved hands together in front of her.

"You're going to get your kids back, marry a good man, and be happy all the rest of your life till you die."

Rebecca was so relieved, she almost looked as though she was going to cry.

"So what are you going to give me? I want it now." Robert suddenly took his bare hand out of his jacket pocket and extended it, palm up.

She backed away involuntarily. Robert was smiling again and she smiled back, swallowing her disappointment.

"I see," she said. "You just have to figure out what the person wants to hear?"

"I think so." He put his hand back in his pocket. It was quite a cold day, getting down into the minus twenties, with a wind blowing.

Rebecca started to walk along beside him again, thinking.

She said at last: "I went to see her and something happened."

She was embarrassed. But he had told her about his dream, after all. She felt she had to tell him about her vision.

"Remember when Haga got hurt? You told us about it the other day. Well, I was there. I was that doe. It happened—well, I think it happened while I was visiting the medicine woman."

Robert turned to face her, amazed. She had turned white when he was telling about it the other day; he remembered wondering why.

"It really happened."

"I wasn't sure whether I ought to tell you."

"Why not?"

"Well—saying you had a—a vision of somebody. They might get the wrong idea. They might think you were saying that because you were trying to—"

"I had that dream with you in it," said Robert. "And I told you."

They smiled at each other. Then Rebecca looked around her, almost as if she didn't know where she was, as though she had been back briefly in that world of her vision.

Their conversation had been so absorbing that she hadn't realized she was home. They were standing outside the trailer.

"Come in," she said. "Are you hungry?"

"No," said Robert. He spoke shortly. "I'd better not."

He couldn't go into her house, not with everyone gossiping about them.

"Why not?" Rebecca was wondering suddenly, anxiously, if it had been a mistake to tell him.

Robert didn't want her to know why not: it might get between them just when they had discovered they could really talk to one another. But he saw the expression on her face. She had the wrong idea already. He remembered that intelligence is just how you use information.

"This morning I heard that you and I are carrying on together," he said. "My sister-in-law told my other sister-in-law, and she told me."

"Sarah? And Roseanne!" Rebecca was horrified. "Well, now at least I know what they're saying." She spoke slowly and he knew that she was intelligent: she didn't want it to get between them either.

◆ II. DENE CHRISTMAS ◆

"Seven Die of Gunshot Wounds, Twenty-Three Presumed Burnt in Fire." Robert lay on the upper bunk in the shack, reading *Time* magazine out loud to Haga.

"Maniacal Sect Leader's Threat of Communal Suicide Prompts FBI *Action.* Oh boy!" He turned a page.

Haga had been cooking all morning. First he had carefully scraped the hair off a caribou head, and now he was boiling it in a large pot on the stove.

It was Christmas Day.

"Look at this picture, Haga. Federal investigators hold hooded suspect at gunpoint beside site of mass grave. Another serial killer, I guess."

Haga came over to look.

"How can those whitemen stand it?" he remarked. "I'd be scared to live down south. With those murderers everywhere—you can't hardly walk to the store or go out of your house to a card game without getting murdered."

"There won't be any trees left down there pretty soon," Robert said. "The rivers are all polluted."

"Boy, what a place to live! No wonder so many of them have to come up north."

"Yeah, and now the Americans are trying to get hold of our water." Robert had just been reading an in-depth perspective on this subject.

"Our water?" Haga was alarmed. "How are they going to get it? It's up here. Not down there."

"They'll dig trenches, probably," said Robert. "You know, like the Panama Canal."

"To take away the Big River?"

"Maybe they'll build a tunnel." Robert was not just teasing Haga. He had been trying to figure out how they would do it himself.

"You know how the water goes into the Ramparts above Sans Sault? It kind of all just pours down in there?"

Haga looked up at him, his mouth open.

"It'd be like that. Only the water would disappear into a big hole."

"But what would happen to the people who live in Aklavik?" Haga protested.

"Well, I guess it would get dry there, like the Sahara Desert. I wonder whether you could have camels in this country? That would be kind of interesting."

"This is bad, Robert," said Haga. "You know that old prophecy. When the river dries up—the world will end."

"Well, cheer up," said Robert. "The world could come to an end tomorrow if the Americans wanted it that way. So I guess we're kind of used to that idea."

Haga was horrified. "I don't want the world to end," he said.

"Well, it will anyway." Robert put his magazine face down on his chest and looked up at the bare boards of the roof above him.

"It will?" Haga was no longer just horrified.

"In a couple of million years," said Robert. "That's all I meant, partner. A couple of million years."

Haga turned back to the preparation of his soup. The fire crackled. The water in the pot bubbled. It was cosy in the little shack.

Robert turned a page and began looking at pictures from the war in Africa. They were terrible pictures, grisly, haunting.

Then he stopped looking at them and stared again at the ceiling, reminded of something that had happened last night—something that he felt good about for a change.

The Red Baron had finally relented on Christmas Eve and sent in a couple of planes full of turkeys, oranges, toys, wrapping paper, votive candles, snuff, cigarettes, chewing tobacco, formula, baby diapers, and—most important of all—mail. This was how Robert had got his *Time* magazines: a bonanza, four of them at once.

He had been passing by the hamlet office after dark on his way home to the shack, intending to burn a little lamp oil that evening, when he had noticed that the lights were on in the office for a meeting, even though it was Christmas Eve. And a warm, well-lit government office was a wonderful place to read.

Robert ran up the steps and went in, intending to read his way through the hamlet meeting.

Local Government was there: the two officials, Mike and Shelagh. Shelagh was explaining something to Herod, the only other person present, and he was responding patiently.

"We understood from the Red Baron that the strip wasn't being ploughed."

"Yeah, but that was because he never brought in the parts we needed to fix the grader."

"He said he couldn't bring anything in because the strip wasn't being ploughed," she said.

"We needed those parts first," said Herod. "And he never brought them in."

"Well, he was just telling us how he couldn't land the plane on the strip. Because it wasn't ploughed."

"We could stop going around and around right there, I guess," Herod commented. "—We got the parts. Old Elvis Woodcutter went into the Forks and got them with his skidoo."

"Well, it's why we had to postpone your capital plan meeting till tonight, that's all I'm saying."

"Yeah, Christmas Eve." Herod sighed. Then he brightened, seeing Robert, who had already settled down in one of the armchairs, his feet up on a coffee table. "Hi, Robert. Here for the meeting?"

"Nope," said Robert, opening the first of his magazines, the one dated November 3.

The door opened and Billy McCrae entered and took off his parka. He was a member of the Council.

"Good, now Billy's here." Herod was in a hurry to get started. "So maybe we could start talking about that capital plan you guys brought down here for the hamlet."

The two government people were silent. It was not a quorum, only two members of Council, one of them the mayor.

Robert was reading to himself: *Political Chaos in the Caribbean. In the small hours of the morning people take cover and huddle on the dirt floors of the primitive shacks thatched with banana leaves and flattened kerosene tins that are their homes as gunshots reverberate through the slums—*

Gun-toting voodoo men. That would be one to read to Haga.

He began to flip through the magazine, to see if there was anything else like that.

Acid rain. Pollution. Iraq. Saddam was using poison gas again. The bad state of the economy.

The door now opened and Tommy Douglas entered.

"Oh good. Here's Tommy," said Herod. "I'm going to start this meeting. Just to get it off the ground. Take the minutes of the last meeting as read? All in favour?"

"Aye," replied the other two.

"So we'll start with open floor. We're going to go through the capital plan tonight with Mike and Shelagh from Local Government, but first, we've got a member of the general public present. Robert, got anything you want to say?"

Still flipping, Robert had found the pictures from Africa and come to a dead halt. He looked up.

"This is pretty horrible, Herod," he said. "Look at this! Just little kids!"

He got up and went over to spread the magazine pictures out in front of Herod.

"Their legs and arms are just like little tree branches," Herod said, appalled.

"*Children, the most terrible casualties of the 'forgotten war' are left dying on the road by their dead or dying parents in the search for supplies of relief food provided by the* UN. *Some of these children are later dragged into hospitals in the city, suffering from shrapnel wounds or burns, only to be left to die untreated on rat- and lice-infested rag beds in the hallways. There is no medicine for burns, no penicillin, no nursing staff, and there are almost no doctors,*" read Robert out loud.

"Geez." Herod continued to stare at the pictures, swallowing hard.

"God, this is awful," said Robert, reading rapidly to himself. "You know what the awful thing about this is?" he demanded of the others. "It says here that the big problem is that there's no money to send them anywhere near the aid they need. The UN is just about broke, and besides, it's bogged down in this big deal in—what's the name of that other place? Yugoslavia."

"Oh yeah," said the others vaguely. But they were clustered around Robert's magazines, staring hard at the pictures, which were brightly coloured like a centrefold: children, their bloody wounds covered with flies, babies with sunken, haunted eyes, wrapped in white rags with the blood soaking through, the ghastly images of war and starvation.

"Uh—Herod—the meeting—" suggested Shelagh from the sidelines.

"Oh yeah, well, let's get this show on the road again." Herod came back to himself, tearing his eyes away from the pictures. "Anything else from you, Robert?"

Robert took his magazine away with him to the corner where he had been reading.

"I'll just read you this piece here. *The situation once again exhibits how we don't want to stop armed conflict in Africa. For if there were world peace we might have to share our wealth with the poor people of the earth.*"

"You know that really makes me mad," said Herod angrily, staring at Robert with his large, hard-boiled eyes. "People not being willing to share. Especially when it comes to food. There's those poor little orphans and we aren't even willing to give them a little piece of meat?"

"Yeah, it makes me mad too," agreed Robert. "We always shared our stuff. I never heard of Dene people not sharing food."

"Herod. This meeting? Could we—?" Shelagh was getting anxious.

"Oh yeah. Well, I guess that's all the open floor we've got time for." Herod came to again. "So now maybe Mike can get up here and tell us about the hamlet capital plan for next year."

Mike got up and passed around a set of xeroxed handouts showing the breakdown of the capital plan over the next five years. He gave one to Robert as well.

"As you see it breaks down into sixteen categories. Roads, airport, new staff house, and so on."

Herod nodded. "We need a new grader."

"We got the message," said Mike. "Look on page two there."

There was a long pause as the three members of Council present studied the pages of the plan rather helplessly. Robert was also looking it over. He had been so starved for reading material lately that he read everything that came his way—even dry and, in his opinion, largely irrelevant documents like this one.

"I've got an idea," he remarked.

"Okay, shoot, Robert," said Herod.

"The grader's fixed, right?"

"Yeah. Till next time."

"Getting a new grader's going to cost us a hundred thousand, minimum. And it's in the plan for this year. That's what it says here."

Robert flourished the plan, open to page two.

"So what about if you guys take that money and put it into relief for those kids?"

"Then we wouldn't get a grader." Herod was slow to follow.

"Come on," said Robert. "You can still fix the old one."

He dropped the plan on the floor and jumped up, bringing his magazine back over to the table.

Then they were all looking at the ghastly centrefold pictures again and there was a long silence.

Mike had decided that it was time to intervene.

"Well, I'm sorry about this. But you really can't use government funds earmarked for—"

"A hundred thousand isn't going to go very far to help those people," Herod interrupted him. He ignored Mike, looking at Robert.

"Well, look in this budget here and see if you can cut some more things. How about the swimming pool?"

"But we want the swimming pool to keep our kids from swimming in the river," objected Billy.

"Hey, the kids have always swum in the river," replied Robert. "Go down there, take off their clothes and make a little fire. You remember, Billy. That way they can pretend they're real Dene and don't have to live in houses."

"Okay. That's a point. Anything else?" said Herod.

Tommy Douglas now spoke for the first time. His opinion always carried a lot of weight with Herod because he wasn't just a younger relative.

"I don't see that it's real sharing if you just give away the stuff you don't want," he said. "Like when somebody cuts up a moose and gives you the hoofs and a piece of the insides. Why don't you put the whole shebang into relief."

Both the government people present were by now thoroughly alarmed.

Herod cast an ironic glance at them. They were trying frantically to intervene, their hands up.

"It's ten o'clock," he said. "And we've got a rule here that says we don't go on with meetings after ten. So does somebody want to make a motion right now? You, Tommy? All in favour?"

Everyone was in favour. Robert voted as well.

"Okay. I guess we'll just work out what we're going to do without the capital plan budget at our next regular meeting." Herod was already pulling on his enormous tent-like parka, and the others also got up to go.

"Boy, I want to go home! It's Christmas Eve, you guys!"

The door slammed several times and everyone was gone, leaving Government to pick up its papers and regroup. Even Robert was gone; he didn't want to stick around and argue with them about this one.

Of course, as he fully realized now, there had not been a quorum at that meeting, and even if there had, someone in Yellowknife would have found a tricky way to overrule the motion.

But it made him feel good that it had been made.

And this was why he had not got much reading done the previous night.

"Boy, Haga, that soup sure smells good." It smelled so good that he jumped down off his bunk and went to look in the pot.

"There's nothing like soup made with a caribou head," said Haga, lifting the lid for him. "Fish soup is good but you get kind of tired of it in the winter."

They both took a deep sniff of the steam. Then Haga gave the bubbling broth a good stir.

"Nobody wants soup like this anymore, Haga. Not even Dene people. They're all eating pizza."

"And those vegetables," said Haga.

Robert always enjoyed having this conversation with Haga.

"Well, I like an onion in the stew," he remarked.

"But what about lettuce?" demanded Haga.

Robert nodded. "And that broccoli."

"And fruit." This was a real hobbyhorse of Haga's. "What is it anyway? Some kind of candy?"

"Candy?" Robert was only mildly surprised to hear that he thought this. "No, it grows on trees. You know, the way blueberries grow on bushes?"

"Yeah, but it's all kinds of funny colours, like orange and yellow," said Haga.

"Well, blue is kind of a funny colour too, when you come to think of it," commented Robert.

"Well, this here's a real Dene Christmas dinner. Just meat," said Haga. He again lifted the lid of the simmering pot and inspected the contents with pride.

Robert began collecting up soup bowls and spoons, setting the table. They had only a few things of this kind: knives, the sugar spoon, an odd glass they had found in the woods. One of the soup bowls was in fact a metal pie plate, while the other was a chipped blue enamel coffee mug.

Haga dished out the soup with a flourish, using the mug as a ladle. Then they both settled down at the table, eating with their knives and drinking the broth.

Christmas was on Robert's mind now.

"Are you going to visit anybody?" he asked Haga. Visiting was what most people did on Christmas Day.

"Well, I was going to go to my sister's," said Haga. "But she's got so respectable she doesn't want to see me anymore."

Haga's sister was married to the school janitor. Like almost everyone in town, Robert hardly ever thought of the two of them as related.

"She said I'd just go to sleep on the floor like I usually do. She said she was going to wake me up and kick me out if I did that."

"Your own sister." The conservative in Robert was shocked.

"Well, it's not like the old days, that's what I say," Haga complained. "Back in the old days a brother was a brother, no matter how much he snored."

Robert thought now of his own family. It was a mess. He had gone to see his mother the previous afternoon, but she had hardly had anything to say to him. She was in a bad mood because Danny had had a Christmas party without inviting her. She was angry at Michael, now openly drinking and playing cards again, who was sleeping off the night before on her sofa. And she was still annoyed with Robert, both because she was almost always annoyed with him anyway, and also because he had been at Danny's party.

They ate in silence. Finally Haga sat back with a sigh of repletion.

"Was that good!"

Robert got up to get the tea. Still silent, he poured a bit of the hot liquid into Haga's soup bowl—the mug—swished it around and threw it out the door. Then he put a steaming cup of tea in front of Haga, and poured out one for himself into the glass they had found in the woods.

Haga took a spoonful of sugar out of the bag. Robert watched him take another spoonful. Apparently feeling Robert's eyes upon him, he quickly took two more, making four in all. He liked a sweet cup of tea.

"Well, it's Christmas, isn't it?" he said defiantly.

The door suddenly flew open, letting in an arctic blast and three male visitors entered, Robert's cousins, heroic drinkers and card players all of them. Suddenly there was a lot of noise. Someone was singing a Country and Western song about lowdown friends.

"What are you guys doing?"

"Something illegal, I hope."

"Got some cigarettes, Robert?"

"Wipe your feet, you guys," commanded Haga. "You're getting snow all over the floor."

"We came all the way out here to see what you're up to, Haga. There's nothing going on in town."

"Nothing but eating and Church."

"Have you guys got a pack of cards anywhere?"

One of the visitors had sat down on Haga's bed, dropping the long ashes from his cigarette over the blanket. Then he took the remains of the butt and ground it out on Haga's pillow.

"Hey, what's your problem, Haga?"

Haga was getting quite upset with these guys, Robert noticed.

"A beer would taste pretty good right now."

"Why didn't you bring one with you then?" Haga had taken possession of his bed again and was dusting it off assiduously.

Meanwhile, someone else had climbed to the top bunk and lain down.

"Geez, Harold's going to sleep up there! Don't go to sleep, Harold!"

But it was already too late. Harold Woodcutter was a championship snorer, almost in Haga's league.

"For God's sake, wake him up!" Haga was alarmed and astounded by the noises proceeding from the bunk above.

But their visitors were already getting restless.

"Why are you guys just sitting here like this? You got no wives to bug you like the rest of us do."

"Yeah. You could be drinking and smoking and playing cards all day if you felt like it."

"But this is Christmas," said Robert. "We were having Christmas."

"Well, you're not having much of a good time, if you ask me."

"We were eating dinner," Haga told him.

"Caribou head soup. Dene food. Like it was in the old days," said Robert.

They found themselves grinning at each other. In the ordinary course of things they would both have been out roaming the streets in search of entertainment too. But now, in their special position as outcasts and exiles, they were living a life of sobriety and upright virtuous behaviour. It was a strange outcome.

And it was entirely too dull for the taste of their visitors, family men, all of them.

"Okay. I'm going home."

"Nothing going on here anyway."

"Hey, you guys, take Harold with you," pleaded Haga. But they were already gone, slamming the door behind them.

Haga was still nursing his injured pillow, feeling the burned place tenderly with his fingers.

He had never had a pillow till Robert borrowed one for him from his mother, but apparently he liked it now.

The man in the bunk up above rolled over on his back and began to snore in a rich, full-throated fashion, like a caterpillar tractor engine turning over at full throttle.

"Why'd they have to leave Harold behind?" moaned Haga.

"Well, at least they took off," said Robert. "Probably looking for a card game."

He felt a slight twinge as he said this. But it was in the longing for cards, not in any wish to join his cousins out on the road in their fruitless search for something to do on Christmas afternoon.

Harold was still snoring loudly, and the volume, also the absolute regularity of it, astonished Robert, who was more used to the heart-stopping arrhythmia of Haga. Of course, Harold was a big strong man in his prime, and he had probably eaten a dinner of turkey, cranberry sauce, hot buttered buns, mashed potatoes, jellied salad, macaroni salad and two slices of pie sometime within the past two hours.

"Geez," whined Haga.

"I thought you said that back in the old days a brother was a brother no matter how much he snored." Robert gave an ironic shrug.

It was almost as though Haga was getting respectable: he cooked soup for Christmas dinner, he put four spoons of sugar in his tea, he had sugar around to put in his tea, the pillow he was nursing—

But no, Robert thought, taking another look: Haga wasn't going to get respectable. There was no need to worry about it.

▲ ▲ ▲

Robert walked into the village in the late afternoon of New Year's Day and he met his mother at the corner by the road coming from the airport. She greeted him in her usual taciturn way, but she was looking less cross than she had been when he last saw her. He stopped to talk.

"I was just going to watch the stick gambling down at the band hall," Robert said. "I heard some people came over from the Forks to play."

"You were going to watch the stick gambling, were you?" Only the faintest emphasis on the word 'watch' revealed how she felt about that proposition.

"I'd hardly be a Dene man if I could stay away from stick gambling, Ama."

"You could hardly be the son of your father."

"Oh yeah. That's true too." Robert was embarrassed. His mother hardly ever spoke of his father.

He now changed direction and began to walk her home.

Robert sincerely loved his mother, although he wasn't altogether sure what attitude she preserved toward him in return, and never had been sure since he was a teenager. There was so much that he had done that made her sad or angry; even his best qualities, his trickiness and his intelligence, made him resemble his father, and he was aware that this resemblance hurt and offended her.

"Sarah went out," she said.

Robert was able to put the information contained in this laconic remark all together in a flash. Sarah had gone out by plane to the hospital to have her baby—he had heard the plane land and take off while he was walking into town. Obviously it had been a bit of an emergency—probably she had gone into labour early—because Rachel had escorted her to the airstrip, and was now walking back. And almost undoubtedly his mother was going to be looking after his sister-in-law's other children, because his brother Michael would be at the stick gambling.

"You want some help?" he asked. "I guess I could hang around your place with the kids for awhile if you want to go somewhere." It was a heroic offer, for it meant giving up on the stick gambling.

His mother made no reply.

They had reached Rachel's house, a newer one than Robert and Mary Ann's, but not far from it in the centre of town. It was the usual type of dwelling, made of plywood with metal siding, and painted brown. A teepee that Rachel used for tanning hides and drying meat stood outside, a short distance from the porch.

"Come in." She preceded him up the steps.

Robert entered the kitchen, shedding his parka, dusting the snow off his mukluks. Then he stopped short in surprise.

Elvis was sitting at the kitchen table.

He was there quite openly, in his shirtsleeves—he was even wearing slippers. He had a half-full cup of tea in front of him.

Robert was conscious that a revolution had taken place.

Rachel and Elvis had been conducting their love affair for more than ten years, for perhaps as many as twenty. It was clandestine not in the sense that nobody knew about it—for in fact, everybody knew about it—but in the sense that neither of them allowed any acknowledgement that it was happening. They never stood together at feasts or dances, they never spoke openly to one another on the street; Elvis lived in a house of his own down the road, and came to sleep with Rachel only after dark or, in the summer, very late at night. He would never, in the ordinary way, have been seen near her house, let alone inside.

"Elvis! What are you doing here?" Robert said this in spite of himself.

Very embarrassed, he continued, "I mean—Hi, Elvis. I guess you're visiting Ama—Nice day, eh?"

"Give tea to my son," said Rachel.

Elvis had already gone to the stove. He poured Robert a cup of tea and put it on the table in front of him with the sugar bowl.

"Masi," said Robert, still stunned by this development.

Elvis kept his eyes on the teacup, but he was smiling slightly, a little skinny man, quiet and humorous in his demeanour. Robert was quite fond of him—Elvis was his uncle, after all—but only in the context of hunting trips and other male activities. He had never expected to meet Elvis in his mother's kitchen, with the rosaries over the doors, the bunch of plastic flowers on top of the refrigerator, the doily under the sugar bowl.

But he began to get used to it as fast as he could. The other two were having a conversation between themselves about Michael and Sarah's children.

"Is that little one asleep now?"

Elvis said, "Yes. She cried for awhile. I sat with her."

Robert was fascinated by the intimacy with which they talked to one another. The way they were looking into each other's faces, the cozy kitchen in which they were standing, everything about them, in fact, betokened kindliness and love.

"I told the boy to go see the stick gambling," Elvis was saying. "It's good to start watching now."

"Oh yeah," agreed Robert. "It's good to start when you're little. It's like that with poker too."

He was suddenly very embarrassed again as the two elders turned to look at him after this remark, Rachel with disapproval, Elvis with a twinkle in his eye.

"How old is he, anyway?" he stumbled on.

"Four," replied Elvis.

Robert leaned back against the kitchen counter, taking refuge in his teacup, and a silence began to prolong itself. Neither his mother or Elvis were going to help him out with this.

"Boy! Elvis and Haga and I had a real good hunt this fall. Didn't we, Elvis?"

His uncle was smiling. But he still didn't say anything.

"We'd have stayed out even longer if Haga hadn't nearly broken his arm. Wouldn't we, Elvis?"

Robert glanced nervously at his mother. Unfortunately, everything he said seemed to refer to something about him that she disapproved of. Gambling, his friendship with Haga—

He decided to take the bull by the horns.

"Sorry about how Christmas turned out this year, Ama. I know you're mad at Danny—and Michael, too. Not just at me, the way you usually are."

She did not reply, but a slightly softer look crept into her eyes and over her wrinkled face.

"Those're your guns hanging up over there, aren't they, Elvis?" Robert plunged on, trying to get to the point. "So I guess that means you're staying here now? Well, I've got nothing against that."

He felt that he was in the home stretch now.

"When two people—I mean, after all these years when two people—" But as it turned out, this was something he really wasn't going to be able to say out loud to his mother. Even though she was watching him closely, and he had the idea that she knew exactly what it was that he was trying to say.

Robert put his empty teacup down in the sink. "Well, I guess I'll just go along to watch the stick gambling now, Ama." He took his parka off the back of the chair where he had thrown it down.

"I'm coming too." Elvis also put his teacup in the sink.

Elvis was actually the second-best stick gambler in Prohibition Creek, and if it hadn't been for all the other facts about him that Robert had so recently had to absorb, he would have been wondering why he wasn't over in the band hall already, in the centre of a line of swaying, chanting players.

"C'mon," said Robert, on the porch. "I guess the two of us could show those people from the Forks what it's like to lose a lot of money."

"Where's Haga?" Elvis followed him out, hunching his parka over his shoulders.

"I don't know. He was asleep when I left the shack."

"Good," said Elvis.

Robert laughed. Elvis didn't want Haga messing up the stick gambling. He had formed an opinion of Haga's ability to mess things up on their hunting trip together.

Now that he was out of his mother's kitchen, Robert managed to say what he had been intending to say before.

"You staying with her. It's okay with me."

Elvis nodded.

"I'm not like Danny. It's between you and her."

Elvis said, "She'll be glad. She thought you would mind the most."

"Me?" Robert was surprised. He was now taking no account of how long he had thought about this, and how much it had bothered him when he first became aware of it.

"You're the oldest," continued Elvis.

"Oh yeah." Robert laughed with a touch of bitterness. "My birthright."

"The oldest one—they always love that one the best."

Elvis spoke with simple authority, and Robert realized that he would know. He was clearly in a special position to interpret Rachel's thoughts on the matter.

◂ ◂ ◂

They had arrived at the band hall, and the sound of the drumming and chanting inside made the hair on the back of Robert's neck rise. In the absence of his father he was the best stick gambler in Prohibition Creek and he knew the others inside were wondering if he would come, wishing he was already there.

Stick gambling was a game of the utmost simplicity. All that was involved was that a chosen player on a team would try to conceal a small object like a coin in one hand or the other, using a variety of ritualized motions, together with the hypnotic chanting of his team, to confuse his opponents. But to Robert, as to other Dene men, stick gambling was the essence of gambling. It involved everything they loved about cards: bluff and the taking of calculated risks, and the exchange of large sums of money—in the old days, dogs, or even women. A very tricky man was required to be a good player, and he would be up against a whole team of other very tricky men.

Elvis disappeared inside the hall and Robert heard the cries of: "Here comes Elvis!" "Now we're going to beat 'em!" as the drumming became much louder.

But Robert had spotted Danny, standing beside the fire outside, hands in his pockets, his shoulders hunched against the wind. Robert went over to talk to his brother. He felt he had something to say to him.

"I feel kind of funny talking about this, but we did once before, remember? Elvis moved in with Ama. I guess you know."

Danny shrugged. "What makes you think I know anything? Ama's not speaking to me."

Robert had been supposing that Elvis moving in was what was making Danny look so mean today. But maybe he had another problem.

"Was that what you wanted to say?" asked Danny after a moment.

He was now looking even meaner than before.

"Look, why does it matter so much to you?" Robert had decided to go on. "We're all grown up. We've got our own families—at least Michael and you do. We didn't even see each other at Christmas time this year."

Danny didn't answer. Robert continued, "I think maybe she just decided it didn't make sense to go on the way it was, Elvis sneaking in late at night and all that."

As a matter of fact, he realized, he could be blaming Danny for the fact that his mother had let Elvis move in. It was not until Danny had moved back to Prohibition Creek and begun lecturing his mother about her morals that anything had happened at all. And if it hadn't been for Danny, their family would have spent Christmas together. But Robert was not inclined to blame anybody. In fact, now that this had happened, he felt curiously pleased that it had. He remembered the intimacy of Elvis and his mother talking to one another about Michael's kids, the way they looked into each other's eyes.

"Well, heck. Forget I said anything," he told Danny.

And he was also pleased with Danny's intransigence. Danny had painted himself into a corner, in Robert's opinion, and now he seemed determined to stay there.

The drumming inside began to rise to a crescendo. Someone was going to make a guess as to the position of that dime or pebble. Robert was listening, trying to determine what was going on. From the chanting it sounded as if the Forks team was making a killing.

The chanting dissolved in shouts and laughing, and Robert knew that his own team had lost. But that was only how it was going so far; that was only what had happened up till now, he thought.

"Okay, pal, I guess I'll just go in."

Robert went up the steps of the band hall and inside, where he was greeted by a wild chorus of cheers, and cries of "Bobby's here!" and "Now we're going to beat 'em!" And Danny walked in the direction of his own house, although he was not going there.

• 12. BOBBY'S TRIAL •

Two days after the stick-gambling session, at which the Prohibition Creek team had trounced the Forks team, leaving them destitute, and in some cases without parkas to go home in, the police plane landed at the airport, bringing in the court party and Robert's son Bobby with his two friends, all of them charged with assault and theft.

Robert went to court in the morning and watched the trial. Then he went to visit his wife, who had not been in the courtroom.

A strange sight met his eyes as he approached his own house.

The walls had been dismantled down to the bare studs and the tent in the kitchen stood rather starkly out on the bare floor. A puff of wood smoke issued from the chimney, which was still poked crazily out through a window opening.

Robert ran up the porch steps. Mary Ann was in the tent; she opened up the door flap immediately. She had been expecting him.

"Why weren't you in court this morning?" Robert demanded.

He stooped under the flap and entered the tent. It was quite warm in there; Mary Ann had a good fire going.

"I'm not a jailbird," she said. "What am I going to do in that court?"

She was already at the stove, pouring him a cup of tea.

The table made the place a little crowded and Mary Ann had to push it over to one side when she unrolled her bed at night. But though it was small, it was large enough for one person, and Mary Ann was accustomed to tents. Robert couldn't help feeling pleased at how well his plan had turned out.

He stirred his tea for a moment, organizing his thoughts. For he knew that his wife was waiting anxiously to hear what had happened in court that morning. She stood in front of him, her arms at her sides.

"It was a pretty good trial, really. That lawyer didn't do much worse than I would have done myself."

"Not much worse, eh?" she said sourly.

"He got him off lightly. I'd have used the same argument."

"Oh, you would have, would you?"

Robert was used to ignoring the irony in Mary Ann's remarks. Thoughtfully, he continued, "First of all he proved that Bobby wasn't the one who beat up old Arthur. It was that Ryan who did that. He even confessed he did it."

"That Ryan is one of Bobby's friends," said Mary Ann, still standing in front of him.

"Yeah, and that kind of helped too because, on the second charge of assault, it was Bobby who hit Ryan with a two-by-four."

"Helped? How could it have helped?" she demanded.

Robert realized that she was not catching his drift. The idea of argument, especially as it was used in a court of law, would never make sense to Mary Ann. He tried to explain it to her.

"See, he made Bobby look a lot better by making it seem as though he was mad at Ryan because of what Ryan did to old Arthur."

"So it would be all right to hit somebody with a big piece of wood?" Mary Ann was scandalized.

"No." Robert gave up. "All right, I'll just tell you what happened. He was convicted on that charge, and for stealing the beer. But the judge let him off with eight months jail, plus a month at the detox centre, including the time he already spent in jail."

Mary Ann sank down on the other chair by the table and turned her head away. Robert hated crying—in anybody—but especially in women, and even more especially in Mary Ann. "Oh, for God's sake!" he said. He pushed her cup toward her. "Here, have some more of your tea."

Feeling restless and more than a little uncomfortable, because Mary Ann was still crying, he went over to the stove for the teapot to put more tea into her cup. Then when she didn't take it, he stirred the sugar in for her as well.

"Look at it this way. It was a short sentence for what he did. And he's already served almost four months of it. So he'll be home by— probably by breakup time on the river."

Mary Ann took no consolation in this either, and Robert wandered around for a short while in the small area of the tent in which it was possible to stand upright, picking things up and putting them down again: the alarm clock, a roll of snare wire, a box of sewing oddments, a pair of beaded slipper uppers, one of them finished and the other almost so.

"Did you pay your fine?" he asked, putting down the uppers.

Mary Ann looked up. "Yes. I sold a pair of slippers to that RCMP for sixty-five dollars."

"Well, it was nice of him not to cheat you out of the extra fifteen dollars."

There was a pause while Mary Ann wiped her eyes and found a piece of tissue to blow her nose.

It struck Robert that it was a funny thing to say about someone, that it was nice of him not to cheat her out of the extra fifteen dollars. On the other hand, the RCMP constable was a whiteman, after all.

"I saved another forty dollars. I didn't pay the rent," said Mary Ann. "I'm going to start paying it again when they put the walls back on."

Robert laughed. "Wait for the roof," he suggested.

"Maybe I will," she said. "Especially if that Housing secretary comes down here and yells at me again."

"She yelled at me too," said Robert. "She yelled, 'You're fired!'"

"You lost your job?" Mary Ann sounded almost sorry about that.

Robert shrugged.

"Well, it was only a job," he said. "I thought I'd go and get another one with Sasquatch Drilling pretty soon. And make some money to send to Bobby."

She kept her eyes fixed on him now, for this, of course, was the point of their conversation. Neither of these two would have been particularly worried about their financial standing, but for the fact that their son was going back to jail.

Robert said, "I've got about two-hundred dollars. That's what I made from Housing for a week's work."

Wordlessly, Mary Ann got her old purse out from under her sleeping bag and counted out fifty-five dollars, her hands, so skillful with beads, fumbling slightly with the paper.

Robert took out his wallet. "Hey, wait a minute!" he said. "You want me to give it to him? You're his mother. You handle this."

She shook her head.

"But he won't even talk to me, I bet." Robert was reliving some of the horror of his last interview with Bobby in the police detachment office.

"I'm scared to go to that jail," said Mary Ann.

"I could walk you there."

"No! I'm not a jailbird!"

There was no budging Mary Ann when she got into a state like this.

"Okay, okay. I'll go," he said. "Do you want me to tell him anything special?"

Mary Ann broke down again. Clutching the ball of soggy tissue in her hand she rocked soundlessly on her chair, her head averted.

Robert started to leave right away. He thought there was no point sticking around if she was going to behave like this.

But even he felt a little sorry for her. He put his head back in under the front flap. "Stop crying, okay?" he said, in a more kindly tone.

◂ ◂ ◂

There was not much of a procedure involved in getting to see a prisoner in the Prohibition Creek jail. Right down the hall from the main office of the detachment, the cells were familiar to much of the male population of the town, since their most fundamental use was as a holding tank for drunks. The Dene elder employed by the RCMP to stay with the prisoners on Friday and Saturday nights was locally described as "the babysitter."

Robert was in one of the cells with Bobby. Across the way, in the other one, Ryan and his friend were entertaining themselves with a game of rummoli.

Robert had already laid the money out between them on the bare bench and watched Bobby stow it away in his pocket.

"I'm going to get myself another job pretty soon," he said. "So if there's anything you need, pal, you can just write home for it. Cigarettes, or anything like that."

He felt awkward and he was talking fast. Giving Bobby the money had been easy; it was understood between them that he would have to do that, and he expected no thanks for it. The rest of the interview was the hard part for Robert.

"My mother didn't come to court this morning," said Bobby. He spoke tonelessly.

Robert was quick to explain. "Yeah, but that was just because she can't stop crying. You know how she is."

"I didn't want to see you. I wanted to see her."

Robert thought of saying that he had tried to tell Mary Ann that.

But it might suggest that he himself hadn't wanted to come, and since this, in fact, was true, he remained silent.

"Is she all right?" Bobby asked unexpectedly.

"She's fine," replied Robert, startled.

"She's looking after my things? I mean, the things in my room?"

He seemed to have some extrasensory awareness of trouble, and Robert was again taken aback.

"She sure is!—I mean, yes, she is," he replied.

As a matter of fact, Bobby, like Robert before him, was acutely aware how much the fragile truce that was his parents' marriage depended upon him. And a portion of virtually every waking hour he had spent in jail so far had been devoted to worrying about what had become of that; and in particular, how his absence, and now his trial and conviction, affected his mother.

"You still playing cards?" he said. He had been holding on to the thought that his father would never give that up, and that therefore things must have remained the same.

"Sure," said Robert. "—I mean, no," he went on.

"You're not?" Bobby's voice rose suddenly on a note of panic.

The police constable Dave walked past the cell door.

"Police plane has landed," he remarked. "Time to finish up your talk, Robert."

Robert and Bobby both watched him as he walked back up the hall again. Then Robert said hurriedly, "Look, I didn't want to tell you now, but I guess I'm going to have to tell you sometime. Your mother threw me out after you were arrested last fall. So I'm not living in that house anymore." He was speaking almost in a whisper, as though it were a shameful thing, when in fact, as he realized, he was glad all that had happened.

"So I gave up playing cards." Robert forced himself to speak normally again and it sounded good, what he said, even to himself.

There was a look of fear on Bobby's face.

"Is my mother living with some other guy?" he demanded.

"What do you mean?" This idea had never occurred to Robert.

"Your mother wouldn't—"

"Or did you take off on her because of some girl?"

Robert began to protest. "I didn't take off on—"

Bobby had burst into angry tears. "You've got no right to change everything while I'm away!" he raged. "Everything's different and I didn't even know."

"Maybe it's better, though." Robert was very upset himself.

The cop had returned. He began unlocking the cell in a businesslike way.

"Time's up, you guys."

He put a hand under Robert's arm, and reluctantly Robert stood up. Bobby stood up too, crying openly.

"I just want to go home!"

"Come on, Robert," said Dave. "There's nothing more you can do here." He led Robert out and locked the cell behind him.

Bobby had taken up a stance beside the door, gripping the bars, his blubbery face pressed between them. He said to Robert, sobbing, "I want to go home, Dad."

Turning Robert around by again putting light pressure under his arm, the policeman propelled him down the corridor.

▲ ▲ ▲

Robert had no idea how he got out of the detachment. He was not fully conscious until he was some way down the road, walking along toward Mary Ann's house, or rather, tent, in the cold crunchy snow.

Talking to Bobby had been even worse than he had feared.

The thing he was remembering about the interview now was that Bobby had called him Dad. Bobby had given up "Dad" a few years past, replacing it by calling Robert nothing. Now he was calling him Dad again. "I want to go home, Dad"—that was what he had said.

Mary Ann stepped out of the tent before Robert was on the first step of the porch. She looked at him anxiously as he came up, then preceded him into the tent.

"Well, I saw him," said Robert, wondering what he was going to say to her.

They were standing a few feet apart, Robert just inside the door.

"He was okay. Maybe a little thinner."

"What did he say?" she asked.

"He said he wanted to come home." Robert tried to keep his voice level as he told her this.

Mary Ann nodded. "You see?" she said. "I was right to stay in my house."

He had said something else that Robert recalled being puzzled about at the time.

"He wondered if you were living with somebody else. Why was he wondering about that?"

Bobby, of course, was aware of his father's record of infidelity, even though most of that had occurred some years before; it had started when Bobby was an infant and come to an end when he entered his difficult teenage years. But Robert was amazed by his son's suspicion of his mother. Mary Ann had never had another man—or so he had thought up till today.

Mary Ann was looking at him, an expression of outraged surprise on her face. But Robert still wasn't sure, even when he saw her expression. He had used that expression himself in the past; it only worked the first time, he knew. It faded from her face and was replaced by a look of pure malevolence.

"You should have told him about you and your girlfriend," she said.

"Look, Mary Ann—" There was no point pretending now that he didn't know who she was talking about. "She's not my girlfriend."

"Not anymore," agreed Mary Ann. She sat down in a chair and looked up at him, folding her arms.

Robert was looking around. It was really impossible that Mary Ann could be sharing this tiny space with another man. Not without some sign of his presence, at least. And besides, he would have heard all about it from Haga.

"What do you mean?" He did a double take all of a sudden.

"Now she's screwing someone else. That's what Sarah says. She came back from Yellowknife with her baby yesterday. And she's telling everybody."

Scraping her chair around to turn her back on him, Mary Ann took up the unfinished side of the pair of uppers from the table, and sewed down a blue bead on the trim around the edge. Then, as Robert watched angrily, she sewed a red bead, then another blue, then a red—

▲ ▲ ▲

The police plane was gone and it was already dark, but for some reason, Robert hadn't felt like going home to the shack. For one thing, Haga might know some gossip about Rebecca. And for another, he might not. Robert was finding it hard to choose which alternative he would prefer. In any case, he would have to ask; and that was a distasteful thought, even though he knew that he would ask, just as soon as he saw Haga again.

He went to his mother's house and found Elvis there watching a soap opera in the living room. His mother had gone to the store, leaving instructions that he was to watch this program closely and tell her everything that had happened when she got back. Robert was still rather touched by the indications of love and trust between Elvis and his mother and he noticed that Elvis was watching faithfully on her behalf.

"I don't know why people like watching these TV soap operas, Elvis," commented Robert. "They're just about a bunch of rich whitemen having abortions and getting divorced."

It was a comfortable room they were in, well furnished in overstuffed sofa and chairs, store-bought coffee table, end tables and lamps, the Last Supper of Leonardo done in plush tapestry hanging on the wall. Rachel was Dene and therefore not an acquisitive person, and she had been used to poverty all her life, but her daughters, who were grown up and well off, had given her all these things.

"I mean, why do you want to know all that gossip about people who aren't even real?" Robert asked.

Elvis shrugged. "Me, I like *Star Trek*," he said. "Yesterday those Americans turned into devils. They were poisoned by a medicine man with a ray gun."

Robert really liked the way Elvis was telling this.

"A beautiful woman devil was in love with that captain. She put a mask on his eyes and that mask gave him power."

"So what happened?" asked Robert.

"The captain had power from the mask. So he was able to kill the medicine man. He killed that beautiful woman devil too."

A beautiful woman devil sounded good to Robert. "Did he have sex with her?" he asked. "I mean, before he killed her?"

"I think he did."

Robert nodded. He could see why anyone would want to watch a thing like that. Especially someone like Elvis, into whose world view the whole story fit perfectly.

The door into the kitchen banged open and Danny's little girl, Jamaica, ran into the room.

"Come see the baby!" she cried.

"Hi, Jamaica," said Robert. "What baby?"

Even though Danny was not speaking to Rachel, his children were still on terms of perfect freedom and intimacy with her. They ran in and out of her house all day, and this was a normal thing for them to do; Rachel would never have included them in any dissension between herself and their father.

"Sarah brought her new baby over," said Jamaica. "Come see, Elvis. They're in the kitchen."

Elvis looked up, but he was still under orders to find out what was going to happen on Rachel's soap opera. So instead it was Robert who went out into the kitchen.

Jamaica was hanging over the baby, cooing. Sarah had taken it out of the babystrap and set it down on the table. Robert went over to look too.

"Nice-looking baby," he said to his sister-in-law.

Sarah merely nodded, continuing to unwrap herself from her thick winter clothes.

"Lucky we had the airstrip ploughed at Christmas," he continued. "I heard you had to go out in kind of a hurry."

She nodded again, then went to the stove to get herself some tea.

"Where's Rachel?"

"Grandma went to the store," said Jamaica, nursing the baby in her arms.

"I want her to look after the baby tonight." Sarah spoke abruptly.

She was dumping the baby on the grandmother so that she could go to bingo. There was nothing unusual in that, but Robert found himself, oddly, a little indignant with her for it.

"Jamaica, take Crystal in the other room," Sarah ordered.

"Okay," said Jamaica. "I'll show her to Elvis."

Robert now heard the theme music of *Star Trek* filtering in from the living room, and he inferred that this was what Elvis had been waiting for.

"What's that old man doing here?" asked Sarah. She leaned against the counter with her teacup.

Robert shrugged. He was not going to discuss Elvis and his mother with his sister-in-law. She was attempting to pry into his opinion about that.

"You know that's why Danny isn't talking to Rachel. Because of that old man in the other room. The one she's sleeping with." Sarah was watching him closely, still trying to figure out what he thought.

He looked at her without expression; it was easy to do that when you had good cards in your hand.

"Well, I just think it's funny Danny's mad about that," said Sarah. She did not believe that Robert was as calm, cool and collected about his mother and the old man in the other room as he made out, but she also knew something else—and she was sure it was something he wasn't cool about at all. A malicious expression now crossed her face. She went on, "When you think what Danny's been up to himself."

"I guess that's his business, whatever it is," said Robert.

"Come on, Robert. Don't pretend you don't know what I'm talking about." Sarah was very pleased with herself.

"I wasn't pretending." But unfortunately, he was pretending this time. Those good cards hadn't held him for very long.

"You said you liked that girl. You even told me that you like her." Sarah was triumphant.

"Are you talking about Rebecca?" Helplessly, Robert heard himself asking this.

Rebecca and Danny? He didn't want to hear about this. But undoubtedly he had come out into the kitchen to hear it.

180

"Yes! Rebecca's carrying on with Danny now. You used to like her yourself, didn't you?"

"Look, last month you told everybody that Rebecca was carrying on with me. This month it's Danny. But she wasn't carrying on with me. And I don't believe she's carrying on with Danny either." But he felt he was grasping at straws.

"She is! I heard all about it in Yellowknife last week. Everything. Her Dad threw her out of the house. Wouldn't even let her stay there. And she stayed in Danny's room at the Yellowknife Inn."

Robert remembered that Sarah had heard this story while she was still in the hospital, having a baby. There was no defence against people like this.

"That's not all. Did you know she was married and has two kids? She never told us that. She pretended she didn't have any kids."

"Well, I knew about that," said Robert suddenly. "Maybe she just didn't tell you for some reason."

"But did she tell you she's not allowed to have them? Her husband has a court order?"

"Boy, she must be bad," said Robert.

Sarah detected no irony. "Sleeping with all those men—her father kicked her out—and she doesn't even take care of her own kids!"

Robert was looking at Sarah. It now seemed to him a surprising fact that he had wanted to sleep with her at one time; she had been pretty as a girl and he was only about ten years older. But she had lost her looks during the years she had been married to his brother Michael, and it was during these years that she had made it clear, on more than one occasion, that she would be willing to sleep with him.

Sarah's eyes dropped under his gaze; she became flustered and turned away. She knew—she very well remembered what he was thinking about.

"Sarah." Rachel entered the kitchen from the porch and greeted her daughter-in-law with her usual economy of expression.

"I brought you the baby," said Sarah. She was already putting on her parka.

"Again?" Rachel raised her eyebrows.

"I'm going to bingo tonight." She went to the door.

Robert stood against a counter as she left, his arms folded, his head bent. It was an attitude of profound thought, although he was not in fact thinking.

Rachel put her bag of groceries down on the table. She sighed, then went over to hang up her parka.

"First she brings the baby," she remarked. "Then the little ones come over later."

Neither Robert nor his mother bothered to wonder why Michael wasn't babysitting. He had been drinking for several weeks now, so if he was at home he was probably asleep. However, this knowledge added itself to the despair that each of them presently felt.

Jamaica appeared in the interior doorway. "Come play with the baby, Grandma."

"In a minute."

The little girl went over and began helping her grandmother to put away the food in her bag. Rachel offered her a mandarin orange and she sat down on a chair, her legs dangling, to peel it.

"Elvis and I were watching *Star Trek*. That woman doctor made everyone sick." She spoke confidentially to the two of them.

"Doctors make people well, Jamaica," said Rachel.

"That's not what Elvis says. He says no one was ever sick around here till doctors came into the country." She finished peeling the orange and divided it into three parts with scrupulous fairness.

"It wasn't because of the doctors." Rachel took the sections of orange the little girl offered her, looked at them for a moment and then gave them back.

"He says it was," replied Jamaica. "He thinks the woman doctor was mad because of what the captain did last week with that devil woman. What was that, Grandma? Elvis wouldn't tell me."

Rachel stood looking at her for a moment with great fondness. Jamaica was a kind of star among all her grandchildren, smart and quick and pretty, like her own memories of herself as she had been when she was the petted favourite of the nuns. Then an abstracted and slightly sad expression crossed her face as she thought of Jamaica's father.

"You should go home to supper now," she said to the child.

"Does suppertime come before bedtime or after?" Robert asked Jamaica, and she laughed.

"We don't have bedtime now, Robert," she said. "Daddy's always working."

"Aren't you hungry?" asked Rachel.

"Mummy was crying last night," Jamaica replied with great simplicity. "Then she went to bingo. So we didn't have supper either."

The baby in the other room began to cry loudly. Rachel—still looking at this child, but beginning to think about the other—made a noise indicative of hurry and exasperation.

"Better go in there, Ama," said Robert. "I'll help Jamaica get dressed up to go out."

Rachel went into the other room. Robert helped Jamaica put on her mukluks and zip up her parka. Then he too put the orange sections she had given him back into her hand. Like his mother, like Haga, Robert regarded fruit as a treat for children.

The baby in the other room was still crying loudly. It sounded as though Elvis was watching the world news hour now. Robert diverted himself momentarily by wondering what Elvis made of the international situation.

Unfortunately, as Jamaica was gone, he was now alone with his thoughts.

Robert went into the living room. The baby was quiet now. Rachel sat bending over it at end of the sofa, holding a bottle in its mouth. Elvis had turned down the TV and was sitting on the floor, helpfully watching. Wiry and skinny, in a flannel shirt and jeans, he looked a little out of place between the plush sofa and the department store coffee table.

He was one of those people who always had a job. He could have been a trapper, for he had the traditional skills required, but instead he had worked all his life in wage employment, going up as far as the Delta and along the Arctic coast on the DEW line in the fifties. Since then he had worked for the oil exploration companies out of town almost every winter. Presently, however, he had a job as a carpenter with Housing.

"Elvis, I've got something to ask you," said Robert. Robert felt that Elvis would understand the need he felt right now to get away from here and go to work.

Elvis looked up.

"Mind lending me your skidoo? I'm going to the Forks to get a job."

"No problem," said Elvis.

"I thought I'd go to work for Sasquatch. I figure they'll take me sooner or later. Even if I have to hang around for awhile. Somebody'll quit."

Elvis nodded.

"Well, you know what they say: an Indian can never keep a job," said Robert, laughing.

Elvis was still looking at him attentively. After a moment he stood up and stretched.

"Don't take Haga," he advised solemnly.

◂ ◂ ◂

Robert roared away to the shack on Elvis's skidoo, intending to pick up his stuff: his bedroll, coveralls, some extra clothing.

Haga was lying on the bottom bunk, and he preserved a moody silence as Robert came in. He had made soup for supper and Robert had not showed up. He was thinking now that it served him right if it was cold. Robert would just have to heat it up himself, if he wanted any.

Suddenly he noticed that Robert was packing his things. Alarmed, he jumped up off his bed. "Where are you going?" he demanded.

"I'm going to go get myself a job in the Forks."

Robert was irritable. He felt that Haga was acting like a woman, sulking because he was late coming home, bothering him with questions.

To his fury, Haga now began to act even more like a woman. He looked at Robert slyly and remarked, "I guess somebody must have told you something."

Robert was finished with the sleeping bag. He began to drag his coveralls on up over his mukluks and the legs of his jeans.

"Well, I guess it's what everybody is talking about," said Haga.

Robert stopped with the coveralls halfway up and turned around slowly.

"Look, I've been thinking about getting a job. So now I'm going to go get a job. Okay?"

"Oh. Okay." Haga was taken aback.

"All right then. Fine." Robert looked about him. There was nothing else he had to take.

Haga started to roll up his sleeping bag.

"Hey! What the heck are you doing?" asked Robert.

"Getting ready to go," said Haga.

"Look, Haga. You can't come."

"You're my partner," said Haga.

"Yeah. But I'm going to get a job," said Robert. "This is going to be work."

"I'm not too old." Haga was hurt. He was no longer just playing games. Robert didn't see how to cope with this.

But he knew very well that if Haga came this was going to be a tough plan to execute. For one thing, they might not be able to get jobs, the two of them together. Even if they did, he really wasn't sure that Haga could do a job: he was too eccentric for regular work, and the bosses would be whitemen, they wouldn't understand Haga at all.

Haga was even more hurt than before. He sat on his rolled-up sleeping bag looking at Robert with a hurt expression.

"Well, what the heck! Come if you want," said Robert.

"Okay! That's my partner!" Haga jumped up and began to get on with his packing. He didn't have much to pack.

Robert noticed that he was taking the billy.

"Look, they do all the cooking," said Robert, plucking it out of the bag.

One thing about these drill site jobs was that the food was usually pretty good. It was whiteman's food, however: plenty of steak and chops, but also things in the fruit and vegetable line that even Robert had never run across before.

"Ever see a pineapple, Haga?" he asked.

"No. What's that?"

Robert was hard pressed to describe a pineapple. It was one of nature's mistakes, in his opinion. Surprising Haga was certainly a legitimate use that it might have.

"You know, this might be all right—taking you," he said with a laugh.

They turned in the doorway to take one more look at their dark little home. Then Haga blew out the single candle and they were off, roaring away to the Forks on Elvis's skidoo, to make money and get away from it all in the big world outside.

▲ ▲ ▲

Rebecca was in her trailer, talking to herself.

"He said he loved me. But that was in Yellowknife."

Her place was neat and tidy; lately all she did was clean house. At first she had done that hoping that Danny would come over, but now it was to fill in time. She had nothing to do otherwise but brood. For she was angry.

Since they had got off the plane she hadn't seen him, and she had been wondering what he was doing. But she thought she knew what he was doing: pretending it had never happened.

After New Year's she had started trying to do her job again. She had opened up her office; she had even gone to the drop-in centre several times, managing to be there when Danny was not.

She was making an effort to let this thing be the way Danny wanted it. She could even see why he wanted it that way. Of course he couldn't leave his wife and children for her. Danny would never do that. And so, for him, their short love affair in Yellowknife was something, like that kiss last fall, that they were both going to have to forget.

But her psyche had received a severe bruising because Danny now knew all about her. She had told him everything she had longed to tell him before: about her bad relationship with her father, her husband, her kids, her entire history. And he had been her lover; she had expected some kind of help and comfort from him, a cup, not just a drop, of kindness.

She believed that there was something between them that he couldn't handle. Perhaps it was her own recklessness; it was something she was afraid of in herself. She had made him kiss her last fall; she had gone to his hotel room and made him seduce her at Christmas. He was probably afraid of her now, afraid of what she could do to destroy him.

Since they had come back he had not come near her.

The whole village knew that Danny and Rebecca had slept in the same hotel room for a whole week when they stayed in Yellowknife. The whole village also knew that Rebecca's father had thrown her out of his house, and that she had had two kids with her husband, a whiteman, who had taken custody of them away from her.

Rebecca had met the story at the drop-in centre, at the co-op, and in her own office from a couple of welfare recipients. Even the police corporal had made a comment. The counselling program, which she had just resumed, was ruined; no one showed up for appointments any longer.

Everyone in this place thought she was bad. Even Rebecca thought that she was bad, that she had made Danny do it.

Now that her crying phase was over, she had lapsed into dull despondency. It wasn't clear that she could continue in her job any longer if she had lost the confidence of the people in the village. And Danny must hate her now.

"If only I had somebody to talk to!" cried Rebecca out loud.

She went over and stood under the sand picture and stared up at it, hoping to find some comfort in its blandness.

• 13 • A FRIEND IN NEED •

It was a bitterly cold night. The piercing stars lit up the snow and the strange cold bars of the aurora borealis rolled in waves across the sky.

Haga and Robert had just come back home from the Forks.

They were unpacking and the shack was heating up from a good fire in the stove. They still had the stump of the candle to see by; the billy was coming to a boil. But neither of them was much inclined to make the best of things.

"God, I'm stiff all over." Robert sat on Haga's bed, his arms and his head hanging down. His upper body felt as though it were black and blue, he had bruises on his face too, and one of his knees was malfunctioning. All of this came from the fist fight in the bunkhouse, but the jolting skidoo ride back home over the trail from the Forks had been a nightmare too.

"Well, I don't feel too good either," Haga said defensively.

"What a great way to get fired," said Robert.

They had been lucky to get out of the job site so quickly, for it was way north, almost in the mountains. The DC-3 that took them in there with supplies had departed, but after the bunkhouse brawl that occurred the first night, another smaller plane had turned up the following day and taken them back to the Forks. The company had probably paid extra to get rid of them that way.

"I'm just glad to be home," Haga said.

They had only been away three days.

There was a sound at the door, as though somebody was knocking.

Robert and Haga both looked up—Robert in surprise, Haga in fright. It was well after midnight.

"Don't answer it, Robert. It could be a bushman."

"If it was a bushman do you really think he'd knock?"

They both heard the sound of a woman's voice outside calling, "Robert! Robert!"

"It's a ghost!" Haga was now wildly alarmed.

Robert got up and opened the door.

"Thank God you're here, Robert," cried Rebecca. She was standing outside on the doorstep in a cloud of ice fog.

Robert grabbed her arm to pull her in, then quickly slammed the door against the bitter weather.

"I had to come." Her face was wet from the melting frost of her hood fur—or else with tears.

"I couldn't stay home. There's nowhere else I can go anymore."

He had so nearly not been here, Robert realized. It was one of those things that happen in life, as in cards, that you might call luck.

She threw back her hood and took off her mitts.

Haga, meanwhile, was pulling on his socks and boots, grumbling away to himself.

"Hey, Haga," said Robert. "It's just Rebecca."

Haga now donned his parka.

"Okay, okay. She isn't a ghost," he agreed. "But I'm not staying here with a woman either."

He went out, slamming the door definitively.

Robert laughed. "Well, I guess he'll just have to find someplace to sleep where there aren't any ghosts or women," he remarked.

Rebecca still stood by the door. She was not saying anything now.

Robert thought she might be horrified by the barrenness of their living quarters. He had noticed it himself when they got back. The walls were just plywood with the studs exposed, and the floor was also wooden. It was a small dark room, cold and bare; the only domestic touches had been the sleeping bags, still rolled up on the bunks, and what they carried in their packs.

The billy had boiled at last and he went over to the stove to make tea.

"So what's the matter?" he asked, keeping it casual.

"Oh, Robert, I'm in so much trouble –" She followed him over to the stove now, unzipping her parka. "Robert!" she said suddenly, in concern. "What happened to your face? Do you have a black eye?"

"Yeah," he said. As a matter of fact he had two black eyes, but she was only looking at one of them, the one closest to her.

"Where did you get that? You should be putting something on it," she said.

"We were on a job," said Robert, trying to explain the important facts first. "We just got back here a little while ago."

"Does it hurt? Let me look." He turned toward her now and she saw his other eye.

"Ouch!" said Robert, in involuntary response to the expression on her face.

"You have a cut lip too."

"I know," he said.

"I'm going to make the tea," said Rebecca, suddenly taking charge.

Robert sat down while she used one of her mitts to take the billy off the stove. She set it down on the table and put in the two tea bags he had laid out there. Then she peered into the tin mug and the glass they had found in the woods and decided they were clean enough. There was even some sugar left in the bag. She poured out the tea.

"Masi," said Robert.

"Were you fighting?" she asked. "That doesn't seem like you, Robert."

"We got a job with Sasquatch," he replied. "The first night some guy in the bunkhouse started picking on Haga. Then Haga threw a punch at him, and the whole crowd of them piled on him at once. I didn't think that was fair."

"Well, it wasn't," agreed Rebecca.

"So after that, we both got fired," he concluded.

"That wasn't fair either!" she exclaimed.

"Well, you know what they say about an Indian: he just can't keep a job," said Robert with a laugh.

Rebecca looked at him gravely. But after a moment she smiled. She had come a long way out of her misery, sitting here with him.

Unlike Robert, she was getting a sense of security just from being here in the little shack. She was sustained, even borne up by the circle of light cast by the candle, the cheerful warmth of the stove, the taste of the hot sweet tea in her mouth, and even more, by the sound of another person's voice, speaking to her.

It seemed as though she had emerged out of weeks of near insanity and suddenly become herself again, making tea, talking to Robert.

"So why'd you come out here in the middle of the night?" he asked, casual again. "It's pretty cold out there."

"I just had to talk to somebody." She bit her lip. " I was going crazy at home. And it wasn't just cold—I'm afraid of bushmen too –"

She laughed nervously. "Now I don't want to tell you."

She had really almost forgotten that this was the point of her being here.

"I know what it is anyway," said Robert quickly. He stood up with his teacup. "Well, I think I do."

"The whole town knows, don't they?" Rebecca spoke dully.

"I guess so," he said. "But maybe you'd better tell me what really happened."

She nodded, looking at him sadly.

It had all started when Danny and Rebecca went to the workshop in Yellowknife. They had arrived in the airport about noon, shared a taxi into town and thereafter parted company, for Danny was staying in the Yellowknife Inn with the other delegates to the workshop.

"I went home," she said. "My dad wasn't there, but I saw my mother and one of my sisters."

Elijah McCrae lived out at the end of the Yellowknife islands, in the house next to the Pentecostal mission.

"After that I took a taxi and went to see my—my husband and my kids," she went on.

They were living in a high-rise uptown.

At first her husband wouldn't let her in the door. But she had pleaded with him, and he almost had to let her in; the noise in the hall was attracting attention.

The children were crouching, petrified, on the far end of the sofa. Rebecca sat down on the floor; she got out the presents she had brought them: a beaded belt for Peter, her son, and a Raggedy Ann doll for Megan, her little girl. But they wouldn't take them, they wouldn't even reach out to touch them when she unwrapped them herself, and all the time their eyes rolled in the direction of Mike, her husband.

He had turned them against her; he made no attempt to keep the facts of their history with her away from them. Neither of them could really remember the time when she had had custody; she had been away in Fort Smith at Thebacha for three years. Before that, when she was going through detox, or trying to get through it, Mike had gone to court and taken them away.

"See," said Mike sarcastically. "Mummy brought you some nice presents. She's going to go away now," he added.

He hated Rebecca; he had reasons to hate her, for she had destroyed his life too, not merely her own. She had made him miserable after they got married, partying and sleeping around. Then she had become a drunk and made him pay for her habit, prying money out of him, stealing it when she couldn't get it any other way. And she had had these two children, whom, as far as he was concerned, she had never loved; she had parked them with him, deserted them, and now they were entirely his, as he saw it.

Mike worked underground in the gold mines, and with his two children he had to maintain this expensive apartment, which cost him half his salary, plus pay for daycare. Rebecca had never contributed a cent until lately. When he received her letter he had torn up the cheque and sent it back. The only thing he had now was the children and he was determined that she was never going to get them back, no matter what she did. He loved them; he loved them even more when he thought that he was all they had.

After a while she left. She went out into Yellowknife on Friday night, and wandered around for some time, going into the bars and seeing people she knew, but not sitting down with them, just vaguely flirting with disaster, while her mind worried at the problem. Would she ever be able to get them away from Mike long enough for them to see that she wasn't the way he depicted her? Would she ever be able to create a home of her own in which they could live, at least part of the time, and get to know her?

Finally Rebecca went home. She had lost track of time. It was after midnight when she started down the hill, nearly closing time for the bars, and as she couldn't get a taxi, she walked. A drunk came stumbling out of the alleyway leading to the old Hall of Fame. He almost bumped into her, sloshing a cup of whiskey down the front of her parka. Then he grabbed her shoulders.

"Rebecca?" he cried drunkenly. "How ya been?"

"You knew him?" said Robert in surprise.

"I don't remember. He was someone from Rae, I think. I used to know everyone," Rebecca said defensively.

Shuddering, she disengaged herself and walked on her way. He tried to follow, but he was too drunk. He fell down in the road on a patch of ice.

"And then when I got home, my dad was waiting up for me."

"Was he mad at you or something?"

"No. But he got mad when he saw the way I looked." There was some sort of plastic string in her hair; at one of the bars she had been in they had been spraying the stuff around. And when he smelled the whiskey that had been spilled on her coat, he turned her out of doors. He didn't rant at her, he didn't pray, at least not while she was still present. He merely turned her around and marched her out the front door, and a moment later she heard the lock click.

Rebecca arrived back at the Yellowknife Inn around 1:00 A.M. Her walk back up the hill had taken her a long time and she was freezing, as well as semi-hysterical. She got Danny's room number from the desk clerk and went straight up there.

"So then—that happened," she said and fell silent.

Robert had been listening intently. His amour-propre was somewhat soothed by the fact that she had applied to him for help. Although he had not been admitting it to himself, jealousy was predominant among the emotions he had been experiencing when he first heard the gossip about Rebecca. It was not that he was any kind of a man for Rebecca, as he told himself—but he certainly didn't want his brother Danny to have her.

However, he had not thought—or, at least, he had not thought up till now—that having an affair with Danny was something that could have hurt her. But it seemed, from her reluctance to talk about it, that it had. Robert had never really believed that women had much of a conscious existence at all. He was learning differently from Rebecca.

"Did you think you were in love with him?" He was almost afraid to ask.

"I don't know," she said slowly. "Perhaps I did. But now I think I was just—trying to make myself feel better. By getting someone to want me." She was still groping her way toward some understanding of what had happened. At first it had seemed, because of what she had done, that she must be in love with Danny.

"You must think I'm bad," she said.

"You're bad?" said Robert, coming to grips with this instantly. "What about him? He was sleeping with you and he's got a wife and kids."

"But it was my fault," she said. "I made him do it."

She had known that Danny was trying to stay away from her, ever since that kiss in the fall. She had gone up to his room, and when he answered her knock on the door, she had thrown herself into his arms, she had pressed her lips against his. She had known what she was going to do beforehand; it was a crime of intent.

"You made him do it?" said Robert. "You couldn't have made him do anything."

Ordinarily he might have been willing to swallow a tale of seduction. But in this case, strangely enough, he was completely on Rebecca's side, and he saw that there was more to it than that.

"He has a lot of problems too. He's a very complex person," she said.

"He's complex, but you're bad, is that it?" Robert was feeling much more cheerful now that he knew Rebecca wasn't in love with Danny.

"His wife doesn't understand him." Rebecca was even afraid of Roseanne now.

"His wife doesn't understand him? Did he tell you that?" Robert seized upon this joyously. "That's the oldest line in the book. You didn't fall for that one, did you? I mean, his wife doesn't understand him! Look, my wife doesn't understand me either, but—Feed 'em fish!" he added.

Rebecca was silent. She knew Robert was trying to ensnare her in one of his tricky arguments.

"Did he tell you that?" he demanded again.

She nodded. He had, as a matter of fact. They had ended up discussing Danny's marriage, in the bed of that hotel room, far more than any of Rebecca's problems.

"But I think it's true," she said.

"Well, it's one thing for it to be true and it's another thing for him to tell you. I mean, think about it. What if I said something like that? Wouldn't you think I was just trying to get you into bed?" He was triumphant.

"No," said Rebecca.

"What? Of course that's what I'd be trying to do!"

"But Robert, you just said it yourself." Rebecca had a very good memory. "You just said your wife didn't understand you a minute ago."

"I did?" Robert was ambushed. He paused, thinking. "Oh yeah—well, I guess I did," he said.

Suddenly Rebecca laughed. A charming wrinkle appeared high up on either side of her nose when she laughed. If they had been debating the point she would have won.

But to Rebecca it was not really a debating point. She knew—she remembered that she had been in desperate straits when she went to Danny's room. And it was true that he had not helped her—he had not helped her at all. His guilt had so consumed him that he had only wanted to blame his wife.

She was feeling angry at Danny, because he had dumped her; he had left her worse off than before. But now she also realized that he had been completely self-absorbed right from the beginning of their affair.

Robert, meanwhile, was having a different thought. After a short silence he remarked, "So maybe I'm not the kind of man you can trust either."

"I trust you, Robert," she said.

But he was not sure he was entirely happy about this. It was strange to sit across a table arguing with a woman when she wasn't mad at you, to have her say "I trust you" when you had never made love to her.

"That's why I came out here," she was explaining. "I had to tell someone what happened. Someone who would try to understand. And—who would contradict me when I said I was bad!"

They both laughed. Then he yawned.

"You must be tired if you came all the way from the Forks tonight," she said. "Does it hurt anywhere else? Besides your face?"

As a matter of fact he hurt all over.

Rebecca yawned too.

"Could I stay overnight?" she asked. "I don't want to go home."

Again, he was taken aback. But he was pretty sure this had no hidden meaning. She wasn't asking him to sleep with her.

Somehow that seemed wrong as well, however. Shouldn't she at least expect him to want to?

"I know you won't tell anyone," she said. "Besides, my reputation couldn't get any worse than it is now."

Robert didn't answer. He had a lot of mixed feelings.

Rebecca got up from the table and wandered over to the bunk beds.

"Is this Haga's bed? The bottom one?"

But Robert was struck by a sudden determination that she was not going to sleep in Haga's sleeping bag.

He jumped up from the table too, before she could sit down, pulled Haga's bedroll off the bottom bunk and bundled it up on top. Then he pulled down his own sleeping bag and opened it up to arrange it on the bottom.

"What are you doing?" Rebecca was watching this curious manoeuvre in perplexity.

"It's just that—if you're going to sleep here—you're going to have—my blanket," said Robert, panting.

"Does Haga have fleas or something?"

Robert finished laying out the sleeping bag, unzipped it, fluffed up the pillow. "There," he said.

The candle was burning low, but at least there was plenty of wood. Robert went to dump three or four big chunks into the stove, then adjusted the draft to his satisfaction.

Rebecca had shed her parka already. She sat down on the lower bunk to remove her mukluks.

"I'll just take off some of these clothes before I get in," she remarked cheerfully. She was taking off her sweater.

Robert hesitated, then climbed into the top bunk, groaning because of his bruises, his knee.

"Poor Robert," said Rebecca down below.

Her nonchalance was making him question his own self-respect.

He had been attractive to women, plenty of women; he was still attractive to women, surely? Rebecca seemed to have forgotten that he was a man.

He had neglected to blow out the candle, and he began arduously to climb down over the end of the top bunk again.

Rebecca remarked, "I'd better blow out the candle." She got up to do it, and Robert sank back against Haga's pillow with another groan.

They were in the dark together. Robert lying still above, could feel her barest movements down below. She had pulled the blanket up; she rolled on her side and snuggled down, doubling the pillow under her cheek.

Then she laughed.

"This is a very strange way to go to bed with a man," she said.

◆ ◆ ◆

Right after he woke up Robert had gone out to chop wood. He came in the door with an armload, dumped it in the wood box and opened the stove door. Rebecca was still in bed, but she sat up, stretching and yawning.

"Good morning, Robert."

He turned around and they smiled at one another shyly.

"I was asleep," she said in surprise.

"I know." She had not woken up when he crawled down out of the upper bunk, when he made up the fire, nor when he had come in before with a pail of snow to melt on the stove.

"It's unbelievable." She stretched again luxuriously. "I haven't slept at all for days. I just stayed at home all the time, crying and well— eating." She laughed. "I must be getting fat."

Robert was finding it strange to contemplate a woman whom he hadn't slept with waking up in his sleeping bag.

"I was afraid to go out, really," she continued. "Roseanne—and that Sarah—are even getting up a petition against me."

He hadn't slept with her, but on the other hand, he was feeling good about that. The phenomenon to which she had alluded last night when she said that she had thought she was in love with Danny after they had gone to bed together was very familiar to

Robert. He had noticed that this frequently happened to the women he had gone to bed with. He knew that Rebecca was already confused and unhappy, and he had the virtuous sense that he was making her feel better, not worse.

She had mentioned eating. But there was no food in the house. Robert put some water in the billy. "At least we could have tea," he remarked.

He fed a handful of little sticks into the stove and the fire began to crackle.

Rebecca was still in bed, lying against his pillow.

"This is a nice place, Robert. I didn't know it was like this out here."

Robert looked around in surprise. But in daylight, with a good fire going and the beds made up again, it didn't look too bad to him either.

"I wasn't expecting this. Everybody thinks—" She laughed.

In town, the fish store shack was thought to be a veritable den of iniquity. Robert and Haga were supposed to be out there drinking patent medicine and making homebrew, sleeping anytime they pleased, without a darned pair of socks or a clean shirt to their names. It was a good example of what could happen to a man if he left his wife, as the wives frequently remarked.

"What everybody thinks is usually a lot worse than the way anything is," Robert remarked.

Rebecca was looking at him thoughtfully. It was strange that he had ended up living this way, when he was so smart, so good-looking, apparently so sure of himself.

She suddenly began getting out of bed in a hurry. Robert started to turn away, but then he saw that she was wearing a lot of clothes, a T-shirt, jeans, even her white socks.

"Your face!" she was saying. "I wasn't thinking at all last night. We should have been putting snow on your black eyes."

"They're only black eyes. They'll go away by themselves," he protested.

"No! I'm going to get some snow."

She pulled on her mukluks and went out the door.

It now seemed to Robert as if he had dreamed all this sometime, and perhaps was still dreaming. Rebecca here, getting snow for his eye: it had all the absurdity and lack of sequence of a dream, without surrendering thereby any of the conviction of reality.

Rebecca came back in.

"Here. I made a snowball."

He appeared to be there in the shack, seeing the usual things around him. The snowball was cold, and he felt the warmth of the stove, the wooden floor under his feet. He heard her voice, talking to him—

There was no way you could discern waking reality from dreams, at least, not while you were having them. He knew this from the dream he had had about her before.

"Here. Sit down. I'm going to pour the tea." She was already busy doing so.

"Masi," he said automatically.

Rebecca sat down or appeared to sit down, and Robert took, or thought he took, a sip of tea.

"Is anything the matter, Robert?"

"This just seems kind of unreal, that's all."

But surely he could never have dreamed up the messy snowball he was holding in his right hand, that was melting all down the front of his shirt.

"I know what you mean," said Rebecca. She was smiling at him, her cheek in her palm, her face flushed from the warmth of the stove. "It seems unreal to me too—sitting here with you in the morning. Almost as if we were a married couple."

She was slightly embarrassed to have said this. He might take this the wrong way.

"Of course, I didn't mean—because, well, we didn't, did we? But still—"

He probably couldn't have slept with her anyway, he was thinking, what with the condition he was in last night. The way he was feeling right now, however, was an entirely different proposition.

He certainly could, but he wasn't going to.

"I slept all night," she was saying.

"You look good," agreed Robert. Seeing her the way she was, with her eyes clear after her long sleep, the pure oval of her face, the delicate flush of her cheeks, he was really thinking that she was beautiful.

"I mean," he corrected himself, "you look as if you slept pretty well."

"I felt safe."

"Well, you're with me." He had the good feeling that he was protecting her.

But again he had to change this. "I mean, there's nothing to be afraid of."

She jumped up and went over to the window. Standing there, she tried to make a little hole to peep out through the frost flowers and the thick rime, blowing on the pane and rubbing away at it with her fingers.

"I decided something before I went to sleep," she said.

She turned around and Robert looked at her interrogatively.

"I decided I was going to quit my job."

This was not what he wanted her to decide at all.

"But what will you do then?" he demanded. "Will you go back to Yellowknife?"

"Oh, I don't know!" she said. "But it will be better than staying here." She made a little gesture as though she were flinging the whole problem away from her.

"I don't think you ought to."

"But they've even got a petition up against me. To get me fired."

"Think anyone's going to fire you for sleeping with somebody? That's your personal affair. They can't fire you for that."

She came back now and sat down, as she had been sitting before, across the table from him, resting her head on her elbow. "Are you going to argue with me, Robert?" she said.

But Robert was too upset to respond playfully.

"Okay, you're unhappy here. But how is it going to be there? That's why you ended up sleeping with Danny, isn't it? Your Dad, your kids."

She had her eyes cast down toward the tabletop, listening to what he was saying. She nodded mutely.

"Besides," he went on, "you were doing something good here."

Rebecca looked up in surprise.

"I think Danny's doing something good here too. Even if I don't like the way he's doing it," said Robert. He was rather surprised to hear himself saying this, even more surprised to realize that it was true.

"But now I can't do anything," she said. "And he can't either. I spoiled it for him. It would be better if I went away, wouldn't it? Maybe people would forget all that if I wasn't here."

She was talking like a whiteman, in his opinion. She thought she could get away. Robert knew that when a whiteman came up north and screwed-up, he just thought, "Well, so what? I can go somewhere and start over."

But with Dene people it was different. They couldn't get away; there was no other place for them to go. And no one was going to forget either. The whole Dene Nation was only a few thousand people, all of them related somehow. Whatever you did, everyone knew, or would find out, sooner or later.

"How can I do my job if people won't even speak to me? I was going to get Roseanne to start a nursery school next summer. But now she probably wants to kill me." Rebecca was arguing a little, almost in an idle spirit. She had finally taken a resolve that helped her and she didn't expect him to change her mind.

"You were going to start a nursery school?" Robert was surprised.

"Roseanne has a lot of experience as a daycare worker. And this place really needs a nursery school," she went on.

"It does?" Robert disagreed violently with this proposition.

"What's that got to do with AA and all that?" he asked. "I thought you and Danny were trying to get everyone to go dry."

"Well, you have to start with children. Because someone who has a happy childhood—"

It sounded like brainwashing to Robert.

"Your mother should take care of you when you're little. Not some school," he said.

Rebecca sat up straight. "But what if your mother plays rummoli all afternoon and goes to bingo at night? And what if your dad drinks a lot and stays away from home all the time?"

"Your family is the most important thing to you no matter how bad they all are." He felt very strongly about that.

But Rebecca had a strong opinion about this too.

"Well, if that's true," she said, "it'll be true even if the kids go to nursery school—But they'll have a better chance to play there, and somebody will be looking after them."

It occurred to Robert suddenly that this crazy nursery school idea really mattered to her. He made an adroit right face.

"So stay here and start a nursery school," he said.

Rebecca was taken by surprise. Then she burst out laughing. It was one of his tricks.

"What does nursery school make you think of, Robert!" she demanded. "I bet you think of jail! Jail or residential school."

"Or Church," he agreed.

"But really it's just fun. Puzzles and picture books and playing with toys—"

"Well, I guess Danny's against it." Robert was curious to know whether he was or not.

Rebecca wasn't, in fact, very sure at all what Danny thought. She had brought it up a few times, but Danny had put her off. They didn't have the money.

"All I know is that you're against it," she said. "But you're against almost everything, Robert."

Robert got up and began to walk around, a little restless. Rebecca had turned the tables on him and he had to defend what he thought.

It was true that he was that way—against almost everything.

"Why is that?" She was watching him alertly. Robert's physical being, his black eyes, and his tough, handsome face too, had temporarily dropped away. She was speaking to the deepest part of him, in which, she knew, there lay a kind of malaise.

"Maybe it's the way I am." This conversation was cutting very close to the bone for Robert.

"But why is that the way you are?" she persisted.

"It's the way all of us are," he replied. "We had to do everything the whiteman told us. They made us have Church and schools—even their houses. We had trapping. For their hats. Now they don't want hats or something. The only place left is to be against it all." He stopped talking abruptly.

"But we have to change that, Robert," she said. "That's the attitude that's keeping us down."

Robert shrugged.

"But we have to. We won't survive if we don't." Rebecca spoke passionately.

"Well, we survived a long time."

"Yes!" she cried. "We made it. And now here we are. We have to do something better now."

"We'll make it no matter what they do to us." Robert was sure of this, at least.

"I can't live in a world like that." Rebecca had stood up too, almost hating him for his negativism.

"Yeah, but you do live in a world like that, Rebecca." Robert shrugged again. He turned away and began to enlarge her frost hole at the window moodily.

"So you think I shouldn't quit, but there's nothing I can do?" she said to his back.

Robert didn't reply.

"I think I can do a lot if I get the chance," she went on.

Getting the chance; that was the whole problem, of course. They were right back where they started from, in Robert's opinion.

"I can't change the world," she was saying. "But I could give some people here a—a better deal."

He heard her falter, and it made him turn around. Rebecca was standing in the middle of the floor staring at him, her hands clasped, her eyes blazing with the passion of her argument.

"I've been through a lot myself," she said. "I know what it's like."

"That's true," he said.

He had never known a woman like this before.

"So you're going to stay, aren't you? And start that daycare thing," he continued, trying to speak casually.

All at once, Rebecca began to smile, a sweet smile, engaging and amused.

"I should throw this tea out the door." She went over to the table and picked up her cup. "I didn't drink any of it."

She took the cup to the door, opened it, and threw her cold tea out onto the snow.

"You are going to stay, aren't you?" he persisted.

"Why do you keep trying to make me say yes to that?" she asked.

"I'm not trying to make you say anything."

She had shut the door again, and she stood with her back to it, her teacup in her hand.

"Do you want me to stay, Robert?" she asked.

"Yes."

"All right then, I will," said Rebecca. She laughed.

Then she began to put on her mukluks, her sweater, her parka.

"I'm going to walk you home, okay?" said Robert.

"Okay."

• 14 • THE PETITION •

Robert left Rebecca outside her trailer and continued on his way into town, walking along the road briskly, in high good humour.

The universe was a pretty well-organized place, or so it seemed to him this morning. Rebecca was going to be alright now, because of the kind of person she was. And as for Danny, he would be getting his comeuppance somehow, Robert was sure of it.

A truck drew up beside him and stopped. It was Herod, offering him a lift.

Robert got into his truck, which was new. The insurance company had come through with the money for the old one, and Herod had brought the new one into Prohibition Creek over the rough winter road from the Forks.

"This is pretty snazzy, Herod," he remarked, shutting the door and settling into one of the bucket seats. "Red—that's my favourite colour too."

They turned out the road to the airstrip. Herod liked to drive around town, keeping an eye on things.

"So I guess we won't be getting a new airport soon," he commented. "Not likely, anyway."

"But I thought the Band was going to trade the airport land for that piece with the fish plant on it. What happened?"

Robert was looking out the window at the wasteland of tree stumps that marked the approach to the end of the runway. They were unfortunate in that there was no high land around town, so the airport was in a muskeg.

"Well, the Band wrote the Department of Indian Affairs. Then DIAND wrote to the Lands Office in Yellowknife. Then the Lands Office wrote Local Government. Local Government wrote to the Cooperative Association of the N.W.T. And they all wrote back to DIAND—Well, that's about where it stands now."

"So what seems to be the problem?" Robert asked.

"Well, it's your outhouse," said Herod.

"There can't be any problem about my outhouse. Not if the Band gets the land." That had been the object of making the trade, from his point of view.

"Yeah, but the Feds won't let the deal go through. They think the fish plant just put in new employee washrooms. Because of your outhouse."

"But—" Robert was struggling for comprehension of this absurdity. "The fish plant hasn't been operating for fifteen years!"

Herod shrugged. "That's what I tried to tell 'em."

"Did you write a letter too?"

"Nope. I called 'em up."

"And what did they say."

"Said I should write 'em a letter." Herod stared moodily across the smooth white tableland of snow, blowing up wispily in the small wind, that was the airstrip. The big grader had broken down again after New Year's, but the Red Baron had finally got the skis on his Beaver, so they still had some kind of air service.

"Look, I could just withdraw my application for that outhouse."

"Forget it," said Herod. "The file on that is already an inch thick."

He backed up the truck carefully amongst the drifts and began to drive back into town with his customary equanimity.

"Going somewhere special?" he inquired.

"Nope. I'm kind of looking for Haga, that's all."

"Did you boys have some kind of disagreement?" Herod asked tactfully. Like Rebecca, he had been shocked to see Robert with two black eyes. Robert's tough-guy looks derived from his broken nose, but that was a hockey injury from twenty-five years past, as Herod knew.

"Nope. We went on the job with Sasquatch. Got fired after we were jumped by a bunch of redneck whitemen."

"Haga went with you?" Herod said. He shook his head. "You shouldn't have taken Haga," he said.

They had come back into town and were passing the big new blue and yellow police detachment. Robert said, "I guess I'll get out here, Herod. The cops'll probably know where he went."

"Oh yeah," said Herod.

Robert got out of the truck and stood for a moment at the foot of the long flight of steps leading up to the office. He didn't want to go in there. The place had bad associations for him. Taking a deep breath, he ran up the steps.

The cop, Dave, was there. He was getting himself a cup of coffee from the machine that stood hospitably on the counter of the main office.

"Oh, hi, Robert. Want coffee? I just made some fresh."

"Sure," said Robert.

Dave poured out a cup for him, pushed the cream and sugar in his direction. The police were always delighted when somebody from the community came in for a cup of coffee. Robert was rather surprised to be put in the category of casual visitor.

"You wouldn't be looking for Haga, would you?" said Dave.

Robert nodded.

"Sometimes I think we should take a fee for the babysitting we do."

"Well, I guess Haga wouldn't be able to go to jail if it cost anything," said Robert, stirring his coffee.

Haga called out from the cell down the hall, "That you, Robert?"

"Take your time," suggested Dave. "He already had his coffee at breakfast time. My wife made it and I brought it over here for him."

"Busy these days?" asked Robert.

"It was busy at Christmas." The policeman moved into the chair behind his desk with his coffee cup. "A lot of people started partying again. This town is going down the tubes," he added.

Robert shrugged. "Well, it's a job for you guys. Keeping the cells filled."

Dave shrugged too. "For this I went to college and had two years of specialized training with the Force."

"Yeah, but sometimes you get a case. Anything doing on who wrecked Herod's truck?"

Since he was here he thought he might as well find out about that, although he was pretty sure there wasn't anything. Herod would have told him already.

The cop took his nose out of his coffee cup.

"Your brother Michael wrecked Herod's truck. I guess you know that, Robert. But can I prove it?"

Their eyes met.

"He was wearing his gloves. It was November. A pretty cold night."

"Too bad," said Robert unsympathetically.

Dave returned to his coffee. "You know, this is the kind of thing that's keeping you people down," he remarked.

"It's a funny thing but somebody already told me that this morning," said Robert with a laugh.

Dave sighed. He took his feet down off the wastebasket. Then he got up and stretched.

"I'll go get Haga," he said. "You can take him out."

They didn't usually kick the drunks out until the afternoon;

by then they had had the time to get the alcohol out of their systems.

Dave paused on his way out the door. "Robert, I wish you'd sign up for that special constable course. I know you're a smart guy." He went down the hall, not waiting for an answer.

"Yeah, but I have a negative attitude," Robert called after him. Somebody else had already told him that too, he recalled, smiling to himself.

He could hear Dave down the hall, jingling the keys.

"Thanks, partner." Haga was looking pleased to see him. But his expression was considerably obscured by his contusions; Robert was horrified to see the mess his face was in. No wonder the police had taken him into custody.

"Seeing the two of you together, I can't help noticing—You been fighting, or something?" The cop was looking critically from one to the other.

"Yeah, but not with each other," said Robert. "Sasquatch Drilling fired us the other day after some deal in the bunkhouse."

"Haga went on the job too?"

This conversation was going to happen again and again, Robert thought.

"Boy oh boy! Let me guess." Dave was rubbing his hands. "Somebody jumped Haga and you cut in on the wrong side. Is that how it went?"

"Yeah. Roughly."

"Didn't anybody tell you not to take Haga? I thought you'd have had more sense."

Robert shrugged. Then he laughed.

"Come on, Haga. Let's go," he said. Then he added, "Bye Dave. Thanks for your coffee."

You couldn't help liking the guy in a way, he was thinking. It was tough, being a cop in a place like this.

Robert and Haga went out the door, down the steep flight of steps, and with one accord began crunching through the snow toward the co-op. Haga spent most of his time loafing around the steps in front of the store, when he wasn't out at the shack sleeping. And Robert wanted to see if he could get any more credit; they were out of food, even out of necessities like candles, and the tea would soon be gone.

A small group of people were standing clustered together outside on the steps. Robert recognized his sister-in-law, Sarah, holding a long white piece of paper in her mitt.

She gave it to somebody and he signed it, then passed it to the friend who was reading over his shoulder.

"What in heck—?" said Robert. Then he remembered Rebecca saying something about Sarah starting a petition against her.

He strode across the street to the store, speeding up suddenly. Haga trailed behind him.

"Hi Robert," said Sarah. "Want to sign this petition?"

"Are you kidding?" He took it from her. "Let me have a look at this thing."

"Petition to fire Rebecca McCrae—For her immoral behaviour?" he read. "Who thought that one up?—What's this?" He was caught up short suddenly.

Haga's name, printed characteristically in crooked capital letters, appeared about halfway down the page.

"Oh yeah," said Haga, catching up. "I already signed it last night."

"You what?"

"Hey!"

Robert had turned around and seized a fistful of the front of Haga's jacket.

"No!—Robert, old buddy—!"

Haga tore himself away and ran off down the street, yelling with fright.

Robert looked after him as he disappeared in the direction of the snowy riverbank. Then he laughed. Haga was jealous, that must be it.

Sarah rescued the petition and gave it to somebody to sign.

Robert was no longer paying attention to the machinations of Sarah. Forgetting even that he had been intending to go to the store, he began to walk back out to the shack. In spite of all the things there were to feel bad about today—Bobby in jail, Michael's behaviour, the absurd bureaucratic confusion created by his outhouse, that stupid petition Sarah was raising—he was feeling good. He was feeling very good.

▲ ▲ ▲

Danny was in his office in the band hall, just down the road from the store. He was acutely aware of what was going on outside on the co-op steps.

He was in a terrible state, and had been since before Christmas.

His home life was disorganized; since Roseanne had found out about his affair with Rebecca, she had been unwilling to wash clothes or cook meals. The kids ran wild, with Roseanne neglecting everything. Sometimes she even screamed abuse at him in front of them.

But his emotional state had been bad before she found out. If anything, it had been even slightly worse then.

Danny was utterly at odds with himself. His homecoming had been a bitter one, since at that time he was still in love with Rebecca. But here he couldn't see her, he couldn't even go near her or else he would make love to her again. And he couldn't do that here.

He had been having a strange time in Yellowknife. Having lived there for years, he had been looking forward to going back for a visit. But Yellowknife was a government town full of transients, and everything was different, even though it was only six months later. The people he knew in his old office thought he had done something retrograde, going back to his hometown to become a backwoods chief, and there really wasn't much to talk about with them any longer. Danny ended up sitting rather dismally with the other loafers in the coffee shop for a few hours, then retiring to his room with a detective novel.

By that time he was very much looking forward to the workshop starting the next morning.

It was well after midnight when someone knocked on the door.

"Who is it?" All kinds of people knocked on doors late at night in this hotel.

"Rebecca."

"Rebecca!"

Danny took off the glasses he used for reading and got out of bed in his pyjama pants.

It was Rebecca and she was a mess. She looked—and smelled—as though she had been drinking. But a moment later she was sobbing out the whole disconnected story—her husband, her kids, her father—she had nowhere to go—

And then she was in his arms. Sweet Rebecca, pressing her cold trembling lips against his. And he was kissing her, drawing her inside, putting her down on his bed.

He had tried—he had tried so hard—to stay away from her.

Danny was a stubborn man; he was still clinging to the idea that he loved Rebecca. However, he knew he couldn't have her. And this was not just because of his principles or because he cared about his family. Rebecca herself had done things he couldn't accept: stealing money and liquor, experimenting with drugs, sleeping with strangers for drink or money. She had wrecked her marriage, deserted her kids.

The idea was growing on him that she was bad. Sometimes, in the violence of his emotions, it even seemed that he hated her.

But in his rational mind, Danny knew that what was going on outside on the steps of the co-op was unfair. Whatever Rebecca had done to him, she shouldn't lose her job for it. She had been doing the job and doing it well since the fall, and he was also conscious that the very things in her background that repelled him, that he was afraid of, made her stronger in her role as a counsellor.

But there was no way he could intervene to stop this. If he intervened it would only strengthen the campaign against her. Maybe they would turn on him as well.

There was no way the Department of Social Services would fire Rebecca for what she had done. Sleeping with a married man was not a crime; it was your own business whom you slept with.

But this campaign in the village might make Rebecca decide to quit of her own volition. There was nothing left for her to do here; her ability to counsel was destroyed. In fact, Danny's whole program was in ruins. So many people had started to drink again at Christmas and had been encouraged to go on by hearing of this scandal, that it might take him years to pull it together again.

And that was what he wanted most of all. He wanted to be chief in Prohibition Creek, and he wanted to get his wife and kids back.

"If only Rebecca would quit," Danny said violently. "If only she just weren't here any longer!"

◂ ◂ ◂

Since Haga and Robert were broke and all the work to be had in the village these days was with Housing, there was not much point in going into town. On the other hand, Robert was restless out at the shack. He hiked into town to visit his mother. She had given him some candles and a box of tea, so he took her a rabbit from Haga's snare line.

She wasn't home, but Elvis was.

Robert put his rabbit, stiff in its snowy fur, down on the kitchen table. His mother had been baking bannock, and there was an appetizing smell in the room. She had made a lot, twelve dozen, the way she used to when he was a child. The flat round cakes, studded with raisins, were cooling on plates and racks all over the room. Robert thought he would hang around until his mother returned; she would probably give him some to take back to the shack.

"Not working today?" he said to Elvis.

"Nope," said Elvis. "I quit."

Robert nodded, going for the teapot. Etiquette forbade further inquiry. In any case, he was familiar with the scenario and didn't really need to ask.

The contractor doing the rehabs had started out with a local hiring policy, but the jobs were almost all taken now by workers from down south. This always happened, even when the contractor was the Band Development Corporation. There was a slightly riotous atmosphere in town and the drinking and partying centred around the trailer where the southern carpenters were living.

Elvis was a good worker, but he had hardly ever had a job in his own hometown.

"Well, I got fired by Sasquatch," Robert remarked by way of commiseration.

"I know." Elvis nodded solemnly. "You took Haga."

Robert thought he must have had this conversation with everybody now.

He leaned against the counter beside Elvis, his teacup in hand. He didn't feel like drinking tea; he was drinking tea all the time these days. The oil-heated room seemed a little too warm, and despite his walk in the cold weather, he wasn't refreshed and energized. He felt that he was getting fat, although a person could not get fat living on wild meat.

The problem with being unemployed at this point in the winter was not so much economic—for the woods were full of rabbits—as metaphysical. There was nothing to do but hang around.

"So what are you going to do now, Robert?" asked Elvis.

"I don't know. I'm just—waiting for something that's not going to happen." Robert shrugged.

This life of inaction was driving him crazy. And there was a particular type of inaction that made it seem worse than usual.

He had not seen Rebecca since parting with her outside her trailer three days before. He was constrained from going there and hanging around: it would not help her get out of the mess she was in, and in any case, his own dignity forbade it. He was not going to hang around a woman.

"You ever see that old cabin my father made at Rocher River?" asked Elvis, off on a track of his own.

"Sure."

Robert was still thinking about Rebecca. There was just nothing he could do about Rebecca, even though he seemed to be thinking about her all the time these days.

"You've been out there?" Elvis went on.

"When I was a kid. With my dad and Ama. They used to take all of us out hunting and trapping back then."

Robert knew he was in love with Rebecca. When he thought about it, he realized he had been in love ever since he had had the dream about her when he was out hunting at the Gravel River. But Robert had never had much use for love. "I love you" was something people usually said as a prelude to hurting each other, in his experience.

"I must have been working in the Delta, those years," said Elvis.

"Yeah, you used to go out of town a lot back then," agreed Robert.

"I didn't have a wife and kids," Elvis said. "I didn't have anyone to take to the bush."

"Well, I don't have a wife anymore. My kid's gone too."

Although he still did have both of them, in another sense, and it was a bad situation, worse, really, than Rebecca's affair with his brother. For Rebecca could write Danny off; Robert thought she already had. But he couldn't write off Mary Ann; they had been married for nearly twenty years and had a son who—It was hopeless.

Elvis now left off leaning against the sink and walked around in front of Robert, attracting his attention.

"Want to go trapping?" he asked. "To that camp at Rocher River?"

"Trapping? Oh. Okay," Robert said, coming to.

Rachel now came into the kitchen from outdoors. She removed her parka and hung it up, taking in the rabbit on the table without comment. Then she turned around and looked at their two faces searchingly.

"You're going?" she said to Robert.

He had already agreed and it had been an easy thing to do; but Robert now perceived that his mother and Elvis must have talked this over before. It accounted for why she had been making so much bannock.

His mind began to work on the problems to be overcome.

"We'll have to get gas on credit, I guess. Where are we going to get the traps?"

"I have traps," said Rachel.

They were Robert's father's traps, left behind when his father had moved to Yellowknife to take up the life of a gambling man.

"We can get an advance from the game warden at the Forks," suggested Elvis. "We'll get a better price from him than at the store."

"It's a long way to Rocher River. Take a radio." Rachel was fearful because she knew the risks. A person could die of pneumonia or blood poisoning; there were a thousand accidents that could occur, the chance of exposure if you got wet, or drowning from falling through thin ice. Being mauled by a wild animal improperly caught in a trap, or having their own dogs turn on them. Bushmen might be nearby and come into camp, or a meteor might fall on it; they might be in a hunting area proscribed by the old-time medicine men or—

"I guess we'll see whether we can get a radio from the Game Warden," said Elvis.

"And buy supplies in the Forks once we get our trapping advance."

"Tea. Rice," said Rachel.

"Tobacco. Matches," Elvis went on.

"When are you leaving?" she asked.

"Tomorrow morning," said Elvis.

Robert was still trying to catch up. "Tomorrow morning?" he said. "Oh. Okay."

He was feeling good suddenly. Going trapping, staying out in the bush with Elvis. Away from this town, away from gossip and trouble and people bothering you. Eating dry meat and bannock, and fresh caribou meat too, if they were lucky; the very thought made his mouth water. This was the right thing to do. He put on his parka.

"Oh yeah." Elvis spoke casually. "Tell Haga he's not coming."

"Sure you don't want to take him?" Robert asked, poker-faced.

"I want to be out there for a month or so." Elvis did not regard this as a joke. "If we take Haga we'll be back here in a week. Bringing him to the nurse."

"Okay." Robert laughed.

"Good," said Elvis.

It was only when he was already outside and on his way home that he remembered that telling Haga that he wasn't coming was not going to be easy.

It was a mild day for January. He took the way out of town that led him past Rebecca's trailer, the same way he had come in. There was a trail of fresh footprints in the soft snow on the porch, leading down off the steps and away, into town. He had just missed her, going to the post office.

Robert tramped into the bush, on the old wood road that led to the fishplant, thinking of Rebecca saying, "I trust you, Robert," her sparkling face turned up to him; Rebecca the next morning, sleeping in his bedroll on the bottom bunk, the pillow doubled under her cheek. His bitter heart had been soothed by these things, and now he wanted to tell her he trusted her too, he wanted to hold her in his arms and look into her face—but more than anything else, he wanted to know what it would be like to be lying under that blanket with her.

A raven was sitting in a dead tree on the edge of the clearing, making a sound like a clock striking, its eyes half closed in admiration of the beauty of its voice, and Robert threw a chunk of snow at it.

He found Haga lying on the bottom bunk, as usual. He was not asleep, even though his eyes were shut. He was almost as tired of looking at the inside of the shack as Robert was.

"What are you doing, Robert?" Haga still didn't open his eyes.

"Oh—nothing." Robert was pacing around, trying to summon up the initiative to tell Haga he was taking off.

"You're kind of restless all the time. But I know what that's because of."

"What? You don't know what it's because of," Robert said.

"Oh yes, I do know what it's because of." Haga was really enjoying himself.

"Look, you don't know anything about me." He went over to glare down at Haga. "You don't know what's on my mind at all."

"It's that girl," said Haga. "That's what's on your mind."

They had already had a discussion like this three days ago, when Haga had finally come home after Robert found out he had signed the petition. One reason why Robert wanted to go to the bush with Elvis was to avoid having to talk about Rebecca with Haga.

"You've been crazy about her since last fall. She slept with you last week." Haga was sitting up, listing these things on his fingers. "And ever since that happened, you can't even sit still," he concluded.

"Look, Haga, I haven't been crazy about her since last fall. And if she slept with me, well—what of it?" Everything in this speech was a lie, but he couldn't help that. "Why do you have to talk about it all the time?"

"You don't need to worry. I'm not talking about it to anybody else. I never told a soul that she spent the night here that time."

"Well, good," said Robert, his mind returning to the main problem he had right now, breaking the news that he was going to leave.

"Except that cop," said Haga.

Robert began to glare at him again. Haga was thinking hard now.

"And—oh yeah—that woman who gave me the petition to sign."

"Right. You never told a soul." Robert turned away and walked impatiently over to the window. The faint mark of Rebecca's breath was still imprinted in an aureole around the tiny hole in the frost made by her fingers.

"Look, Haga, I'm going trapping. Down by Rocher River."

"Okay." Haga sat up in surprise and something like enthusiasm. "When do we start?"

"Sorry, pal," said Robert. "You aren't coming. Elvis asked me."

"Oh yeah." Haga spoke sullenly. "It was his gun that nearly broke my arm that time in the mountains."

"It'll only be for a little while. Say—a month or so."

"Well, I don't care," said Haga. He lay down and composed himself for the grave, his arms crossed on his chest, eyes closed, his face in the rictus of death.

"When I come back, at least we'll have some cash again."

"I don't care about how rich you get," Haga said. "That doesn't matter to me."

"We'll be able to afford tobacco. Even cigarettes."

"A good friend is worth a lot of cigarettes."

Robert was beginning to feel sorry for him again. "Yeah. I guess you're right," he said. "Sorry, partner. But Elvis just wants to take me."

Haga had turned his face to the wall.

Robert spent the rest of the afternoon doing chores. There was a little sewing to be done, and he knew how to handwash socks. Haga didn't get up to cook, so he just ate a bannock that his mother had given him, and put another one on the table for Haga to eat later, when he stopped sulking.

He was having a struggle with himself over whether to go and say goodbye to Rebecca. He thought she might be surprised and hurt if he didn't. But he couldn't imagine going to her place, knocking on the door, telling her the innocent fact that he was going trapping. He felt as shy as a teenager about seeing her; while the cynical adult in him shared Haga's opinion that he was crazy.

It was a relief when it got dark. He was not going to visit Rebecca after dark.

Finally he thought he was tired enough to sleep. Days like this could pass in a kind of waking dream; he had shown more initiative this afternoon than in a whole week of days.

"Blow out the candle, okay?" He was already in the bunk above, getting ready for a long restless seance with Rebecca behind closed eyelids.

Haga sighed. He got out of bed, blew out the light, stumped back to bed and got in.

He spoke into the darkness.

"Well, I was alone all the time before. It doesn't matter to me."

"Come on," said Robert. "I'll be back pretty soon."

"For a guy like me, no wife, no kid, it was kind of like—a home here, for a while."

Robert was really feeling bad about this. And he thought that what Haga said was true. It had been pretty homey here in the shack, right up until the night Rebecca had slept there on the bottom bunk with the pillow doubled under her cheek.

"Heck, I'm sorry, Haga. It'll be like that again."

"No, it won't," said Haga. "You just think I'm a crazy old fool. Want to get away from me now."

"No, I don't."

Haga groaned.

"Look, pal—" He paused desperately. "Want to do something for me while I'm away?"

"Sure," said Haga, brightening. "What?"

Robert was still trying to think of what.

"Maybe you'd like me to—I know what you'd like me to do," Haga was triumphant all of a sudden.

"What?" Robert was alarmed. Haga had had an idea.

"Keep an eye on your girlfriend, of course. You know what I mean."

"I guess so—What do you mean?" It was such a bad idea that he was having trouble grasping what it might involve.

"Well, like—keeping an eye on her, that's all."

Perhaps it didn't involve all that much after all. Robert laughed.

"Sure. Why not?" he said. "It can't do any harm."

It couldn't do any harm unless she noticed he was doing it. But most of the time people didn't notice that Haga was around unless he was asleep. And aside from the way he snored, he didn't do any harm at all then.

The fire in the stove crackled.

Haga, pacified, was already beginning to breathe deeply and irregularly.

Robert was alone with his thoughts again, wrestling with them.

He was glad he was going to go. If he stayed in town it would be like waiting around for Rebecca to look at him. He was already doing that, passing by her trailer, reading the footprints in the snow.

What if she already was in love with him too, perhaps without knowing it? Could he just go away without finding out? Was that because he was afraid of what might happen?

He was completely unsure of himself.

And he was in a fever, like a young man, almost like himself as a teenager, when he thought of her sleeping in his bedroll, under this blanket where he was lying now, where he could still detect the faint, clean, soap and shampoo scent of her skin and hair.

◆ 15. LO, THIS DREAMER COMETH ◆

Rebecca was in her office talking on the phone to her boss in Yellowknife. She had just found out that Social Services was going to conduct an investigation of her work in Prohibition Creek.

She was not behind in the paperwork. In fact, there was hardly anything for her to do, since there was no more counselling and the AA meetings had stopped. Her job had dwindled to mere record-keeping on the welfare cheques.

She hung up the phone. Actually, her boss, who was a woman named Marcia, was quite sympathetic. They were not going to fire her over a personal matter. It was merely a response to the wishes of the community to make sure that her work was being done well; it was for her own good, Marcia thought, to answer a complaint thoroughly.

Rebecca leaned back in her chair and stared at the acoustic tiles on the ceiling, unattractively stained with water from leaks in the roof.

She was talking to Robert again in her mind. Why had he had to go trapping right now, just when she needed him? Perhaps he didn't care about her at all. But she knew he cared about her.

Somehow, in spite of all precaution, people in town had learned that she had spent the night out at the shack with Robert. And they had put the obvious interpretation on it, just as she had known they would. The gossip had now even spread as far as her boss in Yellowknife.

Sick of the claustrophobia of her little office, Rebecca got up and flung open the door.

"Haga!"

Haga was humbly crouching on his heels beside the trailer with his back against the skirting. Taken by surprise at her sudden appearance, he cleared his throat again nervously, a long horrible noise like a death rattle.

"Haga, what is this all about?" cried Rebecca. "I saw you all day, everywhere I went. You even walked me home. And now here you are—still here!"

"Yeah," Haga agreed.

"Why are you following me around?" she demanded, very agitated. "What are you doing here?"

"Robert took off on me." Haga was morose.

"Yes. He did," she said, thinking to herself, he took off on me too.

"But before he left he said," Haga continued.

"Said what?"

"He told me to, that's all."

Rebecca was not used to discussions with Haga. She looked at him impatiently. "Told you to what?"

"He told me to look after you," said Haga desperately. He stood up.

Rebecca suffered a moment of astonishment. "You?" she said.

Haga was standing, an aggrieved expression on his face, looking up at her from the area of trampled snow in front of her office.

Then she suddenly began to laugh with relief and happiness.

Robert did care about her, that was perfectly clear. The proof was that he had left her Haga, while he was away.

She ran down the steps and began to propel Haga up and inside. The least she could do was make him tea. And even if he wasn't someone to talk to, he was supposed to be looking after her; he could sleep on the floor of her office while he was doing that, rather than crouching outside against the skirting.

◂ ◂ ◂

Elvis and Robert were both asleep in the cabin at Rocher River. Although it was now late February and the days were getting longer again, it was still the deepest part of the winter from the point of view of cold. The tiny cabin was wrapped in frost outside and in: the ceiling was coated with rime and icicles hung like stalactites from the beams.

It was a very small place, much smaller than the lean-to of the fish plant, a cabin for one, or at most two, people. Robert and Elvis with their heavy down and blanket-cloth Arctic sleeping bags almost filled the place up, Elvis sleeping on a makeshift bunk that also functioned as a table, and Robert on the bare packed earth of the floor.

Robert had been here last at this time of year when he was twelve years old, with his whole family: his father, his mother, himself and the two sisters that came after him, as well as Danny, then a toddler, and Michael, a young baby.

It had been a winter when they had not seen the track of a single large animal. Robert's mother and sisters had supported the family on rabbits from a snare line; some nights the whole family—seven people—sat around a stew made out of a single rabbit. They had had fish too, and fish in profusion when the spring finally broke the river. The fur price was low—the way it was this winter—but that had been the way they lived.

All was now silent, only broken by the deep breathing of the two men.

Robert was dreaming. He dreamed of Rebecca standing in the shack in the morning light, the way she had been the last time he saw her.

"Why did you run away, Robert?"

"I just didn't see what I could do." He spoke aloud.

"Don't you care about me at all?"

"I care about you, Rebecca." And then he woke up.

"Dreaming again, eh?" remarked Elvis, now also awake.

"I guess so," said Robert.

He opened his sleeping bag and got up on his knees to replenish the stove, which was almost out. He put in a few big chunks, then opened the draft; the place was so small that the ancient half-broken oil-drum stove could heat it up in no time.

There was a little light in the room now from the intermittent flicker of the fire through the draft hole of the stove. It was light enough for Robert and Elvis to see by, for their eyes were attuned to starshine and moonlight; there were still only six hours of full daylight to work by.

Elvis yawned and opened up his own sleeping bag to stretch. "Brrr," he said.

"Don't get up, Elvis. Everything's frozen yet," said Robert.

He got back into his own bedroll and lay down with a groan of discomfort. Then he began to think about the dream.

Robert had spent a month now dreaming about Rebecca every night. And he spent most of his waking time thinking about the dreams—on the long trail while they were laying the traps, or back at the cabin, thawing and skinning the bodies of the animals, marten and fox and wolverine, and setting them on the stretchers.

He had put together in his mind every scrap of knowledge he had about her or her family, including things heard and half understood when he was a child about her father, his wild history of drinking and womanizing before he became a Protestant evangelist. Robert divined many things about Rebecca in this: she was the oldest in the family and therefore, like himself, the rebellious one, the one who had been through everything with the parents. He remembered what she had implied about the breakdown of her marriage too, and in dreams he saw her in scenes of degradation: passed out, befouled with her vomit, giving herself to men whom she was too drunk to remember later.

But there was idealism in her character, a character that he understood now came from her crazy religious nut of a father. And somehow, slowly, she had pulled herself out of the slough she was in and with her quick intelligence, her spirit, her sense of humour, had created another Rebecca, who was that beautiful, sparkling woman he had been talking to in the shack. "Do you want me to stay here, Robert?—Then I'll stay."

Robert had been in a fever of desire and indecision when he left Prohibition Creek; but now he was sick with love.

He felt Elvis's eyes upon him.

"Cold weather for trapping, isn't it?" Robert said.

Elvis laughed. "Well, we've all got our own problems, I guess," he said

Robert rose on one elbow and they were almost face to face; Elvis was grinning down at him from the edge of the table.

"What do you mean by that?" Robert sat up farther, prepared to deny everything, whatever Elvis had heard him saying in his sleep.

"It's still too cold to get up," said Elvis. "Tell me a story, Robert."

"A story?" said Robert, surprised. It was a strange request from Elvis, with whom he had an entirely practical friendship.

Like all the old people Elvis did everything by taboo. When they killed an animal for fur they first knocked it unconscious, then reached up under the rib cage with their fingers to dislodge the heart. They were trying not to damage the fur and the spirits were satisfied only if they killed it this way. Other animals like moose and caribou could never be clubbed or beaten with sticks. And there were ways of setting traps, particularly for the larger, more intelligent animals, for wolf and wolverine, that reflected an ancient understanding of animal personality. Robert had learned a lot from Elvis, even on this trip, about the old ways of doing things.

If there was an old-time story to be told, it seemed more reasonable that Elvis should be the one to tell it.

"You're a real good storyteller—like your dad," said Elvis.

It was also strange, the way Elvis occasionally remarked on that resemblance, in view of his relationship to Robert's mother.

Robert began, almost absently, "There were two brothers."

So many stories began that way.

"But they had different mothers," Elvis said, unexpectedly taking over the story. "The older one's mother died of TB when he was only three."

"Then his dad married again. The younger brother was born when the older one was five," Elvis continued.

"But the younger one's mother died of TB too, didn't she?" Robert contributed. Elvis had his full attention now.

"He never had a mother," said Elvis.

Robert remembered that there had been some girls too. But they had been in his grandfather's third family. The old man had been a patriarch: there were thirteen living children, from three wives. But only one child had survived in each of the first two families, in each case a boy: his father, the eldest, and his uncle Elvis.

"The younger brother never had any mother but the older brother," said Elvis. "The older brother started taking care of him when he was a baby."

"He must have looked after him when they went to that school too," said Robert, his own memories of school coming back to him in a rush of bitterness. He had been separated from his sisters when they were put in the girls' residence; he wasn't even allowed to see them.

"He always looked after him," said Elvis gravely. "But the older brother was a crazy guy," he went on with a reminiscent smile. "He liked stick gambling and poker more than just about anything else—except chasing girls."

Robert grinned. "I guess he was a good-looking guy, that older brother."

"Yeah," Elvis agreed. "The younger brother was skinny and kind of ugly."

"Come on!" said Robert.

His uncle just laughed.

"The older brother got married," said Robert. He knew that Elvis was leading up to this and it was the part of the story he wanted to get to as well.

"That girl was an orphan," said Elvis. "Both her parents died of TB."

Those had been bad times.

"The younger brother got married after a while too. But his wife and kids died of TB."

The record of how bad those times had been was locked in the memory of the old people like Elvis: the waves of epidemic disease that had decimated the Athapaskan bands, from the twenties till the end of the fifties, and left behind a legacy of grief.

No family had been left intact. First came flu and measles, which could strike and kill half the people in a settlement in a few hours. Then came TB; and this epidemic rended the families, taking the sick away to sanatariums in the south, and leaving parents, husbands and wives not to know, sometimes for years, who had lived and who had died.

It had been a holocaust; a whole society almost destroyed—for society was the family, first and foremost, to the Dene.

"So the younger brother went to stay with the older brother and his wife," Elvis continued. "She was a real good one, smart—and she was good-looking too."

"Yeah. I guess she must have been." Robert could not remember that. He could only remember his mother crying after they had been deserted and then working like a man and wearing the clothing of a man.

"So maybe I know what happened to the older brother and his wife," said Robert, impatient to get on.

"Maybe you do."

He realized that he didn't really know it, not from Elvis's perspective, at least. He had just been in a hurry to get his father's cruelty behind them, as an understood fact, something that didn't need to be discussed. But it was Elvis's story.

"Tell me what happened to the younger brother, Elvis," he said.

Elvis lay down on the bunk above, and Robert couldn't see his face any longer. "The younger brother really hated that pretty girl at first," he said slowly. "But after the woman had a couple of kids, the older brother didn't pay any attention to her anymore. She was unhappy and the younger brother felt sorry."

"Maybe he wished he still had a wife and kids himself."

"I think he couldn't stand to see what was happening to the woman. She was a good woman," Elvis said.

Robert hesitated. But he wanted to know. He was getting the chance to know.

"Was he in love with her a long time? Even before the older brother took off?" he asked.

"A long time," Elvis replied.

"I guess she must have been in love with him too," said Robert still tentative.

"Not with that skinny little guy!" Elvis peered over the edge of the table again, with an expression of mock surprise and they both laughed.

"She didn't want to be," Elvis spoke soberly a moment later. "God wouldn't let her do anything about it."

Robert had been relying on that all along. It was the main consideration for his mother, what God would let her do.

"She made that guy stay away from her," Elvis went on. "He had to go work in the Delta. They wasted a lot of time."

Robert thought of all the years that Elvis had worked away from home.

"A long time later—a long time—she finally let him move in." Elvis paused. Then he said, "But she made him go away again. She made him go trapping."

"She did?" Robert had thought that it was Elvis's idea to go trapping. "Why was that?"

"Because of the way one of her boys was acting. He didn't like it the way that old man moved in with his mother."

Danny. The hypocrite, Robert thought.

Elvis was now giving Robert quite a penetrating look, from the edge of the table.

"Do you think they should have wasted any more time, Robert?" he asked.

"No," said Robert. "No, I don't."

At once Elvis sighed, and lay back down, crossing his arms under his head.

A thin daylight was now creeping in through the chinks around the door of the little cabin.

Robert got out of his sleeping bag and began rustling around to start the day.

He pulled on his pants and his vest.

Then he fixed the fire again and put the billy on for tea. He rummaged through the bag of food, and found a piece of dry meat and a bannock for both of them.

Elvis was now also fully dressed and sitting on the edge of the table.

"I guess I'd recognize Ama's bannock if I was eating it in a space capsule," remarked Robert, munching.

"So would I," said Elvis.

Robert poured tea out of the billy, sitting cross-legged on his bedroll beside the stove.

"Masi." Elvis reached for the sugar bag, put a spoonful of sugar in his tea and stirred it with deliberation.

"Now tell me your story, Robert," he said.

"My story?" Robert had forgotten that he was supposed to be telling a story. Elvis's revelations had taken it off his mind.

"There were two brothers," repeated Elvis, starting him off.

There seemed to be a good reason why so many of the stories in the Book of Dene began this way.

"They were in love with the same woman," said Robert, surprising himself with his own words. "The younger one was married. But he slept with her anyway," said Robert.

Because he had lived so much of his life away from home, Elvis usually didn't know any gossip. He could identify Robert and Danny as the two brothers, but Robert thought he wouldn't know much else about it.

"The older brother found out the woman didn't care about the younger one," Robert went on. "And he—Boy!" he broke off suddenly. "Do you really want to hear this story?"

Elvis folded his arms. "Yeah," he said.

"He wanted her himself." Robert managed to say this. It was like coming to terms with his dreams. He hadn't said any of this out loud before, except when he was talking in his sleep.

"So what did he do about that?" Elvis asked.

"Nothing," said Robert.

Big fat nothing, he thought.

"Is that the end of the story?" Elvis was looking rather disappointed.

"Look," said Robert desperately. "I helped you tell that story we just had. Maybe you could give me a hand with this one."

"Let's see," said Elvis. "This guy was married, right?"

"Yeah, and his wife hated his guts. So she threw him out." Robert thought for a moment. "She'd never have him back. He wouldn't go back."

"But maybe he cared what everybody would think," said Elvis. "If he took up with that other woman."

"He didn't care what they'd think," said Robert.

"You said she was his brother's woman."

"She wasn't really his woman. She just made a mistake, that was all. She'd had kind of a crazy life."

"Well, maybe the girl didn't like this guy enough," Elvis suggested. "Maybe he couldn't get her anyway."

"He wasn't sure," replied Robert. "But he dreamed about her all the time. She was always talking to him in his dream," he went on.

"What did she say?" Elvis was looking at him with interest. The elders attributed a great deal of significance to dreaming. And he had been a witness to the amount of dreaming Robert was doing just lately.

"She told him things about herself. She asked him things too. And when he answered her in the dream he couldn't lie."

"This story is getting better," Elvis murmured.

"Another thing that happened was she appeared to him one time as a caribou doe. And he couldn't shoot her. You were there when that happened," he said to Elvis, who was listening with an open mouth.

He began to tell this part properly now, as a story. The clear mountain air on the ridge. The doe and the two little ones. And Haga being bowled over by the kickback of the gun.

"But how did you know it was her?" asked Elvis. He only meant, by what sign or supernatural means, for he was not a bit skeptical; he remembered, he had been there.

"She told me about it afterwards. About how she had been that doe. How she saw us and everything. The two little ones were her two kids."

"This is a really good story, Robert," said Elvis.

"Yeah," said Robert. "Except that nothing happens at the end."

They had finished eating and drinking by this time and the daylight was much stronger. The cabin had no window, but the light found its way in anyhow, around the door and through the broken chinking of the logs. A broad beam of bright spring sunlight fell between them, and tiny particles of ice from the ceiling sifted down through it with the iridescence of a thousand prisms.

Robert began to pack up the food bag again. They were late getting out on the trail this morning and there were forty miles of traps to visit in one direction, fifty in the other.

Almost thirty years ago, as a child of twelve, he had gone these rounds with his father. They had used dogs; it was one of the last winters his family had kept dogs. It had been one of the last good times between his mother and father too; in the bush they worked together cheerfully, and there had been an equality between them, for the work the man did on the trapline depended on the sewing, the fishing and the snare line of the woman.

A whole way of life had been and gone, and although Robert remembered what it had been like to some extent, cold hard work and cramped at night in the tiny cabin with the baby crying, he thought that the life then had been better than the one he was living now.

He and Elvis were two lone men, perhaps both destined to become lonely old men, driven out here together almost as if they were being ostracized by their own people. It felt as if they were the last human beings on earth; they were among the last who would be willing to make their living this way.

"You know, we've been out here a long time," said Elvis, watching Robert put the lard can, the sugar bag and the billy in his packsack.

Robert nodded.

"We've done pretty well. You can't make money out of trapping any longer anyway."

"Well, if they still wanted fur, we'd have made something," Robert said. If that way of life he had been thinking about still existed, they would have made enough to sustain it.

"I want to go home," said Elvis.

Robert laughed. "You don't want to waste any more time, is that it?" he said.

"Yes." Elvis laughed too.

"Well, I think you're right about that," said Robert.

They could go around and get the traps in a day, he figured. Then if they travelled all night they could be in the Forks by next day, sell their fur and—

"Get back to Prohibition Creek tomorrow night?" said Elvis.

"I guess so." Robert had begun to roll his sleeping bag.

"You'll tell me the end of that story some time?" said Elvis, rolling up his sleeping bag too.

"Well—if it turns out to be a good one," agreed Robert.

"What do you mean? A story like that, with dreams and people turning into caribou—it's a good one," said Elvis.

▲ ▲ ▲

Rebecca had spent the month of February doing her job as best she could. On her own hook she applied for a grant for a nursery school, receiving help on this project from nobody. It was not really part of her job to do so, but she had a lot of spare time and the community needed a nursery school.

The drinking in Prohibition Creek this winter was worse than ever; this was to some extent a cyclical thing, but the ruination of Danny's programs had contributed to making it unusually bad.

Danny had started the AA meetings again, but on some cold nights only he and Rebecca showed up. And they were barely speaking to each other, for Danny maintained a front of coldness and austerity; and Rebecca was angry at him for this too, very angry, even though she knew why he was doing it.

She talked regularly on the phone with her boss, who was still purportedly conducting an investigation of Rebecca's work. It was taking the department a long time to reach a conclusion; Rebecca knew that this was because they had nothing to investigate. Her reports were on time, and her personal life was none of their business—in any case, she had no personal life. They were really just waiting to see whether Rebecca would resign or be driven out of the community.

Now it was the end of February and neither of these things had happened, but they both still could.

She hung up the phone and said in a small voice to the air in front of her, "Help!"

Haga suddenly woke up on the floor in front of the desk where he had been dozing in a cross-legged position.

"No drink, no tobacco for a whole month," he groaned.

"Think how much healthier you are."

He dragged himself up to kneel with his chin on the edge of the desk. "Healthy!" he exclaimed.

"Here, do you want some vitamin C?" she asked, opening her desk drawer. "The nurse gave me these vitamin pills for my cold."

"No." Haga spoke dismally.

"Well, you like taking things. I just thought I'd offer," said Rebecca.

But what she said had given Haga an idea.

"Got any painkiller?" he asked. "I like that kind with the picture of the doctor on it."

Crushed by the expression on her face, he sank back onto the floor in front of the desk.

"Well, I just thought I'd ask," he muttered. "There's no harm in asking, is there?"

The days were now becoming longer, and the sun of spring

streamed in through the window. Rebecca was longing to be free of the box she was in: this job, this office. The only thing that kept her here was the thought that Robert was coming back sometime.

He had left her Haga, and that must mean he was coming back.

"I don't want much. Just something for smokes."

"If I lent you money you'd spend it on drink," Rebecca said.

"How could I get drink for five dollars? You can't even get a cup of homebrew out of people for that these days," he whined.

"You'd go buy that painkiller."

"Bernard keeps it behind the counter."

"Then you'd buy some yeast and make something," said Rebecca.

"But you have to get a letter from the chief to buy yeast at the store." This was one of Danny's institutions.

"You'd get it somehow," she said.

"Please, Rebecca," He remembered that pleading sometimes worked. Not on Robert, but possibly on this girl. "Just for smokes."

"I don't believe you." Rebecca folded her arms, adamant.

Haga took another tack.

"Robert would believe me," he said. "He'd lend me the money, anyway."

Rebecca caved in suddenly. "Oh all right! But just for cigarettes."

She went into her living quarters for her purse while Haga made a mental note to mention Robert early and often.

"Swear that it's only for smokes." Rebecca was holding out the five dollar bill. She snatched it away suddenly.

"I swear."

Haga's conscience was clear. Ever the optimist, he was thinking that he would buy cigarettes, and then if he met somebody with a cup of whiskey they would have something to smoke as well as drink.

"Gee, thanks."

Rebecca realized that even a pack of cigarettes cost more than five dollars at the store. All of Haga's vices were too expensive for him.

He got up fast and stumbled out the door before she had a chance to change her mind.

Then she was talking to the wall again. And thinking about Robert.

16. FIRE IN THE FISH STORE SHACK

Elvis and Robert had delivered their hundred martens, ten foxes, twenty mink, two wolverines and a lynx to the game warden at the Forks.

This was a method of selling fur that replaced the old Hudson's Bay Store system; the Game Department dealt directly with the fur auctioneers in Winnipeg. The trappers made a little more money, cutting out one of the middlemen, and what was more important, they were no longer the prisoners of the store.

The only problem was that they got no other money from the game warden aside from the advance that covered expenses; the cheque from the fur auction would not arrive for a month. So they were still poor when they arrived back in Prohibition Creek at midnight the next night; poor in the goods of this world, although somewhat richer in the spirit.

"It's kind of late," said Robert. He was standing in the snow by Elvis's skidoo in front of his mother's house. "I guess I'll just take my stuff and go out to the fish store."

"You could camp overnight with me and Rachel." Elvis was already anxiously scanning the lightless exterior of the house.

"Nope," said Robert. "I kind of got the idea—from somebody—that you'd like to see her all by yourself."

Elvis laughed. "Masi, Robert," he said. "It was a good trip."

"Masi, Elvis. It sure was."

Elvis was untying the toboggan. "You can take the skidoo," he said.

Robert got his pack off the sled. Then he got on Elvis's skidoo and roared off.

As he approached the other end of town he noticed a strange flicker of light against the cloud-occluded sky. It was an orange light and wisps of black smoke were rising through it.

This was no natural celestial phenomenon: it was fire.

In wonder at the sight, Robert had slowed the skidoo almost to a stop; when he suddenly realized what he was seeing, he gunned the machine and flew up over the snow bump on the lip of the ditch and onto the wood road; then he paused and shouted over his shoulder to whoever might be awake in the houses behind him, "Wake up! The fish store is on fire!"

He reached the clearing and flung himself off into the snow. The roof of the main building was already well ablaze. The exterior of the shack was not yet on fire, but there was fire somewhere inside, for he saw the flicker of flame behind the window panes.

"Haga! Haga! Are you in there?"

There was no answer.

But Robert knew he was inside. There was no doubt in his mind that Haga had set the place on fire—from a candle or the chimney, by carelessly setting the drafts of the stove and going to sleep, or with his smoking in bed, if he had been lucky enough to bum some money for smokes from somebody.

It looked impossible to get in, with fire behind the windows. Robert pulled up his parka hood, damped his mouth and nose with his scarf, furred all over with frost from his breath, then seized the latch of the door and opened it a crack. A gust of smoke and hot air came out of the crack like the breath of a dragon.

"Haga!" shouted Robert.

But again there was no answer, and he knew he was going to have to go in.

"Haga, are you here? I can't see a thing." He was crawling across the floor. It seemed as if the fire had started against the back wall, where the lean-to adjoined the hulk of the ruined main building.

A moment later he came up against something soft, like a bundle of rags, lying in the middle of the floor. Robert felt it over blindly; it was discernibly a human body, whether dead or alive. A moment later it moaned.

"Come on, pal. We've got to get out of here fast."

He began dragging and lifting the body in the direction he had come from. He could still see nothing; he didn't dare pick Haga up and make a run for it because of the clouds of choking smoke.

"Which way out?"

Suddenly there was a huge explosion. Glass tinkled as the windows were blown out of the shack, and with a whoosh the fire was all around them.

Robert heard his voice, unrecognizable in panic, shouting, "Got to get out of here!"

Picking Haga up and slinging him over his shoulder, he burst out through the flaming door. Then he ran heavily across the snow and dropped Haga by the edge of the clearing.

"Wow! That was a close one," said Robert, standing up straight to look at the lean-to, now engulfed in flames.

He was dimly aware of the fire siren in town. But they would never be able to get the fire truck down the road, even if it were worth it for what remained of the fish plant.

The fire, Robert was almost sure, had started in Haga's bunk. The explosion must have been caused by the remains of the oil furnace in the main building; there had been a tank in there with some oil in it. When the fire got that far, it blew up.

He turned to Haga, who was still lying, a limp bundle, in the snowbank.

"You okay, Haga?—Haga? Haga?" Panicking again, Robert began to shake him.

Then he bent over his face, trying to hear whether he was breathing.

He had moaned once inside, Robert remembered. "Breathe, okay?"

Haga made a slight noise like a cough.

Rejoicing, Robert took off his parka and wrapped it around Haga. He himself was wearing padded coveralls, but in any case, he wasn't cold. He had no physical sensations at all just at the moment.

The blazing building had begun to collapse upon itself. But meanwhile, the fire siren was slowly coming closer. A moment later, the fire truck pulled into the clearing, grandly preceded by the grader, and followed by Herod, driving his new red pickup. It was like a parade.

Instantly there was a confusion of shouting, as the Fire Department began arguing about what to do first.

"Here's the hose. Crank her out."

"Okay, it says here there's seven steps to starting this pump."

"Never mind reading the directions. Get Herod."

"Here I am," said Herod. "Ready to turn her on?"

They started right in again.

"Nope. Somebody's got to hitch up that hose."

"Anyone know how?"

"Okay, she's hitched up," said Herod. "Now I'm going to turn her on."

He stood back proudly as the hose filled and stiffened, and three young men ran to pick up the business end and direct it toward the timbers burning high above them against the night sky.

"You're never going to put that one out, Herod." Robert, feeling a sense of dislocation—so many people suddenly, so much shouting and confusion—had staggered over to talk to him.

"What are you doing here, Robert?" asked Herod in surprise.

"Mind if I borrow your pickup? I want to take a friend of mine to the nursing station."

Herod went over with him to look down at Haga, still unconscious, but visibly breathing now, his smoke-blackened face pillowed on Robert's parka ruff.

"He okay?" Herod asked.

"I don't know."

"You look pretty rough, Robert. Got a burn on your face. I guess you don't know."

Herod glanced at the fire-fighting operations. "Look, I'm going to take you," he announced with sudden decision. "I already knew we weren't going to put it out. Thing was, though, I thought the boys could use some practise."

Together they slung Haga into the front seat of the truck. Then Herod drove slowly back down the newly-plowed road into town.

About an hour later, in the nursing station, Robert was staring at himself in a bathroom mirror down the hall from the nurse's office.

Jane, the nurse, was having quite an argument with someone on the telephone.

"Yes, I know all about the condition of the airstrip here," she said. "That's what I said. Smoke inhalation, burns on the hands and face, unconscious." Her pipping, educated English accent made her sound like the Queen broadcasting to the Commonwealth on Christmas Day.

"I'd call the Red Baron back myself, but I have a patient, do you understand? I have two patients. All right, get the doctor to do it then." Twenty years in the North would have made a tartar out of Jane had she not been a tartar already when she arrived.

She put the phone down with a slam and came out of her office.

"All right, Robert, let's see your face," she said, catching sight of him.

"I was looking at it already," said Robert.

He had two ugly raw patches on his cheeks above the line where his scarf had been protecting his mouth and nose. They looked bad, but he thought they would probably heal like frostbite.

"Take off the wet pack." She removed it quite gently. "Too bad. You might have some scarring from that," she said, the pale creamy skin of her forehead wrinkling up with concern.

Jane could be very nice to people when they were sick.

"You should go to the hospital with Haga."

Robert shook his head. "I've got to stay here," he said. "Is Haga going to be all right?"

"Don't worry about Haga, Robert," said Jane, still gentle. "The good Lord looks after him—Why, I have no idea," she added, turning away with a shrug.

Outside was the sound of the fire truck returning with its siren winding up and down slowly on an off-key note. A whole troupe of people entered the nursing station and stood milling in the front hall.

Several of them, seeing Robert, came over to pat him on the back. He was the hero of the event.

"Want to get in the truck, Robert?" Herod now re-entered the nursing station. "I could take you home."

"No thanks, Herod. I'm going to stick around here awhile longer. I want to see my buddy get on that plane," said Robert.

A plane was coming in overhead. The Red Baron had relented.

"It's probably that Beaver again, though," someone said.

"Probably the Red Baron just wants to wreck it."

"Then he'll be able to blame Prohibition Creek when he collects on the insurance."

"He told the hospital he'd sooner send one of his planes to hell," remarked Jane, coming briskly down the hall with Haga on a rolling stretcher.

"I ploughed the airstrip yesterday," said Herod. "It's just that it's—"

"It's too short, the lights aren't working, and there's a ski jump at the west end," Jane said crisply. "I know all about the condition of the airstrip—Let's go, Herod. Robert, are you coming too?"

They carried Haga out on a stretcher and put him in the front seat of Herod's truck. Jane drove slowly to the airstrip, followed by Herod and Robert in the fire truck, a cavalcade of skidoos behind.

"Are you sure you're not going, Robert? He doesn't have an escort," said Jane.

Robert shook his head.

"Goodbye, old pal. Get better in that hospital, okay?"

They were packing Haga into the back of the Beaver, still on the stretcher.

Then the pilot slammed the door of the fuselage, hopped up into the cockpit and slammed that door as well. The plane began to taxi out, down the short, dark runway.

"Come on, Robert," Herod said. "Haga'll be okay. I'm going to take you home now."

They climbed back into the fire truck and drove slowly into town. The siren was still rising and falling mournfully. No one could turn it off, not even Herod. The problem was that he had not been the one who turned it on.

"The boys haven't had much practise, that's the trouble," he remarked.

Robert was exhausted, too punch-drunk to care much about anything. But when Herod pulled the truck to a stop he suddenly noticed that he had taken him to his own house, the one Mary Ann still inhabited with her two tents.

"Here you are," said Herod in a businesslike tone.

"Wait a second. I thought you said you were taking me home."

"I did."

"But this isn't your house." Robert was still confused.

"No, it's your house. Come on."

He got out of the truck, slamming the door. Robert got out too.

A moment later Mary Ann came out of her tent wearing a long flannelette nightgown, her hair in a braid.

"Why are you driving in the fire truck?" The siren had announced their arrival effectively.

"There was a fire at the fish store, Mary Ann." Herod was looking up at her from the bottom of the porch steps. "Robert saved Haga's life," he continued. "He dragged him out of the burning building. I just brought him home."

"Home?" said Mary Ann blankly.

"Yeah. This is his place, isn't it?" Herod was trying to be persuasive. These were two very stubborn people, he knew, but they were married in the sight of God, and as far as Herod was concerned, what God had bound together, man should not put asunder.

Neither Robert nor Mary Ann were looking at each other. They were both staring in annoyance at Herod. Robert would have begun to walk off, but Herod grabbed his wrist.

"Come on, you guys."

Robert detached his wrist from Herod's grasp.

"Aw heck," said Herod, giving up. "I'm just going to leave you alone. Work it out, all right?"

◆ 17. A NEW HOME ◆

Robert woke up late the next morning in Bobby's tent. Sunlight came pouring through the clean white canvas of the walls and roof; for a moment he was confused. Then the pain of the burns on his cheeks made him remember.

He had come back to Prohibition Creek last night from his trapping expedition with Elvis, and he had been intending to go find Rebecca right away this morning and see—just see—whether he meant anything to her. But now his plans were in disarray: his face was disfigured, at least temporarily; and he had no place to take Rebecca to, in case she decided—

This thought made him sit up energetically. He had to get a place fast, in case she decided what he hoped she would decide.

A moment later—for he did not have to dress, having fallen asleep in his coveralls—he was standing rather awkwardly outside Mary Ann's tent on the platform that had once been the kitchen floor.

"Mary Ann? I just came by to say thanks. For letting me stay in Bobby's tent."

"Do you want tea?" she asked from within.

"No thanks. I've got to get going. I've got to find myself another place now that the fish-store shack burned down."

"What other place is there?" Mary Ann put her head out the door and Robert took a step backwards.

"I don't know," he said, shrugging.

She regarded him in suspicious silence. She didn't want Robert getting the idea he could stay here forever, no matter what Herod thought about it.

"Well, this is your place, not mine," said Robert, divining her thought. "Maybe they'll put the walls up again soon," he went on. "Then you won't even need a tent."

"They're going to make the house all different inside," she said gruffy.

"I guess you're worried that Bobby won't like that."

This had been on her mind. She looked at him anxiously.

"Well, never mind," said Robert. "After you take down his tent, everything in his room will be just the same."

"Did you make his bed?" she demanded.

"Yeah." He hadn't, although it had been neat enough the way he left it.

"Well—I guess I'll be going," he said.

She had stepped out and was already heading for Bobby's tent to tidy up after Robert.

It was a kind of symbiosis they had and they both hated it: that Mary Ann asked Robert whether he had made the bed even though she didn't trust him anyway, and that he bothered to lie, even though he knew she would check.

Now Robert ran down the porch steps and crunched off through the snow, feeling a burden lifted from his shoulders. He had been pretty sure that Mary Ann didn't want him back and would never make up, but she had just confirmed it for him very satisfactorily.

She was a strong-minded woman. He had never thought this was such a good thing until now.

Rebecca was out that morning as usual, following her planned walkabout through town.

She was passing the fire truck garage, midway between the store and the drop-in centre. Herod was out in front sitting in the cab of the truck, tinkering with the siren which was still sirening up and down, but very slowly and hoarsely. She went over to talk to him.

As with all scandals in a settlement like Prohibition Creek, whom you were on speaking terms with often depended upon what your last name was. Rebecca didn't understand this very well, as an outsider and a city girl—but while she was a scarlet woman to the Woodcutters, her Metis relatives, the McCraes, were naturally all on her side.

Of course, Herod was too dignified for gossip. He liked Rebecca, pure and simple; and he had been getting very fond of her lately since she had been coming to see him so often.

Rebecca went up to the cab, and stood on the running board. "Hello, Herod."

The siren quit suddenly.

"There," said Herod, pleased with himself.

It started again, more faintly.

"That was quite a noise last night," said Rebecca. "I heard the siren going for hours."

The siren stopped again.

"There," said Herod, less pleased.

"You're having trouble with the siren, are you? Was it a false alarm?" she went on.

"Nope," said Herod. "The fish store burned down."

"The fish store?" she said in alarm. "But Haga was living in the shack out there."

"Yep," said Herod.

"Is Haga all right, Herod?" Rebecca was alarmed.

"He was unconscious," said Herod absently. "And he had some burns. They put him on a plane for the hospital. But the nurse thinks he'll be okay."

"He was in the shack?"

"Yeah. Robert got him out of there right after that old oil furnace blew up."

"Robert?" Her voice rose and broke. "But Robert is away trapping."

"Well, he got back. Lucky for Haga."

Rebecca was rendered speechless by the news for a moment.

"And Robert? Is he—Is he—?" she stammered.

"He just got some burns on his face."

Rebecca had begun to cry in relief, pleasure, delight that he was safe; and also in empathy for his injuries, and fear—dread, really, of what was coming next. It was like one of those fortunately-unfortunately stories where something bad succeeds something good so fast that a person cannot tell how it is all going to end. And it seemed to her that this was just like the story of her life so far.

Herod didn't notice. He was still staring at the switch in perplexity. If a thing could fix itself, it could just as well unfix itself in a moment.

"After we got Haga on that plane I took Robert home. I figured Mary Ann would make it up with him finally. Every woman loves a hero."

Just as he had feared, the fire siren started up again suddenly and with renewed vigour. Losing patience, Herod gave it a hard thump and it quit immediately.

"You were telling me—" Rebecca had swallowed her tears, even though this was the double whammy she had been dreading "—about Robert and Mary Ann."

"Well, he spent the night."

"He spent the night with her?"

"Yeah." Herod flicked the switch to ON and the siren started. It sounded pretty good. He flicked it back to OFF and it stopped—just like that.

"So they made it up?" she asked.

Herod shrugged. "Must have."

Rebecca turned away abruptly and began to walk home.

Herod gave the siren another thump, an affectionate one this time.

"Yep. I think that's fixed again," he said. He turned to address Rebecca, but she was already gone. Then he craned out the window of the fire truck and caught a glimpse of her walking away.

Herod was not being entirely ingenuous in telling Rebecca that Robert had gone back to his wife. He didn't know whether Robert had gone back to Mary Ann or not, but he had heard something, first of all about Rebecca and Robert, and then, more recently, about Rebecca and Danny, and he wanted to set his niece on the right track. She was in a fair way to take after her father—Herod also belonged to one of those "two brothers" stories—and that was a shame, in his opinion.

◆ ◆ ◆

Robert had gone out to the fish-store shack to pick up Elvis's skidoo from where he had left it the night before. He passed by Rebecca's trailer and noted from the disposition of footprints that she was still living there, but he did not pause to see if she was at home. He had a plan to carry out.

The fish store and the shack were completely gone, leaving a gaping, blackened hole in the snow. Robert gazed at it for a moment, feeling an unexpected sorrow at its destruction. So much had happened to him while he was living in the shack. He was hardly the same person he had been when he had first swept it out with the stump of a broom.

A moment later he hopped on Elvis's skidoo and roared off. There was no time to waste. He had to find or borrow or make some kind of home for himself fast.

All at once he stopped and jumped off the skidoo. There was an old teepee frame down by the lakeshore, a picturesque and somewhat melancholy reminder of the almost prehistoric times before the fish plant had been erected, when Robert's people, his grandparents and great grandparents and a thousand years worth of ancestors before them, had camped by the lake and fished.

The teepee itself was only about twenty years old; the canvas that clung to it was tattered and rotten, but the poles were still sound, and someone had put a little plywood around the bottom to keep the wind out. Probably kids, Robert surmised, investigating further, and finding a beaver house of charred sticks, broken beer bottles, cigarette butts, and discarded clothing, including one rubber boot with the moccasin still in it.

Without giving it much more thought, for this was certainly the only private residence he was likely to find on such short notice, Robert kicked the mess on the floor out the door, and taking an axe from his pack, went to cut some spruce boughs to make a clean mat around the fireplace.

"I wonder what Rebecca will think? It's not exactly a palace," he said, about an hour later, standing back to inspect the results of his labour.

He had to take the skidoo back, go borrow a tarp from the band hall so as to replace the rotten canvas flapping around the poles, and get cleaned up and change his clothes at his mother's place.

He laughed, beginning to get excited. He wanted to see Rebecca right now, to bring her out here and find out what she would think about living in a teepee. He wanted to see her there, sitting on her heels in front of the fire.

◄ ◄ ◄

Rebecca was at home, packing. She was crying. Now she paused in her activities to cry more violently.

Robert had come back. But it was a bitter thought. He had come back to go home to his wife.

He had never even kissed her or made any suggestion that he was interested in her. That idea had been all in her imagination. It had started after she spent the night at the shack; then for some reason while he was away she had imagined he was thinking of her, that he really cared for her, and had just gone away while he figured out what to do about it.

However, he had probably just been thinking about going back to his wife all the time he was away.

With considerable determination she stopped crying .

Her last errand was to go see Danny and tell him she was leaving. It would be a short interview—she had a plane to catch.

"Goodbye trailer. I hated living here."

◂ ◂ ◂

After she left, Danny sat wrapped in his own bitter thoughts.

He was not as hypocritical as Rebecca and Robert thought he was. He had told Roseanne that his affair with Rebecca in Yellowknife had been all Rebecca's fault and now he had to follow through on that, because he wanted to save his family. The problem was that he couldn't stand himself. Even if he had made the right decision, he was no longer clean and pure and single-minded, the way he had been in the fall.

Seeing Rebecca filled him with a seething mass of emotions: desire, shame, fear, anger. But now that she was gone forever all he felt was self-disgust.

The door of his office opened for the second time that afternoon, and Robert entered.

He started right in. "Danny, I want to borrow that tarp—" Then he broke off.

"Hey! What's the matter?"

He had noticed that Danny was a kind of ashen-grey colour, and he sat upright and motionless in his swivel chair; for a moment Robert was wondering if he might have died in that position.

"Nothing," said Danny.

"Are you kidding?" said Robert. "Tell me."

"All right. Rebecca just came here to say she quit her job."

"What?" Robert had sat down, but he stood up again right away. "Where is she now?" he demanded.

"Going to the airport, I guess."

"The airport?" Robert was still coming to grips with this information. "I just heard a plane landing. When I was coming over here."

Danny shrugged.

Robert stared at him for a moment, his thoughts whirling. Danny stared back curiously, not understanding what was on Robert's mind, but grasping that he was agitated.

"What about that tarp? You want it for something?"

"Yes!" shouted Robert, running out of the building. "No! Hey, sorry, but I've got to go right now."

"Well, can't you even take the time to close the door after you?" Danny grumbled, crossing the big room.

He held the door open for a moment, looking out. Robert was running furiously down the street, then up the road that led to the airport, still keeping up a wild turn of speed.

Why was he running like that? Danny wondered. And then, into his mind, which had been focused for so long on his troubles at home and with himself, with his conscience, came a strange new thought.

Robert running to the airport. After Rebecca?

◂ ◂ ◂

Rebecca had been just in time to get on the plane. There were four other passengers; the plane was full.

Don slammed the back door after her, then got into his own seat up front and began running up the engine.

Suddenly Robert's face appeared in the cockpit window beside the pilot. He had jumped up on the ski strut, in spite of the wild wind from the propellor. Then he began beating with his mitts against the curved Perspex of the windshield, making it clear that he wasn't going to go away.

Rebecca, in the back, didn't know what was going on; she craned forward. She was thinking that there was something the matter with the plane; or maybe it was Don, trying to scare everyone.

The pilot had reduced the power. Now he put the parking brake back on. He got out, and there was an altercation outside.

Suddenly Rebecca was able to make out through the window of the passenger beside her that Robert was there, and it looked for a moment as though Don was going to punch him in the face.

But Robert stood there, explaining patiently, his hands at his sides, and with a violent gesture, Don turned back to the plane and opened the door of the fuselage.

"C'mon," he said to Rebecca. "Out you get." He grabbed her wrist and began pulling her out of the plane quite roughly, dragging her across the legs and knees of the person sitting by the door.

She understood that he was taking revenge on her not only for this strange interruption but for her behaviour last fall. She felt his anger and contempt in the hand he was squeezing, and all the way up her arm. He hated her as a woman, as a native, and as a native woman who preferred another man.

"You want her?" he said. "Here." He projected her into Robert's arms.

"Okay," said Robert, holding onto Rebecca.

"What are you doing?" she cried angrily, twisting her head around to see Robert behind her. "Why are you doing this?"

Don was slamming the door to the fuselage. A moment later he hopped up into the cockpit, revved the engine and taxied out. Whatever Robert was saying was lost in the wind and prop wash.

Robert released his grip on Rebecca and began to walk her, holding more sedately to her elbow, over to the trees beside the runway.

"Did you have to do that, Robert?" Rebecca was furious.

Robert was still breathing hard.

"My suitcase is on that plane. You just made a fool of me." She was too angry to cry.

"Come over here out of the wind." He drew her into the mouth of a path in the trees.

The plane began its take-off run from the other end of the airstrip, coming fast up over their heads.

"Robert, this isn't like you," Rebecca shouted over the noise. "What are you trying to prove?"

He was still in a wild physical state, having run half a mile from town and having nearly got into a fist fight; and the aircraft noise overhead was at an inhuman pitch.

"I needed to tell you something." The sound of the aircraft was receding. He drew her further into the bush. It was calm in there, and somehow secure.

Rebecca had begun to cry now. "It doesn't matter what you have to say to me, Robert."

The plane was a million miles away now, as far as he was concerned. What he had to say to her—he was not going to say it in words.

There was a hushed silence all around them, deep snow on the path, on the branches of the spruce trees.

Robert took her in his arms and began to kiss her on her pretty, angry upturned face, her wet cheeks, her astonished mouth, that softened and opened slightly under the pressure of his lips and tongue.

Rebecca had been crying, but now she began to laugh. "Was that what it was?"

"Yeah. That was it," he said.

Her face was still turned up; he was kissing her again. It was a splendid kiss.

There were bush noises all of a sudden; the subtle, muted noises of small birds in the spruce trees and the mice under the snow. A flock of snowbirds settled on the ground almost at their feet, in among the withered branches of the Labrador tea.

"I ran all the way to the airstrip," Robert said.

It seemed scarcely possible to Rebecca that such a thing could have happened, that he had come and got her off the plane at the eleventh hour. But there was reality in the arrogant curve of Robert's lips, the flare of his nostril, the tight, possessive way he was holding her.

"I dreamed about you the whole time I was out there with Elvis," he said.

Robert had not been sure he would tell her this. It made him vulnerable, letting her know that she had so much power over him. But the feeling he had in the dreams was upon him now, and he had to tell the truth.

"It wasn't just that I saw you. You talked to me," he went on. She was listening, wide-eyed, her mouth a little open. "And I told you things I didn't even know about myself."

"I was talking to you, Robert. I talked to you all the time when I was alone."

They stared at each other, hardly daring to believe that it was true. Then they started to kiss again spontaneously.

"Are you in love with me?" Rebecca removed her lips, still gazing into his eyes.

"Yeah," he said.

"Am I in love with you, Robert?" she asked, resting against him happily.

"I'm pretty sure you are," he said.

All at once he took her hand and began to lead her down the path.

"Where are we going?" She wasn't sure where they were in relation to the town and she thought they could be going to the shack. But then it occurred to her that the shack had burned down.

"I've got an old teepee out by the lake," he explained. "I started fixing it up this afternoon. I went into town to borrow a tarp from Danny and that was when I heard you were leaving."

She stopped short, her high-heeled leather boots ankle deep in snow on the path, and he turned around to look at her.

"But you spent the night with Mary Ann, didn't you?" The pressure of Robert's mouth on her own, the clasp of his arms, had driven this completely out of her head for a short while.

"She let me sleep in Bobby's tent," replied Robert, considerably startled.

She looked at him blankly, and he realized that she didn't know what he was talking about.

"I mean the tent we set up in his room. I had to have a place to sleep. It was kind of late after they got Haga out on the medivac."

To his horror—although, on second thought, he was happy about it—she burst into tears again.

"Did you think I moved back in with Mary Ann?" he asked.

"Yes! That was why I was going, Robert. I thought you went back to your wife and I—I didn't believe this would ever happen."

"Well, it would have happened a lot sooner if it hadn't been for that doggone fire."

She had stopped crying as suddenly as she started, and Robert was kissing her again, rather more urgently than before, because they were getting close to the teepee.

All at once Haga's dog began to bark at them. She was still tethered out by the remains of the shack; Robert had forgotten about her till now. Rebecca hung back, tugging slightly on his hand.

"Don't be scared. It's only Haga's dog, Lassie."

"But I'm afraid of bushmen too," she said.

They came out into the clearing and she began to walk at a brisker pace, freed from the terror of the woods.

"Don't you think there are bushmen, Robert?"

Robert had delivered her to the very door of the teepee now and he didn't have time to think about this question. Maybe some other time he could explain his complex views on the subject: the certainty he had out in the bush that there were other intelligent beings surrounding him, not all of which he could sense directly—and the feeling he sometimes had that he was not independent of all that, but only a function of a larger intelligence comprised by the whole.

He stooped down to enter the teepee.

"Come in." He had paused, holding up the flap. "It's my house."

It was dark in there despite the rents in the canvas. It was a gloomy day; unusual for the end of February, it had turned out to be a lowering, cloudy afternoon. And it was already after four o'clock.

Rebecca entered hesitantly and stood just inside the door, while Robert knelt down and began lighting a fire.

She continued to watch as he put on more wood and began setting up the grate and the billy.

She was wearing good clothes for travelling—not jeans, but polyester slacks, a white cotton blouse, a little jacket she had bought to go with the slacks, her parka and leather boots.

Robert looked up, saw her there, and remarked: "I'll have a good fire going in a minute."

She was afraid; her eyes were very large and dark as she watched him doing these things that were really a woman's job. He was a little anxious about what she was thinking.

"My dad always said I'd end up in a teepee if I didn't mend my ways." She gave a shaky laugh.

The fire was now going strongly. Robert got up off his heels and went to her, still standing by the door.

"Come sit on my blanket. Then you won't get your clothes dirty," he suggested.

He brought her to sit on his sleeping bag and she came readily enough. But he was still nervous of her reaction. There was no place else that he could take her but this teepee.

"It's kind of a mess in here," he remarked.

"You haven't really had time to set up housekeeping yet." She turned her head to look directly into his eyes.

"I was trying to do that before I—well, before I brought you here."

He put his arm around her, and she settled in against him.

"And now you brought me here," she said softly, looking into the fire, and Robert knew that she was all right. She had merely been frightened by the unfamiliarity of the teepee, and the bush all around them. But she trusted him; she wasn't scared when she was beside him like this.

"I think I'll put some more wood on that fire," said Robert.

He had already made an astoundingly large fire for a teepee which because of its design—even one in such poor condition as this—tended to warm up with a minimum of wood. So he settled for pushing the fire around a little, then sat back down beside Rebecca.

Rebecca had been watching him do this dreamily. She turned her head as Robert put his arm around her again. "I looked after Haga while you were away, Robert. He thought he was taking care of me."

Robert was startled. He had forgotten about his last conversation with Haga.

"He did?" he said.

Rebecca laughed.

"Well, you told him to, didn't you?"

"I did?" Robert had drawn a blank. Perhaps he had. He didn't remember how he had gotten out of Prohibition Creek. It had been hard—that was all he knew now.

"He said you did," Rebecca said.

"What did he do?" said Robert cautiously. "I mean, to look after you?"

"He hung around. I let him sleep on the floor while I was working," she replied.

"He snores pretty bad," said Robert.

"I didn't mind. He was lonely without you, Robert."

"He just didn't have anybody to bum smokes from," said Robert in cynicism.

"I lent him some money the other day," she said. "I made him swear he would only use the money to buy cigarettes."

Robert was now staring at her in consternation and surprise.

"Oh no!" she cried. "That's not how he burned down the shack, is it?"

"I think so. He was probably smoking in bed," Robert said.

"Then it's all my fault!"

"Are you kidding?" Robert tried to hold her down in the curve of his arm. "Haga would have found some way to burn down the shack even if you hadn't given him the money."

Rebecca turned toward him suddenly, kneeling up and freeing herself from his arm completely.

"You saved his life, Robert. Herod told me."

Robert was glad she had heard. He would never have been able to tell her about that himself.

"It was a brave thing to do. You're a hero."

The tears in her eyes did not disturb him at all.

"It's not such a big deal. I'm always having to save his life," he remarked.

Rebecca put her hands up to Robert's face, touching it tenderly.

"Robert," she said, almost whispering. "The burns on your face. I cried when I heard about them." Two big tears were tracking down her cheeks, but again he did not find this in any way annoying.

They were kissing again, kneeling against one another. Something new and important was about to begin; they both knew it.

Then Robert broke off their kiss to lay her on the sleeping bag against his parka, thrown down there where he had taken it off when he came in.

He knelt above her, staring down at her, at her beauty, her slim ness and smallness. For a moment he hesitated, seeing again the good clothes she wore, her smoothly combed hair done up on the back of her head. He had washed at his mother's house, but the clothes he had on were still those he had been wearing in the bush, and they smelled of the bush, of animal blood and campfires and spruce pitch, all things unfamiliar to Rebecca.

She held out her arms to him with a small cry of desire and at once he came forward to lie upon her and kiss her lips, her closed eyes, her neck, to unbutton her little jacket and her blouse.

To Robert it seemed like an old-time courtship, as though he had won this woman and brought her to this hastily prepared place to convince her with his body alone that she was his. He had nothing else, only the clothes he wore, his bedroll and the scanty contents of his pack.

A moment later he raised himself up to take the clip out of her hair and pull it down onto her shoulders—so that Rebecca would look like the Dene girl he had seen so many times in his dreams.

• 18. THE LAW OF THERMODYNAMICS •

Robert was up early as usual. Rebecca had still been asleep when he went out to chop wood. He remembered what she looked like when she was sleeping from before, that time at the shack, her innocence.

But this was different from the night she had spent at the shack. Everything was different between them now, and he was still vibrating with excitement.

He came in with an armload of wood and put it down neatly beside the fire.

Rebecca was sitting on his bedroll, cross-legged and fully dressed. She had been brushing her hair, but she put the brush back in her purse as he came in.

He went to lay a stick of wood on the fire, feeling almost shy. "You weren't cold—during the night?"

He knew she hadn't been cold. He had kept the fire well stoked during the intervals when they were not sleeping or making love.

At one point they had even had tea, although neither of them had been able to finish drinking it.

He wanted tea now.

He put the billy on the fire, then rummaged in his pack for tea bags and the sugar. There was still some bannock in there, old and hard, and he got it out. "Want one?"

"Yes, please. I'm hungry," she said, putting out her hand for it.

Robert was about to give her one of the biscuits. On second thought he took her hand instead, and turning it around, stared down at the inside of her wrist where the blue veins showed under the coffee and cream of her skin.

He was secretly dying for her again, remembering the way she had been during the night. But she was hungry and he wanted her to eat too.

She picked up the bannock nonchalantly, where it had fallen onto the sleeping bag between them and Robert went back to his tea-making.

Rebecca looked up through the smoke hole of the teepee with admiration. Even in its tattered condition with the grey, mildewed canvas barely clinging to its poles, it was aesthetically satisfying as a dwelling, and surprisingly comfortable when you lived on the ground, without the square corners of conventional furniture.

She was also impressed by Robert's easy ability to keep the fire going, to make the space around him neat and cozy. She had never been with a man who had his skills; and she believed that they were only the outward manifestation of a whole life-system that she knew nothing about, that made it possible for him to go to the bush for weeks or months as the impulse took him.

"You know how to live in the bush, don't you, Robert?" she said.

"I'd better. I'm Dene." Robert sat beside her, one knee up, consuming his bannock, and Rebecca admired his profile, like a peregrine falcon, with the slightly flattened shape of his broken nose.

"You go off hunting and trapping for weeks with Haga or Elvis," she said. "I never really knew anybody who could do that before."

"Well, I didn't do it much, the last few years. But I always knew

I could, if I wanted to. My dad and Ama used to take us out from when we were little kids."

"I wish I could go with you sometime." It was part of a secret fantasy of hers to go to the bush.

"You can," he said simply. "I want you to come."

They were very conscious of each other, although they were merely sitting side by side, eating, like children or a pair of old people.

"When I was growing up, people still used to go with their families and stay till Christmas," Robert said. "Then they'd go out again in the spring and stay through the breakup."

No one did that now; everything else had changed as well. No one would be willing to go for the winter, the way Robert had done long ago with his mother and father, taking even the baby.

However, even for his family that had been an unusual thing to do, going out so early after Christmas. Even back then the children had had to go to school in town; families didn't go to the bush until breakup time, for the fish runs.

The school was part of the ruination of his society, in Robert's opinion. Literacy was the forced introduction of another language; the truancy laws had separated families, or made them unable to pursue their livelihood. The real old-time Dene had educated their children without schools.

"There's a place out in the mountains I'd like to find some day," he remarked. "They call it the mountain where the boys died."

Rebecca was listening to him, her face sparkling with interest, ready to hear the story.

He didn't really know this story, the way it began or the way it ended. His father had told him about the place one time, that was all.

"I think that back in the old days sometimes a boy went out to live by himself for a while, after he got to be fourteen or so. Maybe it was a kind of a test. To see if he could do it. And then afterwards that boy always knew, see? That he could do it if he had to."

"But they died, you said."

"There was one place where a lot of them went, I guess. A mountain. And none of them ever came back."

"But Robert, that's horrible," said Rebecca.

"Well, maybe it is," he conceded. "But when my dad told me, I wanted to go there."

His father had told him about it when he was around fourteen himself, and beginning to get into trouble. Perhaps it had been as a kind of threat that he had told him—Robert knew that he had been just about out of control already; or else as a strange joke. But whatever it was, threat or joke, the idea had made a deep impression on him.

"Did you want to see whether you'd be able to make it?"

"I used to think about it a lot. What I'd do." He was staring into space. It was still an attractive idea.

Rebecca shuddered. But Robert, turning to look, saw that she found it fascinating as well.

"I always thought I could have made it," he said.

She nodded. Rebecca fully understood the idea of a personal test. Even though it was frightening—and she was afraid in the bush even right around town—she was a brave person too.

"Do you know what I'd like to do sometime?" he continued eagerly. "I'd like to go live in the mountains. Not even the way it was when I was a kid. Really to live out there."

"You'd have to have some things from the store. Like tea, and—and gas," she said.

"And shells," he said. "But I guess you could still make enough out of fur to pay for that. Want to come?" he added casually.

"Yes," she said. "I'm Dene too, Robert." She spoke with that passion that he had seen before, when they argued about the nursery school.

He was glad she felt that way about being Dene. Going to the bush was in her blood, after all, even if she had never done it before.

Robert was very excited suddenly. There was nothing to stop them.

"Would you really do it, Rebecca?"

"Yes," she said again. They were both taking this very seriously all of a sudden.

"We don't have a skidoo," she said.

"That's okay," he replied. "We can walk. They used to in the old days. They walked all over those mountains."

They could take some dogs, Robert was thinking. He thought he could still drive dogs. The rivers would be a problem after breakup, and they would have to teach themselves to make bark canoes or skin boats. In the past, his people had made enormous boats, forty or fifty feet long, involving eight to ten moose hides, sewn together with sinew and caulked with spruce pitch, to bring down their furs out of the mountains for trade.

"I don't know how to do anything. I barely even know how to sew," Rebecca spoke ruefully; even though she could use a computer, she really felt for the moment that she didn't know how to do anything.

It was true that the Dene women in her background had highly specialized skills. The sewing they had to do was continuous, not only on clothing, but on packs, sled covers, and dog harnesses. One of the things that made it almost impossible for a man to go out and live alone for long was that he couldn't sew well enough.

"You're smart enough to learn." That really was the main point, he thought.

"I'll have to learn everything right from the beginning. I wasn't brought up the way you were."

It was incredible to Robert that Rebecca really wanted to come with him. There was no one else in Prohibition Creek who would have entertained the idea for a moment, not even people like his mother, or Mary Ann, who had the skills.

"My wife was brought up like me," Robert said. "She even knows how to hunt."

Rebecca was instantly burning with jealousy, partly because of the way he said "my wife."

"But she doesn't want to," he continued. "She just wants to sit in a house with an oil furnace." Robert was pondering. "Of course she went to that school in the Forks. They told us it was better to have a house and live in town. Nothing Dene people did was any good according to them."

"But didn't you go out on the land together?" Rebecca demanded.

"Nothing like what we're talking about."

They had gone on hunting trips sometimes and to the camp at Joker Lake. But after Bobby was born Robert had taken up poker—and women. As part of her stoical, obstinate response to that, Mary Ann would never go anywhere with him.

"I wish Mary Ann didn't know how to do all those things," Rebecca cried in her jealousy.

"Well, she'd never go do them," he said, surprised.

"But maybe I'm the wrong person to take. You should take her instead."

"Mary Ann would have thought I was nuts. Besides, you said you'd go." Robert still hadn't picked up on her agitation.

"Did you love Mary Ann?" she demanded. "Did you marry her because you loved her?"

"Yeah. At least, I did before I married her. But I was a crazy guy in those days."

"What's the matter?" he asked a moment later.

"Can't you tell that I'm jealous, Robert?"

Robert was bewildered. He believed he had just been explaining, at least partly, what was awry with Mary Ann.

"You said that you loved her."

He thought, not for the last time, that it was going to be difficult having a woman he couldn't lie to.

"You must have cared about that guy you married, too," he pointed out.

"Yes," she said reluctantly. "But—but it wasn't like this."

Robert was jealous himself all of a sudden. He didn't like that whiteman; in fact, he despised him. How could she have been in love with him? And what about all those other men, including his brother Danny?

But he saw at once that this was unreasonable. He had made a mess of his marriage and screwed up his own life in somewhat the same way Rebecca had screwed up hers. There was no point in reproaching her for that.

"Nothing has ever been like this, Robert," said Rebecca. She was looking at him sadly, understanding what had been on his mind.

She wanted a new start. She was not going to screw it up again. And she felt it was true that nothing had ever been like this.

It was a surprise to him that he could follow her thoughts just as easily as she had been following his.

They smiled at one another suddenly.

Robert began putting the food back in his pack and clearing up around the fire.

"I guess we'll need to get ammunition at the store," said Rebecca. "And things like matches and thread."

Robert was looking critically at her clothes. "Your parka's okay," he said. "Those boots wouldn't last a minute. We should take another blanket. I wonder whether I can get credit on the strength of that fur cheque?"

"I have some money in my purse," Rebecca said. "And there's my pay cheque. I guess I'll still be getting that."

Robert looked at her in surprise.

"Well, I had a job until yesterday," she said. "I didn't even tell my boss I quit yet."

Since yesterday he had forgotten everything except her physical immediacy, the lovemaking of last night. Then there was the way they sat here now, working out this plan: close together although not touching; but close enough, apparently, to be aware of each other's very thoughts.

Danny was the only person she had told that she was leaving, he thought.

It was suddenly very clear to Robert how impulsively she had acted the day before. It was only because she had heard he was going back to his wife that she had jumped aboard that plane. She had not really quit her job at all.

"I couldn't stand it any longer anyway," Rebecca said. "My boss was doing an investigation because of that petition against me. She was going to come in here next week with the results."

"She was, was she?" Robert was thinking furiously.

"So I probably would have been on the plane to Yellowknife anyway."

It was very hard for him to turn back from the realization of that plan they had just been making; it had been in the back of his mind for so many years.

"What were you going to do when you got there?" he asked her, knowing the answer.

"I was going to try—one more time—to get my kids back."

"But you wouldn't have got them," said Robert.

"No," she agreed. "Not if I lost my job."

"That's what you want, isn't it?" Robert continued. "To get your kids back?"

"Yes."

"So you can't quit." Robert was just following out his reasoning.

"But they're going to fire me anyway," she pointed out.

"No, they're not," he replied. "I saw that petition. They'll never fire you for that. And you did a lot of work here."

"I was still doing my work."

He rose onto his knees. "Well, okay. I think you should go to your office this morning. Look, it's early yet."

They both looked at Rebecca's watch. It was 9:15.

"But Robert—What about going to the mountains?"

"We're not going. It's a big daydream, that's all." There would probably never be another chance. If Rebecca got her kids she would no longer want to go with him, not in the way they had just been speaking of. It was a simple dilemma, and they both knew which choice was the right one.

"No, it isn't. You want to go out there. To try to live out there."

He wanted to test himself, Rebecca knew. But he also wanted to do it because he thought it would be a better life, the best kind of life that he could live. Robert was an idealist too, in his own way.

"But I'm not going to do it," he said. "I'm going to stay here."

"Because of me, Robert?" There were tears in her eyes.

"Because of you, Rebecca."

◂ ◂ ◂

"What you do in your private life is up to you, Rebecca," Marcia was explaining. "There was never any question of firing you for that."

It was a nice warm day at the end of February, only about minus twenty degrees, with a high blue sky. Rebecca and her boss were walking from the trailer downtown to the band hall.

"The only question was whether you were doing your job."

"I showed you all the work I did," said Rebecca. "It's just that so many people stopped going to AA after Christmas."

"Well, Rome wasn't built in a day," Marcia remarked.

A whole week had passed since Rebecca had been rescued by Robert in her impulsive attempt to escape from Prohibition Creek. No one knew that anything like that had even happened except Danny and Don, the pilot of the plane, and neither of them were talking.

In the meantime, although she still worked out of the trailer, she had taken up residence in a teepee, a considerably improved teepee, with new poles, a new canvas tarp, a fine spruce mat covering the floor, a big woodpile, an outhouse that had been moved down, lock and stock, from the fish store.

The Complaints Department had taken over her affairs entirely for the time being.

And Robert had been very busy. He had reset Haga's snare line and begun doing a little ice fishing with Elvis, but most of the time he spent dreaming up ways to make his new place better and more comfortable so that Rebecca would like to live there; for he had made a vow never to reside in an oil-heated and government-supplied house again. Every evening when Rebecca finished work, he was waiting for her outside the trailer to walk her home through the bush to the teepee, where he could talk to her and make love to her in the intervals.

It was lucky for them that they had met when they had, when they were both making big changes in their lives. As it was, their paths had come to an intersection just at the right moment in history. Even more massive changes were on the way—signalled, curiously enough, by the fact that Robert had recently learned how to use a washing machine. Rebecca showed him. He washed all of the filthy things he had been wearing in the bush, and then, since she was busy, her clothes as well.

Rebecca and Marcia were actually on their way to a meeting in the band hall. Marcia stopped briefly outside the door.

She was a little woman with a little high voice, who used these features to commanding effect. Most people felt clumsy and ineffectual beside her, even slim, clever Rebecca. But Rebecca believed, nevertheless, that Marcia was sincerely trying to help her.

"I'm a little worried about you, Rebecca," she was saying in her small, fluting voice. "Do you think you can handle this?"

Rebecca nodded. She was, in fact, terrified of going to this meeting, but she knew it had to be got through. It was the final test: if she could get through this, however it went, her ordeal in Prohibition Creek would be over.

"You're not being put on trial or anything," Marcia said. "And after all, you can always be transferred if the people here don't accept you."

But they both knew that it was a trial, and that Rebecca would never be a social worker at any Dene settlement in the Western Arctic if this community rejected her.

They entered the hall. It was a public, not a Band meeting, and a large number of people were present, sitting on the benches around the walls. A table was pulled out into the middle of the floor at which Danny, Elvis and several other members of the Band Council were sitting. She and Marcia went to sit at the other end of this table.

"All right," said Danny, speaking over the hubbub. "Let's get this meeting off the ground."

The noise in the room subsided.

"First of all, this is Marcia from Social Services," Danny went on. "She called this meeting to discuss the Drug and Alcohol Program. Let's hear from you now, Marcia." His voice was dry and strained. Rebecca knew the meeting was an ordeal for him too, but he wasn't the one on trial, only a perjured witness.

Marcia had stood up: "—just like to say that Prohibition Creek is our star community. You people have done a lot this year with your drug and alcohol abuse prevention program. The new chief has been a real leader in this area."

Danny bowed his head in acknowledgement, his face expressionless.

"I received a complaint about your Social Services employee in February," Marcia went on. "So I came in to discuss it with her. I'm happy to say that her work has been very well done. We went over the files together yesterday and today."

There was a constrained silence in the hall.

At this moment—and it was like a film to Rebecca—Robert entered the hall, walked coolly across the floor and pulled out a chair for himself to sit with the Band Council.

Rebecca had already been looking for him in the audience on the benches by the wall—where Sarah and Roseanne were sitting. She knew that he was intending to come and support her, but it had not occurred to her before that he might do something destructive here, possibly even break up the meeting.

She watched apprehensively as, unzipping his parka, Robert pushed back his chair and lounged beside the table, gazing first at Marcia, and then, penetratingly, at Danny.

Everyone else was looking at Danny too. He cleared his throat.

"If that's all you want to say about that, let's go on to the next item."

Still no one spoke; and the embarrassed pause continued. Robert shifted his gaze to the ceiling.

"There's another thing I wanted to raise at this meeting," said Marcia.

"Well—go ahead," said Danny. Rebecca detected a note of relief in his voice. The actual cause of the complaint had not been mentioned by Marcia, and no one else had spoken up. Not yet, at least.

"You have an application in for a nursery school." Marcia was really changing the subject.

"We do?" Danny said blankly.

"As you know, these are hard economic times and the Department of Social Services is having cutbacks in all program areas." Marcia turned to Rebecca. "But I gather that this project has a lot of public support," she went on. "Which is why I really wanted to take it up at this meeting."

"So?" Danny was angry, although he tried to disguise it. He smoothed his eyebrows.

"Your application did not go through. The Nursery Schools Program was only a pilot and we've had to cut it altogether."

"Too bad," said Danny. He sat back in his chair.

"So if you want a nursery school here you'd have to find the money in your Drug and Alcohol Program budget," she continued.

"You mean, we'd have to take the funding out of our own pocket?" He was furious again.

"It's all government money, Danny. Just a question of your priorities." Marcia was looking at him, bright-eyed, her head tilted like a bird. She was surprised to be receiving conflict from this unexpected quarter.

For Danny was now speaking very definitely.

"The Drug and Alcohol Program has to come first. We can't afford to lose any of the money in that budget for anything else."

"Is that how everyone feels?" Marcia looked thoughtfully at the men clustered around the opposite end of the table: Robert, slouching with one knee up, Elvis sitting neatly and unobtrusively in his chair, his face expressionless, Michael, looking sulky and hungover, Danny, once again smoothing his eyebrows in simulated boredom.

There was another uncomfortable pause at the table and in the audience. No one was going to speak up for the nursery school.

"Mind if I say something?" asked Robert, looking at Danny. "I don't really care how you spend the government's money. But I'm against having a nursery school."

There was a very definite stir along the walls as he said these words. A woman said, "What does he know about it?"

Another, behind him, said, "Shut up, Robert."

Robert turned right around to talk to her directly.

"Now those women who play cards all afternoon aren't even going to have to feel bad about neglecting their kids," he said.

"I guess there are men who play cards all the time too, Robert," remarked another woman on the opposite side of the room.

"Yeah, there are. But a woman's job is to take care of her family."

Rebecca intervened, speaking in a low voice, but firmly. "Women can have different jobs than that, Robert."

"They can," he agreed. "But they shouldn't neglect their kids."

He was only saying what he thought. But Rebecca had thought about this too.

"Some kids in this town are being neglected," she said. "A lot are being looked after pretty well. But all the kids would be better off with a nursery school."

"All we ever throw at the kids these days is school. School and more school," said Robert in disgust.

"A nursery school is a different kind of school, though. It's a play school."

They had the same argument once before; they both remembered that very well.

"You know what I was reading in *Time* magazine?" he demanded. "It said that the way you play—you know, when you're a little kid—has more to do with what you'll do when you grow up than anything else."

"That's why having a nursery school is such a good idea, Robert. If the little children have a secure place to play, with lots of games and toys—they'll have a better chance to grow up happy." She knew she was right.

"They'll grow up into whitemen, you mean." Robert, of course, always thought he was right.

While Rebecca and Robert had been speaking to one another the stir in the room had grown. Whatever hostility there had been against Rebecca had been supplanted entirely by annoyance with Robert.

"Be quiet for a change and let her talk." It was Sarah who spoke, quite suddenly.

"You always had a big mouth, Robert," somebody else snapped.

Several loud arguments had started among the spectators along the wall.

Robert looked at Rebecca and shrugged. They would have had to shout at each other to go on talking.

"I made the application for the grant. Here are some copies if anyone wants to look at it." Rebecca stood up to get them out of her bag.

There was a rush on the table to pick up copies of the application.

Robert took advantage of the comparative silence, as they began to read, to sum up his position.

"All I say is, bringing up children is something that the parents should do."

"Yeah. Look at your own kid, Robert," someone shouted rudely. "Your kid is in jail."

"It's the only way we're going to keep our Dene customs." Robert looked around, strangely unperturbed.

People were really reading the application, turning pages.

Danny didn't have a copy.

"I don't see the point of this discussion if there's no funding for the project," he said.

"As I told you, funding could come out of your drug and alcohol budget," said Marcia in her high, child-like voice.

"How much would it be, though?"

"It isn't very much money for something that could make a lot of difference," said Rebecca. She pushed her master copy of the grant application down the table for him to see, but he left it lying there.

"No," he said. "That's just all there is to it." He glared at her.

"Okay, Danny." Rebecca sat down submissively. But she was secretly furious, not only with Danny for cutting her off, but with herself, for letting him do it.

Other people at the meeting who were not directly in line with Danny's glare, were not so inclined to give in.

"That's just the opinion of Danny and Robert Woodcutter," said a woman.

Another woman was demanding, "Where's the Band Council on this? Couldn't you have a vote?"

"It would only be a vote in principle," said Danny. "How to spend the drug and alcohol money is up to the local board."

"Well, have a vote in principle, then," she shouted.

"Okay." Danny was white with anger. "Anyone on the Band Council want to make a motion?"

No one at the table moved. Elvis was immobile, Michael grimaced, Robert looked around alertly for a moment, then slouched as before.

"They're all men," grumbled somebody from the benches on the wall.

"All Woodcutters." It was the woman who had called for the vote.

Danny said smoothly, "Well, I guess that's that. Anything else, Marcia?"

She shook her head. Then she looked at Rebecca and whispered, smiling, "Better luck next time."

The trial was over. No one had even mentioned the petition they had raised against Rebecca in January. And there was—it was now a proven fact—a lot of public support for a nursery school. There might even be a next time for it to come up.

Danny was going on.

"—There is one other thing that just happened. I got a call from DIAND. It's about the fire at the fish plant last week."

Robert sat up straight again.

"They said they heard about it from the Cooperative Association. Apparently someone over there was going through the insurance claim sheet and he noticed that they could make a claim for a new male and female employees' washroom. Even though the rest of the building was a wreck."

"A claim for employees' washrooms," Robert repeated in disgust.

"Just wait," replied Danny. "That didn't seem right to this guy, so he looked up the file of correspondence."

"You wouldn't think that would help him." Robert laughed.

"Yeah, but this guy was kind of keen about his job. So he finally got hold of a copy of your original application, Robert."

Robert thought of the three page form, blank except for his name at the top, and "The Great Outdoors" pencilled in somewhere below.

"The upshot of it was, he called Indian Affairs, and told them that the Cooperative Association wasn't operating the fish plant anymore, and besides, it burned down. So then they gave us the go-ahead to trade the airport land like we wanted."

"So we're getting an airport?"

Some people in the audience now began to cheer.

Robert was still trying to grasp this strange result, which seemed to be the consequence of Haga burning down the shack.

He had read in *Time* magazine that, according to the laws of physics, systems have a natural trend toward disorder. And when you contemplated a system like this one, involving the Hamlet Council of Prohibition Creek, the Band Council, the federal Department of Indian Affairs, the territorial Department of Local Government, the Lands Office, the Cooperative Association of the N.W.T. and a big insurance company, probably located in New York or London, it seemed that only chaos could come of it.

But Prohibition Creek was getting an airport. Thanks to Haga— a system all to himself, in profound, but perhaps countervailing, disorder.

"This meeting is adjourned," announced Danny, and indeed it had already started to break up, some people still cheering and hooting.

Rebecca walked Marcia back to the trailer, and then out to the airport, where the Red Baron's Beaver was waiting to take her to the Forks. Marcia said goodbye, and then turned her attention, childlike and ever so slightly flirtatious, upon taciturn Don, the pilot.

The days were now much longer, and there was still bright sunshine on the snow when, back in town, Rebecca locked up her office and took the wood road leading to the fish-plant clearing and the lake.

It was a pleasant walk in broad daylight. The grader that preceded the fire truck the night the shack burned down had scraped the path into a real road again, and although there was no thaw yet earth and moss were visible underfoot. All around her was quiet broken only by the rustling, creaking noises of the frozen trees that Rebecca no longer construed as threatening.

She walked slowly, thinking about the meeting.

Danny was wrong if he thought he had put a stop to the nursery school. But his opposition to the nursery school was not really the point, as she saw full well. Danny had been surprised and unprepared when it came up, but he was against it primarily because it was her project.

He was still hoping that she would go away. He had been waiting since January for her to quit her job. She remembered how he had seemed to take it for granted, that day in his office, that she was going. And now she contemplated with anger how he had run the meeting, how he had made himself invulnerable by being its chairman, and the ease with which he had cut her off and made her sit down.

At this point, Robert ran up behind her on the path and, first throwing a packsack down in the snow, embraced her with bear-like arms. "It's me. Not a bushman named Robert."

Rebecca had twisted around, startled, but not at all frightened, and they were kissing.

"I was just getting some whitefish from Elvis. See?" he said a moment later, picking up the packsack and giving her a glimpse of scales and a fishy tail through the top.

"I'm hungry." Rebecca leaned on his arm. She was ravenous.

"I'm going to cook them right away," he said.

Robert did the cooking, partly because he acquired all the food in the first place, but also because he liked giving Rebecca the experience of eating meat and fish done properly over the fire.

They had begun walking along side by side.

"So you didn't get fired," he remarked.

"No," she said. It still surprised her.

"And nothing bad happened at the meeting."

Rebecca remembered the apprehension she had felt when he came into the hall about what he might do on her behalf. She had not had any previous experience of Robert's way with meetings.

She looked at him and a smile began to form on her lips.

"I guess that was because they were all looking at the application you made for the nursery school instead." He returned her glance limpidly.

Rebecca began to laugh.

"Did you go to the meeting to argue against the nursery school, Robert?" she asked.

"No. But since I was there—" He couldn't help grinning a little.

Rebecca stopped short on the path, and as he was holding her hand, he stopped short too.

"Why did you go to the meeting, Robert?" she asked.

"To make sure you were going to be okay," he replied.

Rebecca laughed again, happily. "Well, I was okay. You did make sure of that," she said.

The Complaints Department had once again thwarted the workings of the second law of thermodynamics.

• 19. MICHAEL •

The fire in the teepee had burned low. The flame shadows hardly flickered on the dark, inward-sloping walls above. Robert had one arm across Rebecca as she lay between him and the fire, holding the sleeping bag up over her bare shoulder. They were both asleep.

"Robert! Robert! Come quick!" A child was calling from outside.

Robert woke up right away.

"What is it?"

The child outside called, "It's Michael! Michael drove Herod's truck off the cliff again."

Robert sat up quickly. "Is he hurt? Is he alive?"

"He's still in there." The child was running off again.

Rebecca came to as Robert gently but hurriedly tried to draw his other arm out from under her neck.

"What's going on?" she asked, still half awake.

Robert was pulling on his shirt, his jeans. "Michael drove Herod's truck down the bank again."

"Again?" said Rebecca blankly. Then she too struggled out of the sleeping bag and began to dress herself. "Wait. I'm coming with you. Maybe they'll need somebody to help look after the kids."

It was the thirteenth of March—a date Robert never forgot.

At the opposite end of town from the wood road, and where the lake emptied into the Kalonde River, which was its outlet, there was a little cliff, between twenty-five and thirty feet high, a good place for daredevil boys to climb and slide in the winter as Bernard had been reminding Robert. The promontory above was a trysting place of lovers, and there was a bench up there for old people to sit and view the river and the lake behind.

The scene of the accident was the beach at the foot of the cliff; it was brightly illuminated by the headlights of the police truck and some skidoos.

The truck lay on the roof of its cab, upside down. It didn't look as if anyone inside there could be alive, for the cab was crushed as though the truck had been partially through a cruncher at a wreckers. The police were trying to get Michael out.

Robert had run all the way from the teepee, leaving Rebecca behind him once they reached the edge of town, and now he came sliding and stumbling pell-mell down the cliff path, almost into the arms of Dave, the cop.

"Tell me what to do, okay?" gasped Robert.

"There isn't anything. We're going to open the can. But it might take awhile." The policeman indicated car jacks, metal cutters, an axe from the fire department. Herod, Danny, and a couple of Robert's cousins were working with these things under the direction of the other policeman.

"Is he—?"

"No one knows. He would have been safer in jail—after last time." Dave turned away to the others, but then he turned back. "Sorry, Robert," he said. "He's your brother."

The truck looked as though it had rolled several times. The beach was strewn with icy boulders that had punctured it in places, and the cab was not crushed equally on both sides. The rescue team was trying to get in from the offside, removing the door, cutting open the roof. On the driver's side there was only a six inch aperture where the window had been.

"Come here," said Dave. "Maybe there's something you can do. Just talk to him. See if you can get a response."

He crouched beside the cab and put his face down beside the sawtoothed glass of the dark hole.

"Michael," he said softly. "We're going to get you out. We're workin' on it. Just hold on. Keep it up, buddy." He stood up, dusting snow off his knees. "Like that," he suggested.

Robert lay down in the snow beside the broken window of the overturned cab. It was pitch dark inside, and he could hear no sound over the metallic pounding and crunching from the other side.

"Just let me look at you, pal," he said, seeing nothing.

There was no response.

"Hold on. You've just got to hold on," he repeated rather desperately.

He went on talking to him, saying the policeman's phrases over and over. He had to keep reminding himself that Michael was in there at all.

Michael was twelve years younger than Robert and he could hardly remember him in childhood as anything but a kind of nuisance. And he was still the baby now; he had not grown up and become a competitor like Danny. All the same, Robert felt a special responsibility for Michael because he knew that he himself had been Michael's model when Michael became a teenager. Michael had never known their father; he had got his card-playing, his drinking habits, and his unreliability with women from watching Robert.

There ought to be something he could say to Michael that would have more meaning than "Hold on" and "Keep it up," just as though he were the policeman talking to him. There ought to be something between them besides this nullity.

He remembered now with despair how he had known that Michael wrecked Herod's truck the first time and did nothing more than feebly warn him about gossip. He ought to have told him something better than that. He had no authority over Michael, but he remembered the way his father delivered advice, enigmatic, sometimes threatening, something to ponder. If Robert had ever said anything to make Michael think a bit, that would have been between them now.

"You're still there, pal. You're in there all right."

All at once Michael said faintly, "Robert."

He even knew who was talking.

"Yeah, it's me," said Robert. "You're looking good."

"Where am I? I can't move. What's all that noise?"

"Well, you're kind of stuck there for a while, pal. But they're getting you out."

"Am I going to die?" He was panicking.

Robert thought quickly.

"You know what I read one time? If a person can ask whether he's going to die, it's a pretty good sign he isn't."

Jane, the nurse, was kneeling beside Robert. "Is he talking?" she asked. "Did he say something, Robert?"

Robert nodded, his attention still focussed entirely on Michael. He had to create that bond, the one that wasn't there, and he had to do it now. He even had the feeling he might keep Michael alive if he did that.

"Ask him if he's in pain," whispered the nurse.

"Does it hurt, partner?"

"No. No, I can't feel anything—I don't even know where I am—What happened?" Michael spoke faintly.

"You drove Herod's truck down the bank."

The nurse put her hand gently on Robert's shoulder for a moment. Then she got to her feet and walked around to the other side of the cab, where they were finally beginning to remove the door.

Robert continued to talk, saying the same things over mechanically, that Michael was all right, that they were getting him out, that he was going to be fine, when really he wanted to ask, "Why'd you do this a second time?"

It didn't make any sense.

But Robert was thinking that Michael had known they all wanted him to feel bad the first time. He thought they were all mad at him. And they were. Everyone in town knew he did it, even Herod. He had really wanted to get caught.

Ordinarily Robert wouldn't have been able to make this connection at all. But lying here in the snow, with his face between a chunk of ice on the beach and the broken window, he could suddenly divine how if you did bad things and people didn't stop you, you would go on and do worse things, hoping they would stop you then.

He was still talking and in Michael's responses there was beginning to be a hint of physical distress.

There were some ripping, tearing sounds as they got the door off its hinges and dragged it away from the truck. There was light in the cab from the other side now, and Robert could see Michael jammed in under the dashboard; it was incredible that he had not been crushed, his head smashed to jelly, in the total destruction of the roof.

"Now we're getting there," said Dave. His head and shoulders came through the aperture on the other side, temporarily blocking out the light. "Just hold on, buddy," he added, speaking to Michael.

"Stay with me, Robert," said Michael, panic in his voice again.

"Sure," said Robert, stretching out flat in the snow and putting one freezing hand under his cheek so he could get his face right up against the hole where the window had been.

It still took them a very long time to get Michael out of the cab. They had to carry him by hand on the stretcher to the nursing station; it was impossible to tell how badly injured he was, but the nurse wouldn't let him be lifted into the front seat of a truck, or jolted on the back of one.

There was a horrible moment—from Robert's point of view—when they brought Sarah into the nursing station and finally let her see Michael.

When she saw him on the stretcher, pale, feeble, motionless and—Robert hated to admit this to himself—shorter, as though he had somehow been compressed by the crushing of the cab—she began to scream hysterically.

Jane ordered Herod and Danny to wheel Michael off down the hall to an examining room, then turned around and spoke crisply to Robert.

"I'm going to go to Michael," she said. "If you want to do something now, Robert, help your mother."

"What am I going to do if he dies?" wept Sarah in Rachel's arms. "Oh, what am I going to do?"

And Robert, who would a hundred times rather have stayed with

Michael, or not been there at all, had to take his mother and the ugly, noisily weeping Sarah into the kitchen of the nursing station, where he found an electric kettle, a teapot, tea bags, sugar and mugs, and made tea for them all.

▲ ▲ ▲

Rebecca had gone to Rachel's house, but finding nobody there, she had gone to Michael's house. Sarah was already gone and Rachel had deputed Elvis to stay and babysit. He was in the living room with the baby, who was awake.

He would have been far more useful to the police at the scene of the accident than many of the other men who were there, but Elvis was an unassuming man. Since Rachel wanted him to babysit, he became a babysitter.

"Oh! Elvis." Rebecca was surprised to see him. "I—I heard about Michael's accident. I could stay with the kids. If you want to go to the nursing station."

"They're all asleep anyway. Except this baby." He gave her the baby, and for a moment they looked at one another with interest. Robert had told them each a great deal about the other by now.

"The bottle is in the other room," said Elvis. He had been trying to feed the baby, but all she did was play with the nipple. It reminded him of Michael, whom he had fed many times as a baby. He had been a fussy eater too.

"I'll stay here till you come back." Rebecca cuddled the baby, having memories of her own.

"Masi," said Elvis, going out.

▲ ▲ ▲

After a long weary while for Robert in the kitchen of the nursing station the plane came for Michael. He was still alive. Sarah, calmer now, was going with him as an escort—but only because she insisted and he agreed, for half the Woodcutter clan would have gone with him: his mother, his two brothers, his uncle all wanted to go.

What would happen next, no one knew.

The plane took off, the trucks and skidoos departed the airstrip for home. It was seven o'clock in the morning, getting light already, and Robert was walking back into town by himself, glad to be alone for a while.

He was thinking about dying—what it would be like to face death, the actual process of doing it. It might be what Michael was experiencing right now.

His mother would be praying, he knew. Experimentally, he tried to pray himself. It turned out he could still do it. But it was a little mechanical, like, "Hold on, buddy—just hang in there—keep it up."

But that had been what worked apparently, when Michael was still in the cab.

He wanted to see Rebecca suddenly, to ask her if she ever prayed. He remembered that she had said she was going to look after the kids. A moment later he was coming in through the kitchen at Michael's house.

Rebecca was in the living room, sitting on the floor, playing with the baby, who found her a delightful new toy, much more exciting than Elvis, and would not be put down for a minute.

Robert stood in the doorway and Rebecca looked up at him apprehensively.

"Was it very bad?"

"Yeah." He came over to kneel beside her.

"How's Michael?"

"Maybe he's going to die. I guess no one knows yet."

"I was praying for him," she said. "Even though I never do, usually."

Robert was amazed. He had just been intending to ask her about this. He still hadn't got used to the way Rebecca kept up with him.

"Could you hold the baby for a moment, Robert?" she was saying. "I want to give her the bottle again."

He took the baby and for a moment, like Elvis, he was thinking of Michael. Rebecca was getting the bottle, putting in formula, shaking it, all those things the older children learn to do for the last baby when the mother's milk has dried up because the father has left her.

Then Rebecca came back with the full bottle and sat down beside him again, and he asked:

"What do you do when you pray?"

He had remembered that the Protestants prayed differently; they didn't use the rosary and they seemed to say, embarrassingly, anything that came into their heads at all.

"I just say some words—into the air," she replied. She went on hesitantly, "I'm not sure there's anybody I'm saying them to."

"Well, I'm pretty sure there is somebody," said Robert. "But him and I don't see eye to eye on a lot of things." He was thinking of what had happened to Michael tonight. If he had been God, he wouldn't have done that.

The baby seemed to be looking purposefully at the bottle in Rebecca's hand.

"I'll take her again, Robert."

She took the baby and Robert put his arm around her, getting them arranged so that she could lean on him while he rested his back against the edge of the cot that served as a sofa. The baby had taken the nipple eagerly and begun to suck.

"There, that's good," breathed Rebecca.

"She'll probably go to sleep on that," he commented.

"Finally."

They sat there in silence, watching the purple, furiously sucking baby slowly grow heavy and content, then gently relinquish the bottle nipple as she fell asleep, a trail of milk flowing from one corner of her open mouth.

Robert was fully alive to the tenderness Rebecca was feeling, which he knew derived from her memories of her own children, and which he himself shared, remembering Michael and Bobby. Some of the raw anguish he had just been experiencing had gone away, with Rebecca leaning on him like the Madonna, Michael's baby cradled against her breasts.

"It's nice, holding a little baby, isn't it?" she whispered.

The baby burped suddenly, and a blob of curdled milk came up on the bubble.

They both laughed, and Rebecca held the baby up against her shoulder, patting her back.

Somehow she couldn't bear to put Crystal down. She rearranged herself so that she was leaning against Robert again, with the child in her arms.

Robert was still thinking about God.

Just because God had the power to force you into things, did that make it good, what he did? It was simply impossible to think that what God had done to Michael was good, even if you believed he was trying to teach him a lesson.

If Robert had been God he would have stopped 'Bad' right from the start; he would never have invented it. They would still be living in the Garden of Eden now, although, with himself, a Dene, as God, there would have been some additions to that: snow, fire and a teepee for Adam and Eve.

But still, it was an important question, whether what the man in the long black dress told you was necessarily right. Just because he could force you, that still didn't mean you had to believe it. It was not as though Robert had just found this out now; he had known it years ago, and it still made him angry—what that man could make you do.

Elvis silently entered the house through the kitchen.

He came into the living room and stopped short, seeing Robert and Rebecca sitting together with the baby.

In spite of what he already knew, he was quite surprised.

Robert looked up. "Hi, Elvis. I'm sitting here with Rebecca."

"So you are," said Elvis dryly.

Rebecca also looked up. "The baby went to sleep after Robert came in."

Elvis surveyed them, a twinkle appearing in his eyes.

"Rachel wanted me to get the kids. But maybe I'll just go home, eh?" he said.

"Sure. We can bring them over when they wake up," said Robert.

Elvis lingered for a moment. "Remember that story you were telling me in the cabin at Rocher River, Robert?"

Robert laughed.

"That sure was a good story you told there," Elvis said, going out.

◆ ◆ ◆

It was a lovely morning late in March, and the thaw was coming. The sun rose now before six and shone, hot and bright as summer, on the reflecting snow. Robert and Rebecca were sitting in the doorway of the teepee, drinking their morning tea.

"Have some more tea, Rebecca." He proffered the billy.

"Okay. But I have to go to work in a minute," she said, looking at her watch.

"Yeah. But it's kind of nice here in the morning, isn't it?"

The clearing was full of little birds, sparrows and Lapland longspurs, flitting around in the low branches of the trees and hopping down to pick up seeds on the ground. The songbirds were beginning to migrate through, just a few so far, but they were harbingers of the ducks and geese, and hearing their trilling voices made Robert dream of the spring hunt. Going out by skidoo on the sticky snow over the lake ice, crouching in the willow bushes on a sandbar while the long trailing flocks passed overhead calling to one other; the shots and intermittent shouts of the hunters; and the first bird, split and spitted on a stick, roasted right there over the fire, then crammed, crunchy and hot, into the hungry mouths of three or four cold, triumphant men.

The spring hunt was, of course, completely illegal; it was also one of the most contentious issues on the table in any land claim or aboriginal rights negotiations with the government, and came up regularly in debate. But even a kilometre out of Prohibition Creek the game laws were virtually unenforceable, and the smell of burning feathers would shortly be on every wind.

"I have to go see Danny today," Rebecca said, putting down her cup.

"What about?" demanded Robert. He was not jealous of Danny—right now he had quite convincing proof that there was no need to be jealous of anyone—but he resented the idea that Danny had any authority over Rebecca.

"There's a new grant program for women's shelters," she said. "I want to ask him about putting in a proposal. And—I need a character reference."

"A character reference? From Danny?" Robert was contemptuous.

"I want the court to lift that injunction. So my kids can visit me."

"Yeah, but why Danny?" said Robert.

Danny was still the chief, although it seemed as though there was no chief right now. Aside from the public meeting that had been Rebecca's ordeal, he had held no Band meetings since Christmas, and no one knew what was happening.

"What about your boss? Or your teachers?" Robert went on. "Can't you get letters from them?"

"I did," she replied. "But it depends on what the community leaders say about me too."

Obviously Rebecca McCrae could get a recommendation from Herod McCrae. But she needed one from somebody whose last name was Woodcutter.

"Why don't you let me give you a reference?" said Robert.

Rebecca laughed. "A reference from the Complaints Department?"

"Why not? After all, I know what you're really like."

"What would you say in your letter?" Rebecca asked him playfully.

But Robert was thinking of how he sometimes saw Rebecca in the teepee at night, thinking, her face grave in the firelight, her eyes cast down. She was full of passion, he knew; she wanted to do things, to make her mark on the world.

"Oh, I don't know," he said. "I guess I'd say that you're full of crazy ideas. That you're trying to change this place around and it might even work."

Rebecca was surprised and touched. For she had felt that Robert didn't, and fundamentally never would, agree with her in what she wanted to accomplish.

Robert knew that their little place, like the whole world around it, was in the grip of change. He could never be in favour of that, for he was deeply conservative, but he was also helpless to stop it. So it was his ambition now—he had turned all his clever, calculating attention as a poker-playing man to this end—that Rebecca was going to get her way in whatever changes did take place.

Rebecca got up to go.

"What are you going to do today?" she asked.

"Hang around the nursing station and bug Jane," replied Robert. "Haga might be coming back any day now."

◂ ◂ ◂

Danny was in his office, as usual, getting the paperwork done. The government agencies he had to deal with, DIAND and the Department of Social Services, were pleased with the Prohibition Creek Band, the way they read about it on paper.

To curb Rosanne's boredom, he was getting her to do some of his typing. They had started to love one another again lately, and although neither of them knew it yet, she was pregnant again—entirely in accordance with the prophecies of the medicine woman in the fall.

Roseanne finished typing a letter and looked up. Danny was tapping his fingers on the blotter, looking out the window at the brilliant snow. The signs of thaw and the sound of the birds outside was making him feel restless.

"What is it?" she asked.

"Oh, I don't know. I'm just fed up," he replied. "I wish I could just go someplace where I didn't have to think about all this stupid paperwork."

She knew that Danny held himself totally responsible for Michael. Michael had survived the medivac to Yellowknife, and then another medivac to the Camsell Hospital in Edmonton for surgery, and he was staying there for therapy and rehabilitation. No one yet knew whether he would recover any function in his arms or legs; the best prognosis was that he would end up permanently in a wheelchair.

It was his program that had made Michael reform himself in the fall, but at the time when Michael most needed the extra support, Danny knew that he had not been there for him. He had been taken up with his own problems. And he felt it was his own fault that there had not been an active AA after Christmas.

To Danny, the functioning of Prohibition Creek was virtually continuous with his own brain processes. He had turned his attention away for a while and everything had fallen apart.

If it had not been Michael—if it had been another one of the people he had been counselling in the fall—it would have been easier to take up again where he left off. But Michael was his own brother, the child closest in age to himself; he had always been responsible for Michael, ever since he was two years old. He knew everything about Michael, how he had started to go wrong, when he had told his first big lie, when he had got caught for shoplifting, when he had had his first girl in the old teepee out by the lake—everything, in fact.

He recalled the joy he had felt when Jane came around the front of the wrecked truck and touched his arm to tell him that Michael was alive, that he was talking to Robert. Then Michael, pale and compressed on the stretcher in the nursing station, telling Danny that he loved him—he loved them all. He thought he was going to die, and so did Danny, who cried with him then.

Roseanne was still watching him, his impatient and compulsive gestures, the loud sighs he gave, even though he said nothing. He really needed some time off, she thought. He was going to pieces over Michael.

The door opened and Rebecca came quickly across the outer room toward Danny's office. Roseanne swung around in the swivel chair and began to work over a fresh letter at the keyboard.

"Oh—hi, Roseanne," Rebecca faltered. She had stopped short in the doorway of the office.

Roseanne said nothing. She continued to type.

There was a short pause. Nobody was going to help anybody else through the awkwardness of this.

"Have you seen this, Danny?" Rebecca was holding out a fax. "It's a new program. For women's shelters in small communities."

He didn't reach out to take it, so she stepped forward to put it on his desk.

"I think we should apply."

Danny shrugged.

"More paperwork," he said.

There was another awkward pause. Then Roseanne said, "Let me see that. Is it for a real women's shelter? Where a woman could stay with her kids?"

"It's just another program they'll cut the funding for in a few months time. Like the nursery schools." Danny began smoothing his eyebrows.

"But I think we need this," said Rebecca. She spoke firmly. But she was looking at Roseanne. Roseanne was reading the fax all the way through.

"And when the funding is cut," Danny continued, "people will be screaming to use our alcohol and drug program money for that too. We can't afford to take a cent out of the alcohol and drug program."

"I'm going to apply for it anyway, Danny."

Rebecca hadn't forgotten how Danny had cut her off and made her sit down at the meeting when they had been discussing the nursery school. Strangely enough, that was the thing she would never forgive him for.

"Most of the programs we have are for men and teenagers," she went on.

"Those are the people who are abusing drugs and alcohol," said Danny. "Look at Michael. He needed help earlier. And a lot more help. Now he may never walk again." He turned his back on her and went to the window.

He blamed himself, Rebecca saw. But she had been through this with Robert, who also blamed himself. It was natural in a way, but it was also irrational, she considered. The larger a man's ego, apparently the more he hated himself for things he couldn't prevent.

Roseanne had finished reading the prospectus, but she continued to stand beside the desk, gazing down at it. "If only we'd had this shelter for Sarah," she murmured.

Rebecca nodded. A place to go where they could take their kids would have made a difference to a number of women in town.

"It seems almost as though Michael was punished." Danny spoke grimly, with his back still turned.

"Well, if somebody was punishing him, then his wife and kids got punished too," said Roseanne. "They got punished first. And they're still getting punished."

She looked, for the first time, at Rebecca, and Rebecca met her glance.

"There's something else I have to ask you," Rebecca said a moment later, to Danny's back.

"Ask." Danny turned around.

But Rebecca had shifted her attention back to Roseanne.

"I—I never told you," she said, "but I have two kids."

Roseanne nodded. She knew this, of course, as did everyone in town.

"They're in the custody of their father. And there's a court injunction preventing them from staying with me. He got that," she continued, "because I—deserted them a few years ago. And I neglected them when I had them."

Roseanne knew this too. She continued to watch Rebecca, surprised.

"I want to get them back now. I need a character reference for the court. From a community leader. My boss thinks it should be from Danny."

No one spoke. Danny still had his back turned.

"It has to say that I've been completely sober here, and that I've been working steadily for six months."

Rebecca continued to look at Roseanne. "I just want my kids," she said.

Roseanne met her eyes steadily. She was an independent thinker. In spite of her dislike and anger, she had been on Rebecca's side at the meeting when they talked about the nursery school. And she knew that Rebecca was going to apply for this new women's shelter whether Danny wanted it or not.

"I'll type that letter for you, Danny," she said.

◂ ◂ ◂

Robert usually went to the nursing station and hung around, as Rebecca knew, not because Haga might be coming back any day now, but because he wanted to glean all the information he could about what was happening to Michael. He borrowed the nurse's medical encyclopaedias and texts, and bothered her with hypothetical questions that Jane, who was a compassionate person but used to her own eccentric solitude, answered as patiently as she could.

On this day, however, it turned out Haga really was coming back from the hospital.

Robert and Jane were at the airport, waiting for the plane.

Depending upon how much money they had, patients sometimes had a way of getting lost in the bar at the Forks on the way home, but Robert was pretty sure Haga was still as broke as he had been when he went out, unconscious on a stretcher.

It was the Beaver on skis, as usual, but Robert had the eyes of a duck hunter and he spotted something different about it at once.

"Oh boy," he remarked. "I think that's the Red Baron himself in the cockpit."

"Well," said Jane dryly. "A perfect opportunity to talk to him about—quite a number of things."

They looked at each other for a moment, formulating the same long list of complaints: the big holdup before Christmas, the terrible mail service right now, the way the potatoes always froze on the way to the store, the fact that they had to call him three times before he'd send in a medivac.

"Are you really going to say any of that stuff?" asked Robert. Jane was a tough customer, but the Red Baron was a wild man; he was famous for his temper all over the Western Arctic.

"He shouts at one so," she murmured.

Robert nodded. "Sure gets mad fast, that guy."

The Red Baron pulled up stylishly around them and shut off the engine in a swirl of flying snow particles. Then he jumped out of the cockpit and went to open the door of the fuselage. Haga was packed into the very back seat, behind four large cartons of sliced bread, two sacks of frozen potatoes, and a single pathetic bag of mail which had got tossed on as an afterthought.

The Red Baron, a short, dapper man with a red beard, began busily throwing all these things out into the snow.

"Hello, Jane. Robert," he said over his shoulder. "Potatoes froze again. Too bad. It's the way they pack 'em," he added, delivering one of the sacks into a snowbank.

"Is that a bag of mail?" asked Robert.

"Found it in the warehouse behind some other stuff," agreed the Red Baron, throwing it for Robert to catch. "Here's that crazy burn patient of yours, Jane," he added.

"Haga!" cried Robert, dropping the mailbag in his joy as Haga, good as new, came out crabwise by the footrest on the strut.

"Now there's a touching scene." The Red Baron stood back beside Jane to watch.

They were embracing, then slapping each other on the back.

"Haga, old buddy!" cried Robert, almost dancing in the snow, he was so pleased.

"Well, that's that." The Red Baron dusted off his hands, and turned around to address Jane. "Hope you don't have another medivac soon, because that strip's going to be a mudhole. But if you do, be sure you try to get that fancy King Air from Yellowknife again."

Jane gazed at him bravely.

"You think a plane with a fancy pressurized cabin and Captain Know-It-All at the controls is a safe bet on this airstrip at night, no lights and sixteen hundred feet long if it's an inch?" he shouted furiously. "I'll tell you what—there isn't another operator in the North besides me that would be willing to wreck his equipment in a place like this. And you can tell the doctor I said so."

He jumped up into the cockpit and slammed the door, then started the engine and taxied off.

"Right," said Jane, speaking into the whirlwind of flying snow in her face. "I'll tell the doctor."

She turned to Haga. "How are you, Haga? All better?"

She took his hands, which were still done up in bandages. "You'll have to have the dressings changed on those every day, you hear?"

Then she looked sternly at Robert, who nodded.

"But the first thing we're going to do," he said to Haga, "is get rid of the taste of those vegetables you were eating in that hospital. We're going to go right home and cook up a piece of moose meat."

"Home?" Haga looked at him sadly. "They said I burned it down."

"Well, I got a teepee—" Robert broke off to say goodbye to the nurse, who was getting into her truck to drive back to town. Then he began to walk Haga across the end of the airstrip toward the path leading to the lakeshore clearing.

"Where are we going?" asked Haga, surprised.

"I got a teepee and—Oh yeah, something else happened too, Haga."

"Am I going to like it?" Haga asked, somewhat pathetically.

Robert was wondering about this for the first time. "I don't know," he said.

Haga had once been so jealous of Rebecca that he even signed a petition against her. And even though he had been hanging around her while Robert was away trapping, Robert wasn't sure Haga was going to like the way things were now. For they were utterly different. Everything had changed.

"Well, you know Rebecca," he began cautiously.

"Sure. I know Rebecca." Haga was beginning to get a little frightened. Robert appeared to be trying to break something bad to him.

"Well, see, when I was out there with Elvis—I couldn't stop thinking about Rebecca. I even dreamed about her all the time. So now Rebecca and I—" Robert suddenly gave up on the roundabout approach. "She's staying at the teepee," he said.

A lightbulb went on in Haga's brains. "Oh," he said. "You mean you and Rebecca are—?"

Haga broke off, not exactly out of tact. But he knew that any vocabulary item he had for what was going on here would only make Robert mad.

"Yeah," said Robert, with a sigh of relief.

"Well, I already knew that," said Haga. "She stayed overnight at the shack that time, remember? But you know what, Robert?" he continued after a moment.

"What?" said Robert.

"Remember that giant woman who was married to the dog? The one I saw that time on the spaceship?"

"Yeah."

Haga's voice sank to a whisper. "I saw her again in the hospital. She was dressed up—Robert, she was dressed up—like a nurse."

• 20. BOBBY COMES HOME •

Later on in the day Haga and Robert were lounging beside a little fire in the teepee. They had suspended a large chunk of moose meat from an improvised spit and they had been gorging themselves, cutting the cooked pieces off the sides. Now, even though their appetites were sated, they nevertheless continued cooking collops, turning them over on the grill with the points of their knives.

Rebecca was stooping in the doorway under the flap. She couldn't help noticing that a feast of very memorable proportions was going forward.

Haga raised am arm reddened with meat juices. "Hi, Rebecca."

"Haga! I'm so glad to see you I could—I could almost kiss your lips!" she said, going down on her knees to embrace him.

"Hey! Almost, okay?" But Robert relaxed as Rebecca now sank into her customary position beside him.

"Have some meat," he said to her. "Have this piece. I was keeping it for you." He had been saving the tenderest piece he could find for her on one side of the grill.

"Masi."

It always gladdened Robert's heart to see Rebecca eating meat. She ate fastidiously, holding the meat in her fingers and tearing it off in neat small bites, exactly the way a Dene woman should.

"This is delicious," she said, her mouth not even full.

The gross banquet he and Haga had just been enjoying was fading already into a pleasant memory. Haga too had noticed a change in the atmosphere. The rich, full-blooded, unbuttoned afternoon of eating was over.

He cleared his throat. "Nice place you got here," he said.

"Robert fixed it up beautifully, didn't he?" Rebecca said.

"This place looks too respectable for old Haga." He spoke mournfully.

"What? It's a teepee," said Robert.

But Haga was getting sadder by the minute. "Maybe you'd like me to go out and get my own teepee or something," he said.

"Of course not."

Haga was familiar with the decline and fall of civilization. It had begun this way with his sister, when she got married.

"They have to have their own bedroom," he said. "That's why they like living in houses. It's these new ways they have, I guess."

"New ways?" Robert laughed.

But then he thought about Rebecca and himself, the exciting secret life they were having alone together at night. He didn't need a bedroom for that. But it wasn't clear what it would be like to have Haga around all the time.

"Yeah," he said, a little nervous. "Well, I see what you mean. What do you think, Rebecca?"

Rebecca was bemused. "About what?" she said.

"Do you mind if Haga stays here?" Robert was really seeing the argument against it for the first time.

"Of course not."

"I mean, do you mind if Haga sleeps here?" he asked.

Rebecca laughed. "He'll be asleep, won't he?" she pointed out.

Robert laughed too, in relief. "Oh yeah," he said. "I guess you already know about the way he snores."

Rebecca knew Robert would have found it a real dilemma if she said she didn't want Haga to live there. Robert had been through a lot with Haga, and in some strange way he felt they were brothers. It would have gone entirely against Robert's principles to make him get out.

But in any case, Rebecca was fond of Haga herself now. She too had been through a lot with him. And she still felt sorry that she had ever lent him any money for smokes.

They were going to form a household together.

It sometimes seemed to Robert that society, like the universe, was all broken up into pieces, almost like a puzzle. You picked them up and turned them, then turned them again, and sometimes, surprisingly often lately, it seemed that they fitted. It was like the cosmic scheme that had made him build an outhouse in the fall, that had got Haga to burn down the shack, that was going to get Prohibition Creek an airport. It occurred to him that he had never explained his theory about all that to Rebecca and he began to tell her now.

They all were laughing, even Haga, who somehow came out as the hero of the story, the way Robert was telling it.

◂ ◂ ◂

The night of that same day Danny went to visit his mother. His footsteps on the frozen dirt of the road made an echoing lonely sound. He ascended the porch steps, then hesitated.

"Ama? Are you here?"

Rachel came out of the living room.

She was not very happy or very well these days. She had been looking after Michael's kids since Sarah was still away, living in a hostel in Edmonton in order to stay with Michael. She had a lot of help from Elvis, and even Robert. But she was finding it hard to cope with small children, and with the grief she was feeling for Michael.

Her family seemed to have fallen apart, in spite of all her efforts through the years. Her girls were gone to other settlements with their husbands, but what had befallen her with her sons represented, in every case, a personal and moral failure.

"Could I have some tea, Ama?" Danny said gruffly.

She nodded and he sat down while she brought him a mug. They were both rather afraid of each other, of further damage they might do.

"I don't want to fight with you anymore, Ama," he said.

"I wasn't fighting," she replied.

Danny took no notice. "I realized I was being a fool," he went on slowly. "After—what happened to Michael."

She sat down across the table, folding her hands at her waist like a nun.

"I'd be nothing without my family," he said. "Your family is the most important thing, no matter what they do to you."

She waited to hear what else he would say. But Danny, strangely enough, wanted her to talk.

After a moment she spoke, shyly and formally.

"I was an orphan. I never had anything except school till I got married. I wanted to have a family more than anything else in the world."

"Well, you made one," said Danny. "You were the one that did it—not Dad."

"He never had a family either. He didn't remember his mother," she said.

"That was a bad thing, I guess," he conceded.

"He never cared about anyone but his little brother," she went on.

She seemed to be trying to explain something that he still wasn't sure he was ready to accept. But there was at least something he could grasp in what she said.

"I have a little brother I kind of—kind of care about too," he said.

Rachel looked at him a moment longer, at the tears Danny was not ashamed to shed before her glistening in his eyes, and then she dropped her face into her hands and cried with him.

A moment later Danny was kneeling on the floor beside her, hugging her shoulders.

"Everything is getting to me, Ama, even my job. What I need is some kind of, I don't know—spiritual renewal," said Danny.

"You need to go to the bush," she said. "The bush is our place."

"I was the one that stayed in school, remember? I don't think I could go by myself."

"Nobody goes to the bush alone," said Rachel. "Take somebody with you."

"Who?" asked Danny.

The TV in the other room was switched off and Elvis came out into the kitchen. He leaned against the kitchen counter, looking carefully away from Danny the way an experienced woodsman avoids looking directly into the eyes of a wolf or bear.

"Do you want tea, Elvis?" asked Rachel.

He nodded and set about getting it for himself, while Danny watched, surprised by how at home Elvis was here.

"It's a good time for muskrat at Joker Lake," Rachel said to Elvis. "The fish are beginning to run."

Elvis was looking into her face. He had been yearning to go to Joker Lake for days, and he knew that the only thing that had been holding Rachel back from coming was her problems with her family. Now she was going to solve those problems in one stroke, and he was with her all the way.

"Do you want to go to Joker Lake, Ama?" Danny asked.

"I always want to go to Joker Lake in springtime. If someone will come with me."

"We'll take the kids," said Elvis.

"Will you come too, Danny?"

Danny had been looking down abstractedly at his hands on the table, but now he looked up, understanding at last.

"Yes. Yes, I will," he said.

◂ ◂ ◂

The next morning Roseanne and Danny were in his office again. Danny was wearing his parka over a pair of coveralls. He was all ready to start for Joker Lake, just as soon as Elvis came by to pick him up. Rachel and Elvis wasted no time at all when they decided to go to the bush.

He was giving Roseanne some last minute instructions, for he was intending to be gone more than a month, till after the breakup.

"—So all you have to do here is get the mail. Answer the phone when you're in the office. You can call me on the radio if anything really urgent comes up."

A skidoo drew up outside and Danny kissed his wife goodbye.

He went out the door and the skidoo drove slowly off on the long jolting trail—Elvis and Danny riding pillion in front, Rachel and the three children in the toboggan behind. A bag of flour and a can of lard, the hand-crank sewing machine, fish line, guns and shells—it was all they were taking, for the Joker Lake camp was already well-stocked with necessities, and the bush would be supplying them with so much food shortly that they would not know what to do with the surplus.

Roseanne watched them disappear out of sight. It was a warm day, the snow thawing, and there would be water on the trail, maybe even mud. It made her feel cold even to think of how wet they would be before they arrived.

She shut the door and went back inside, crossing the dimly lit main hall to Danny's office. She sat down in the swivel chair behind the desk and looked at the equipment: the teleconference phone, the computer and printer, the fax, the Xerox machine, the neat desk with the empty In box.

"So that leaves me—the chief of the Prohibition Creek Band," she said to herself. "What should I do first, I wonder?"

As a matter of fact she became very busy almost immediately.

Rebecca's boss, Marcia, had found some money left over in an administrative account of the Nursery Schools Pilot Project Fund, and since she had seen with her own eyes how much support there was in Prohibition Creek for a nursery school, and since she was ardently in support of initiatives like this one, on behalf of an oppressed and seldom heard-from group of women, she sent it to Rebecca. And Rebecca, as she had always intended, delegated the whole project to Roseanne, who really had a great deal of experience as a daycare worker and organizer.

Rebecca then contributed her trailer to the new nursery school, as she wasn't living there, and its lighting and heating were already fully funded by the government. Roseanne took over her office, and as a matter of mutual agreement, Rebecca began to operate out of Danny's office, since someone had to be there to answer the phone.

It was a marriage of convenience in the beginning, but shortly the two women discovered that they could work well together, and that they agreed about many things.

Robert got a job in the last week of March, with a contractor doing a gravel haul for the hamlet. It was only for a short time, driving a dump truck over the ice road across the lake to a quarry, but he made a little money. His fur cheque had arrived, but by this time he had spent most of it in advance, getting credit at the store to buy Haga a new sleeping bag and some clothes.

They worked day and night on the gravel haul. Driving conditions were actually better at night, when the temperature sank into the minus twenty degree range. But at the end of the day, when the sun was low on the horizon and reflected off the meltwater on the road with a blinding radiance, it produced a stupefying heat in the cab of the truck. When Robert came home, he would cast off his coveralls, drink a bowl of Haga's soup, and fall instantly asleep in Rebecca's arms, if she happened to be there.

It was satisfying to be at work on a regular basis, even for a short time. Robert had not often been employed in his own village; there were only a few steady jobs. But the old Robert, living like a European aristocrat on his winnings at cards, had always thought of the people who held these jobs as drones.

When the contract came to an end, he and Haga began to do a little fishing, making use of rifts in the ice on the lake that always formed in the same places at this time of year. Spring was coming; the geese and ducks would be here at any time now, and after them, the breakup.

Robert went to Mary Ann's house to borrow her father's shotgun. It was a house again with a roof and walls, he was pleased to see. She had even taken down the tent in the kitchen.

Robert was standing in the porch, not knocking, but giving her a moment to get adjusted to his being there in the doorway.

She looked up at him with displeasure.

He knew she wouldn't exactly be glad to see him. The strange and scandalous news had recently come to the ears of the respectable citizens of Prohibition Creek that Robert Woodcutter was living with their social worker.

"What do you want?" She got right to the point.

"The gun," said Robert in the same spirit.

He might have been embarrassed, but this was not an afternoon call he was making; he needed the gun.

Robert had gambled away his own guns some years before, and since Elvis had taken his with him to Joker Lake he had no one to borrow from. But every shotgun in town was presently being kept oiled and loaded for that moment that was coming, when the first duck would be sighted overhead.

She got up silently from her beadwork at the table and went into the other room.

Robert came farther into the kitchen and, to allay any feelings of awkwardness, began looking around at the amenities. There was a faucet over the sink, and he ascertained, upon experiment, that a hot-water heater had been installed. The furniture now looked very old and battered in the presence of the huge new refrigerator humming in a corner, the large gleaming new stove.

"Here." Mary Ann had returned and she put the gun into his hands.

Robert was wondering whether he had to say thank you. The gun was virtually his anyway. Mary Ann had not done any hunting with it for fifteen or sixteen years; Robert had used it, although only occasionally in recent years, throughout that time. But still, it was her father's gun. And what had kept Robert from gambling it away was a fugitive respect for the old man.

"Masi," he said, for the sake of that ghost.

And a ghost was present in the whole exchange for it was the unconscious understanding of both Robert and Mary Ann that he would continue to hunt for her. Robert could not leave his wife and start fresh. Mary Ann would always be here; and there was nowhere else for him to go.

"Bobby's coming home," Mary Ann said flatly, sitting down.

"When?"

"Tomorrow." Mary Ann had got this information from the police. She and Robert had to depend upon word of mouth for any contact with Bobby, since neither of them had a phone.

Robert had been looking forward to this news, and dreading it at the same time, for months. He sat down slowly opposite Mary Ann and put the gun on the table, looking at the newly laid linoleum floor.

He was a fatalist, however. He knew that whatever was going to happen now would happen; in a sense it had already happened.

He looked up again. "What the heck am I going to tell him, that's all I'm wondering."

"About your girlfriend?" A grim smile appeared on Mary Ann's lips.

"No! About himself, his life—all that. What you were saying in the fall, Mary Ann. I've got to talk to him."

"Tell him not to drink," she replied. Her smile was gone. "Tell him to stay away from those bad boys."

Robert contemplated the absolute fatuity of this. You couldn't tell young men things like that, or rather you could tell them all you liked and it would make no difference.

The things Robert's father said had never done anything to stop Robert when he was Bobby's age. It was only now that he thought of them.

He was afraid of the way Bobby was acting and the way he had been talking last summer. He had even vowed to kill Robert. The fact that he had called him Dad during their last interview did not prevent Robert from remembering how violent Bobby had become.

He looked into Mary Ann's eyes and saw that she was afraid too—and she had no confidence whatever in him. He was no kind of moral example for her son, as far as she was concerned, and she was unconvinced that Robert would say anything to Bobby. Or that it would do any good if he did.

"I'm going to try, anyway," said Robert, divining her thoughts. He stood up to leave.

He picked up the gun, and it gave him a good idea.

"I'll take him duck hunting."

◂ ◂ ◂

Haga and Robert went fishing that afternoon. Robert took the shotgun, cleaned and oiled, and both of them kept glancing upwards from time to time, hoping to see those little ducks coming down from the moon.

There were no ducks, but they got a load of fish out of one of the rifts, just dropping an unbaited hook and line off the edge of the ice. They loaded these onto a toboggan, which they prepared to drag back over the mushy snow on the surface of the lake.

"What's the matter?" asked Haga out of the blue.

"The matter?" said Robert.

"You aren't talking. It isn't like you, pal."

They took up the harness rope of the toboggan together and began to drag it side by side, squinting in the sunshine reflected from the pools of water on the ice.

"Bobby is coming home tomorrow," said Robert.

"So what's wrong with Bobby coming home? I thought you'd be glad."

"I am glad," said Robert.

There was a silence broken only by their panting breaths and a faint crystalline tinkling of the honeycombed ice falling into the water from the edge of the rift behind them.

"So I guess he'll find out about you and Rebecca now," said Haga.

"Yeah."

"You think he'll be mad?" Haga was ruminating.

"Sure he will. Me leaving his mother to go live with another woman."

"Well, I guess I see what you mean," said Haga. "Except you didn't leave Mary Ann to go live with Rebecca. You left Mary Ann to go live with me."

This was a hair-splitting argument worthy of Robert himself.

Robert now dropped the traces of the sled in exasperation.

"So what's your problem?" Haga asked.

"Oh, I don't know. I've got to talk to him—about his life." Robert was still feeling desperate about it. "I know I've got to talk to him. But what am I going to say?"

They deposited most of the fish in Robert's mother's freezer. Haga went home to the teepee taking a good-sized one to cook over the fire.

Robert went to pick up Rebecca at the band hall. He entered her office, sat down opposite her and put his feet up on the desk. She was on the phone.

"No, I'm sorry, the chief is still out of town. When he comes back—Okay, I'll find someone to represent us. Yes, I know it's important. I'll go myself if I have to. Okay. I will."

She put down the receiver.

"Hi," said Robert.

"Hi yourself, Robert," she replied.

Robert thought she looked good in the swivel chair, alert, bright-eyed, on top of things. He made a kind of complementary statement, lounging in front of her.

"What was that all about?" he asked.

Rebecca made a gesture as if tearing her hair out.

"Oh, I don't know. The federal government is pretending aboriginal self-government is in the constitution when it isn't. The chiefs are having a meeting in Ottawa."

"Danny's still in the bush."

She nodded. "And I can't go. But someone has to. Why don't you go, Robert?"

Robert laughed. "You'd send the Complaints Department to Ottawa?"

Rebecca laughed too. But she was serious. She had no patience for the sort of politicking involved, but it was right up Robert's street, she knew. Why had no one ever thought of making use of his talents for the purpose before?

"Well, you're the chief now," said Robert.

He was only partly joking. She was doing all the work, after all.

"I just wish Danny would come back," she remarked.

"No, you don't," said Robert.

He had come through the band hall on the way to her office. It was full of women and kids, some of whom seemed to be living there; Rebecca had already started up a women's shelter, before they even got the money. And what was Danny going to say when he found his wife running a nursery school in the old DPW trailer?

Strangely enough, Robert had almost come around to Rebecca's way of thinking about these things now. The nursery school had thirty children in it. And the band hall really was full of women and kids.

"Danny will probably like what we've done when he sees it," said Rebecca. "And Roseanne thinks—she thinks that when Sarah and Michael come back—They'll be all dried out—"

"Thinks they might run your shelter, eh?"

"Well, it would be a life for Michael," said Rebecca.

"A life in a wheelchair," said Robert.

They got up to go home. But once out the door they heard an extraordinary groaning noise as though the earth were in labour and pushing to give birth.

Robert took Rebecca's hand excitedly and led her through the willows behind the band hall and down to the river.

The ice hadn't broken yet, but it was grinding, periodically emitting that sound, a colossal chthonic straining.

They stood there watching, fascinated, almost mesmerized. The rushing water under the ice was pushing relentlessly, and the surface had become fluid: quivering, heaving and breaking. One could stand and watch this for hours in a kind of dream, poised on the brink of a change that might bring with it mountainous jams of ice, floods that could drown out the lower part of the village, and then, finally—tomorrow or the next day—summer.

They were not alone; all along the riverbank people were standing to watch.

"Bobby's coming home tomorrow," said Rebecca.

She had heard this from the police, but she wasn't sure Robert knew yet.

"So you'll be seeing him," she said.

"Seeing him," said Robert glumly.

The ice emitted a prolonged sigh, as loud as a shout, and they both turned to look. But the breakup of the river was a process, not a single event, and whatever had happened was invisible on the surface.

"Is there something wrong?" Rebecca asked after a moment.

"Just about everything I ever did, I guess."

But something was worrying her too. She had been thinking about it off and on since she had seen the police.

"Do you think he'll be mad because I'm living with you?" she asked.

"Yeah," said Robert.

With one accord they turned away from the river and began to trudge toward the teepee and the still hard-frozen lake.

"This'll be one more thing he has against me. One big thing, I guess," said Robert.

They reached the wood road at the end of town. The top two or three inches of the muskeg were thawing and big puddles stood in the path where the grader had scraped as far down as permafrost.

"Maybe—maybe we could pretend—" Rebecca was thinking hard. "You could move into your mother's place. And I could go sleep in my office." She meant the chief's office in the band hall.

Robert stopped where he was, up on a snowbank, dodging a puddle.

"Ama's house? Your office? Are you kidding?"

"Well, we could still—see each other sometimes." Rebecca was up on a snowbank on the other side, clinging to a branch as she made her way along. Neither of them had rubber boots.

"See each other!" said Robert.

"Just in the beginning. Then later on—after he's been home for awhile—"

Robert jumped down off his snowbank and crossed over to her side.

"Hey, wait a minute, Rebecca. We're not going to do that. I don't want to pretend this didn't happen."

He put up his hand to help her, but she slid down into his arms instead and they stood there embracing, oblivious to their wet feet.

"I did just about everything wrong up to now," he said. "This is the only thing I did right."

◂ ◂ ◂

An oddly assorted welcoming committee met Bobby at the airport the next day. Haga was there, Mary Ann and Robert; the police arrived at the last moment, and brought Rebecca. She was the social worker—but really, she had come because she couldn't bear not to be there, even though she had no role to play.

Haga wanted to persuade Bobby to come to the teepee right away; he was remembering the banquet they had had to celebrate his own return.

But Bobby only wanted to go home. He barely glanced at Robert, as he got into the back seat of the police truck to ride into town with his mother.

Robert looked desperately at Rebecca and Haga, who were standing there together and then went over and got into the back seat too, in spite of the fact that he knew there were no doorhandles on the inside.

Mary Ann led the way into her new house.

"Everything is here," she said. "Your volleyball, the rosary over your door. Nothing has changed."

"They fixed the porch." Bobby spoke listlessly. He looked around his bedroom.

"Yes," said Mary Ann, pleased that he had noticed nothing else. She went out of the room to make tea.

Robert called after her, "Hey, Mary Ann, that isn't all. You got running water. Double windows. Insulated walls. Heck, you lived in a tent all winter."

"She lived in a tent all winter?"

"Yeah. She didn't want the carpenters to mess up your room when they rehabbed the house. So she set up a tent right here."

Robert suddenly realized that Mary Ann did not intend to tell Bobby anything. He realized that she had not forgiven him, she would never forgive him, but she thought that Bobby would prefer to have the card-playing absentee father he had had before to no father at all. And now that he was here, now that he had followed them home, maybe she even expected him to move in. She would not tell him to get out again if he did.

Robert saw that he had to tell Bobby everything now; there was no alternative. So he sat down on the bed and did that.

He told him about moving out to the fish store with Haga, about giving up drinking and poker, and about how he had tried to make a living at various jobs last winter. He told him about the trapping at Rocher River and about the fire at the fish plant when he came back, and how he had fixed up the teepee. He told him about Rachel and Elvis, and what had happened to Michael, and how Danny had gone to Joker Lake in his despair. Then he told him about Rebecca; he even told him about his dreams and Rebecca's vision, although he didn't believe that Bobby would care about any of that.

Bobby listened restlessly.

"So you went with that woman," he said in the end.

"Yes, but everything is different with me now, I told you."

"Look, if you're going to give me some routine about being sober, I heard it already." Bobby spoke in a surly voice, his hands clenched. He turned away to the window.

"I'm not giving you any routine," said Robert, speaking to his back. "Something happened to me. Something good."

"You took off on my mother."

"No. She told me to get out. And I'm glad she did. She was right. Maybe I owe it all to her in a way." He could say this now and he even meant it.

"All what?" Bobby turned around with a sneer.

And now Robert didn't know what to say. It was his own cynicism confronting him, eighteen years of it, staring him in the face. How could he tell Bobby that he himself was making a new start, that he was happy. It sounded naive to him too.

He tried. "What I have now—in my life. It's good. You could have something like that."

"By giving up booze?" snarled Bobby. "Why should I? What's it to you?"

He said these last words in a mean whisper.

And Robert driven to it at last, replied, also in a whisper, "You're my son. I love you."

▴ ▴ ▴

Robert knew that nobody could really help Bobby until he decided to help himself. He wouldn't change by a single choice or decision, or by any mere advice that Robert gave him. This was only the beginning of his very long life (for the medicine woman had been right about so much; she was probably right about that too) and there were many more false turns for him to take, and many blind alleys down which he had to walk.

However, at the end of the week Bobby had been duck hunting with Robert and Haga three times and that scene that was always in Robert's imagination at this time of year, of the first duck being cooked on one of the beaches of the lake, had actually taken place, with the three of them standing around the fire, cramming the crackling skin and the dark juicy meat into their mouths with greasy fingers.

After that, as soon as the Kalonde River was negotiable by boat, Bobby went to stay with his grandmother at Joker Lake, and Elvis took over his education for a while.

Rome was not built in a day, as Marcia had so casually remarked.

But love is not a worthless thing, especially the love of parents, which bears all things, believes all things, hopes all things, endures all things—as some very smart man once said.

• 21. THE MONSTROUS REGIMENT • OF WOMEN

It was June and Rebecca's various projects were prospering. The women's shelter, like the nursery school, got temporary funding simply in virtue of the pressure exerted on the government by its existence. AA meetings were better attended now that the long winter was over. The Pentecostals still operated the drop-in centre, and Rebecca even had some people approach her for counselling.

Robert had gone to the constitutional conference in Ottawa. He was away for a week and a half in May. He had never been so far away from Prohibition Creek. In fact, the only other real city he had ever seen before was Edmonton, where he had once gone, over ten years before, as a medical escort for Mary Ann's father, when he was dying of cancer.

As for the conference, Rebecca was correct. It was right up Robert's alley.

He returned, having done a good deal of damage to everyone's presumptions in caucus, and having met all the major players, including the Prime Minister, with whom he shook hands.

It was a local joke that Rebecca was the chief and Robert the minister of foreign affairs.

Then Danny came back from Joker Lake. He came down to the band hall to take over his office again the next morning.

"What's all this stuff?" He spoke quite roughly to Rebecca, as he sorted through the paperwork on his desk. In fact, he was furious.

"Receipts from Robert's trip to the Aboriginal Self-Government Conference in Ottawa. I was keeping them all together in that file, Danny." Rebecca was packing up her own things to move, she wasn't quite sure where yet.

"Robert went to Ottawa? Who decided that?" Danny was looking like a thundercloud.

"I did, I guess," she said. "Everyone on the Band Council was too busy."

"I'll have to talk to him." Danny still spoke angrily. "It's too bad that came up while I was away. What else?"

"Here's the expense sheet for the nursery school." She knew he was going to be angry about that now too.

He sat down in the swivel chair and looked at it, smoothing his eyebrows.

"I already told Roseanne we're going to close that down. So we'll pay the bills and that's it."

"You're going to close the nursery school?" Rebecca sat down too, quite suddenly.

He shrugged. "We can't afford to run it."

"We got some money. We're hoping they'll find some more. And in the end, if we keep it running, the government—"

"I'm not arguing with you about this," said Danny. "I had the argument with Roseanne last night. The nursery school is closed. What else?"

"The shelter—" Rebecca began.

"What shelter?"

"You remember, I was going to apply for funding for a women's shelter? We've been using the band hall."

She was actually quite sure he had heard about it. It was controversial, especially since she was using the band hall; as with the nursery school, however, all the opposition to the women's shelter was male.

"It's just a temporary thing," she said. "Till we get a house."

"Well, get a house," he said. "But you won't use the band hall any longer."

Danny's anger shouldn't have surprised her. If Rebecca had been a less fair-minded person she would have realized that he simply hated her now, and that he resented the success with which she had been doing his job.

Now she was getting angry in return. She had always had to give in, all her life, to a man like this, and Rebecca hated to give in.

"It's a good thing I got back here," he was saying. "I never expected all this to happen. I left Roseanne to answer the phone, that was all."

"After she started the nursery school, we agreed that I'd work here," Rebecca responded. "And it turned out there was a lot of stuff that had to be done while you were away," she went on.

"Well, now I'm back."

"Yes. You are." Rebecca picked up an armload and started to leave.

"Wait," said Danny.

If that was all the heat she was going to give him he could see that there was room to make a concession.

"I hear you're doing a good job organizing for the Canada Day picnic, Rebecca."

"Thanks," she replied briefly, going out.

By the next day Rebecca had moved back into her office in the old DPW trailer. Robert was waiting for her to walk her out to the teepee.

"I guess everything's going to be different now that Danny's back," Robert remarked.

Rebecca hadn't said anything about it, but he knew it must be so. And now she was working again in this office.

She nodded, putting her forehead down against his shoulder.

"Danny's the kind of guy who has to have things go his way," Robert remarked.

And although he didn't know it, this was one very important difference between Robert and Danny Woodcutter, both of them arrogant men. Danny had the mentality of a leader; he just expected people to follow him and was angry when they presumed to question his decisions. Whereas in Robert's mind, he was completely on his own; he never expected anyone to follow him anywhere.

There was rather a long pause in their conversation, because Robert was kissing Rebecca.

Then she said, "I feel like doing something."

"Doing something?" repeated Robert, not really sure what she was getting at.

"I mean, like not letting Danny get away with this. He wrecked all my projects," she went on. "The nursery school, the women's shelter—" He had even been furious about Robert going to Ottawa.

"What are you thinking you'll do?"

They went out the door together. Rebecca was locking up.

"The chief election is next month. Are you going to run?" she asked.

"I always run," he said.

"Maybe you'll win this time, Robert. I can't believe they'll let Danny get away with this."

Robert laughed. "But everyone knows I'm against all that stuff too," he said. "Schools and shelters and centres."

"Then—I was thinking—" She spoke almost timidly. "I might run, myself."

Robert was momentarily shocked.

"You can't do that," he said.

"Why not?"

He didn't have to give it much thought. She was the wrong sex, non-treaty, didn't come from Prohibition Creek and had no interest in politics.

He laughed and shrugged, not taking her seriously.

"You can't, that's all."

They continued on their way to the teepee in silence, Rebecca wrapped in her own thoughts, while Robert, who was rather hungry, wondered if Haga was there already and whether he would have cooked something.

◂ ◂ ◂

Prohibition Creek always had a big celebration on Canada Day, and since, unlike New Year's or Father's Day, it was a holiday without emotional significance to anyone, nobody did much drinking. With good organization there were a lot of games and contests that the adults could enjoy as much as the children.

This year, Rebecca had put her heart and soul into the Canada Day celebration and the games lasted nearly all day. They finished up with an enormous picnic on the baseball field, that ranged across the entire culinary spectrum, from Spam sandwiches and hotdogs all the way to moose nose.

Danny was reading out a list of prizewinners through a megaphone.

"First prize for the sack race: Elijah McCrae; egg and spoon: Amanda Woodcutter; tea boiling: Mary Ann Woodcutter; canoe race: William Woodcutter's boat; and in baseball, Band against the Hamlet, of course it was our team, The Prohibition Creek Band—us Woodcutters!"

There were resounding cheers.

"Us Woodcutters," echoed Rebecca. She was standing right behind Danny and it seemed to her as though she had been standing there all day—behind him.

"Thank you very much to all who made this event a success," he finished up. "Enjoy your food now. And come again next year."

Rebecca began packing things up quickly. Now that it was all over, she wanted to get away fast.

"Hey, what are you doing?" Danny was interfering again, even in her getaway.

"I had some balloons as consolation prizes," she said. She was holding a bunch of them in her hand.

"Here, give them to me," he said. "Maybe I can do something with them later."

Rebecca gave them to him.

"This is entirely your show, isn't it, Danny?"

"Somebody has to take charge," said Danny sharply.

"Somebody has to get this place back on the rails."

"Yeah, that's true. It went off the rails while I was away." He was very well aware of the gnawing anger she felt.

"No, it didn't," said Rebecca.

"Yes, it did," Danny replied. He put his megaphone down on the picnic table as if to walk away.

But Rebecca was still facing him, in an argumentative stance.

"Well, it seems to me we did a lot. People were very involved. There wasn't much drinking," she said.

"I started the AA here," Danny told her.

"But I helped you. And I'm the one with the social work training."

"That's fine. I appreciate the help. But you aren't the chief."

"No. I'm not," she said.

"Somebody has to take the responsibility. That's what I realized when I was in the bush," he said.

He thought about this a lot out there. He still felt that what had happened to Michael was his fault. But it had made him feel a little better just to admit that. He thought no one else would have shouldered the blame.

"There's going to be an election soon, isn't there?" said Rebecca.

"Even if I don't want the job, there just isn't anyone else," he said.

"Don't you think anyone else will run?" she asked.

"Robert," said Danny. Then he went on, looking maliciously down at Rebecca, "Somebody ought to tell him he's wasting his time."

"Danny, I'm going to run against you too," she said.

She had not actually planned to say this, at least not this way or at this time. But it gave her enormous satisfaction to see the malicious look wiped from his face to be replaced by bewilderment, surprise, shock, protest and finally anger.

"Are you trying to screw me up?" he demanded.

"No. But maybe I want to say something, Danny."

"Listen to me, Rebecca." He spoke quickly and decisively. "I know you're mad because I put a stop to that nursery school scheme of yours. And to the shelter in the band hall. And maybe because of other things too. But you can't run for chief. You're aren't one of us."

"I'm a McCrae," said Rebecca.

"A Metis. And you're not even from here. You don't know anything about this place."

"I was here all winter. I was counselling, Danny. I listened to people."

Rebecca had never argued this aggressively with anyone but her father. And Danny was rather like her father, she couldn't help noticing.

"But there's another thing," he went on. "You haven't got what it takes," he went on.

"What do you mean by that?"

"A chief's got to be a leader. He's got to be an example to everyone else. And he has to be a man."

"There are woman chiefs." There were, in Inuvik, in Arctic Red River, once even in Tulita.

"Somewhere else," he said. "Not here."

"Maybe this will be the first time then, Danny," she said. "I'm starting my campaign right now—at this picnic."

"Your campaign?" Danny repeated these words in disbelief.

◂ ◂ ◂

Robert had seen Rebecca leaving the baseball field and he ran after her on the soft dirt road, past anemones and gentians in the ditches on either side. He caught up with her as she passed by the store.

He had just heard some disquieting news.

"I'm going to my office," she said. "I thought I'd take a minute to—to think about things."

"Rebecca, I just heard something at the picnic. Are you saying you're going to run for chief?"

"Yes," she said. She stopped walking and they stood facing one another.

"You didn't tell me," said Robert.

"Yes, I did. The other day. But I hadn't really made up my mind then."

"You made up your mind without even telling me?"

"Robert, Danny's taken over everything! He even took over the picnic. And I organized it."

Robert already understood why she was angry. The way Danny was behaving was typical, in his opinion. He was entirely on her side about all that; it was a matter for the Complaints Department.

But this other thing was different. If Rebecca was going to go around saying she was running for chief, she would make a fool of herself. She was making a fool of him too.

"You can't run for chief," he said.

"Why not?" Rebecca was wearing white clam diggers and a baseball shirt with "Hamlet" printed in black marker on the back. She put her hands on her hips.

"You don't even belong to this band."

"Yes, I do. My family came from here. You know the new rules, Robert." Changes to the Indian Act made band membership a question of local acceptance.

"The rules don't make any difference. You wouldn't win. You probably wouldn't get any votes."

"Well, you're running. And you aren't expecting to win either," she pointed out.

"Yeah, but that's different," he said.

It was hot northern July. The dust was thick and white on the road under their feet; no breeze stirred the air.

"What's different about it?" Rebecca said.

He didn't know how to answer that question, where to begin. It was very different. He ran in the spirit of Esau, who should have been a chief, if things had not gone wrong with him from the beginning. But in his opinion Rebecca was just messing around. She might even get hurt.

"You know what I think is different?" she said. "I think it's because I'm a woman. That makes it different."

And now Robert made a big mistake.

"Well, you're my woman," he said.

"Are you telling me I can't run? Because of our—our relationship?" she demanded.

"I guess I am." He spoke almost in surprise at himself. Robert was not accustomed to telling people what to do.

"I'm not your woman, Robert." She responded fast.

"What? You are," he replied.

"No, I'm not. I don't belong to anybody." She turned away and began to walk quickly in the direction of the trailer.

Robert now realized that he hadn't thought this through. It was against his principles to forbid people to do things. He should have thought of some tricky way of dissuading her.

"You don't want me to be chief. No. You don't even want me to run for chief. Because this place belongs to you and your family—not to outsiders like me."

For Rebecca, this argument with Robert was like a continuation of her argument with Danny. They were both leaning on her in exactly the same way.

"Hey, wait a second, Rebecca! I didn't mean that." Robert was still trying to think of a good way out.

"You did, Robert. You did mean that."

He was walking along beside her and she quickened her pace. They were almost at the trailer now.

"Hey, Rebecca—" Robert had realized she was heading for her office, so she could go in there and slam the door on him. Whatever he was going to say, he had to get it out fast, before she disappeared.

She paused on the doorstep and looked down at him from the top of the steps. She was almost a foot taller in this position.

"You can run and you don't care whether you win because you're running on principle," she said. "Well, you aren't the only one who can do that, Robert."

"Rebecca—!" he protested.

But Rebecca was no stranger to scenes in which people said or did things that were final—that were apocalyptic, in fact.

"Well, thank heaven I still have this office," she said. " And I can sleep here. So maybe I'll see you sometime, Robert. After the election."

She went inside, and just as he had expected, she slammed the door.

◂ ◂ ◂

Robert walked out to the lakeshore in a vacancy of mind and spirit. He had not been angry himself, and he was still not sure exactly what his quarrel with Rebecca was all about. She was mad at Danny; he had interfered too clumsily in that and now she was mad at him.

But of course she could not run for chief. In that area he was sure that he was right.

He had almost reached the teepee when he realized that there was somebody behind him on the path.

It was Danny. "I want to talk to you," he said.

"Well, come in."

They entered the teepee. Robert sat down but Danny remained standing.

No one in Robert's family had yet acknowledged that Robert was living with Rebecca. Robert was, of course, unrepentant about it, but as Danny took in the unmistakable signs that Rebecca was staying in the teepee: her clothes, drying underwear, one of the romance novels to which she was addicted lying open and face down on the pillow, there was a slightly awkward moment.

It was even more awkward, since Robert was conscious that Rebecca might not, in fact, be living with him any longer.

"Rebecca just told me she's going to run for chief. At the picnic. Did you know about that?"

Danny had been behind them on the road. He had seen them talking in front of the trailer. But then Rebecca had just gone inside. He was not aware that they had been quarrelling.

Robert gave an interior sigh of relief.

"You want tea?" he asked.

"No," said Danny. He changed his mind. "Okay. Masi."

Robert began making the fire.

"She won't win," Danny said.

"I guess not," agreed Robert. He perceived with something like glee that Danny was appealing to him.

"A chief isn't just somebody who can handle the office work and—and organize picnics," Danny went on. "He's got to be a leader. Rebecca couldn't be a leader—not of these people here. I know there are woman chiefs but—"

"We never had one," said Robert.

"The chief has to have a position on national issues. He has to be able to make speeches. Rebecca hasn't thought about any of that stuff. She even sent you to Ottawa while I was away."

"That was a strange thing to do," said Robert.

But Danny was too upset about this to attend to minor ironies.

"And when I came back here," he continued, "I found my wife working in a nursery school and the band hall full of women and kids. Then when I make Rebecca go back to her own job, she starts running for chief."

Danny had felt her to be his competitor from the moment he got home. And he was taking her seriously now; he knew she really wanted to be chief.

"None of those projects of hers has any funding," he went on. "We haven't got enough money for what we're trying to do already. Look what happened to Michael."

That was actually the point as far as Danny was concerned, and he stopped, unable to explain further because of the bitter lump rising in his throat.

Robert was surprised to discover himself sympathizing with his brother. Not because of anything Danny had said so far, but because he realized just how deep and strong was Danny's misery over what had happened to Michael.

"God, if only I could have prevented that. If only I'd started earlier—soon enough." Danny was still standing up, staring into the flames of the little cooking fire.

There was a long silence between them.

"Here's your tea," said Robert at last.

"I don't want this," said Danny once more looking around him in disgust at the teepee, neat enough except for Rebecca's drying brassiere, her paperback book.

"Neither do I," said Robert. "I'll throw it out the door." He took the cup.

Danny hesitated. Then he said, "Can't you tell Rebecca to cut it out?"

It was what he had come out here to ask.

Robert was suddenly very taken aback. It struck him as a truly horrible fact that not only did he agree with everything Danny had just been saying, but he had already done this: he had already told her to cut it out.

"She's your woman, isn't she?" Danny was taking his silence for resistance.

"So you think I ought to tell her what to do?" asked Robert.

"Sure you should." Danny shrugged.

Then, without another word, he turned away and began to walk home. He was not going to have an argument with Robert about that.

◂ ◂ ◂

Some hours later Robert and Haga were having supper. It was twelve o'clock at night, but this did not discommode them; it was still bright enough to read a newspaper at one o'clock in the morning. In this latitude, the whole summer was a long delightful day; no one went to sleep unless he felt like it, and there was enough time during the period one was awake for five or six meals.

"Where's Rebecca?" Haga asked suddenly.

He was not conscious of a twenty-four hour clock, but Rebecca's nine to five schedule had a certain rhythm to which he had become accustomed.

Robert was lying on one elbow on the other side of the fire with a moody look on his face. As Haga continued to look at him interrogatively, he sat up and shrugged.

"Where were you all day anyway?" he asked. "I didn't see you at the Canada Day picnic."

"Harold gave me a cup of whisky," Haga replied. "I must have gone to sleep on the beach. When I woke up I had my head on a nice smooth stone."

Robert could almost envy Haga. He had been having a terrible day himself. The worst part was the evening he had just gone through, during which it had gradually become apparent that Rebecca was not going to give in and come back.

"So I came home and cooked a piece of moose meat. Then you're not hungry and she doesn't show up," Haga complained.

Something about Robert's expression gave him pause.

"Did you two have a fight or something?" he asked.

"Or something," said Robert.

"Women, eh?" Haga said, after a long introspective pause. "We're better off without 'em." He had decided to try to cheer Robert up. "Look at how much better off you are without your wife."

Robert stared at him in annoyance.

"And my wife," said Haga, trying to get on a footing of solidarity. "Me, I'm better off too."

"Your wife?" Robert was surprised. "You had a wife?"

"Well—I think she married me." Haga had forgotten exactly how people did this. It required the intervention of a priest, he was sure of that, but he had had this wife a long time ago, and priests were always all mixed up in everyone's business back then.

"Who was she?" Robert had summoned up enough interest to ask.

"Sunny MacDonagh. You know her."

"What?" Robert was not merely surprised now, but astounded. "She's the MLA."

"Yeah, but this was before she got into politics."

"Why the heck did a woman like that marry you?"

"She must have liked me."

Robert was staring strangely at Haga.

As a matter of fact, it was the first time it had occurred to him that the MLA was a woman. He himself had not voted for her, but that was almost beside the point. She had been the MLA for over ten years now. And she had once been Haga's wife?

"Well, it was a long time ago," said Haga, responding, apparently, to his incredulity. "Before she quit drinking. After that she up and left me."

Sunny McDonagh did not come from Prohibition Creek and Robert couldn't help wondering if Haga had got her mixed up with some other woman. But then he discarded this thought. Haga might not remember whether he had been legally married, but the woman's identity was a detail that surely would not have escaped him.

"Women should stay out of politics. But you can't tell them anything," stated Haga.

"Yeah. You can't," said Robert glumly.

"You're a man. You know better. But they don't get it. They can't accept that." Haga warmed to the theme.

Robert was looking moody again, but he continued.

"Now we've got all these women chiefs. Even the Prime Minister was a woman till this one came along and kicked her out. I mean, sure, women can talk. But what about having babies? And doing the cookin'? They don't have time for that anymore."

It had finally come to Haga what was going on. Robert and Rebecca had not just had a quarrel. Rebecca had taken off on him. Like his wife, Sunny McDonagh.

"So what's it going to be like around here? Just you and me? No women?"

Solidarity was required.

"Well, that's great, pal. We're better off without 'em, that's what I always say."

Robert had his eyes closed. Maybe he was tired, Haga thought.

There was a piece of meat drying up on the side of the grill where Robert had left it.

"Mind if I eat this last piece here, partner?"

"Go ahead."

◂ ◂ ◂

The next day Sarah came back to Prohibition Creek.

Michael's therapy was progressing; it was now known that he would never walk, but the doctors were still making progress with his upper body. It was time for his wife to go home and start preparing for the life they would lead together in the future.

She was walking into town. She had left a cardboard box containing a CD player in the airport to be picked up later. Michael had insisted on sending it as a gift to his kids, despite their ages—four, three, and less than one—and Sarah had bought it with money donated by the village. Her other luggage was scanty: a small suitcase and a shopping bag full of candy—also for the kids.

Sarah looked around her at the familiar scene on the walk from the airport, the dry ditches lined with the brilliant wildflowers of high summer: wild roses and yellow cinquefoil, and tall clumps of purple fireweed. Behind this the stunted trees of the muskeg, ravens wheeling in the high blue sky over the dump, the low-lying buildings of the village just visible as she topped a little rise in the dusty road.

It was like coming back to life again.

It seemed as though she had been in purgatory for months; long waits in corridors and impersonal rooms, doctors who treated her as if she understood much more than she did, and others who talked to her as though she were a fool, her hostel with its horrible whiteman's food, being afraid even to go out because of the ugly things she saw on the streets; and Michael, with his white face, suddenly relying on her for everything.

And now once again she was in her own place. It was all still here. She was home.

And home to some very strange news, which she heard first of all from her mother and then from Roseanne and some other women friends. Rebecca had started a nursery school and a women's shelter but Danny had closed them down again. And so now she was running for chief.

◂ ◂ ◂

Robert brought his mother and Sarah's kids from Joker Lake back to Prohibition Creek by boat.

The first thing he saw, coming up from the river, was a Canadian flag flying on the mast over the band hall. It was Treaty Day.

Sarah, Roseanne and Danny were down on the beach to pick up the kids, but Robert was feeling rather alienated from his family—from everything, in fact, these days. He didn't hang around, but went straight up the bank and into the hall to collect his money.

Both cops were there, in their red dress uniforms. Like the flag, it was kind of a statement they made.

Robert always liked to make a statement himself on this occasion.

"Hi," he said to the clerk. "I just came to collect my bribe for another year."

She was a pretty young Dene woman, a fact that might have interested him in other years.

As it was, he was just playing his usual role; walking through his part, in fact.

"Here you go," she said with a smile. "Five bucks. Compliments of the Queen."

"Thanks. Too bad it won't buy me a pack of cigarettes any longer, isn't it?"

She laughed, even the cops laughed, and Robert, his duty to his ancestors discharged for another year, went back out the door and down the steps to the sunlit lawn in front of the building.

In the seventies and the early eighties there had been considerable controversy over whether they should take treaty money, but because of the constitutional vicissitudes of Canada and internal disputes among the Dene themselves, they had gone back to doing it again. Although this might be the last year, if the land claim came through.

If the land claim came through: they had said that for so many years.

Bobby was standing by the fire with some men who were arguing about the land claim and Robert went over to join him, even though his heart wasn't really in it. Management boards, square miles of land and money—it was all they were talking about.

"You guys remind me of the people at that conference in Ottawa," he remarked. "Indians thinking like whitemen."

"So you think they should be allowed to take our land away for seventy years and not pay us?" Danny had walked up from the beach and was standing there now too.

"No," said Robert. "But money isn't what I want to get out of this."

"You want the land back, right?" said someone else.

"Yeah, but that isn't all."

"So what else do you want?"

"I want them to leave us alone," Robert said.

"Well, we're going to get self-government too," said Danny. "It's coming."

"No, it isn't. Self-government is when you're free. When nobody can boss you around. Not when you have a bunch of boards and councils and committees."

Danny shook his head. "You're never going to be free then. Not that way."

"I guess not. But you asked me what I want. That's what I want. So maybe I can just say it, at least."

He looked at Danny, who nodded after a moment, and there was a sort of murmur from the older men around him too. Robert had no constituency to speak of, but these people understood him; they knew what he meant.

Robert had turned his attention on the hall again. Billy McCrae and his younger brother Donald were going up the steps.

"Hey, what are they doing here?" he asked, surprised.

The McCraes were, of course, admitted to the Band because of their intermarriage with the Woodcutters, but as the Metis faction, they usually eschewed most Band functions, especially Treaty Day.

Danny was also watching the McCraes go into the hall, his face clouded.

"Come here," he said to Robert.

They went around the corner of the building.

"You couldn't get Rebecca to quit running for chief?"

"Nope," said Robert. They were standing beside a tangle of raspberry bushes in the shadow of the hall. He picked a berry and began to eat it.

"Well, do you realize—she might win?"

"Nope," said Robert again.

"Do the arithmetic," Danny said impatiently.

Robert shrugged. "The Woodcutters are going to vote for you."

"That's about thirty votes. The wives might not vote for me, though."

Robert nodded. Rebecca plainly expected to get a lot of support from the women.

"Then there's the McCraes," said Danny.

And suddenly the true significance of the McCrae boys going into the band hall on Treaty Day burst upon Robert.

Rebecca was a McCrae. And just as the Woodcutters would vote for Danny, the McCraes were going to vote for Rebecca.

He was doing the arithmetic now.

In spite of himself—in spite of the bewilderment and sorrow he was feeling about the way Rebecca had walked out on him, and in spite of his realization that she was making a mess of the traditional balance of power in Prohibition Creek—Robert couldn't help grinning. Rebecca had more political acuity than he had given her credit for.

"Now that you mention it I guess you've got something to worry about there," he said. He picked another raspberry.

Danny hesitated. Then he said, "Look, Robert. Why don't you drop out of this?"

"Why? You think that might give you the edge?"

"I need all the support I can get. And you're my brother."

"But the people who vote for me are never going to vote for you," Robert pointed out.

Danny reacted angrily. "Who are they anyway? The other people who don't want any government at all?"

"Yeah. All ten of us," said Robert.

"So you won't quit?"

"I already told you. Sometimes you have to say what you want. Even if you're not going to get it."

Danny walked away, and Robert, losing his taste for raspberries immediately, as he seemed to have lost his taste for everything these days, also walked off, in the opposite direction.

◄ ◄ ◄

Slowly, a week passed, and it was the day before the election.

Rebecca was in the post office getting her mail. Bernard was in the habit of looking letters and parcels over closely as he passed them out, and announcing what they were; it was a kind of service he performed for everyone, literate and illiterate alike.

"There's a big envelope from Social Services," he was saying. "Then there's a postcard from somebody in Yellowknife. Says she's going to Hawaii. Must be a friend of yours, eh? And something else—just an ordinary envelope. From the Justice Department."

"Oh thanks." Rebecca pounced upon the last thing as he passed it through the wicket and turning away, began to tear it open at once.

Haga was standing there behind her.

"There's something here for you too, Haga," said Bernard.

"For me?" Haga was surprised.

Bernard turned it over, looking at it carefully before he handed it to Haga.

"It doesn't look like a summons."

"Haga! Look what I got here!" Rebecca seized his tattered sleeve in her excitement. "It's a letter from the court. My kids can come for a visit."

"Your kids," said Haga, remembering. "What the heck are you going to do with them now you're back living in that office?"

"I don't know," said Rebecca. She paused. "But at least they can come, Haga."

They were now standing side by side out on the steps of the store.

"We were going to take them to Joker Lake, me and you and Robert, remember?"

"I—I remember."

Robert and Haga and she had spent many happy hours, over tea, sitting in the sunshine in front of the teepee, or eating one of their huge meals, discussing what they would do with Rebecca's kids when they came for a visit. And now none of that would come true.

Haga had been looking at her rather censoriously. But now he remembered the letter in his hand.

"What's this say, Rebecca?" he asked. He gave it to her.

Rebecca unfolded the letter and began to read.

Dear friend,

Since we met in the Yellowknife Hospital, I have had the warmest feelings of regard for you. Can it be our friendship was born only to wither because of the many miles intervening between us? Please extend my hope that our acquaintance might yet blossom into the rosy flower of love.

Your sincere admirer,
Amelia McCrae

> *P.S. I was the one that sneaked you a smoke that day when there was vegetable soup for lunch.*

"A nurse?" Haga had jumped down off the steps, a look of alarm on his weather-beaten features.

Rebecca was staring at the letter in some surprise. "Amelia McCrae is a cousin of mine. She's not a nurse. She works in the kitchen at the hospital."

"Oh." Haga was relieved. "Is she big and fat—with long hair?" he asked. "That was the one that sneaked me a smoke."

"Amelia must be sixty if she's a day." Rebecca continued to gaze thoughtfully at the letter in her hands. "Well, I guess it's never too late," she remarked.

"I'm fifty-five," said Haga. He and Robert had figured this out once.

"Well—maybe she's fifty-five if she's a day," said Rebecca, coming out of her reverie and handing back the letter.

"What am I supposed to do now?" Haga asked, rather pathetically.

"Write back." Rebecca began to smile.

She had almost forgotten how to smile just recently.

"But I can't," he said.

"Get Robert to help you." Just saying his name made her stop smiling. Instead she wanted to cry.

"Robert? He's no use."

He had Rebecca's full attention. "What do you mean?" she asked.

"He just lies around on his back all the time," Haga complained. "When you say something to him he gets mean or else he isn't listening—He's been that way ever since you took off on him and went into politics."

Rebecca picked one of the tall grasses that stood beside the steps of the store and turned it in her fingers, pretending to be indifferent.

"I guess Robert was in love for the first time in his life," said Haga, undeceived.

She dropped the grass stem. "Did he say—something like that?"

"Naw," said Haga. "He doesn't talk about it at all. That's another first for Robert."

Rebecca looked at Haga, her lips quivering.

"Well, you're going to beat him in this election, aren't you? I guess he feels pretty lousy about that," said Haga.

"I'm not in the election to hurt Robert."

"No," Haga agreed. "But that's what happens to a man when a woman puts the big boots on."

"Oh, Haga! What can I do?"

It struck neither of them as in any way unusual that she was soliciting his advice. Even though this was the first time anyone had ever done that.

He shrugged.

"Win the election, I guess."

"I'm not going to win," she said, startled. She had never worked this out; she was quite as naive about local politics as Robert had thought at first.

"Yes, you are," said Haga. "Your whole family's going to vote for you."

Haga didn't need to count heads. He had known that big changes were afoot the moment he saw the McCrae boys at the band hall getting their five-dollar bills.

"But I don't want to win if Robert is going to feel that way about it," she said slowly.

"Well, he already feels that way," said Haga. "So I guess it's too late."

◂ ◂ ◂

Late that night Robert and Haga were lying on their bedrolls in the teepee. Neither of them was asleep. Haga was on his back holding his letter, which he had got by heart now, open above his face. Robert rested on one elbow, slowly whittling a stick.

"Amelia," remarked Haga. "That's some kind of a name."

"Yeah," said Robert.

"You think she really could have fallen for me?" he went on. "Just because she sneaked me a smoke that time?"

"Maybe," said Robert.

"What do you mean, maybe?" Haga demanded. "Listen to this letter: she hopes that our acquaintance might yet blossom into the rosy flower of love."

"Yeah," said Robert.

"Heck, you're not even listening." Haga was disgusted.

"Yeah," said Robert.

"Maybe you'll listen to this then," said Haga. "Rebecca got a letter today too. From the court."

Robert said nothing, but Haga could tell he was paying attention all of a sudden.

"Rebecca," Haga repeated. "That one, remember? She's going to get her kids up here now."

Robert was thinking of their plans. Rebecca had been intending to get some days off and they were going to take the kids to Joker Lake where they could experience the freedom children ought to have: running around camp day and night, in and out of the boats, going fishing and swimming and berry picking; maybe he'd get a moose with any luck and they'd have some big meals. There was a lot a person like him could show an eight-year-old and a five-year-old: how to make huts and lean-tos, how to use a .22 calibre rifle, how to set a net—

But none of that was going to happen now.

The dreary evening dragged on. Haga yawned.

"Sure is dull around here," he remarked.

"Yeah," said Robert.

"You're not much company, that's for sure. Think I'll go out."

"Yeah," said Robert.

Haga had been tucking the letter carefully under his pillow. Now he turned around. "I wonder whether he hears anything I say at all. Do you hear anything I say at all, Robert?"

"Yeah," said Robert.

Exasperated, Haga lifted the door flap of the teepee and went out.

Robert was still thinking about Rebecca's kids. He had been here all this time, just hanging around town, waiting for the letter from the court, so they could take the kids to the bush.

In fact, he had worked on so many small hamlet works projects this summer that he knew they were thinking of taking him on the payroll as a Labourer—the job even had a title.

Robert didn't want to have the job of Labourer.

The fact of the matter was that he didn't want anything anymore—not if he couldn't have Rebecca.

How could he have her if, in order to get her back, he was going to have to admit he was wrong about something?

He just couldn't seem to get started.

But the election was tomorrow. And after that it might be too late. He had to do it now. Even though she was probably going to tell him to go jump in the lake. And even though she was probably already asleep. It was way after midnight.

Robert groaned and got up, lifted the flap of the teepee to go out.

There was somebody coming down the hill from the burned-out fish plant, moving quickly through the bushes.

"Rebecca!" Robert was astounded. "What are you doing here?"

She was looking rather wild; as a matter of fact, she had been reliving some of the terror she had felt on the first night she had gone to visit Robert at the shack, when it had been cold and dark and she was alone for the first time in the bush. Now it was only dim, and she knew the path well, but she could still remember what that night had been like.

"I was just going over to the trailer. I thought you'd be sleeping."

Her appearance here, just as he was going to go look for her, suddenly seemed to him all of a piece with the other things that signified their supernatural connection: his dreams about her, her vision, the way they seemed to anticipate each other in everything.

"I couldn't sleep," said Rebecca.

She had been standing waist-deep in the low Arctic willows on the slope, but now she advanced timidly a little closer.

"Robert, there's something I have to tell you," she said.

"Me too," said Robert. "I have to tell you something."

It was amazing how this kind of thing happened.

"I—I think I decided not to run anymore." Rebecca spoke tentatively.

But Robert had also begun to speak:

"I should never have tried to tell you—"

They heard each other.

"You decided what?" Robert spoke first.

"Robert, I only went into the election because I wanted—"

"I guess I know why," said Robert.

"Danny thinks he can act like God. And he thinks only a man can be chief." Rebecca spoke with energy. "But I was doing his job all the time he was away."

"Well, I guess you proved you can do it, all right," said Robert.

"And there's so much more I could do," she went on. "A home in town for elders—"

Robert was scandalized.

"An old people's home? Our families are going to kick out the elders?"

He could see that Rebecca was getting kind of excited about this, however.

"Kindergarten in Slavey—"

"The kids would speak Slavey if they didn't have to go to kindergarten."

"A clinic with a midwife—"

"The midwife would just be some whitewoman," he reminded her.

They stood staring at one another. It was long past the meridian and the sky was beginning to brighten into full daylight. The lake was like a mirror in the pale soft pink light, with the morning star and the moon fading above.

"Well, I'm going to drop out, Robert." Her manner was gentle, almost listless, in comparison to the energy with which she had been speaking before.

"No! Don't do that," he said.

"What do you mean? You told me not to run."

"Yeah, but you shouldn't drop out because of that."

Rebecca was tongue-tied. She had come here to tell him she had decided to quit. She knew he wanted her to.

And now Robert knew he had a choice. He could go on and say what he had been intending, or else he could go along with her, and let her quit.

He spoke slowly, after a moment.

"I guess I kind of think people should do what they want to do."

Rebecca came a little farther downhill out of the willows. But she was doubting that he meant what he said. And was it even really true?

"Even when it bothers someone else?" she said.

"When you run for chief it's bound to bother someone else," he said. "The way Danny is running bothers you."

"It does!" agreed Rebecca.

"And me running—that bothers almost everybody."

She burst out laughing. Then she walked out of the willows and stood in front of him, smiling. She was waiting for him to say something more, though.

"You got pretty mad at me," he said. "You didn't even give me time to think."

They looked into each other's eyes.

"You're just about as stubborn as I am, Rebecca," said Robert. "Don't you know—it's kind of hard for me—to say I was wrong?"

She put her arms around his neck and he began kissing her. He broke off after a moment, a thought striking him.

"Sure is a new experience. Kissing a chief."

Rebecca was still smiling, although there were tears on her cheeks.

"I'm not a chief."

"Yeah, but you're going to be."

He was going to grab her and kiss her again, but she said, "Are you sure you don't mind? Haga said it's no good when the woman puts the big boots on."

Robert laughed. So Haga had been giving her some of his advice as well.

"That's just some kind of bug he's got. His wife went into politics."

"His wife?" she said.

In Robert's opinion, she had picked the right thing to be surprised by.

"But when you think about it, it's no good when the man puts the big boots on either," he remarked after a moment.

"That's true," she said.

They started kissing again.

The little songbirds had woken up and were twittering in the low bush all around them. From east to west over the glassy water of the lake the sky was bright with pale early morning summer light.

The day of the chief election had dawned.

But neither Robert nor Rebecca were thinking about the chief election anymore.

"Come inside." He spoke rather urgently.

He took her by the hand and began to lead her toward the door of the teepee.

Rebecca laughed. "Are you telling me what to do again, Robert?"

"Yes." Robert took the time to say this although he knew that speech between them on this point was by now quite unnecessary.

◂ ◂ ◂

Robert was sitting outside on the steps in front of the band hall. The sounds made by the drummers warming up came through the open door behind him.

He was in a reflective mood. May the best man win; that was what he always said. What he always used to say.

Herod's truck pulled up and he jumped out.

"Who won, Robert?"

"Rebecca," he said.

Herod's face was a study in conflicting emotions. Robert thought Herod probably felt much the same way he did himself.

"How'd the voting go?" he asked.

"Danny got forty-one votes. Rebecca got forty-two. Oh yeah—and I got ten." It was a funny thing—Robert was still wondering about that. Why had he got ten?

"Well, I never thought I'd live to see this day. The McCraes never had anything to do with the Band before."

"Better go in there, Herod," Robert suggested.

Herod hesitated. "I don't know how I feel about this," he was saying. "It just don't seem right."

Behind them, Rebecca began making her speech.

"She's speaking English," Herod protested.

"That's what she speaks," said Robert.

Herod paused a moment longer.

"Well, she's my niece," he said. "I guess I better go in." And he lumbered in the door.

Robert was undeceived. Whatever Herod might think of the new order as it was emerging, he had voted for Rebecca.

Haga approached across the lawn.

"Haga, old pal," Robert said. "Come sit on the steps with me."

"You don't look mad."

"I'm not," said Robert in surprise.

Haga hung back, however.

"Sure about that?"

Robert suddenly grasped the cause of Haga's apprehension.

"Rebecca and I made up last night," he said.

The agony he had been going through last week seemed like ancient history to him now. He felt fine about Rebecca winning the election. He had even voted for her himself.

And he felt fine in general. A little tired on account of having had no sleep last night—but that was all.

Haga sat down.

"I guess Rebecca's not going to have much time to spend with her kids now," said Robert. "You and me will just have to figure out what we can do with them around here."

"Maybe I won't be here," said Haga unexpectedly.

"Why not?"

"Maybe I'll be in Yellowknife."

"Yellowknife?" Robert now remembered Haga's letter from Amelia McCrae. "But wasn't she the one who looked like the Woman That Married the Dog?" he inquired.

"That was someone else. Besides, a woman writes you a—a passionate letter like this, you got to do something."

"Do you think you're in love?" Robert was staring at his friend in disgust.

"Why shouldn't I be in love? You're in love," responded Haga with dignity.

There was no reply to this, even though Robert felt that the comparison was inexact.

They continued to sit side by side in dreamy silence for a few minutes.

There were voices now behind them. Danny made a graceful speech of concession. He had to: the McCraes were a formidable new faction. Then Rebecca, who still didn't realize what a genie she had released from the bottle, made a graceful reply.

There was something Robert still couldn't understand.

"I got ten votes," he said. "I just can't figure it out."

"You always get ten, don't you?" said Haga.

"Yeah, but this time I didn't vote for myself," said Robert. He shook his head. "Maybe somebody made a mistake."

And suddenly Haga was able to show, by the depth of his perspicacity, just how much events over the past few months had touched him, had made him a finer person with a new, more delicate range of feelings. Ready, in fact, for love.

"Heck, no," he said. "That's not what happened, Robert. You want to know what happened?"

"What?"

"Rebecca voted for you."

"You think she did?" Robert asked.

"I know she did," Haga replied.

And it was entirely clear that he was right.

"Well, maybe this'll be the end of the Complaints Department," he continued. "With you all tangled up with the new chief and me off in Yellowknife."

But Robert wasn't so sure about that.

The Band had suddenly gone haywire with a bunch of McCraes in charge and the land claim was coming toward them now for real.

In his view, things were shortly going to be in a broader, deeper, taller, meaner mess than ever before.

No matter what happened, he felt sure there would always be a Complaints Department.

◂ ◂ ◂

This, of course, is not the end.

Billy McCrae replaced Rebecca as chief in a surprise coup that took place in November of that year. Then the land claim arrived, and Billy was replaced by Elvis, whom just about everybody trusted, and in the following July, Danny was re-elected. The nursery school had opened again under Rebecca as chief and continues to this day, in one half of a derelict house the other half of which became the home of the women's shelter.

As for Robert, in January he was offered a job on the staff of the First Nations Constitutional Committee in Ottawa, on the recommendation of some people he had met there the previous May, and Rebecca went with him. She started in the BA program at Carleton University—but never got to finish the degree. For when she and Robert returned to the North in the summer—after he lost that job—she ran for the N.W.T. Legislature from her own district of Yellowknife, and won.

Her ex-husband left the North on account of the strike in the gold mine, and Rebecca got her kids back, in a fairly amicable joint custody arrangement, which later became full custody after he married another woman in Sarnia.

As for whether Robert and Rebecca managed to stay together in the long run, the reader will not have forgotten that it was prophesied that Rebecca would get her kids back, marry a good man, and be happy until she died—although of course, it was Robert who made that prophecy, not I.

For I will now tear off the mask and inform the reader that I, as the author of this book, am the old medicine woman; I foresaw this, I made it happen, and this story is only one of many I could tell.

Susan Haley's first two novels, *Getting Married in Buffalo Jump* and *A Nest of Singing Birds*, were made into movies for CBC-TV. Her third novel, *How to Start a Charter Airline*, draws on her experience of owning a charter airline in the Northwest Territories for nearly fifteen years. Susan now lives in Black River, Nova Scotia.

◂

Some of the traditional stories used in this book were found in *The Book of Dene* (Government of the Northwest Territories, 1976).

The chapter "Dene Christmas" previously appeared in *The Gaspereau Review*, as well as in the anthology *Home for Christmas: Stories from the Maritimes and Newfoundland* (Goose Lane Editions, 1999).

The chapter "The Outhouse" previously appeared in the anthology *Fresh Tracks: Writing the Western Landscape* (Polestar, 1998).

The chapter "Lo, This Dreamer Cometh" previously appeared in *Inland Shores: New Writing from America, The Pacific, and Asia.*

Copyright © Susan Haley, 2000, 2005.

All rights reserved. No part of this publication may be reproduced in any form without the prior written consent of the publisher. Any requests for the photocopying of any part of this book should be directed in writing to the Canadian Copyright Licensing Agency.

Typeset in Adobe Jenson by Andrew Steeves. Jenson is based on the work of the fifteenth-century typecutter Nicholas Jenson. Printed offset at Gaspereau Press.

Gaspereau Press acknowledges the support of the Canada Council for the Arts, the Nova Scotia Department of Tourism, Culture & Heritage, and the Government of Canada through the Book Publishing Industry Development Program.

The first edition was published in 2000 under the ISBN 1-894031-26-1. This is the revised second edition.

2 4 5 3 1

Canadian Cataloguing In Publication Data

Haley, Susan Charlotte, 1949–
The complaints department

ISBN 1-894031-98-9

1. Tinne Indians—Fiction I. Title.
PS8565.A4334C66 2005   C813'.54   C2005-90394-7

GASPEREAU PRESS
47 CHURCH AVENUE
KENTVILLE, NOVA SCOTIA
CANADA B4N 2M7